DANGER IS IN THE UNWEAVING

DANGER IS IN THE UNWEAVING
HOUSE OF THE SPIDERKING™
BOOK TWO

MICHAEL ANDERLE

DON'T MISS OUR NEW RELEASES

Join the LMBPN email list to be notified of new releases and special promotions (which happen often) by following this link:

http://lmbpn.com/email/

This book is a work of fiction. All of the characters, organizations, and events portrayed in this novel are either products of the author's imagination or are used fictitiously. Sometimes both.

Copyright © 2024 LMBPN Publishing
Cover Art by https://fantasybookdesign.com
Cover copyright © LMBPN Publishing
A Michael Anderle Production

LMBPN Publishing supports the right to free expression and the value of copyright. The purpose of copyright is to encourage writers and artists to produce the creative works that enrich our culture.

The distribution of this book without permission is a theft of the author's intellectual property. If you would like permission to use material from the book (other than for review purposes), please contact support@lmbpn.com. Thank you for your support of the author's rights.

LMBPN Publishing
2375 E. Tropicana Avenue, Suite 8-305
Las Vegas, Nevada 89119 USA

Version 1.03, April 2026
eBook ISBN: 979-8-89354-265-3
Print ISBN: 979-8-89354-266-0

THE DANGER IS IN THE UNWEAVING TEAM

Thanks to the JIT Readers

Christopher Gilliard
Sean Kesterson
Diane L. Smith
Dave Hicks
Dorothy Lloyd
Veronica Stephan-Miller
Jeff Goode
Jackey Hankard-Brodie
Peter Manis
John Ashmore
Jan Hunnicutt
Paul Westman

Editor
SkyFyre Editing Team

CHAPTER ONE

Vicky tore a piece of packing tape off the roll with her teeth and slapped it on the cardboard box Elana held shut. "Another one down, all the rest to go," she announced.

Elana rolled her eyes. "That was funny the first time. *Maybe* the first five times. Thirty boxes in, it is *not* funny anymore."

Vicky beamed behind her thick-rimmed yellow glasses without a hint of apology on her face. "Ah, but it's *distracting*."

Elana raised an eyebrow and gestured at the disaster around them. "From *what?* You're *pointing out* how much we have left to do!"

Her best friend raised her index finger in the universal expression of "Ah, but!" and replied, "I'm keeping you focused on how not-funny I am instead of how much we have left to do."

Elana blinked as Vicky pulled a Sharpie from her hair and scribbled an imprecisely itemized list on the side of the box. "Okay, I admit you have *half* a point."

Vicky chortled, capped the Sharpie, stuck it back in her hair, and hefted the box. After she'd secured it in the stacks that covered most of the back living room wall, she grabbed the next flat box and folded it into position, then held it for Elana to tape. "Half a point's all you need to win. That said, I'm sure I could distract you with something else if you'd prefer."

Elana groaned. "God, *anything* would be better than this." She looked up from taping the bottom of the box, and her eyes widened. "Oh, fuck. That's your mischief face. Fuck, no, *I take it back—*"

"Too late," Vicky crowed. "You've opened Pandora's box!" Ignoring Elana's continued protests, she leaned in close and whispered, *"Tell me everything you know about vampires."*

Elana flipped the newly folded box right side up and bent back the open flaps. "If I did, they'd kill you," she informed Vicky. "But I can tell you a few things as long as you promise not to blab."

Vicky made a show of crossing her heart. "I am the *picture* of discretion."

Elana scoffed. "You are a *travel blogger.*"

Vicky put a hand over her heart and one to her forehead and mimed as though Elana had stabbed her through the soul. "Being a successful travel blogger requires *insane* amounts of discretion! Otherwise, you'd *never* get little local places to let you write about them!"

Elana snickered at Vicky's melodramatics despite knowing they were at least forty percent feigned for effect. The woman had a knack for defusing a situation and lightening the mood, and Elana desperately needed that right now.

Elana had already arranged with Jerry that the boys would move all her stuff two days from now. That meant she had to have it all *packed* by then.

She and Vicky had been packing for five hours—it was nearing half past midnight—and there was no end in sight. That was because Vicky had directed Elana to pack from the outside in. "Bedrooms first, then move to the common areas," she'd declared.

When Elana asked why, Vicky had explained that packing the least-used rooms first meant they cleared greater square footage faster, and it *felt* like you were further ahead than you were. It *also* resulted in gathering all the random shit that had migrated into other rooms into one place, which made for easier packing of "miscellaneous" boxes.

Vicky had moved over a dozen times and was used to living out of a suitcase as someone who traveled for work. Her advice was proving invaluable. Without her recommendation of packing a month of living supplies in a suitcase—or in Elana's case, in her dimensional bag—Elana would have ended up haphazardly ripping open boxes to get a couple of items here and there, and the new house would have been unlivable within a week.

Vicky had shown up with moving supplies, two cases of assorted vodka coolers, and enough snacks to feed an army. One of the garbage bags at the front door was half full of nothing but chip bags. The rest were full of junk Elana couldn't believe she still had.

It hadn't surprised Vicky. "That's what happens when

you live somewhere for decades," she'd told Elana. "Junk drawers are the bane of my existence. I allow myself one junk *pocket*, and I adhere to the KonMari method *zealously*. No joy? *Sayonara*."

The fact that a large portion of Elana's belongings were technically her father's tempered this approach. She hadn't cleaned out his things after he died since they had lived together until his death. Moving meant dealing with all of Elana's stuff and Jeremiah's. Vicky was as unfazed as ever. She left Elana to pack her month of stuff and disappeared to box up Papa Bishop's things into neat rows of boxes labeled Storage.

Seeing the wall of boxes marking her father's worldly possessions had been the first major blow to Elana's composure. She'd been holding it together until then by focusing her freakout on the drive to pack and telling herself it was perfectly normal to be nervous about moving house. Everyone got nervous about moving, right?

When she'd stopped in the middle of the living room, clutching a box of spare linen hard enough her fingers indented the cardboard, Vicky had gently taken the box from her hands and replaced it with a mozzarella stick she'd heated up in the toaster oven.

The mozzarella stick had opened the floodgates to a torrent of Elana's confessions. Elana had poured her heart out to her best friend about her fears of posthumously disappointing her dad by not following his dreams. She'd worried about whether she was engaging in wishful thinking by imagining that her mother had left this trail of clues for her.

Most of all, she'd lamented losing her humanity and

place in the world. Vicky had sympathized with Elana's parental issues. She reassured her that Jeremiah would have wanted her to be happy and that from everything Elana had said, it sure *sounded* like Tessa had deliberately laid these breadcrumbs. She'd also straight-up called Elana ridiculous for those last existential fears.

Vicky had poked Elana with a tea towel. "Get a grip, girl. Dry those eyes. You're not entering a convent. You're moving to Haven. Didn't you see *Crazy Rich Asians*? It'll be just like that, only with vampires. It'll be *great*."

In the present, Vicky tugged on the roll of packing tape in Elana's hand. "Earth to Lana. Come in, Lana. Don't tell me you're *brooding* again."

Elana shook herself and handed Vicky the tape. "Sorry. No. Well, kind of. Just…lost in thought."

"What about?"

Elana gestured vaguely around herself. "Everything. It's a *lot*, Vicks. Like… I'm training with the Arbiter of Shadows, who I swear is trying to turn me into the next Jackie Chan. Or Michelle Yeoh, or—I don't know who the coolest female action hero is, pick whoever. On top of that, I'm cramming my head full of Haven's political nonsense. You think *our* government's bad? Jesus…"

Vicky stowed the packing tape on the stacks of boxes and began methodically wrapping all the knickknacks from the living room shelves in bubble wrap, then sealing them with Scotch tape. When she sufficiently padded each tchotchke, she tucked it into the box at Elana's feet. "I hope you're *sleeping* in all that."

"Like a rock, most nights. Except the days when I finish on a political note. Those keep me up until all hours."

Vicky rocked back on her heels and eyed Elana. "Help me wrap—it'll give your brain something else to do—and tell me something about vampires that has nothing to do with the politics."

Elana sank to the floor and picked up the first gewgaw within reach, a glass figurine of a ballet dancer Elana had received from her grandmother when she was five. *Why am I keeping this?* Then she realized she'd be heartbroken if she gave it away.

"It feels like everything has to do with politics," she grumbled. "I train to get better at defending myself from nobles who want to kill me, then spend the afternoon reading about all the ways those same nobles want to fuck each other over—which is what leads to people wanting to kill me."

Vicky narrowed her eyes. "I thought you were being melodramatic, but you sound awfully serious."

Elana exhaled forcefully. "I wish I *was* being melodramatic. Honestly, Vicks, I've been giving you a sugar-coated version of events. I don't want to put you in danger. These people are crazy."

Vicky quietly finished wrapping the star-shaped crystal box and nestled it amid the plastic bubbles surrounding porcelain, wood, and glass. "Then why are you going? Why not leave? Walk away. If it sucks, hit the bricks."

Elana carefully placed the ballet dancer in the box, then picked up a wallet-sized photograph of her mother in a pewter frame. "I think I'd better start from the beginning again."

Two hours later, Elana drained the second wine bottle into her glass and sat back against the wall of boxes with a heavy sigh. "There you have it. Everything I know and everything that's happened. My mom became a vampire instead of dying, then secretly turned me into one and left a trail of breadcrumbs to lead me to the conspiracy that almost certainly killed her. Please don't say anything to anyone or Valeria will probably make me kill *you* if she doesn't do it herself."

Vicky stared into her empty wineglass for several long seconds. At length—still staring at the last drop of transparent yellow liquid—she inquired, "Is Mr. Sexy Voice as sexy as his voice?"

Elana blinked at her. She blinked again. "*That's* what you ask? After all the doom and gloom and bullshit—you ask if Matt is *cute?*"

When Vicky glanced up to meet Elana's eyes, the hint of a devilish smirk turned up the corner of her lips, and she winked. "It's two in the fucking morning, Lan. I've had four glasses of wine, three vodka coolers, and split six bags of chips with you. I'm ordering pizza because I'm pretty sure this is turning into an all-nighter. When it gets here, we are gonna talk about the *stupidest shit on the planet* because *oh my fucking* God *you need a break.*"

Elana was too stunned to reply, so she watched while Vicky ordered the pizza on her phone. After she tossed the smartphone aside into the mess of bubble wrap, Vicky rose unsteadily to her feet, went to the kitchen, and came back with two tall glasses of water.

Vicky sat, put one glass of water beside her, then held the other out to Elana until she took it. Then she chugged half of her water in one go. She smacked her lips, wiped them with the back of her hand, and wrapped her dark fingers around the glass.

"*So.* Is Matt Richelieu the sexiest man alive or not? Do vampires have sex the same way humans do? Are they cold like in *Twilight?* Are they all into blood play? *Do they sparkle?*"

Elana held her glass of water in one hand and her glass of wine in the other as giggles built inside her at the increasingly absurd questions. When Vicky's last question prompted the memory of Matt's recounting of the body glitter craze, she snorted and slopped water on her jeans. She met Vicky's gaze, and after a moment of held breath, they both burst out laughing.

When they calmed down enough to speak, Elana answered. "Matt's definitely attractive, but I don't know if I'd call him the sexiest man alive. I *tend* to like my men a touch scruffier, y'know? I *will* say that I had a few terribly inappropriate thoughts shortly after he rescued me from the guy who almost killed me, but in my defense, Matt ran toward me through a forest of cherry blossoms with a sword in hand. No woman who has *any* interest in men could ignore *that.*"

Vicky chortled, then waggled her eyebrows. "Only would've been better if he'd been in a kilt and there were bagpipes in the background."

"You and your Scotsmen."

"What can I say? I'm a simple girl. I love a man in tartan, blue paint, and not much else. Now answer the rest of the questions."

Elana abandoned the last of her wine for now and

sipped her water. "I haven't read or heard anything that suggests vampires have sex any differently than we do. I have *no* idea if blood play is in vogue. Funnily enough, I have *not* had much time to dive into the kinky history of vampires."

Vicky *tsked*. "What are you *doing* with your life? Get on that! Possibly literally!"

Elana snorted again. "Unlike some people I could name, I am quite content being vanilla, thank *you*."

"God, you're so boring." Vicky rolled her eyes, then flashed Elana a mischievous smirk. "Okay, but the glittering. You haven't denied the glittering. And are they cold?"

Elana shook her head. "If anything, I'd say they run a little warmer than most humans. But about glittering..." She broke into a devious grin and recounted Matt's story about the body glitter craze, finishing with, "He says he still has some. I plan to strongarm him into going as Bella and Edward to whatever Halloween party gets thrown."

Vicky had grown increasingly rapt as Elana told the story and guffawed when she reached its conclusion. "Oh my *God*. That's *amazing*. You *have* to send me pictures."

"If I'm allowed to, I certainly will..." A *buzz* sounded underneath the pile of bubble wrap and packing paper. "Who the hell is texting me at three in the morning?"

She fished the phone out, and her eyebrows rose as she scanned the screen. "It's Valeria."

"The Arbiter of Shadows?" Vicky's eyes widened. "That can't be good, not at this hour."

"Actually..." Elana opened the message and read it. "Uh. Wow."

"Share with the class!"

Elana showed Vicky the screen. "Speak of the devil. There's a gala in three days, and she wants me to attend."

Vicky skimmed the text and gasped. "You're gonna be presented like a debutante and everything! Holy shit! Tell me you get a plus one."

"I have no idea."

Vicky beaned Elana on the head with a ball of crumpled paper. "Well, ask her then!"

"Okay, okay!" Elana quickly tapped in the question and sent it. A moment later, the reply scrolled in. "She's asking me why the hell I'm awake at three in the morning, and she says… Holy shit, Vicky, she said yes."

Vicky squealed. "Did you ask if you can bring me?"

"Of course! All the other vampires I know will probably get their own invites, so…" Elana laughed and dodged a second paper missile.

Vicky did a little happy dance, still sitting on the floor. "I get to go to a vampire ball, uh-huh, uh-huh, yes I do…" She paused in her victory dance and eyed Elana. "You realize this means we're going shopping, right?"

"Well, duh."

CHAPTER TWO

Both women crawled out of bed the next morning by nine with headaches and fuzzy tongues. Plans to make breakfast were quickly abandoned, and they opted to take an Uber to the fanciest brunch spot in town. Elana briefly considered driving them herself, then decided she had no desire to drive her Emeya before the Advil kicked in.

Elana paid the driver with her black card and left him a sizable tip. When she and Vicky exited the car and stepped onto the sidewalk, Vicky elbowed her.

"Black card?" she intoned, eyebrows raised. "Dang, girl."

Elana chuckled. "Had you not seen it yet? Yeah." She waved the thin black rectangle between her fingers before slipping it back into her wallet. "That's what you get when you're in the *royal house*."

Vicky shook her head in astonishment. "God*damn*. I still can't believe that. I swear, this is a real-life *Princess Diaries*. You seen Julie Andrews yet?"

"That's what *I* said! And yes, before you ask, brunch is on me."

Despite the name, Chez Antoine was not a restaurant specializing in French cuisine. Its menu featured a smorgasbord of classic brunch dishes dripping with grease and loaded with calories. What set it apart from every other hangover cure was that they used truffle shavings on their eggs benedict and Moet et Chandon in their mimosas.

Elana ordered the Belgian waffle platter, Vicky opted for the Southwestern omelet and home fries, and they requested a bottomless pot of cold brew coffee. While Vicky picked at the complimentary fruit salad, Elana sipped her chilled coffee and lowered the blinds a few more inches to block the searing summer sun.

"Do you have a place you usually go to buy your fancy outfits?" Elana inquired as she sat back down and speared a strawberry in the bowl.

"Here? No. I have a list of my favorite boutiques in NYC, LA, and Paris—oh, and Rome. The couture there is to *die* for—but in little old Ashford? Not a chance. Honestly, until I saw the pic you sent of the dress you wore to the reparations meeting, I didn't think there was *anywhere* here that did fashion on that level. I assume you're taking us there...unless it was a shop in Haven?"

Elana grinned. "Nope. Zizi's human as human can be." Her brow creased. "As far as I know, anyway."

Vicky perked up with curiosity. "Zizi? Who's Zizi?"

"Just you wait."

An hour later, with takeout boxes under their arms, the best friends summoned another Uber and were soon on their way to Pax Vesta. When they alighted from the car, Vicky eyed the dusty storefront with deep skepticism.

"You're sure this is the place?"

"A hundred percent sure," Elana confirmed. "Although I didn't think to look ahead and see if they were open. We might have come all this way for nothing."

Sure enough, the door was locked. Elana groaned. "Well, *damn.* Sorry, Vicks. I have no idea what else is around or when Zizi opens. He hasn't listed any business hours."

Vicky made a moue and nudged past Elana on the top step. "There's a bell. I'm gonna ring it."

"Wouldn't that be *super* rude? If he's obviously closed..."

"He doesn't have to *answer*," Vicky chided. "It can't hurt to try. Plus, you're super rich now. Super-rich people get a pass on being super rude. Isn't that how it works?"

"That is an absolutely despicable social convention, and I have no intention of following it," Elana protested, trying to block Vicky from the doorbell. The shorter woman ducked under Elana's outstretched arm and pressed the button.

The shrill ring was audible through the closed door and continued as long as Vicky held down the button. She did so for two seconds, then released it and rocked back on her heels. "Now, we wait. We'll give it sixty seconds, then ring again, and if after another sixty seconds nobody answers, we leave."

Elana bit her lip. "If you say so."

The *shunk* of a deadlock interrupted Vicky's second ring. The door opened a hand's width, its progress halted by the chain lock across the gap, and Zizi's shock of platinum blond hair appeared above a pair of sunglasses dripping with rhinestones. He clasped a silver satin dressing gown around his wiry form, and the bunny faces on his slippers wore sleep masks.

"We're closed." His tone was as tart as his pinched lips suggested. "Come back in..." He glanced at his wrist and huffed when he realized he wasn't wearing a watch. "Come back when I'm not brutally hungover."

He moved to close the door, but Vicky shot her hand out to stop it. She blurted, "I have half of a fresh Southwestern omelet special from Chez Antoine ready and willing to be sacrificed in the name of fashion, a best friend with deep pockets, and a vampire gala to attend in two days. Rumor has it you're the best game in this hick town, and that bears out based on the honest-to-little-baby-Jesus fact that I would not only pay good money for those slippers, but I might kill a man for your glasses. I'll write you up in the *Traveler* if you let us in early."

Zizi narrowed his eyes behind the tinted lenses. He looked Vicky up and down, then glanced at Elana. Recognition dawned on his face, and one plucked eyebrow rose. Then he closed the door without a word.

Elana exhaled heavily. "Damn. Good try, though—"

The *shink* of the chain lock sliding open cut her off. Vicky flashed a triumphant grin at Elana as the door opened again, revealing Zizi with a hand on a hip.

"I'm the *only* game in town worth talking about," he informed them. "Welcome back, Miss Bishop. How did the dress go over?"

"Like a dream," Elana assured him. "Thank you so much for doing this."

"Your friend makes a *very* strong case. Omelet, please." Vicky nudged the door closed behind them and handed over the takeout box, which Zizi snatched. "You're welcome to browse the racks, but *wash your hands first*," he warned. "I do *not* want greasy fingerprints on my babies. Bathroom's *there*. Zizi will be back. Ta-ta."

He disappeared into the back, leaving Vicky and Elana alone on the atelier's display floor. Vicky beelined for the door Zizi had indicated, emerged a minute later with freshly washed hands, and went straight to the closest mannequin. It sported a gown that shimmered and sparkled in iridescent greens and blues even in the dim light.

Elana deposited her container of waffles on a stool near the door and also went to wash her hands. The little bathroom contained only a sink and a toilet, but it matched Zizi's heavily styled sensibilities. The mirror over the antique porcelain pedestal sink was easily four feet high, taking up most of the wall space and making the room feel twice as big. Its ornate oxidized copper frame matched the crown molding's curlicues and swooshes, and the textured wallpaper had been faux finished in a distressed maroon. Even the burnished brass soap dispenser could have been a century old.

When Elana re-emerged into the atelier proper, Vicky had moved past the second mannequin, which displayed a suit with enough ruffles that it could have passed for period clothing if not for the heavy floral embroidery done entirely in silver and green sequins. The third held a floating diaphanous dress that reminded Elana of a thundercloud.

"This man is *magic*," Vicky declared. "Why does no one know about him? He could be headlining runway shows in Europe!"

Elana shrugged. "Maybe he doesn't want to. Maybe he likes anonymity."

Vicky leveled a scathing look at her best friend. "Honey, nobody who designs like *this* wants to be anonymous. It's more likely he's hiding from the mob."

Elana blinked. "Are—are you *serious*?"

Before Vicky could respond, the curtain at the back swished aside, and the man in question appeared. Gone were the satin dressing gown and bunny slippers, replaced by a burgundy smoking jacket and trousers in a darker shade of the same over a black dress shirt and mustard-yellow tie with an Atlantic knot. He'd spiked his hair, and his shoes were leather of the same dark red as the rest of the ensemble with a steeply pointed toe and black stitching.

"There's no *way* you ate already," Elana protested. "We're not in a rush, and you're already being way too kind by opening…"

Her voice trailed off at Zizi's dismissive wave. "Fashion waits for no man, woman, or hangover," the slight man informed her as he strode toward Vicky. She was examining the fourth mannequin—an eye-popping wrap dress in fluorescent teal and pink. "That is *not* your color, dear."

"Not at all," Vicky agreed. "But I can appreciate the clear influence of Mornay's spring 2022 line on a silhouette straight out of Chantrelle 1956. Pairing those with that daring of a color combination is *inspired*."

Zizi paused two steps away from Vicky and the

mannequin, crossed his arms, and leaned back on one foot. "*Someone's* got more than a silver tongue."

Vicky winked at him. "Any chance you have something that says, 'I'm the coolest human in the room, bar none,' maybe with shades of Van Rijn's 1992 fall collection…in yellow?"

Elana thought Zizi might have fallen in love.

The designer recovered in record time and glanced between Vicky and Elana. "*The* coolest human in the room?" he repeated. "Are you not attending, Miss Bishop?"

"Oh, I am," Elana confirmed. She ignored the blush rising on her cheeks. "But, well…"

For the second time that morning, comprehension spread over Zizi's face like the rising sun. Unlike Jerry, for whom shock had followed understanding, Zizi's expression morphed into eager anticipation. Elana immediately understood why Zizi eked out a business in Ashford, and judging by Vicky's raised eyebrows, she'd figured it out too. A break in Haven was worth more than a dozen Paris runway shows.

"I *see*." He shifted to look her over. "Gala. Evening, then. And you said in two days?"

"Yes. I know it's short notice, but we only found out late last night."

Zizi waved it off. "You've engaged the best. Depending on your budget…"

Elana bit her lip and ran calculations in her head. "Five figures, tops?"

Zizi's eyes widened a degree, then returned to their normal half-lidded cool. "Eminently doable. Let's get started, ladies."

CHAPTER THREE

The next day, Elana left Jerry and the crew loading boxes and furniture. The stunningly bewildering meeting between Vicky and Zizi resulted in Elana commissioning a bespoke couture pantsuit for the upcoming gala and Vicky gaining a new friend for life. Not to mention another trip to the lingerie boutique where she dropped another thousand dollars on the underwear set Zizi had recommended. She drove to Haven with boosted confidence and music blasting through her Emeya's stereo with the bass cranked loud enough that the floor trembled.

She felt more in control of her life than she had in weeks. Undoubtedly, some of that bravado was due to an overabundance of caffeine, a distinct lack of sleep, and the elation of spending incomprehensible amounts of money. It was a damn sight better than feeling sorry for herself and jumping at shadows.

Elana turned down the volume out of courtesy as she approached the gate and waved gaily at the attendant. He smiled, scanned her car, and waved her through. If Elana thought about how creepy it was that Haven's biometric sensors were sensitive enough to recognize her through her vehicle, she got *Big Brother* vibes that did *not* jive with her deeply ingrained sense of personal privacy. She elected on a regular basis not to think about it. Whether that would come back to bite her in the ass, only time would tell.

She drove to the Citadel, parked outside its ring wall, and continued on foot. The lady in the long gown stood at the rebellion memorial again. Today, her gown was a soft silvery green that reminded Elana of the underside of willow leaves. Her hair remained in the messy beehive, reminiscent of Helena Bonham Carter in at least half of her movies.

Elana glanced at her phone. She had a few minutes before she was supposed to meet Matt. That was enough time to say hello.

She approached the woman from the left and politely paused a couple of steps away. She said nothing at first, instead examining the memorial more closely.

The Rebels' Memorial was an eight-foot hourglass that turned over every new moon. Dust gathered from the ground they stood on filled it—pulverized concrete, glass, and metal from the first incarnation of Haven, destroyed by the SpiderKing to wipe the slate clean after the rebellion. A force of new initiate vampires, American colonists given the Rights, allied with their human friends and tried to overthrow the SpiderKing and his arbiters. On this very spot, the SpiderKing had set off bombs that turned the entire city to rubble and ash, including every person who had turned against him.

The unflinching response had sent the SpiderKing's message loud and clear across the globe. Fuck with the SpiderKing and your sorry ass *will* be annihilated.

Elana watched the shimmering grains slide through the hourglass in a tiny, constant stream. The frame was carved from polished, shining obsidian, and the SpiderKing's sigil was inlaid in opal on each base. Eight spindly obsidian arms stretched from base to base, twisting and crossing around the hourglass in an intricate webbed helix.

The hourglass said that while time would continue unceasing and unabated, its passage remained within the SpiderKing's grasp…or perhaps it simply meant the SpiderKing would never forget the rebels. Either way, it was a powerful reminder.

"Makes you think, doesn't it?" Elana quietly volunteered.

The woman to her right glanced at Elana, then returned her gaze to the trickle of dust. She folded one white-gloved hand over the other. The latter held an emerald-encrusted clutch. "My son's ashes are in that hourglass."

Elana felt as though Gustav had socked her in the gut. "Oh. Uh…I'm…I'm so sorry."

"Don't be," the woman replied airily. "He was a traitor and a cheat, and an embarrassment to his House. It's hardly a loss to our bloodline."

Elana resisted the urge to squirm. This was *not* the conversation she'd had in mind. "I see. Still, I can't imagine it's easy to lose a child."

"It isn't. That is why I come to see him every day—to remind myself of what a failure he was and how disappointed I remain."

A chill ran through Elana's heart. This woman was *something else*. She let that declaration spin into silence before venturing, "I'm Elana Bishop. It's nice to meet you."

The woman looked aside again, and this time she met Elana's gaze. The woman's eyes were the same piercing green as her handbag but a cold green—one more reminiscent of the depths of the sea than verdant, lively forests.

Her long eyelashes lowered, veiling her eyes. "Sarah. Sarah Goldin, of House Viverri."

Sarah's eyebrows rose a degree as she finished her sentence, and Elana's breath caught in her throat. It was a clear request that Elana finish the pleasantries by offering her House in return. While Sarah's words said she was a loyal Havenite, something about her didn't sit right with Elana.

Unfortunately, snubbing standard pleasantries was *not* the way to make friends and influence people in Haven. Elana had neatly painted herself into a corner.

"House of the SpiderKing," Elana politely replied as neutrally as she could manage.

Sarah's eyebrows twitched up another degree. "I was unaware His Royal Highness had…adopted another heir. Congratulations."

Elana abruptly wished Cathy were there. The old vampire's social sensibilities hadn't failed her yet, and she would have immediately known whether Sarah was on the level. As it was, Elana was forced to rely on her intuition, and her intuition told her it was past time to get the fuck out.

"Thank you." Elana gestured slightly toward the hourglass. "My condolences on the loss of your son. Losing family is hard no matter what happens around it, and I can only imagine how hard it is to grieve for centuries."

"Yes." Disdain crept into Sarah's eyes, and she managed to look down her nose at Elana despite being a couple of inches shorter. "I can only hope the same indignities and sorrows are not inflicted on the *young*."

Elana bit her tongue to keep from grimacing. "Again, thank you. Now, if you'll—"

"Miss Bishop."

The cool voice of the Arbiter of Shadows sent an ice-cold spike of "Oh, *shit*" down Elana's spine and froze her in place. The hand that came down on her elbow gripped with shocking intensity.

"Arbiter Draven!" Elana exclaimed.

"Mister Richelieu is waiting for you."

Elana frowned. "I didn't think I was—" She caught the flash in Valeria's eyes and redirected. "My deepest apologies. I was speaking with Madam Goldin and lost track of time."

She turned back to Sarah and bowed politely. "A pleasure to make your acquaintance, ma'am. I wish you a pleasant day."

Sarah inclined her head. "And to you, Miss Bishop."

Elana held the bow for exactly as long as was polite, then hurried to catch up to Valeria, who had abandoned her and was striding toward the consulate. The moment they were in the building, she spoke up. "What was *that* about?"

Valeria huffed under her breath, then shook her head. "Not here."

Her tone was sufficiently sharp to worry Elana further,

and both women remained quiet until they were in the upper levels of the New Moon wing. Only after they entered the meeting room where Matt was waiting for Elana—arriving precisely on time, as Elana had known she would—did Valeria turn on Elana and throw her hands up. "I thought you would have *known* not to engage with her. What happened to reading all the Haven tabloids?"

Elana goggled. "She never showed up in anything *I* read. I don't know who she is. I take it she's bad news?"

Matt hissed through his teeth. "Sarah Goldin keeps herself *well* out of the tabloids ever since the rumormongering in the nineties, Valeria. Unless Elana went back and read the old editions, she wouldn't have known."

"And who reads *old* tabloids?" Elana added. "Even I'm not *that* bad of a gossip. But now you've got my attention, so who the hell is Sarah Goldin?"

"A *snake*," Valeria spat. Then she took a breath and let it out very slowly. Before she inhaled a second time, she was back to being the unflappable Arbiter of Shadows. "House Viverri is one of the oldest, snootiest, and most *infuriating* Houses in the world. They are infuriating because they maintain a strict non-engagement policy in any inter-House squabbles. Their official line is perfectly trim and proper without a branch out of place. You can't *prove* anything, but it's a well-known, entirely open secret that their cadet lines—all disowned on paper, of course—are the *de facto* rabble-rousers and wet work men of the vampire world."

Elana's eyebrows drew together. "So they're what, the vampire mafia?"

"To put it very bluntly, yes, in a way," Matt agreed.

Elana sank into a chair, still frowning while she tried to work this out. "Okay, so they're a House that double-crosses worse than the rest. Is that why you, or we, don't like them? Sarah said her son died in the Haven rebellion and that he was a disappointment to the family. That doesn't sound *treasonous* to me, but she *did* give me the heebie-jeebies."

Matt snorted. "She's only disappointed in him because he *failed*—but if she says it the right way, nobody can call her out on her bullshit."

He put his elbows on the table and leaned toward Elana. "Viverri plays the long con. They're interested in power but not responsibility. They cultivate a pristine outer face, but scratch the surface and you find rot underneath."

"They sound like Veridian. Are the Houses related?"

Valeria clicked her tongue. "That's my cue. Enjoy yourselves." She wheeled and left the room without another word.

Elana looked between Matt and the door. "I am so confused."

Matt smiled wanly. "Plausible deniability."

"Oh. Right."

"To answer your question, it wouldn't surprise me if Veridian and Viverri were related, but it would be impossible to find out." Matt scowled. "House Viverri has made *very* sure that no record of their cadet lines exists. There is one *singular* line of Viverri. It does not branch. It does not waver. Any scions born or turned that would alter that line and *pfft!*" He swirled his hand and pinched the air. "That poor unlucky soul is disappeared."

Elana stared. "But it's an open secret that they run the vampiric criminal underworld? How the hell does *that* work?"

"Oh, they're *extremely* well-paid to keep their mouths shut and do their jobs." Matt looked as though Elana was asking him to eat pickled lemons. "It ultimately serves Viverri's goal of building a reputation of being terrifying and omnipresent if everyone on the 'dark side' whose family is unknown is rumored to belong to their House."

Elana drummed her fingers on the table. "Are they good at their jobs?"

"Unfortunately, yes."

"Then why does the SpiderKing allow them quarter in Haven?"

Matt's scowl hardened. "Because on the surface, they're squeaky clean. They build, run, and supply *hospital ships.* They're fanatically devout. They say *all* the right things and never miss an opportunity to contribute to charity or public works. They're impossible to touch."

"But the SpiderKing must know better than anyone that they're rotten."

"I've no doubt. Doesn't mean he can act on it without proof." Matt's grimace deepened and he brought up the interface in the tabletop. "Which brings me to the reason I asked you to chat."

"None of the leads have panned out, huh." Elana sighed and rolled her chair over to peer at the documents projected on the table. "No solid proof."

"No solid proof," Matt echoed. "Which means we have two options right now, in short."

"Give up or keep going. The same choices we always have."

"Almost." He tapped one of the windows to expand it. Over a dozen small pictures appeared, all portraits of people Elana didn't recognize. "I think this is the best place to strike. If we can prove that House Veridian is linked to the names in this file, we'll be a big step closer to actually doing something about them."

Elana pulled the window in front of her with a swipe and examined the pictures. "These are missing persons cases," she murmured. "All vampires. There was a minor panic about a vampire serial killer for a while back in the nineties. I remember listening to a true crime podcast about it. *Fang the Ripper*. Terrible name, uninspiring host, but the story fascinated me."

She frowned again and counted the pictures. "There are too many victims here. The East Coast Staker was only linked to eight cases. I count at least thirteen."

Matt chuckled darkly. "Human media is dumb when it comes to vampires. If you expand the timeline to a vampire's lifespan, you get a *lot* more hits."

Elana blushed. "Oh. Duh." She squinted at the pictures again. "So, what's the plan? You think House Veridian is linked to the East Coast Staker?"

Matt shrugged. "I wouldn't have ever guessed it—honestly, I'd have put my money on Viverri before Veridian—but this is one of the files your mother linked to in her encoded journal, so I have to assume they are. She's been right on every other hypothesized link so far."

"We haven't verified this one yet because…"

"Because doing so will require us going over to the *dark side* I mentioned earlier."

Elana sat up straight. "You're a lawyer. Can you even *do* that?"

He snorted. "You must not know many lawyers. These days, I'm a guardian—a peacekeeper in the employ of the Arbiter of Shadows. I do a *lot* of work that most law-abiding citizens would consider under the table at *least*."

She narrowed her eyes and leaned in. "Okay... Then why haven't you already done whatever you'd need to do?"

Matt rolled his chair closer to Elana's and looked her very seriously in the eyes. "Because I needed to know that *you* were okay with it. Valeria's investigating your mother, but you're investigating the conspiracy your mother found. If that changes, Valeria's word will be final, but until then, it's your call which lines we cross and when."

"I assume you've already done everything you can legally."

"Yes."

Elana held Matt's gaze while she considered her response. House Viverri and House Veridian were only the *most* morally egregious Houses she'd met or learned about in her short time in Haven. Most Houses skirted the law somewhere like most *humans* did when you came right down to it. Sure, most people obeyed the law most of the time, but Elana didn't know anyone who hadn't rolled a stop sign or rounded a number up or down to make accounting a little easier. When it didn't hurt anyone, was there any real harm in it?

On the flip side... When morally bankrupt people did awful things in secret, and the people attempting to bring them to justice had no way to shed light on those things without resorting to technically illegal measures, weren't those measures justified? Didn't the ends justify the means in that case?

That's a slippery slope.

She bit her lip. "Illegally obtained evidence wouldn't hold up in court, would it? Would we count on whatever we found leading us to something that *could* be used?"

Matt lifted a shoulder. "It certainly wouldn't hurt, but in Havenite courts the burden of proof is less concerned about provenance and more about factuality. If you obtain evidence via sketchy means but the evidence is irrefutable, it still counts."

"You think this evidence would be irrefutable?"

"I think that if it isn't, it will *lead* in that direction."

Elana thought she could feel metaphorical rocks tumbling away down the slope of her life. She only hoped it would be worth it when she brought her mother's killers to justice—and possibly the killers of many more if this hunch was correct. "Do it."

Matt wasted no time. He cracked his knuckles, then brought up a command line interface on the tabletop and typed into it rapid-fire.

Elana watched the lines of code flash across the screen. "You're a programmer, too?"

"Couldn't *not* be, in this line of work. Picked it up around the turn of the millennium."

"How are you ever going to go back to dispatching guardians?"

He chuckled. "I'm sure I'll get bored with playing detective eventually. For right now, though…"

Matt continued typing as he narrated his steps aloud for Elana's benefit. "We'll take the encoded ciphertexts from your mother's files that pointed to these names. We'll use them as passwords to break the encryption on the secure database hidden in the Cayman Islands—with a backup in Amsterdam—that *another* of her files pointed to, hidden behind over three dozen shells and proxies.

"We'll disable the auto-shred feature by jamming it with a few petabytes of garbage data pulled from the last twenty-four hours of weather recording from the canopy. Then we'll log in using the handle and password we've gleaned by elimination during the decryption process, do a keyword search for anything referenced in your mother's files, and...*voilà. La victoire est la nôtre.*"

He hit Enter with the air of the cat who has swallowed the canary. A black screen replaced the command line interface, which lit up with a visualization of a soundwave as a recording played.

"*The latest wave of disappearances has been noticed.*" The voice was vaguely masculine, but several layers of filters masked its true nature.

"*Do better to hide them, then.*" The second voice was lighter in comparison. Perhaps feminine or a higher-voiced man.

"*If you do not want to be noticed, then Veridian would be well-served to—*"

"*Do not say that name here!*"

A moment of silence followed, then the first voice stated, "*Taking targets with less frequency would be more effective if more resources are not forthcoming.*"

"*Take fewer, then. We cannot spare more resources at this time. Hart is the goal.*" The second voice sounded peeved.

"*Very well. I will be in touch.*"

The recording ended. Elana's heart thudded. "They said my mother's name."

"It could have been the common noun. There's no proof it related directly to your mother."

"No. It has to be. What's the date on that file? Can you tell?"

Matt grimaced and tapped back into the command line interface. After a moment, he shook his head. "The metadata was scrubbed. It's all blank. I can't even tell when the file was uploaded, which is a bit of a feat, honestly. Whoever set up this server was good."

Elana gripped the edge of the table. "Is there anything more on the server?"

"Working on it… Yes, but nothing immediately usable. Everything I see here has been encrypted in multiple layers of file types—audio files saved as images saved as plain text, which has been ciphered into hex or worse. It'll take time to make any of it comprehensible."

She grinned. "But once you do, it's game over for Veridian, right? There's no way they'd hide innocent shit behind this many locks."

The crease in Matt's brow deepened. "Maybe, but…"

"But what?"

He paused his typing and focused on Elana. "Unless we have a smoking gun that directly connects a current living member of House Veridian with your mother's death, everything else will be circumstantial. Allowed in court, yes, but still circumstantial.

"If we had Valeria's public backing on the initial accusation, we might sway enough opinion on the consulate to convene a grand jury to indict House Veridian and win the right to investigate further. Without that smoking gun, Valeria can't throw her weight behind us. She *cannot* lose. You have to understand that."

Elana sighed. "Okay, then what else do we have to do? Hope for the Holy Grail?"

Matt clicked his tongue and returned to typing. "If you were your mother and had history *and* lineage on your side, I might say we go ahead with the accusation regardless and take our chances…but you're not. Not yet. We need allies. The more people we can win over…"

He glanced at her. "I'll set up a few meetings. Did Valeria tell you about the gala?"

"I went shopping this morning."

"Good. You are gonna need to schmooze like you've never schmoozed before."

CHAPTER FOUR

Later that afternoon, Elana stood with her handful of friends amid the perfectly stacked boxes filling her new home. She popped the cork on a bottle of champagne to cheers and applause.

"To new beginnings!" Vicky exclaimed, raising her flute so Elana could fill it with the bubbling wine.

"To new friends," Matt suggested as he did the same.

"And to a new life," Cathy finished with a smile.

Elana filled her glass and set the bottle in a bucket of ice. "I'll drink to all of that."

They all toasted, drank, and sat in the small circle of chairs Elana had put out minutes before they arrived.

"You gonna hire help to unpack?" Vicky chuckled.

Elana shook her head. "Nah. I'll just do it bit by bit. I want to know where everything is and figure out for myself what I put in storage that I want out…"

"But you have *so much money*," Vicky protested in shock. "At least tell me you're hiring a cook!"

Elana snorted. "I am *so* not at that stage yet."

Cathy crossed her ankles and adjusted her fluorescent purple and green paisley skirt. "It's always better to manage things on one's own, regardless of money or status. Otherwise, it's that much easier for bad actors to take advantage of you."

"Hear, hear," Matt chimed in and raised his glass again.

Vicky shook her head in wonderment. "Man, I *wish* I had the kind of cash where it wouldn't buy me happiness anymore. To live like that, even for a month—I can't even imagine."

Elana eyed her best friend over the rim of her champagne flute. "That could probably be arranged."

"Don't you dare tease me, Lana."

"I'm not!"

The doorbell rang, interrupting further conversation, and Elana hopped up to answer it.

"I thought you said Valeria couldn't come," Matt spoke up as she walked by his chair.

"She can't," Elana confirmed. "She said she's busy. This is probably the catering."

It was. Three trays of fresh sushi from Elana's newest discovery in Shestoi, delivered by a young man with a long ponytail that Vicky eyed salaciously from the living room.

Elana hip-checked her on the way back. "You're terrible, Vee, quit it."

Vicky chortled as the door closed. "I didn't even catcall him! No harm done!"

"You're a *menace*. Here, have a hand roll."

"Don't mind if I do."

The knot of friends and acquaintances devoured the delicious array of fish and rice, served on a bed of crushed ice covered with thin leafy greens with containers of soy, ponzu, and unagi sauce on the side. Bouquets of julienned cucumber and pickled ginger encircled by wasabi rosettes filled the center.

After they'd eaten their fill, Elana took her friends on a quick tour of the bungalow. When they reached the basement, Vicky put her hands on her hips and eyed the unassuming white walls and low-pile gray-speckled carpet.

"I gotta say, Lana, this is way *less* fancy than I expected. Where are the granite countertops? The crystal chandeliers? The antique vases, the uber-fancy security system complete with an impenetrable panic room? Where's the *money?*"

Elana snorted. "This is a starter home, Vicks. I'm not there yet. Also, do you have any idea how expensive construction materials are these days? And *labor?*" She whistled under her breath. "I could bankrupt myself in weeks if I went too nuts. As it is, my first plan is to install modular, climate-controlled storage down here." She motioned at the large dehumidifier unit still in its box in a corner.

"For your new clothes, no doubt," Cathy commented, and Elana nodded. "Very wise. Do you need contractors? I have a list."

"I'd love to take a look."

"I can recommend someone to build you a panic room," Matt added. "You know, in case you're feeling paranoid."

Elana hummed. "Well, if anyone *else* jumps me, I just might give you a call…"

Cathy started. "What do you mean, 'if anyone *else?*'"

"Oh—um…" Elana winced. She still hadn't had a chance

to check with Matt whether Cathy was connected to House Veridian. Unfortunately, Cathy was also terribly perceptive. "It's hardly housewarming party conversation…"

"Do I look like I give a damn about *social propriety?*"

"Seeing as one of the biggest reasons I wanted to be your friend was to *learn* vampire social propriety…yes?" Cathy gave her a scathing look, and Elana lifted her hands in surrender. "All right, I give. A couple of assholes jumped Matt and I in Senkyem. They didn't manage to do us any lasting damage."

The spark in Cathy's eyes could have started a fire. "Have you found out who had the audacity to target a member of the *royal House?*"

"Not yet. The guardians are investigating."

"We got blood samples," Matt volunteered, then briefly met Elana's gaze and shook his head a fraction of a degree. "We'll have a lead in time, I'm sure."

Cathy scoffed. "They'll have masked their DNA, mark my words. You'll find nothing." The vampire matriarch put a hand on Elana's elbow, setting her mismatched bangles a-jangle. "I'll get you in touch with my preferred contractor for a good panic room, my dear. If nothing else, it's where you hide your valuables."

Elana raised an eyebrow. "Isn't the point that a panic room is unlocked until you get in? Wouldn't that be an *unsafe* place for your valuables?"

"Not if you install a high-quality safe in it first. Then you turn the panic room into an escape pod. Something goes awry, and *pop!* Out you go, away into the stratosphere, and you come down with a splash in the Atlantic where your hired submersible picks you up."

The room fell quiet as everyone stared at Cathy in stunned disbelief. When her deadpan expression cracked with the hint of a mischievous smile, Elana groaned and smacked her lightly in the upper arm.

"Cathy, you're *terrible*."

Cathy grinned. "A little absurdity makes the centuries much more pleasant. My uncle was the most dour, bitter man you ever did see. Lived nearly a millennium but did he enjoy it? No, sir."

She patted Elana's elbow again. "In all seriousness, though. Be careful. There are more than enough Houses in Haven, let alone the rest of the world, who will want you out of the picture by any means necessary for the sole reason that you are your mother's daughter. Don't give them the satisfaction. I like you too much."

Vicky broke the ensuing awkward silence with an overly cheery, "So, who's looking forward to the Initiates' Ball?"

A couple of hours later, Matt and Elana were alone in Elana's new bungalow with the end of the bottle of champagne. The last piece of sushi was gone, Cathy had flittered off home, and Vicky had driven away in her Haven town car with only a modicum of squeeing over the cute chauffeur.

Elana split the bottle between their flutes. "I keep

meaning to ask you about Cathy. Do we know if she's connected to House Veridian at all?"

"She isn't." He caught himself and corrected, "Not to my knowledge. House Lucciola is *old*, which means it's connected to most Houses *somehow*. I highly doubt Cathy is connected in any way she'd be aware of. She's quite scrupulous about her alliances. She wouldn't give you the time of day if she didn't think you were worth it."

"Do you know how old she is?"

"I haven't got a clue, and I am *not* stupid enough to ask."

Elana sighed, drank half her glass in one swig, and let her head fall back on the pile of boxes she was sitting against. "Then it isn't the end of the world that she knows someone's after me, right? She's on the good side?"

Matt contemplated the bubbles in his champagne and thought for a long moment. "She's certainly on *your* side, I'd say, but that doesn't tell us anything about her loyalties in the big picture. My gut says she'd have nothing to do with whatever Veridian is planning, and my gut is *usually* right. I'll do some digging."

"I hope your gut *is* right. I get the feeling she would be a powerful ally."

"She would. We'll need to be sure she's safe before you divulge the whole story, but like I said, Cathy Smith doesn't make friends lightly. Alliances, even less so. She keeps to herself nearly universally, but she has enough connections and clout that when she throws her weight behind something or someone, it means a lot.

"On that topic…" Matt crossed his legs. There was something odd about a man in a three-piece suit casually sitting cross-legged amid a forest of cardboard boxes. He drained his glass. "I've set up meetings with three heads of Houses that I've vetted as being excellent potential allies. Ravenwood, Stormhaven, and Rothschilde."

Elana smiled. "The first two sound like names out of fantasy books."

"Not everyone can be part of a distinguished House like the Richelieus." Matt winked. "Besides, you're one to talk, being in the *House of the SpiderKing*."

She snickered. "Fair. Why these three?"

"Their politics and social activities are reasonably aligned with your morals and areas of concern. They have no connections to House Veridian within at least four branches of the main House line, and they agreed."

Elana raised an eyebrow. "Are you saying other Houses *didn't*?"

He chuckled and shook his head. "I didn't chance asking anyone who wasn't likely to agree this time. It would have made for bad gossip. This way, we keep generating *good* gossip."

Elana blinked. "I didn't realize I was generating gossip at all."

Matt stifled a snort of laughter. "Oh, Elana, everyone who's *anyone* is talking about you. You showed up out of nowhere and were inducted into the House of the Spider-King within the month. You have frequent one-on-one training sessions and personal meetings with the Arbiter of Shadows. You disappear into the King's Archives with a high-ranking guardian on a regular basis.

"You bought a house in Zevenda in your first month after making friends with one of the most reclusive matriarchs in the city. You regularly make significant purchases at luxury boutiques in Premier with your black card...*but you don't talk to anyone.*"

Elana opened her mouth, paused, closed it again, then finished her champagne, set the glass down, and stared at the floor. "Well, when you put it *that* way…"

Matt chuckled softly. "You're a magnet for gossip. Nothing gets vampires' attention faster than something that smells interesting. Not only are you an enigma but you're also tied to an arbiter. *Two* arbiters, although we're making sure that remains *uncommon* knowledge. Any connection to the consorts ratchets up the interest exponentially. Add it to the fact that you haven't gone out to do any networking, and you have a recipe for intense curiosity.

"The rumors about who you are and why you're special are probably significantly more outlandish than the truth, but the truth is still pretty damn juicy. Therefore, anyone with two brain cells will want to talk to you. The trick is picking people who don't *just* want to talk to you so they have more to gossip about." He rolled his eyes. "Too many people are only in it for the gossip and don't think anything will come of it."

"I take it Ravenwood, Stormhaven, and Rothschilde are *not* among that cohort."

"Not in the slightest. All three are Houses with either deep or strong veins, as we'd say."

"Long lineage or a wide power base?"

"Pretty much."

"Vampire slang is creepy sometimes."

"You haven't heard the half of it."

Elana drew a deep breath and let it out very slowly.

"*Okay.* So. I'm gonna talk to three super important Houses and get them to, what, back me when I accuse House Veridian of killing my mother?"

"To put it simply, yes—either that specifically or convincing them House Veridian is acting against their interests, and they'd be well-served by backing you." He finished his champagne and set his glass beside Elana's. "I'd recommend reading up on each House so you don't make an utter fool of yourself speaking with their respective heads."

"You are *horrible* at giving pep talks."

Matt smirked. "Sorry. Not part of guardian training."

She raised an eyebrow. "*Pretty* sure it's part of being a *social* worker."

"Mm. Haven't done that in a while."

Elana glared. "I think you like putting me on the spot. Speaking of, when do we start?"

"Right now."

"*What?*"

"You'll want to change."

CHAPTER FIVE

Elana pored over the e-books Matt had sent to her phone while they shot through the North Carolina landscape in his Audi. While House Ravenwood maintained a residence in Haven proper, their manor house sat on the outskirts of Pisgah National Forest.

The vampire House's purchase of the land had been hotly protested by the human population farther afield, but the locals, it was said, mostly appreciated the Ravenwoods' custom. The Ravenwoods employed numerous human contractors to maintain their grounds and work their lumberyards, which naturally boosted the local economy. The biggest draw was the vampire tourism.

Ravenwood Manor was the epitome of a Gothic Revival mansion. Pick a campy horror film from the eighties on, and you could film it somewhere on its grounds or in its vaulted halls. It cost upward of seven million dollars to build over five years, included over a hundred rooms, and covered nearly two hundred and fifty thousand square feet in five stories.

The exterior featured locally quarried light gray stone in mesmerizing patterns, hand-laid and filled with a dark gray mortar. From afar, figures resembling constellations or tangrams could be made out like tracing figures in the clouds. Most agreed a stampede of stallions adorned the wall closest to the exterior stables, and it was universally agreed that a raven stretched its wings over the entrance hall. Beyond those, what one saw in the Ravenwoods' walls was a deeply personal affair.

Thick, old-growth trees surrounded the mansion. The Ravenwoods kept lumberyards, but only in specific locations well back from the main roads and well-hidden from prying eyes. The human contractors who worked those lumberyards told stories of trees grown faster than nature would allow without soil failure or wood weakness, but they only felled the trees. They didn't grow them. The location of the Ravenwood nurseries was a jealously guarded secret.

"Where *do* they keep the nursery?" Elana inquired as Matt threaded along the winding forest road toward the estate. "Does anyone know?"

"Underground." He flicked his headlights on and grimaced when it did him little good. It was that time of the summer evening when the sun had barely set, and the twilight's quality desaturated all color. Add the flickering light between the tree trunks, and Elana would have sworn they were driving through a rotoscope.

She frowned. "Really? That seems like a silly place to keep a tree nursery."

Matt chuckled. "Haven controls its weather, and you're complaining that we can't grow trees underground?"

"Fair point." She slipped her phone into her purse. It was another Hermès bag, and Vicky had turned positively green with envy when she'd seen it. *It's not fair,* her best friend had lovingly complained. *You don't* understand *what you're buying.*

"Most of the Ravenwood residence is underground," Matt continued. "Ravenwood has always liked to dig deep. Their Old World branches made their fortunes in mining and forestry, mainly in the Black Forest of Germany. There's also a Russian branch out in Siberia. Nobody talks about them much, though."

"Why not?"

"They're *weird.*"

Elana briefly wondered what could make vampires consider other vampires *weird*. Then Matt slowed and turned a corner between two particularly thick trees and the house came into view.

The setting sun behind them threw its orange rays through the million and one trees they'd driven through and set the intricate stonework alight with figurative flames. Elana's gaze traced a woman in a long veil reaching to the sky up the curve of the south tower, then drifted to a fox trotting along the top of a window on the third floor. It settled on a sprawling fractal pattern of roses that rose from the keystone of an arch above a door to wrap around a balcony and up the spire of the north tower.

"Holy *shit*," she whispered.

"It's gorgeous," Matt agreed. "Trailing vines blossom over most of the front façade in the spring. There's a figure I only ever see at that time that looks like it's picking the flowers. I could stare at the house for hours. Augustus

Ravenwood designed all the stonework himself and hand-picked and trained the masons who would do the work."

"Augustus is…"

"Lady Ravenwood's father. Would have been referred to as Earl Ravenwood in your notes. He was the one who moved to America from the family estate in England, where they moved in the 1700s after the family schism in Germany. Rumor has it they still don't talk to the Rabenholz."

"Sheesh. Is he still alive?"

"No. He finally passed a few years ago."

"What happened?"

"No one knows. It's considered polite not to ask."

"Ah. Gotcha."

Matt coasted to a stop outside the front doors. A wide cobbled walk led from the curb to the banded doors. When Elana got out of the car, the sight of branches and leaves in the mosaic of stones at her feet immediately arrested her attention.

When she finally tore her gaze from the ground, she cast an eye over the walkway and front door. "All the security's hidden, then?" she murmured as Matt drew level with her and locked the car behind him. "Like at your place?"

"Yes," he replied, equally *sotto voce*. "Remember how I said most of House Ravenwood is underground?"

"Yeah."

"I meant it literally. There are at least ten subterranean floors, and they occupy a greater footprint than the above-ground house—and those are only the floors we know about. When we are in Lady Ravenwood's parlor, we will be sitting on top of hundreds of vampires who could swarm us like ants. Do *not* piss them off."

Elana blanched and swallowed. "I'll do my best."

They walked up the path. Matt had instructed her to dress conservatively with a hint of American Gothic, so she'd opted for a calf-length dress in a deep chocolate brown with short sleeves, a collared, button-down neckline, and a thin satin belt in the same hue as the dress.

Sheer black hose and a demure pair of black Mary Jane flats completed the mildly Kate Middleton-esque look. Elana had opted to add a touch of personality by wearing Zizi's fire opal necklace and earrings. A few carefully placed ringlet curls left loose from the chignon tucked at the back of her neck carefully hid the latter.

Matt had changed into a different suit before leaving Elana's. He'd explained it was more appropriate for calling on someone of Lady Ravenwood's status in the evening, but Elana wasn't familiar enough with menswear yet to tell the difference. When she'd expressed curiosity, he'd informed her the navy suit jacket was a "two-button single-breasted notched lapel British suit in worsted wool with jetted pockets." *Okay, I know what all those words mean on their own...mostly.*

He stepped up to the door and lifted the bronze raven perched on a hinge attached to the door. He used its beak to knock twice. The *tock tock* resounded through the heavy oak, and Elana would swear into the stone. She was rapidly getting the feeling it wouldn't take much digging to learn that the American Ravenwoods were as *weird* as the Siberian branch.

A butler who could have walked off a BBC set answered

promptly. His black suit had a subtle sheen that reminded Elana of a raven's feathers. His tie and pocket square were delicately patterned black silk that could have shown feathers or leaves. He was taller than both of them by at least six inches, and while he had no hair on top of his head, his immaculately groomed mustache was thick enough to make up for it.

"Master Richelieu, Miss Bishop," he intoned. "Welcome to Ravenwood Manor. The lady of the house awaits you. Please, enter."

Matt thanked him and offered Elana his arm as they crossed the threshold. She took it and was glad she did because it was all she could do not to trip while gawking at the house's interior. Where the outside celebrated stonework, the inside was a monument to woodworking. The house's skeleton was solid stone, but every piece of furniture and each architectural flourish was hand-carved, hand-polished wood. They were beautiful in elegant simplicity or intricate craftsmanship—or in many cases, both.

The legs of the side tables in the entrance hall depicted copses of trees, and their tops were inlaid like canopies of leaves, all in stained and burned wood. The Gothic arches far above their heads appeared to be draped with real vines at first glance. A closer look revealed they were also whittled and carved. Elana felt like she was in a cathedral that worshipped mountain and forest.

The butler led them up the grand staircase carved in wood and stone to resemble a tree growing from the floor, then down a series of hallways into a back wing of the house. Matt glanced to the side once as though expecting the butler to turn a different direction but said nothing.

The door to their destination was honey-colored and polished to a gleaming shine. It featured a gorgeous, burned depiction of a weeping willow that arched up to the top of the door and draped its lamenting branches nearly to the floor in an invisible, gentle breeze. A small candle burned in a stoneware wall sconce beside the door and gave off a subtle floral aroma. The sconce was carved in the shape of a bowl made of leaves.

The butler swung the door open on silent hinges and gestured for them to precede him. Elana entered first with Matt on her heels. Behind them by a step, the butler announced, "Master Mathieu Richelieu of House Richelieu, and Miss Elana Bishop of the House of the SpiderKing, my lady."

Lady Ravenwood's light soprano voice came from one of three high-backed armchairs silhouetted by the large fireplace. Despite the summer heat, the room did not feel unseasonably hot. "Thank you, Geoff. Bring the tea forward, then leave us."

"Of course, madam."

Elana allowed Matt to guide her toward the other armchairs while she did her level best to unobtrusively take in everything in the room. Lady Ravenwood's parlor resembled a medieval apothecary or alchemist's more than a Gothic study or sitting room.

Cabinets filled most of the walls, their doors covered in detailed woodcarvings of ferns and flowers. Embroidered tapestries that recalled illuminated manuscripts hung on every inch of the walls *not* covered by cabinets and bundles of herbs hung from the open rafters several feet above their heads.

Off to one side, two tables—one of wood, one of stone—stood under hanging chandeliers with dozens of thin, white tapers. All burned with the same mild floral aroma. On the tables sat a myriad of instruments whose purpose Elana could not begin to dream of, except perhaps for creating potions and tinctures. After Haven's high-tech intricacy, House Ravenwood felt like stepping back in time.

Geoff set the wide silver platter with its matching silver tea service on the small coffee table in front of the armchairs with a quiet rattle, which shook Elana from her observations. As she sank into the armchair between Lady Ravenwood and Matt and politely crossed her ankles, the butler bowed to his patron and departed. Elana got her first look at the head of House Ravenwood.

In the firelight, Lady Vivian Ravenwood's long, angular face hid behind her thin black ringlets like a wooden face carved into the trunk of a tree covered in vines. The wrinkles in her skin proclaimed her to be a *very* old vampire, and Elana couldn't help drawing a comparison to tree bark. It wouldn't have surprised her at this point if someone had told her the Ravenwoods were *literally* related to trees.

Her gnarled hands, folded in her lap, were covered in elegant spirals and whorls of wood that wrapped around her fingers and wrists. When she lifted a hand to pour tea into the three cups on the platter, bright blue lines of light flared to life in the carved jewelry. Elana wondered whether they were braces to help with arthritis—whether

Vivian Ravenwood was old enough that not even vampire medical wonders could keep the ravages of time fully at bay.

Vivian's eyes betrayed no hint of age. They were sharp chips of hazel above a thin, hawkish nose, and they examined Elana with hard-won and piercing wisdom. "Very well, shining light. You have my attention. Speak."

Elana abruptly felt like her tongue had tied in knots as intricate as the tapestries on the walls. The severe lack of dates in any discussions of vampire Houses was a serious stumbling block. She'd known House Ravenwood was old and Lady Ravenwood venerable, but this felt like talking to the trees themselves.

She drew a deep breath and let it out slowly. She accepted the cup of tea that Matt handed her and recalled everything she had read about House Ravenwood.

Then Elana took her courage in both hands—along with the tea, which smelled of sharp herbs—and spoke the words she had so carefully crafted on the drive over.

"House Ravenwood proudly stands for justice," she unequivocally stated. "It upholds the rule of law both natural and civil without faltering, and has done so for longer than most people, even vampires, can remember. If a Ravenwood brings a complaint to a higher authority, it is unquestionably a case worth hearing because the unswerving Ravenwood ideals of order and morality run deep. They are taught from birth and siring alike, and only the most upright are offered the Rights of a Ravenwood. Therefore, if House Ravenwood cannot solve an ethical quandary, the knot is tight indeed."

Elana paused for breath and a sip of tea. The brew was sweeter than she'd expected from the steam's scent but had a bitter aftertaste that lingered. It soothed and sharpened in equal measure.

"House Ravenwood brings this passion for justice to every vampire community—indeed, *every* community—where it takes up residence. It is exacting in its adherence to legality and scrupulous in its commitment to equity. It is no surprise that a Ravenwood was the first Arbiter of Light. Your niece's dedication to laying the foundations for Haven's judiciary set a precedent of fairness and equality in Haven's courts that holds to this day."

"Light is ever balanced by shadow," Vivian inserted.

Elana nodded smoothly. "Naturally, and as it should be. It is only fair to take into account the accused's circumstances, intention, and attitude, and so Ravenwood is not without mercy, but when judgment is rendered, consequences follow.

"*That* is what I have come to talk to you about tonight. *That* is why I am here."

"Consequences?" the wizened woman inquired lightly.

"Yes. Consequences for an act I believe to have been wholly unjust, and which has been unfairly ignored. I believe its true perpetrators went unchallenged. Justice was not served. And…"

Elana gripped her teacup to keep her hands from shaking. "I believe those same people continue to act unlawfully without consequence. I believe that if these acts were brought to light, House Ravenwood would agree they could not stand. Therefore, I ask for your assistance in righting this wrong."

Vivian Ravenwood said nothing for what felt like a small eternity. She held Elana's gaze so levelly and with such intensity that Elana could not bring herself to drink her tea.

At long last, Lady Ravenwood broke the silence. "You sound like your mother."

Elana let out a breath she didn't know she'd been holding. "You knew my mother?"

"My dear, everyone knew your mother." A craggy smile stretched Vivian's thin lips. "She was impossible not to know. I suspect you will be much the same way."

The old woman drank deeply of her tea and refilled it before speaking again. "You are speaking of her death, I presume."

"I am."

"You believe it was foul play."

"I do."

"Do you have proof?"

Elana resisted the desire to glance at Matt for encouragement. He'd made it abundantly clear in their conversation before getting in the car that this had to be Elana's show. He was there as personal moral support and a tacit, plausibly deniable expression of support from the Arbiter of Shadows. He was the go-between, nothing more.

"My mother left me papers," she explained. "In those papers, I discovered evidence that my mother was investigating a conspiracy involving House Veridian. Following that trail of evidence led me to further evidence that House Veridian was responsible for my mother's death."

"Tessa Hart died in a drive-by shooting in an inter-House war." Vivian could have been discussing the weather or a terminal cancer diagnosis. She was serene in the same manner as Valeria Draven, except deceptively light instead of deceptively neutral.

"I believe that inter-House war had no true basis and was orchestrated—*manipulated*—by agents of House Veridian," Elana challenged. "My mother's death was ordered because she was too close to the truth."

"That truth being?"

"That House Veridian is gathering power. I don't know why yet—they're very good at hiding—but I am determined to find out. What I have found so far is an insidious web subtly connecting House Veridian to every branch of Haven's inner workings, bar none…including an alarming number of missing persons. Missing vampires, in fact."

Lady Vivian's eyebrow twitched. "I see."

She reached one willowy arm down beside her armchair. The bright blue lines shot up her arm underneath her lacy black sleeve, illuminating its vines and flowers like sunlight through leaves. Elana had been so entranced by the woman's face that she'd barely noticed the intricate lace gown, woven with as much care and detail as all the artwork in the manor. The floral patterns were so organic that the moss green dress could have been *grown*.

Vivian picked up a delicate silver bell and rang it once. A heartbeat later, the door opened to admit Geoff.

"Yes, my lady?"

"More tea, Geoff."

"Of course, my lady."

Elana chanced a look at Matt. He smiled faintly but warmly. This was going well, then. Thank God.

Elana sipped her tea and settled in. House Ravenwood didn't end a meeting until they discussed every last point in thorough detail. They were in for the long haul.

CHAPTER SIX

Elana was nowhere near bright-eyed and bushy-tailed the next morning, especially after sleeping on a mattress on the floor in her new house from three-thirty to seven-thirty AM. She picked up a triple shot of espresso from the first café she spotted in Shestoi before arriving at the Citadel. She didn't even look for Sarah Goldin on her way in. She had to prop her eyelids up with toothpicks to have a hope in hell of surviving this meeting.

She walked into today's meeting room in the New Moon wing too tired to feel trepidation, and thanked her lucky stars that she'd somehow managed to beat Valeria there. She picked a random chair around the boardroom table and settled in to watch stray wisps of cloud float across the morning sky while nursing her coffee and praying for the caffeine to kick in.

As far as Elana could tell, the meeting with Lady Ravenwood had gone well. She and Matt hadn't been shown the door until nearly two in the morning. While Lady Ravenwood was hardly easy to read, she hadn't seemed dismissive. She'd listened to Elana recount Tessa Hart's evidence and connections, the story of the call to the Veridian informant, and the incident in the gardens without so much as an eyebrow twitch. Honestly, if anything, Elana had been worried about *boring* the venerable vampire.

Matt, too, thought it had been a successful trip. "She won't give an answer yet," he'd told Elana in the car once they were away from the estate and weaving through the thick forest, keeping an eye out for deer and other wildlife. "She'll deliberate and consider for at least a day or two. Put it out of your head for now."

That was easy for him to say. *He* hadn't been summoned to debrief with Arbiter Draven at eight in the morning.

The door clicked open, rousing Elana from her reflection, and she turned to face Valeria as she walked in. Today, the arbiter wore a sharp white blazer with thin lapels and ivory buttons, complete with a white collared shirt, white trousers, and pointed white leather shoes. How she didn't scuff them, Elana could not fathom.

Elana greeted her with as energetic a "Morning" as she could muster. Judging by the mild amusement on Valeria's face, it hadn't been convincing.

"Your need for sleep will diminish as you progress," Valeria assured her. "Mornings will not *always* be hell."

Elana grimaced. "How many levels does that take? Never mind, I don't think I want to know. It'll just depress me."

Valeria chuckled once in acknowledgment, then pulled out the chair across from Elana and sat. "You are more direct than your mother."

Elana blinked. "I thought this was a debrief. How do you already know what happened?"

"I have just come from speaking with Mister Richelieu."

"*Christ.*" Elana drained her coffee and set the disposable cup on the table. "Okay. I'm more direct than my mother. Is that a good thing?"

Valeria shrugged a shoulder. "That depends. You will get certain things done faster."

"Like making alliances?"

"Like dying."

Elana's eyebrows shot up. "*Whoa!* That is *not* a good thing!"

"Then either get better at being diplomatic or get better at not dying."

Elana blew out a breath that puffed out her cheeks. "*Okay*, holy shit. Are you saying I did a bad job at the meeting with Lady Ravenwood? Neither Matt nor I got the impression that she wasn't on board. Matt did say she'd take a couple of days to mull it over and decide, but she seemed happy enough when we left."

Valeria shook her head. "It's not your persuasion skills that need work. Mister Richelieu believes that Lady Ravenwood was impressed and swayed by your conversation. He made a *very* good call in bringing you to Ravenwood *first.*"

Elana's shoulders drew together, and she wanted to shrink back in the chair. She felt a little as though she were in the principal's office. "I don't…quite understand. I'm sorry."

Valeria laid her forearms on the table and folded her hands. "Despite maintaining their primary House residence outside of Haven, where they are not bound by Haven law, House Ravenwood has historically sided with the House of the SpiderKing with *extremely* few exceptions...and those exceptions are not on matters of great import. Their values align with his—and indeed, yours—so you might say they are a 'safe bet.'

"You were able to speak as freely and frankly with them as you were because of this," Valeria continued. "Thanks to that long friendship between Houses, that level of familiarity was seen as respect rather than impertinence. In short, you got lucky."

Elana wanted to melt through the chair and the floor to the level below. Her cheeks burned. "Oh, God. I didn't... *Wow*. I *definitely* thought I was being *super fucking diplomatic*." Valeria snorted, and Elana rolled her eyes. "Gee, thanks."

Valeria's stern expression did not waver. "Would you rather I tell you that you were great and not to change anything and have your next meeting result in your quick death?"

Elana scowled. "No. Of course not."

"I didn't think so." She tapped a hand on the table with surprising finality. "Focus on tact and indirect methods of communicating your point. Also—rumors are in the air that something will happen tonight."

"Something? What's *something*?"

"Good question. Be ready."

"Great."

Elana transferred the phone call from her Emeya's built-in sound system to her earbuds as she got out of the car. "Still with me, Vicks?"

"I'm here," Vicky confirmed. "Am I driving myself tonight?"

"No, I'll send a car for you in an hour. How fancy do you want?" Elana walked up her front steps and unlocked her door.

Vicky made a sound that was a cross between a chuckle and a growl of anticipation. "Oh, make it *nice*, Lana. If I have to be squashed under a mile of non-disclosure agreement paperwork to get into this thing, I'm gonna milk every drop of enjoyment out of the experience."

Elana smiled, then closed and locked the door behind her. "Be grateful they're letting you in at all. When I reminded Valeria she'd said I could bring you, I thought she would filet me on the spot."

Vicky scoffed. "Haven's supposed to be this utopia of vampire-human cooperation, isn't it? Could have fooled me. At this point, that sounds like a marketing ploy more than anything else. Or worse, an *election promise*."

"Ooh, *burn*."

"Oh wait! There *are* no elections. You live in a *monarchy*."

Elana shrugged and trotted down the stairs to where all her clothes were being kept in wardrobe boxes, ready to be arranged in the climate-controlled walk-in closets yet to be built. "It's not so bad. I'm beginning to think the Brits had the right of it."

Vicky gasped in horror. "Elana Bishop, *you take that*

back. What kind of American *are* you? George Washington is rolling in his grave!"

"Since when do you give a damn about what *George Washington* would have thought?"

"Point," Vicky conceded easily and laughed. "What do you think, *really*? With all the drama and nasty politics... Your mother died in an inter-House war, for God's sake."

"As far as I can tell, the SpiderKing wants less drama, not more. Did you know only women are *allowed* to be arbiters?"

"Seriously? I thought it had just happened that way. With vampires living so long, there isn't much turnover in the positions."

Elana found the most recent addition to the wardrobe boxes in the last one she opened, naturally. The bespoke pantsuit had been delivered as Elana had been leaving the house that morning, and she'd rushed to shove it in a box before running out the door to get to her meeting on time. In her hurry, she'd forgotten where she put it. She laughed at herself. *Serves me right for trying to be tidy.*

"We both know better than that, Vicks, come on." Elana rolled her eyes. "In all the history of the planet, has it *ever* happened that women have just *happened* to be picked for positions of authority—*once*, let alone *multiple times over?*"

"You might have a point. Huh." Vicky paused. "Is it that he trusts women more? Is *he* secretly a woman?"

Elana shrugged and brought the pantsuit to the dressing mirror she'd asked Jerry to set up and connect. She hung it on the hook on the side, then sat to start her makeup. After a day of research and self-reflection, she was beyond ready to kick back and relax, but tonight's gala was hardly destined to be a light evening out. It was a prime opportunity to network and give the people of Haven a taste of who Elana Bishop was.

"For all I know, he could be," Elana replied. "I haven't found a single person who will admit to meeting him. I have my suspicions about Lady Ravenwood and Cathy Smith, and of course there's Valeria…but no one can tell me, or *will* tell me, what he looks like. So, who knows?

"As to whether he trusts women more…again, I couldn't tell you. But it's in the constitution. Only women are allowed to take the post of arbiter. Men can be consorts and concubines—"

"I still think that's a weird title," Vicky interrupted.

"You're not the only one. But yeah. Men can take lower positions of authority, but they're barred from arbiterships. That gets fun when Old World Houses adhere to the patrilineal style of inheritance."

"Sheesh. I bet there's plenty of resentment bubbling away in those relationships."

Elana smoothed foundation over her skin with a soft sponge. "Undoubtedly."

"Wait a second." Vicky sounded like she was frowning. "This *really* isn't adding up. If the SpiderKing's so damn progressive, and Haven's all about vampire-human cooperation, then why *aren't* more humans allowed in Haven? Why aren't the doors wide open?"

"Think about it, Vicks." Elana leaned in and examined the layer of foundation in the lit mirror. "The SpiderKing can enforce his laws with a velvet-wrapped iron fist, but he can't change anyone's mind. You know how many humans think poorly of vampires—just as many vampires think poorly of humans. It takes a brave soul to stand up to that on either side of the equation."

"I will convince them through sheer charisma to let more humans in," Vicky proclaimed. "I will be a vanguard for my people. Victoire Euphemia Lamarr will be the first human cultural ambassador to Haven. Mark my frickin' words."

Elana laughed as she dug through her makeup bag for her contouring brush. "If anyone could change the state of human-vampire relations via unbridled enthusiasm and not taking no for an answer, it would be you."

"Damn straight. Nothing's gonna keep *me* down. I will wow them *all*."

"I don't doubt it." Valeria's warning flashed through Elana's mind, and she put her brush down. "Shit. I was supposed to tell you earlier—Valeria let me know there might be trouble tonight...just so you know."

"Trouble? What kind of trouble are we talking?"

"Trouble like 'do you have a Kevlar vest' trouble."

The phone line buzzed for several seconds before a mildly stunned Vicky replied, "Uh. I will...I will get one."

Elana made a face at herself in the mirror. "You wouldn't rather cancel?"

"Excuse me? *Fuck* no."

Elana's heart lightened, her grimace shifted to a smile, and she picked up the brush. "Okay. I'm glad to hear that. Honestly, Vick, I'm relieved you'll be there tonight. I don't know if I tell you enough, but I appreciate that you don't beat around the bush. I'm so tired of that, and it happens *all the time* here."

Vicky chuckled. "You can always count on me to be

straight with you, Lana. Did *Lady Ravenwood* give you the runaround last night? Is that what's bothering you?"

Elana traded the brush for another sponge and blended the contouring. "Lady Ravenwood was refreshingly frank when she spoke at all. No, it's Valeria. I don't know what she wants from me. She pushes and pushes but never gives me a *goal*. Why does she care so much?"

Vicky snorted. "Are you serious, doll?"

"Dead serious. What are you seeing that I'm not?"

"It's a classic case of seeing potential. She's grooming you to be her right-hand lieutenant or some shit like that."

Elana stared at her reflection. "Who, me? No way. Not a chance."

"Are you kidding? Think about it, Lana. Now, if you'll excuse me, I have to go buy a Kevlar vest. I hope the Army surplus store is still open."

CHAPTER SEVEN

Kamari Hall was among Octava's premier locations. The building housed a concert hall, a large ballroom, and a more intimate ballroom. Each bore the name of a House Kamari scion—Skopi, Thera, and Sellada, respectively. Since the Initiates' Ball was the biggest event of the summer social season in Haven, it was naturally held in the Thera Ballroom.

While Octava's architecture skewed toward the modern and post-modern, that did not preclude the designers of its myriad edifices from drawing inspiration from other sources. Kamari Hall was modeled after ancient Greek architecture and featured tall colonnades, mosaic floors, and bas-reliefs on the walls.

The art on the walls and floor depicted elegant scenes from art and history, and its smooth white stonework was offset by hanging fabrics in rich, bright colors. Tonight, the Thera Ballroom was draped in shades of blue ranging from deep cerulean to the palest periwinkle. The dozens of people meandering across the floral mosaic floor wore formal outfits that spanned the rainbow and showcased every fashion niche. The Initiates' Ball was the equivalent of the Met Gala without the theme.

Unsurprisingly, Vicky was having the time of her *life*. She'd opted for one of her many trademark canary yellow outfits—a stunning off-the-shoulder chiffon dress with an asymmetrical hem that went from mid-thigh to the opposite ankle. It showed off her curvy, espresso-brown legs, open-toed silver heels, and flawless pearly white pedicure.

Elegant bronze cuffs made of thin metal bands covered half her forearms. A matching thick collar-style necklace brought the viewer's eye to her shimmering gold eyeshadow and lips, not to mention the gold combs studded in her hair.

Elana, on the other hand, had never been to such a formal event. *Certainly* not as a guest of honor. She had to fight the urge to hide behind a curtain every five minutes.

The pantsuit Zizi had selected for her from his back catalog of "little projects" was simple but striking with wide legs and a close-tailored jacket with sharp lapels. One front panel extended below the other to create a triangular, asymmetrical hem. The angular look would have been eye-catching enough on its own, tricking the eye into believing Elana was taller than she was—the stiletto heels helped, too —but on top of that, it was *bright cardinal red*.

"I feel like they're all looking at me," she murmured to Vicky, hiding her mouth behind a glass of wine and side-eyeing the nearby vampires who glanced at her.

Vicky was nonchalantly refilling her plate at the overflowing buffet of hors d'oeuvres. She shrugged. "No shit, Sherlock. You're a brand-new initiate who's been seen in the company of the Arbiter of Shadows. I'd be more worried if they *weren't* looking at you."

She turned away from the table and popped a plump red grape in her mouth. After swallowing, she smiled at Elana. "This is supposed to be networking time, right?"

"I suck at networking."

"It's just small talk."

"I'm even worse at small talk!"

Vicky rolled her eyes. "Chicken. Just follow my lead."

Vicky didn't give Elana time to argue. She swept away from the buffet like a gale-force wind. True to form for that meteorological event, she dragged Elana in her wake and created swirling eddies of activity wherever she blew.

Elana realized later that she'd been talking for an hour, expertly shepherded by Vicky's guidance. She had learned more than she ever wanted to know about the hobbies, business pursuits, and family trees of over a dozen attendees—each impressively powerful in their own way, whether by age, resources, or experience.

Back at the buffet table, they paused for a refill of their drinks and a pit stop. "You're *good*," Elana remarked. "How come small talk's nowhere near as awkward when you're around?"

Vicky chuckled. "Because I've practiced talking to people in this level of society, but it's no different from any other. Small talk is about being curious and caring about people. You don't put them on pedestals *or* in the dirt. You approach folks where they're at, ask what they're doing, show interest, and show you're listening. Soon enough they'll tell you their whole life story."

"You make it sound so simple."

"And *you're* overthinking it—*Whoa!*"

Vicky leaped backward as someone rocketed past her. They hit the table and upended platters of salmon puffs and caviar-topped cream cheese rolls. Vicky scrambled away but slipped in a growing pool of overturned cranberry-lemon sangria and went down hard.

Elana reached for her friend to help her up but pivoted when she noticed the flash of a blade in the hand of the man who had interrupted their discussion. Suddenly, this was no longer a case of a clumsy or unlucky party guest. This was an attack.

She drove her stiletto into the man's back, arresting his movement and slamming him back into the table. The second impact tipped the table over, sending china plates and silver tiers of amuse-bouches cascading to the tile floor to cacophonous effect.

Matt appeared from among the crowd and quickly got Vicky to her feet. The partygoers in their vicinity who had initially turned to look were gasping, exclaiming, and backing up in shock.

"What's happening?"

"Who is that?"

"Is that a knife?"

"This sort of thing would *never* happen at *my*—"

Elana moved in to apprehend the knife-wielding assailant, only to be interrupted by Vicky shouting in surprise. *"Elana, look out!"*

Elana whirled with an instinctive spin kick and got lucky, nailing the newcomer in the chest with her heel. The tall, broad-shouldered man stumbled back with a pained yell, but Elana followed up with a vicious uppercut and a knee to the groin.

Thank God I wore a pantsuit, she reflected while continuing to whale on the man. Her assault was cut short by a sharp pain in her back. She spun again to see the first man up on his feet, covered in smears of cream cheese, soaked in punch, and sprinkled with caviar, but brandishing a knife that dripped with blood.

"Oh, this is not good," Elana muttered.

She dove under the first man's arms, grabbed the edge of the leaning table, and propelled herself over it into a tuck and roll. On the way, she snagged one of the multi-tiered hors d'oeuvres trays and the tablecloth that covered it. When she stood, she dragged the tablecloth with her. The resulting clangor made no few patrons cover their ears in distress.

Elana glanced over and spied Matt shielding Vicky while they backed up. The two attackers focused on Elana while she tore a thick strip off the tablecloth and tied it to the handle of the hors d'oeuvres tray. *Makeshift flail: check.*

She gripped the cloth rope with both hands a couple of feet apart and twirled the flail, building up speed. She and Gustav hadn't had much chance to work on improvised weapons yet, but she had the idea. At the very least, it would be distracting.

The thinner man, the one with the knife, moved first. He leaped over the table, darted toward Elana, and slashed at the arcing tray as Elana whipped it at him. He missed, the tray collided with his head, and he staggered.

The second man strafed to Elana's left, going around the

felled table. He bent as he walked, keeping his gaze on her, and scooped a handful of jellied salad from the floor. This stymied Elana until he hurled it in a wide arc at her feet and it splattered over the tile. The bastard was making the floor slippery as if it wasn't hard enough to fight in stilettos.

Elana kept her tray flail in motion as she continued to back up. This buffet table had been about two-thirds of the way through the room. It was a convenient stopping point for attendees who needed a break from the impressively competent dancing—another skill Elana desperately needed to work on—and networking. That meant she had several yards between the table and the back wall.

The goon ahead of her had grabbed the whole damn bowl of Jell-O, coconut, and marshmallows and was gradually emptying it as he advanced. She would have to run around the slippery area or take her chances with a frontal attack. She didn't like either option, especially since the first guy had recovered from her tray hit and was coming at her around the growing minefield of salad.

"What do you want?" she yelled. Vicky and Matt were approaching the edge of the crowd hurrying for the ballroom exits. If she could distract these two long enough for them to escape, she could either escape or go out fighting.

The first man cackled. The second man grinned and licked lime Jell-O off his fingers. The first man called, "Not obvious yet? Our boss wants you dead."

"Why? What am I to them?"

Jell-O man shrugged. "Not our business. We just like killin'."

Elana rolled her eyes. "Real classy."

She chanced another look toward Vicky and Matt, and

frowned when she noticed that no one in the crowd was leaving. The alarmed hubbub was growing in intensity and rapidly nearing panic. Were the doors stuck? What the hell was happening?

Elana's retreat abruptly halted as she backed into the wall. Both enforcers grinned at her grimace and accelerated their approach.

"Say g'night, Gracie," the big guy threatened.

"Oh, *come on*—what, did you learn how to be a mobster from old movies?" Elana complained. "Seriously? If this is the best House Veridian can throw at me, then it's just a matter of time before—"

The first man hurled his knife at her. She dodged, having seen him wind up, and the knife *pinged* off the wall and clattered to the floor.

Elana took the opportunity to dash forward to her right, giving the treacherous terrain a wide berth as she headed for the knifeless man. He ducked her twirling flail and palmed something on his belt, which he flung her way too fast for her to avoid.

The knife nicked Elana's ankle and skittered across the tiles. She yelped and stumbled, and the hors d'oeuvres tray *clanged* on the floor.

The man laughed and reached for his belt again. Elana refused to give him the chance, so she turned her stumble into a lunge. She looped the tablecloth rope around his neck and turned it into a makeshift garrotte. She slammed the man to the floor with her knee in his chest and pulled the ends of the cloth in opposite directions.

Elana was appreciating his face turning into a tomato when something flat and solid hit her in the back of the head like a two-by-four swinging on the end of a crane. Unbalanced as she was, she flew forward and skidded through the oozing puddle of Jell-O salad with stars dancing in her eyes.

She slid into the overturned table and scrambled to her feet, covered in food. *I sure hope Zizi made this pantsuit machine washable.*

Elana took a step forward, but her vision wavered. Her ears rang, too. It felt like the big man had used her head to ring a church bell.

The small man was preoccupied with hacking and coughing now that his airway was unobstructed, but the big man stalked toward Elana, undeterred. Her eyes crossed, and for a second, there were two of him. Did she smell something wafting through the air? Something extra sickly sweet? She was starting to feel a little sleepy…

The big man was almost within arm's reach now, close enough for Elana to see the smug smirk painting his face. "You're worse than your mother," he jeered. "She only got *herself* killed. Your meddling is gonna kill a *whole lot more*, starting with your little human friend."

Vicky.

The sweet smell was getting stronger. Elana backed up, fell over the table, rolled onto her stomach, and army-crawled away a few feet before scrambling to her feet again. She shucked off her suit jacket and wrapped it around her head, and within a breath, she felt clear-headed again. *What kind of idiot broadcasts their evil plan? Christ, these guys are amateurs.*

Instead of continuing to fight the two goons, Elana dove into the crowd. The attendees were in varying stages of panic or dull-eyed stupor, although Elana saw several who had wised up and covered their noses and mouths with *something*.

What was wrong? Why were none of them leaving? *Where were Vicky and Matt?*

Elana pushed through the mob in the direction she'd seen them last. The hazy air smelled like cotton candy even through her jacket. She elbowed aside a ring of people around the door, all of whom were very obviously looking *away*. She frowned when she discovered Matt kneeling beside a closed door while Vicky *also* looked away. Although Vicky held a knife with a hooked blade like she knew how to use it, despite the fear in her eyes.

"What the hell?" Elana hissed. "Why haven't you left?"

"I'm trying," Matt retorted. "They locked the damn doors and—and *bamboozled* everyone."

"*Bamboozled?*"

"Shut up and cover me!"

Elana whirled and took up a position beside Vicky. She'd lost her flail when the big man had clocked her over the head, so she unstrapped her stilettos and brandished them.

"Why haven't they found us?" she murmured to Vicky.

"Beats me." Vicky's voice quavered, and her terrified gaze flicked to Elana. "Everybody just started acting *weird*."

"You've fought with knives before?"

"When would I have ever fought with a knife?"

"The lean, mean streets of Beijing? Rome? New York City? You're a travel blogger. Don't you skulk in dark alleys looking for greasy spoons?"

"*No!*"

A *click* and a *shunk* sounded behind them, and Matt urgently whispered, *"Come on!"*

"You first, Vick," Elana urged, motioning her friend toward the door. "I'll be right behind you."

Vicky didn't hesitate. She turned and ran on Matt's heels, and Elana pelted out the door after her.

They ran pell-mell and unaccosted through Kamari Hall and out the back door, where Vicky staggered to a halt and doubled over with her hands on her knees.

"I—have to—stop," she panted. "Just—give me—a second…"

Matt's face set in a grim line. "No time," he informed her. Before she could protest, he swept Vicky into his arms and took off running again.

Elana followed Matt barefoot through the darkened Octava streets until he skidded to a halt in an alley behind a museum Elana didn't recognize, especially not in the rain. It had inconveniently started mere moments after they escaped the hall. Not a single ray of moonlight pierced the thick clouds, and while Haven's streetlights were excellent, none stood in this alley. It was dark as dark could be.

A door hidden in the wall swung open at a murmured command from Matt, and he led Elana down a staircase into the same guardian tunnels they'd used days before.

Matt only put Vicky down after they were safely ensconced in a tram car. Then he made a quick circle of the vehicle, pressing unmarked spots on the walls that glowed briefly at his touch.

He sat heavily and sighed. "I apologize for the horrible introduction to Haven, Miss Lamarr. Haven seems to be losing its mind these days."

Vicky wrung rainwater out of the hem of her dress. "Not your fault, Mr. Sexy Voice."

Elana glared. "*Why* did I tell you that?"

Vicky snorted. "I cope with crises via humor. Deal with it, pumpkin. Now, where are we going? Somewhere I can dry off?"

Matt nodded. "I'm taking you both to my condo. Elana, I can send someone to get things from your place. Fresh clothes for both of you, whatever."

Vicky raised her clutch, which was the same color as her dress. She'd managed to keep hold of it through the entire attack. "No need."

Matt narrowed his eyes. "Elana, did you give her a dimensional bag?"

"I lent it to her for the evening," Elana replied innocently. "It matched her dress. Besides, I had a feeling, and I didn't want to carry a purse in case shit went down."

Matt groaned and hung his head.

CHAPTER EIGHT

Vicky commandeered the shower first. Elana changed into clean clothes and tucked her and Vicky's wet—and in her case, food-covered—clothes into a couple of plastic bags, then into her dimensional clutch. Then she flopped onto Matt's couch with a heavy sigh.

"I'm stunned no one's come looking for us," she remarked toward the ceiling.

Matt followed her into the living room from the kitchen and put a steaming cup of decaf coffee on the table near her elbow. "I'm not. The guardians will be busy handling the fallout from tonight's incident, and I already told Valeria that you and Vicky were safe with me."

"But House Veridian operatives? Wouldn't they have figured out we went with you and come here?"

"Certainly possible, but we will have *ample* warning if anyone tries to attack my condo. I doubt it, though. They haven't made it this far with their conspiracy by attacking unwisely. I suspect they'll lay low for a while now."

Elana frowned. "Didn't they just blow their cover?"

Matt snorted under his breath. "Not a chance. This won't even be traced back to them."

She sat up and stared at him in disbelief. "How can you say that?"

"Because there won't be any overt links to them, just like every other incident." He shrugged. "The two guys who attacked you and Vicky will either be House-less, or more likely, from a House that is so distantly related to Veridian it's laughable—just like everyone else on your mother's list. They're probably dead by now, or if not, they will be soon."

"Wouldn't the guardians keep them for a trial?"

"Absolutely, but Veridian plants have a way of turning up dead while incarcerated."

Elana scowled. "Assholes."

"You said it." Matt sipped his coffee. "Everyone else at the gala will have hazy memories of the incident at best, and the security footage will be doctored all to hell."

Elana picked up her mug and slumped back against the couch. "Because of the haze? The cotton candy smell? What *was* that?"

"A biological weapon, essentially." Matt made a face. "Vampires fight dirty, you know that. There were enough high-level vampires in there that Veridian needed to make them all look the other way for a while, or their little game wouldn't have worked. You're Valeria Draven's protégé, for God's sake. If someone had realized what was happening, they'd have been done for.

"They counted on speed and not missing Vicky the first time." He gestured toward the bathroom with his mug. "You're an unknown. They don't know how to leverage or threaten you yet. You have no biological ties. Vicky is the only possible liability."

"You sure know how to make a girl feel special," Vicky sassed from the hallway.

Matt started, then chuckled. "You're *quiet*."

"You have *very* plush carpet, and I get pedicures once a month. Your turn, Lana." Vicky came around the couch into the living room and sat beside her friend. "Not before you tell me what you're on about me being a liability, though."

"You're Elana's only close friend who isn't a vampire, essentially," Matt told her. "I was telling Elana that the people who are after her—"

"House Veridian," Vicky provided.

"Yes," Matt confirmed, although he flashed an unimpressed look at Elana. "House Veridian doesn't know how to handle her. Tonight, they tried to get at her through you."

"Are they likely to try that again?" Elana queried. "If so, I want to give her some protection. I must be able to do that as part of the House of the SpiderKing."

Matt contemplated this while drinking more coffee. "It's possible, but I honestly doubt it. We learned from your mother's files that Veridian doesn't usually try the same thing twice. Also, Vicky is human. She's not exactly a high-value target."

Vicky elbowed Elana. "He's battin' a thousand."

Matt threw up a hand in exasperation. "Just because *House Veridian* doesn't think much of you doesn't mean it's *true!*" Vicky and Elana chortled, and he shook his head. "You two are trouble."

"Always have been." Vicky fist-bumped Vicky, and they grinned.

"I'm almost glad to hear that, actually," Elana admitted. "I was really worried about you being in danger because of me. Knowing that they're unlikely to bother you makes me feel a little better."

Vicky gripped Elana's free hand. "Me too. It's rude as hell but convenient for us." She glanced at Matt. "Real talk though, if I hire a personal bodyguard, can I ask you to vet them?"

Matt snorted. "I think I could manage that."

"Appreciate it." She let go of Elana's hand and patted her knee. "You takin' me home? Or are we both crashing on Mr. Sexy Voice's couch?"

Elana laughed. "I can take you home."

"Actually, I thought I'd send you home," Matt countered. "Sneak you out of the city through the guardian tunnels with an escort, and a car will take you from there."

"Ooh, now *that's* fancy." Vicky grinned. "Lana, you live in a spy movie. A *vampire* spy movie."

Elana groaned. "It's not all it's cracked up to be."

After Vicky had disappeared into the night and Elana had showered, she returned to her cold cup of coffee and sat with it at the kitchen island.

"Spare room's ready for you," Matt announced as he emerged from the hallway.

"Was it not already?"

"My sister stayed the night. I changed the sheets."

"Thanks." She sipped the coffee, then stared into its depths. "I know you said Vicky's probably safe, but I'm still worried."

Matt joined her at the island. "I'd be concerned if you weren't."

Elana set the mug on the island but continued staring into it. "It seems like they're moving so fast. Everything we found in my mother's files indicated they'd been playing a long game for *centuries*. Why now? Why me? I thought we'd been careful."

"We have been. They might have made the connection that you are your mother's daughter, and they're acting preemptively without knowing whether you're on to them."

"They know," Elana confirmed. "One guy, when he was attacking, said something like, 'Your mother only got herself killed, but you're gonna get a whole bunch of people killed.' I don't know what he meant."

Matt shrugged. "It's all fun and games until someone breaks out the stilettos and poison…and occasionally AK-47s. Luckily, most vampires think automatic weapons are lowbrow. He could've been trying to rattle you."

"Maybe." She swirled the coffee in her cup. "What happens when vampires die? Are you—*we*—buried? Or do we turn to dust like in the stories? I've never found a good answer for that."

"That's because we try to hide how normal our deaths are." He chuckled, then paused. "Would you like to see your mother's grave?"

Elana tore her gaze from the reflection of the overhead

light in the coffee and looked at Matt in mild shock. "I didn't realize I could. I didn't even think of it. Can I?"

"I wouldn't offer otherwise."

"Then yes, please. Tomorrow?"

"We can go now if you want."

She frowned. "Won't House Veridian be looking for me?"

Matt waved dismissively. "They won't find us. How do you think we escaped the hall?"

Elana narrowed her eyes. "I *was* wondering about that, now you mention it. How *did* we escape?"

He winked. "High-level vampire shit."

She glared. "You're a tease."

Tessa Hart had been laid to rest in a mausoleum in the Consorts' Cemetery. The very private burial ground in the heart of Senkyem lay hidden behind thick, twelve-foot hedges with cores of woven steel that emerged to form the arching, interlocking gate.

"Very Celtic," Elana commented as they approached the entrance in Matt's Audi.

"The designer is *old* Irish, so no surprise there. Hang on, I have to let us in."

He put the car in Park and got out into the rain. It had lessened to a drizzle since their pitched escape from Octava, but it still required windshield wipers. As a result, Elana couldn't see what Matt was doing at the gate, but after a few seconds, soft orange lights slid along the curved steel knotwork, and the gate untied itself.

That wasn't figurative untying. That was actual.

Matt climbed into the driver's seat and wiped rain from his face. "Always thought that was cool."

Elana was still agape. "You're not kidding."

As they drove through, carved statues on either side of the road lit up with the same gentle light. The statues depicted people and mythical creatures in various poses, similar to ornate headstones or monuments, but each had an eerie realism that the warm illumination emphasized. Elana suspected the overall effect would have been more peaceful than creepy were it not for the rain.

They parked in a lot only big enough for a handful of cars and stepped out into the drizzle. Matt retrieved a couple of umbrellas from his trunk and handed one to Elana. They proceeded up a footpath lit by small topiaries that glowed from within. The pruned bushes displayed the same artistic touch as the statues, although they were cunningly shaped into animals and dizzying geometric puzzles.

Elana peered into the darkness but saw no headstones in the sloping lawn beyond the path. "How many people are buried here?"

"A few dozen. It's a *very* exclusive cemetery. Only consorts can be buried here. Even then, some choose burial in their House plots. Some individuals state in their wills that they must be buried on *original* House land."

He huffed and shook his head. "That can cause problems when the land doesn't belong to the House anymore. There've been a few wars."

Elana grimaced. "Is there anything vampires *won't* go to war about? I'm beginning to think humans get it right when they slag off vampires. It's not the utopia vampire lovers make it out to be."

Matt laughed under his breath. "When we're good, we're really, *really* good—but when we're bad, we're absolutely *horrid*. Your mother's mausoleum is up here."

They were approaching a complex of shadows that Elana had only been able to see as faint silhouettes against the black sky until now, even with her enhanced vision. When they passed some invisible line, the orange light in the topiaries shot forward along the paved path and bloomed into glowing clouds that drifted up the nine massive stones at the heart of the cemetery.

Eight stones stood in a circle with one in the center, a clear analog for Haven. Each stone bore the simplest symbol of their Domains at their tapered tips, all shining in soft orange except for Shadow, which showed only a dark circle. Grassy mounds sloped away behind each monument except the center, which stood alone in the middle of several concentric circles like ripples on a pond.

Elana stepped onto the wet stone first and was unsurprised but still enchanted by the orange light that responded to her footsteps. The glow preceded her by about a yard as she approached the stone bearing Sanctuary's waxing quarter moon.

When she came within six feet of the enormous standing stone, which had to be better than twenty feet tall and ten feet wide at its widest, the outline of a door shimmered into existence, then evaporated into a void. Elana drew a breath and walked into the darkness, aware of Matt's presence a step behind her.

The light followed them in, as she'd expected. The

tunnel was comfortably large, wide enough for Elana to stretch her arms out in any direction and not touch stone. It was not smooth but swirled with carved waves and knots like the front gate.

As they descended into the barrow, the abstract artwork resolved into depictions of human civilization that Elana found no connection between until she realized they were "safe havens." Farmsteads, villages, innumerable places of worship...people in circles around campfires, children playing tag.

The tunnel opened into a circular room so deep Elana couldn't see the other side until the light swooped out ahead of her and rose along the walls to shine out of more waxing quarter moons. Eight more tunnels led out from this central room. None were marked.

"We want this one."

Matt's voice, although quiet, nevertheless made Elana jump. She looked behind her to see him indicating the third tunnel, moving clockwise from the entrance.

She raised an eyebrow. "One tunnel per arbiter? What happens when they hit eight?"

Matt shrugged. "Couldn't tell you for sure, but I assume they dig deeper in the first tunnel and keep going around the circle."

"Fair enough."

Elana proceeded into the third tunnel. It was nowhere near as long as the first, and within thirty seconds, the orange light emerged ahead of her into a simple circular room with more carved stone on the walls and a stone sarcophagus at its center.

Elana approached the sarcophagus with her heart in

her mouth. The lid was sculpted in her mother's image, and like the statues at the entrance, the resemblance was uncanny. Add the glow from within, and Elana was deeply glad the artist hadn't chosen to *paint* the statue. You would have believed that Tessa Hart might rise from the dead. She almost still did.

She forced herself to look away from her mother's stone countenance. Her gaze caught on the walls, which flickered faintly like firelight in the deep orange. Elana saw children everywhere—running in schoolyards, reading books, climbing trees, playing soccer, tearing apart contraptions too small to make out in the dim light...

Everything Elana had done.

Elana swallowed hard, blinked away tears, and looked back at her mother's tomb.

"She left everything for me," Elana murmured into the silence.

"It looks that way." Matt stood a respectful step behind her and to the side. "You okay?"

"I don't know."

"Want to talk about it?"

Elana considered this as she stared at the effigy of her mother. Its eyes were closed, which she appreciated. She didn't think she'd be able to stand it otherwise.

She let her hand drift out and brushed her fingertips along the smooth stone. It was cool, but not cold. She was grateful it wasn't warm.

"The more I see of Haven, and the more I see of my mom's work, the less confident I feel. She saw that something was wrong—or maybe she only felt it, I don't know—

and refused to buckle. She fought for justice until they killed her for it. She fought for *decades*.

"She didn't have to." Elana laid her palm on her mother's forearm. "She didn't choose to become a vampire, at least not as far as we know, but she accepted the curveball life threw her and tackled the challenge with everything she had.

"Did she know they would kill her? Is that why she left everything for me? Or was it just a backup?"

Elana shook her head. "I wish I could talk to her. I wish I could ask her why she picked me. Why did she think I'd be able to continue where she left off? It had to be more than a Hail Mary. She gave me the Rights, *illegally*, before I was old enough to remember her, then kept building this labyrinth of secrets.

"What would she have done if I discovered I was a vampire before she died? Would we have done this together?" Her throat caught, and her voice wavered.

"Would you have helped me, Mom? Helped me understand, helped me see? Because I don't. The moment I think I'm getting it, something else takes me by surprise, and I'm out of my depth again.

"I miss you, Mom." Elana swallowed a sob and hauled in a shaky breath. Matt stepped closer and put a hand on her shoulder, and she did not move away.

"I miss you so much. It breaks me that I don't remember you. How am I supposed to follow in your footsteps? Why did you put so much weight on me? Why did you trust me with this before I could even talk?

"What if I fail? What if I screw up? Not only would I fail Haven and the—the fucking *SpiderKing*—and who said you could saddle me with *royalty* without my go-ahead? *Jesus Christ, Mom*—but I'd fail you! I'd fail you, and I never even got to know you!"

Her voice broke, and several harsh sobs wrenched themselves from her chest. Matt put his free hand on her arm, but she pulled it away.

When the fit had passed, Elana wiped her eyes and gazed at her mother's serene stone face. The sculptor had not smoothed the wrinkles that Tessa Hart had gathered over her handful of decades on the Earth. Tiny crow's feet and the creases of laugh lines were etched into the stone face and would be until kingdom come, Elana presumed.

Tessa Hart smiled in death. It was a faint smile but visible thanks to those carefully reproduced wrinkles. The smile was kind and gentle, not unlike the soft orange light that suffused the space. Elana wondered if the lights were always orange or if they changed based on who was visiting. She wouldn't put anything past a vampire anymore.

Elana gazed at her mother's smile, the hands at her sides, and the lovingly carved children on the walls.

"You trusted me because you loved me," she whispered. "You poured as much love into me as you safely could, then disappeared so they wouldn't find me, and built an arsenal for me that you probably hoped I'd never have to use."

She laid her hand on her mother's cheek and let out a slow, shaky breath. "Okay, Mom. Okay. I'll do it. It might not be pretty, but I'll give it my best shot for you…because I trust you and because I love you, too."

CHAPTER NINE

"It's been a *week.*"

Matt raised his hands in a fruitless attempt to placate his boss. "You know how hard she's been working. She's made *huge* strides in her training. I've lost count of how many history books she's read. She's barely stopped asking either of us questions for more than an hour at a time. You *complained* to me last night that she wouldn't stop pestering you."

Valeria crossed her arms. "She's working, yes. But she's not *making progress.*"

"She's laying low. Can you blame her? Two attacks in less than a week—and she's not wrong when she says she's trying to send the message that she's not interested."

"Which we both know won't work. Have you told *her* that?"

"No. After her visit to Tessa's tomb, she…needed some time."

"I repeat, *it's been a week.*"

Matt sighed. "I know."

Valeria drummed her fingers on her forearm. "Staying in one place for too long is as dangerous as staying out in the open. If you don't get her moving within the next twenty-four hours, *I* will."

He sucked a breath in between his teeth. *"Yes, ma'am."*

Matt slipped into the sub-archive office and waved when Elana looked up from her pile of books and papers. "Just wanted to make sure you were alive down here."

She blinked at him owlishly. The bags under her eyes could have filled an airport carousel. "I texted you half an hour ago."

He shrugged. "I know, but sometimes you just gotta come check on your friends."

"I'm fine. I'm working." Elana tapped the table's glowing interface and zoomed in on a text file. "I've plotted half a dozen more connections between House Veridian and otherwise unconnected Houses—" The interface went dark under her hands, and she started. "Hey!"

Matt lifted his hand from the master control at the top edge of the desk and smiled apologetically at her scowl. "You're turning into a cave dweller. You need a break. I'm kidnapping you before you're forcefully inducted into House Nosferatu."

Elana's scowl deepened. "House Veridian isn't taking a break, I can guarantee you that."

"House Veridian is hundreds or thousands of people strong. You are *one person.* You can't let them rule your life like this, Elana. Please, come with me and take a break."

She glowered for a long moment, then deflated and began stacking the books and papers. "Fine. You win. What are we doing?"

"Since you haven't seen the sun in a week and it's a beautiful day, I thought we'd have a picnic. I already took the liberty of collecting sandwiches from Katz's and a couple of seltzers. All you have to do is get in the car."

Elana tapped the last papers into a neat pile, stood, and stretched. Several vertebrae popped, and she winced. "Ooh. I guess I *have* been down here too long."

"You're starting to look like a shrimp."

"You're so funny."

She followed him through the sub-basement corridor, to the elevator, and through the muted murmur of the main archives. Elana registered the fountain's gentle splashing for the first time in days. Her shoulders relaxed as she released tension she hadn't realized she was holding.

Elana glanced sheepishly at Matt as they exited the King's Archives into the sunny morning. "Sorry. I kinda laser-focused for a while there. It happens sometimes."

He smiled. "No problem. I get it. It seemed like the visit to your mother's mausoleum threw you for a loop. I wanted to give you some time to process, but I think I left it a little long. My apologies for that."

"It's okay. Thanks for caring." She rolled her head from side to side, then pulled back on each hand in turn for a deep wrist stretch. "It felt like I'd just gotten my mother *back*, sort of, by learning about her 'second life.' Then seeing her grave… You're exactly right. It did throw me for a loop."

"Feeling any better?"

"I think a picnic would hit the spot."

"Right this way."

They climbed into the Audi and sped off toward the Citadel, then curved around the wall and turned into Thani.

Elana arched an eyebrow when they passed the entrance to L'Arrondissement. "I thought we were going to your place."

Matt chuckled. "No, we're headed a bit farther afield. You need a change of scenery."

They drove out to the edge of Haven. The districts' layouts differed depending on their purpose, but most maintained the densest concentration of buildings and people along the gate roads and close to the Citadel. The closer to the Wall you went, the more open it became, to the point that the exterior sections of Senkyem and Shestoi resembled farmland more than a wedge of a city-state.

In a similar fashion, Thani's eclectic dwellings were fewer and farther between as Matt and Elana drove. Unlike Senkyem, the "rural" areas of Thani brought to mind a monarch's hunting grounds with carefully maintained green plains, copses of trees, and manufactured ponds.

Elana watched a crow arc across the blue sky. "Is this Crown land?"

"Some of it is. Houses own other sections."

"Does that mean I own some of it?"

Matt chuckled. "Well, you have more right to use Crown land than most, but I wouldn't advise pushing that envelope."

Elana snickered. She already felt more relaxed than she

had all day—all week, even. Matt had been onto something when he suggested a picnic.

They turned onto a road that carved through one of the grassy fields and drove until they reached a wide expanse of thick trees.

Elana raised an eyebrow. "Bit dark in here for a picnic."

"We're going through."

The forest passed in a flash, and Elana was treated to the sight of a three-story mansion in beige stone with a red shingled roof and almost a dozen chimneys. The mansion commanded the landscape even at a distance since perfectly manicured grounds a city block long stretched from the edge of the forest to the manor house.

As they approached, Elana scoured the architecture for clues about which House this could be but found none. The style was busy but functional, featuring balconies, columns, and carvings hanging from the eaves, and when Matt coasted to a stop beside a neatly trimmed oval topiary, she was still none the wiser.

Wryly, she asked, "Do you plan to tell me who you've tricked me into seeing, or are you keeping me on my toes?"

"This is Rothschilde Manor."

Elana drew in a very slow breath. "Oh, I *really* wish you'd told me before we arrived..."

Matt reached behind him and grabbed the basket off the back seat. "Don't worry. Lord Aldric is particularly fond of pastrami on rye."

Elana tugged the seams of her blouse into alignment as she stepped out of the car. She thanked every god she could think of that Cathy had recommended boutiques specializing in low-maintenance clothing. Despite wearing this outfit all day while hunched over a desk, it didn't have a single wrinkle.

The loose, light blue blouse and tan slacks weren't the fanciest look in her closet, but it was appropriate for the time of day and the setting. Her shoes were acceptable—simple white flats—but she wished she'd picked nicer jewelry than gold hoops, and she'd kill for a hair clip.

Matt hooped the picnic basket on one arm and Elana on the other as they approached the enormous mansion. It was more imposing than Ravenwood Manor despite the mesmerizing effect of the forestry family's masonry. Sheer size left an impression, but Elana wondered how the two buildings would compare if one included the Ravenwoods' subterranean levels.

The front doors swung open. Elana glimpsed a marble interior with a red-carpeted grand staircase leading to a second floor before a middle-aged man of average height closed the doors behind him with a twitch of his fingers.

He could have been anyone, Elana realized, although she had no doubt this was Aldric, Lord Rothschilde. House Rothschilde, formed exclusively of those from the centuries-old Rothschild banking family given the Rights, maintained the same realistic, down-to-earth approach to business and networking as the rest of their noble cousins.

"We take a much longer perspective," Elana had read in her research on House Rothschilde. "Responsibility comes with the name. We do not speculate. We preserve." They would not apologize for their wealth or hide it, but they would not flaunt it. Greed was anathema, philanthropy was paramount, and they sought balance in all things… with a conservative upward trend.

Lord Aldric spread his hands in greeting as he approached them. "Mister Richelieu, Miss Bishop. Welcome. I'd invite you in, but it would be a shame to miss this stunning afternoon, don't you think?"

Elana smiled brightly. Lord Aldric's light tenor and obvious enjoyment of fresh air reminded her of her dad's dad, Grandpa Bishop. He'd loved nothing more than to sit outside under a tree and whittle sticks down to nubs while whistling pop songs he always got wrong. There was no physical resemblance. Lord Aldric *looked* like a banker with his round face, glasses, and pressed suit, whereas Pop's nose had been broken three times in the boxing ring and he only wore a suit to his wife's funeral. Still, the *vibe* was there.

"We couldn't agree more," she replied. "Thank you for agreeing to meet with us."

"Always a pleasure to entertain a distant relation. The Richelieus and the Rothschildes go back quite a ways."

Her eyebrows lifted. "Do they? I didn't know."

Matt coughed. "The old noble Houses of Europe don't always advertise their linkages."

Aldric laughed. "Especially if you start trying to track the Habsburgs. Good *luck*."

Elana blushed. "I suppose that makes sense. I apologize for my ignorance."

Aldric beckoned them toward a terrace surrounded by trimmed hedges. A picnic table stood inside, shaded by an umbrella, and elegant flowerbeds nestled at the base of the green walls.

Lord Rothschilde smiled benevolently at Elana as they sat and Matt passed out the paper-wrapped sandwiches.

"No offense taken, Miss Bishop. We in the 'old guard' know all the tricks and sleights of hand that make the tapestries of our history. It wouldn't make the first bit of sense if we expected you to know them all by heart in your first month."

"I appreciate that."

"It's like the 'e' on Rothschilde—you have to get used to adding it after you receive the Rights, but it's terribly important. There has to be *delineation*. Otherwise, you run into issues like 'non-humans cannot own majority interests in financial enterprises controlling over one hundred million euros,' yada yada." He rolled his eyes. "But Rothschildes are not Rothschilds...*technically*."

Elana was happy to bite into her sandwich rather than puzzle out the legal distinction. She exclaimed in impressed surprise, "*Mm*—this is *good*."

"Katz's?" Aldric inquired of Matt, and his smile grew and warmed further when Matt nodded. "Best in the city. You're too kind."

The trio devoured their sandwiches in the silence that accompanied particularly delicious food. After each had polished off the last crumbs and caraway seeds, wiped their mouths, and sighed into their seltzers, Aldric leaned toward Elana with a conspiratorial look. "No one comes to House Rothschilde just to share pastrami. What are you looking for?"

Elana drew a deep breath and flattened her napkin one more time. "Balance."

Aldric raised an eyebrow. "I hope you're not talking about a bank balance."

She shook her head. "Not at all. I'm talking about the balance between humans and vampires."

His skepticism melted away to reveal intrigue. "Go on."

"That balance has shifted from one end of the spectrum to the other over the millennia, as any balance must. Still, it's vitally important that the balance remains as close to the center as possible. We depend on each other more than most of us would like to admit. To keep that balance, the factions within the two populations with the power to affect change have to stay alert…and they need to be kept accountable."

"Accountable to whom?" Aldric quietly asked.

Images from her mother's mausoleum floated in her mind's eye. "To those who come after us."

Aldric set his seltzer on the table. "Which direction do you believe the balance is tipping, young Miss Bishop?"

"Toward vampires, but *not* a faction willing to be held accountable to their descendants. Do you know House Veridian?"

Interest flashed in the unassuming man's eyes. "What of the green house?"

Elana sipped her seltzer, then laid it all out for him. She'd known this meeting would come eventually, if not when, so she'd done her research and planning well ahead of time. She'd confirmed beyond a shadow of a doubt that it was safe to tell Lord Aldric Rothschilde *everything*. It would be necessary to win him over. Rothschildes not only valued balance but also candor. Business behind closed doors was one thing, but if you wanted someone to go all in, you had to meet them there.

If she convinced him to join their cause, it would mean

she was backed by the royal treasury *and* House Rothschilde's private wealth. That would be a *coup de grâce* never seen in Haven. The Rothschildes supported nearly all of the SpiderKing's efforts but had never formally allied with him. They guarded their neutrality scrupulously.

She was coming to the end of her spiel. "They attacked me twice in one week and endangered numerous others in doing so. Whatever I'm onto, they don't want it getting out, and they're willing to risk exposing their operatives to stop me.

"They've spent generations laying the foundations of a plot that I believe will shift the balance between humans and vampires to a greater degree than ever before—and in a way that *only* favors them," she concluded. "This is not in the best interests of *anyone* on the planet. It is *certainly* not in House Rothschilde's best interests. I need resources to stop them. Are you in?"

The round-faced banker pondered her through his simple, elegant glasses. Elana would swear she could see the centuries of carefully tended family values ticking away behind his warm brown eyes. Lady Ravenwood's advanced age had been evident. Elana barely had the first clue how old Lord Aldric was. He could have been fifty, or he could have been five hundred. He had one of those ageless faces.

He offered her his hand. "I'm in."

CHAPTER TEN

The moment they were out of sight, Elana slouched in the front passenger seat of Matt's Audi and let out a huge sigh. "I'm so glad you brought sandwiches, but also screw you for tricking me. That was nasty."

"Heh. Sorry. I was under orders to get you moving, so…"

She rolled her head to the side and arched an eyebrow. "Under orders? From Valeria?"

"Uh-huh. She thinks you've been procrastinating, for lack of a better word."

Elana huffed. "I'd say 'let's see how much initiative she takes after her best friend almost got killed,' but knowing her, I wouldn't have a leg to stand on."

"You're not wrong."

Elana sighed again and stared out the windshield. "Two successful meetings. I think that one went better than the Ravenwood one…although I thought the Ravenwood one went *great* until Valeria raked me over the coals."

"There *is* a hell of a learning curve," Matt admitted.

"Honestly, I think you're doing great. Valeria is…" He made a sound in the back of his throat.

"Is what? Or are you not allowed to say?"

Matt drummed his fingers on the steering wheel. "It's not that I'm not *allowed* to say what I was about to say. It's that I'm not sure it's *wise*."

"Why's that?"

"Because Valeria cultivates a *very* specific persona, and the more people who know it *is* a persona, the less clout that reputation gives her."

"I can keep a secret."

"Can you?" Matt side-eyed her briefly. "You've shared a *lot* with Vicky. I understand it's hard not to since she's your best friend and you're under incredible stress. However, *all* vampires have a responsibility to maintain confidentiality when it comes to Haven's secrets."

Elana straightened and frowned. "Then I need to know what I am and am *not* allowed to share," she retorted. "So far, the 'guidelines' on that have been nonexistent except for the NDA that *I didn't actually sign.* Otherwise, all I've heard is this nebulous 'don't tell the humans anything. It's for their own good,' and if you'll excuse my French, that's bullshit. If Haven *wasn't* so damn tight-lipped, we could do a lot *more* good in the human world. On that, I agree with my mother a hundred percent."

Matt grimaced. "I don't disagree with you in principle, but I do in practice. You don't have the perspective that older vampires do when it comes to the diplomatic release of information—to whom, at what time, and with what conditions.

"There's also the *important* consideration of Haven's

secrets getting back to *other vampires.* You know how horrible Old World Houses can be, Elana. It would be all too easy for one of them to reverse-engineer our technology if they got their hands on it and wreak havoc on humanity."

"All right, I can understand *that* much, but it doesn't change that I need to *know* what I can and can't say. Y'all need to *tell* me because I don't know what to ask."

"Fair enough. We have a couple of hours, so we might as well start now." He drew a deep breath and let it out in a thoughtful hiss. "In terms of technology, things like the dimensional bags are pretty safe to talk about, although I wouldn't *sell* them to humans. They're relatively resource-intensive to create, so producing them in bulk wouldn't work…"

"That's why we don't talk about history in general," Matt concluded as he turned onto Elana's street. "Our living memories are *significantly* longer than humans' are. While you'd think that would result in us becoming respected repositories of wisdom and diplomacy, the opposite is true nine times out of ten. Any time a vampire society has tried it, they've ended up with fanatic devotees within three centuries while the rest of the world decries them as witches or revolutionaries, or worse, *revisionists.*"

Elana snorted. "Oh no, not *revisionists.* How horrible." She groaned and rubbed her eyes. "Man, sometimes we're just dumb, aren't we? Humans *and* vampires."

"We sure are."

She cracked her neck and peered out the window into the dimming twilight. After spending hours in a car, she looked forward to stretching out on the floor mattress.

An uncomfortable silence fell over the car as they pulled up in front of Elana's house.

"Holy fuck," Elana muttered. "Do you see this?"

"I do," Matt grimly confirmed. "Speaking of people being dumb. I'm so sorry, Elana."

Obscene graffiti, words and images alike, marred the façade of Elana's new house. The terminology hardly consisted of clever wordplay, but the gamut of nasty insults was represented in a rainbow of colors across the white stucco. Several front windows were smashed, garbage was strewn over the lawn, and the flowerbeds had been dug up and thoroughly destroyed.

Elana stared. Her heart felt as though it had been carved from her chest, and her stomach had dropped through her shoes. The vandals hadn't torched the place, but they'd come damn close.

She got out of the car and hesitantly stepped forward. As her eyes adjusted to the twilight, she spied the glistening remains of eggs on the side of the house *and* on her beautiful Emeya, parked in the driveway. Looking beyond it, she discovered the garage had been vandalized too.

Elana's blood ran cold, then hot, as she cycled between numb and distraught. She vaguely heard Matt's car door close and his footsteps approach on the pavement.

She picked her way through the scattered trash to the front door. Her throat caught when she saw it hung ajar. The vandals had bashed it in.

"It might not be safe to go in," Matt cautioned her.

Elana shook her head. "If this was supposed to kill me, they wouldn't have left evidence. They'd have broken in and planted a trap, not wrecked all my shit. I won't be surprised if the damage extends inside, though. This is as clear of a 'fuck you' message as I've ever seen."

The first thing they saw upon entering the ransacked house were the words "Humans Go Home" scrawled in bright red spray paint over the living room wall. *Uninventive but effective.*

She knelt in the middle of the floor and gently spread the ripped flaps of a smashed cardboard box. A squirrel figurine lay broken on top of the pile of bubble-wrapped tchotchkes. It had been a gift from her father to her mother, a silly trinket bought on a whim that had been on the fake mantelpiece in their living room for as long as Elana could remember.

Elana sat cross-legged, cradled the broken figurine, and closed her eyes. Matt's footsteps moved away behind her into the kitchen. She heard his sharp intake of breath and knew she wouldn't enjoy what he'd found in there. Probably broken dishes. She'd just started to unpack those boxes.

Matt didn't stay long in the kitchen. He backtracked—Elana heard the crunch of glass under his shoe and winced—and headed down the hall. Doors creaked in succession as he checked each room, then returned to the living room. Based on the rustle of his suit, he either knelt or crouched beside her.

"Elana." His voice was quiet, but the tone was hard as steel. "You with me?"

She didn't open her eyes. "Yeah."

"You can't stay here. It's not safe. I agree with your assessment they aren't likely to have left any further nasty surprises, but...well, your windows are all smashed."

"God. All of them?"

"Almost."

Elana sighed and ran a thumb over the figurine in her palm. A sharp edge nicked the pad of her thumb. She reflexively flinched, although she barely felt the pain. "Does this happen often with newly turned vampires?"

"No. Not at all. This is..." Matt drew a slow breath and let it out in a hiss while deciding how to finish his sentence. "This is not normal at all, for multiple reasons. Do you have a list of everything that was in your boxes?"

"Yeah." She swallowed and nodded. "I have pictures on my phone. Vicky and I wrote on each box what was inside it. I could make a more detailed list if I needed to, using those pics. Do you think they stole anything?"

"Hard to tell. Your dresser's been overturned and gone through, but I know you were keeping the really expensive stuff downstairs, and I haven't been down there yet. The kitchen's covered in broken glass and I don't want to disturb the crime scene any more than we already have."

The porcelain figurine suddenly felt too hot in her hands, but she couldn't move. "Right. I guess we have to call the guardians."

"Well..."

Elana finally opened her eyes when Matt's voice trailed off. The broken squirrel's eyes accused her with their shiny white gaze, and she forced herself to look at Matt instead. "I don't understand. Why wouldn't we call the guardians?"

Matt's brow jutted forward. His set jaw could have cut

stone, and his eyes flashed with contained anger. "Because the guardians should have *stopped* this. The fact that they *didn't* means something is *very* wrong in Haven law enforcement."

Elana's eyes widened. "Oh, shit. You think somebody paid someone off?"

"That's one possibility. Another is that there's a Veridian link on the force with high enough authority that they could make this a non-issue."

A chill ran down Elana's spine. "We hadn't considered that. Now that you mention it, it *is* kind of weird that my mom's list of Veridian contacts didn't include anyone in the guardians. I had vaguely wondered if they were smart enough to steer clear of the cops because the guardians *do* their jobs, but…it's more likely that someone's dirty, isn't it."

"Or at least equally as likely."

Elana heaved a sigh. "If we're not calling the guardians, who *do* we call?"

"We call Valeria, and she handles it. It wouldn't surprise me if she assigns a Chimera squad to investigate."

Elana fell silent and stared at the broken squirrel in her hands. Matt let her have a long moment of thought before he put a gentle hand on her shoulder.

"Come on. We'll go back to my place. Do you have enough in your dimensional bag to keep you for a couple of days?"

"Until tomorrow at least. I can buy something if I need to. I think I left my travel toothbrush in your guest bathroom, anyway."

"Okay." He gripped her shoulder. "This *isn't* normal,

Elana. This isn't how Haven works. Valeria will figure this out, and you'll be fine."

With one more sigh, Elana replaced the two halves of the figurine in the box. "I sure hope you're right."

She sat on the curb in front of the house and waited while Matt made phone calls—first to Valeria, then to someone at the guardians' headquarters. Occasionally, she caught snippets of conversation. "Hundreds of thousands in damages," "Someone should have caught this," "Take it up with the arbiter...and what was your badge number?"

Elana stared at a tiny fragment of something glittery on the pavement. She wished she could explore more of the *good* that Haven had to offer, but the universe seemed intent on shoving her headfirst into crisis after crisis. More than anything else, she wanted a *break*.

The sound of tires on asphalt heralded the arrival of the first guardian car. She looked up to see the same model of black SUV that had shown up to deal with the Runner. It was alone this time, and the black-suited, dark-skinned man who stepped out was not familiar to Elana.

Matt met him at the foot of the driveway. "Kevin. I'm glad you were on duty tonight."

Kevin grunted in acknowledgment. "Anyone left on the property?"

"Not as far as I can tell. Who else is en route?"

"Andrews and Jonasson to start. The CSI squad's supposed to show up in an hour. We'll spell off so the place is under surveillance all night."

"Good."

"The lady okay?"

Elana felt more than saw Matt glance at her as he replied, "She's uninjured."

"Looks like she needs a stiff drink," Kevin opined, not unkindly.

Elana snorted under her breath. She agreed.

A stray eggshell crunched under Matt's shoe as he walked to her. "We can go, Elana. Your house is in good hands now."

Silently, she hauled herself upright and followed Matt to the Audi. She'd wanted to take her Emeya in case the vandals came back, but Matt had assured her the guardians would make sure her car wasn't harmed, and the investigators would need to look at it.

The drive to Matt's place was quiet. They parked in the underground garage and ascended the stairs in silence, and the first thing Matt did upon entering his condo was open the cabinet above the fridge.

"Normally when I offer someone a nightcap, I open the whiskey, but I think tonight's a good night for tequila," he stated. "You in?"

Elana flopped on the couch and stared at the ceiling. "Fuck it. Yes. Make mine a double."

A minute later, he handed her a double shot of amber liquid, which she took after sitting up. She clinked her shot glass against his, then tossed her head back and downed the contents in one go.

She swallowed, coughed, put the shot glass on the coffee table, and fell onto the couch again. "What is my *life?*"

"Astonishingly ridiculous, that's what," Matt agreed after taking his shot in a similar fashion. "I've witnessed dozens of new vampires integrating into Haven society. Not *one* of them has been this fraught. Not even your mother."

Elana groaned. "Great. Guess I'm doing her proud."

"You probably are. You have them running scared, and you've been on the scene for less than two months. Your mother might have stirred up some shit, but you're a bona fide shit *disturber*."

"Yeah, and look where it's gotten me. Forty-eight hours into home ownership and they've completely trashed my place. That four million will disappear faster than you can say… God, I'm too stressed to come up with something clever. I did *not* need this on top of today's meeting."

"Fair enough. Valeria's guardians will handle the house situation, so let's talk about something else. We have one more meeting coming up."

"Madame Lucia Lambra Mor of Stormhaven." Elana drew a deep breath and let it out in a *whoosh*. "As if Ravenwood and Rothschilde weren't intimidating enough… You really saved the best for last."

"You needed a run-up. Besides, the travel plans didn't work until now. So! Tell me everything you know about House Stormhaven."

CHAPTER ELEVEN

Valeria drummed her fingers on her desk and stared at the lines of text that stood out on its pure white surface in sharp black sans serif font. When she leveled that stare at a person, it was only a matter of time before they cracked and told Valeria everything she wanted to know.

Frustratingly, it didn't work on her notes.

Valeria Draven lived for puzzles. This made her an excellent Arbiter of Shadows because her driving motivation was *solving*, not winning. Other facets of her personality that commended her for the job were her unwavering loyalty to the SpiderKing, her negative tolerance for bullshit, and her unshakable moral code. The desire to divine solutions to the most complex enigmas brought the point home.

The best arbiters were selfless. Not self-effacing, not *quite*, but they had to be in it for the job, not the position. Angling for authority was antithetical to the sociopolitical atmosphere at Haven's foundation. *Less* drama, not *more*, was the SpiderKing's official position on the matter, and overbearing egos were *not* welcome.

Granted, that didn't mean there *weren't* any egotistical maniacs who'd held the title. Not every arbiter could be said to have been a paragon of virtue. A certain measure of self-interest was expected, as long as one didn't allow one's ambition to get in the way of performing your monarch-assigned duties.

The Arbiter of Legacy, Carlysle Zilmann, was a prime example of the other end of the spectrum. Zilmann had built an impressive and lucrative career over the decades, and she held onto her gains with an iron fist. She got away with the obvious self-aggrandizing because her record as an arbiter was spotless and successful. She advanced her interests while advancing the king's in equal or greater measure. While Valeria had no use for the woman's attitude or philosophy, she respected the results.

Now, glaring at the notes on her desk as though she could cow them into submission like she could a suspect, Valeria wondered whether a touch of self-interest might have served her well in this case. If she'd built the network of tit-for-tat informants her predecessor had, perhaps she'd have more threads to pull or more corners already open to her.

On the other hand, Valeria had never shied away from a challenge, and the puzzle left behind by Tessa Hart would not be the first to break her resolve.

If she were honest with herself—and she was, scrupulously so—it was the fact that *Tessa* had left this behind that made it so damn frustrating.

Valeria Draven had believed that Tessa Hart was a

friend. Someone she could trust to tell Valeria everything she needed to know and then some. Finding out that Tessa had kept a huge swath of her life a complete secret from Valeria...hurt.

Then again, Valeria wasn't exactly known for her proclivity for asking deep, engaging questions about her friends' pasts. She lived in the here and now, not the past. Especially not when that past was so clearly painful, as it had been for Tessa. Not to mention the very clear "do not touch" signs figuratively plastered all over the circumstances of Tessa's Rights. Valeria knew when to question her boss, and the answer to that was *never*.

Valeria could understand Tessa not telling her about the daughter she'd left behind in the human world. She could even understand Tessa keeping mum about having given young Elana the Rights, especially if it had been an impulsive decision driven by suppressed grief.

However, that was *not* what had happened. Tessa had deliberately chosen to turn Elana, and it had been part of a deep and complex plot to unravel a conspiracy. A conspiracy Tessa had *also* opted not to share with Valeria, even though she was the Arbiter of Shadows. In other words, the person best-equipped and best-positioned to neutralize a threat to the SpiderKing, like, oh, *a widespread conspiracy*.

Had Tessa been concerned that Valeria was compromised? Surely not. Nothing in the files indicated so. Then again, if Tessa *had* been worried about whether she could trust Valeria or the people in Valeria's employ, she wouldn't have chanced leaving any hint of that suspicion where it might come to Valeria's attention.

Valeria growled in the back of her throat and dug the heels of her hands into her eyes. This was *infuriating*, and she'd been at it for weeks now. Add the false Chimera debacle on top, and it was little wonder her workout sessions at the training grounds left more holes in the walls than usual.

Okay, Valeria. Back to the facts. One more time.

Tessa Bishop, née Hart, was taken into intensive care at Grace Memorial Hospital at 2:17 PM on the eighth of June, 1992, suffering from postpartum eclamptic seizures. Newborn Elana Bishop was left in the care of her father, Jeremiah Bishop.

The next time Jeremiah Bishop saw his wife was 11:21 PM that night. She had been pronounced dead ten minutes earlier. Her chart showed that her final seizure had begun at 10:58 PM, and she had flatlined at 11:00 PM precisely. Resuscitation had failed.

Tessa Bishop's death certificate was signed at 12:39 AM on the ninth of June, 1992. Jeremiah took his newborn daughter home after signing the forms that would allow any viable organs to be harvested from Tessa's body and her remains to be cremated.

Valeria had found all this by digging into Grace Memorial's records. That much had been easy. The only trouble was that at some point between 2:17 and 11:21 PM on that Monday in June, *someone* had given her the Rights, and Valeria was no further in discovering who that had been.

You couldn't turn a dead body and bring it back to life. Vampirism was not necromancy. To give someone the Rights, they had to be alive and *stay* alive long enough for the process to progress adequately. Eventually, it would become self-sustaining, and whatever minor ailments the person suffered from before being given the Rights would more or less be eradicated. Something severe like eclampsia—especially in such a late stage—would not have been miraculously cured.

No matter how dead Tessa Bishop might have *looked* to her heartbroken husband and the humans on the medical team, she could not have been. Instead of being cremated, she was undoubtedly whisked away to Haven in a transport either commandeered or driven by the mysterious vampire who had turned her.

From June eighth to August twenty-seventh, 1992, Tessa Bishop, née Hart, had disappeared off the face of the Earth. To everyone in the human world, she was dead and buried as of June eighteenth.

Tessa Hart emerged into Haven society on August twenty-eighth. She was registered as a member of the House of the SpiderKing, and all records of her Rights were sealed under royal order. Naturally, this was a curiosity and thoroughly debated behind closed doors, but few were stupid enough to question the king's will openly. Perhaps she was a distant relative or someone the SpiderKing wanted to protect. Tessa made no secret that she was a turned vampire, not born, but that didn't preclude her being related to the House in other ways.

The raised eyebrows never went *away*, but Tessa quickly made a name for herself that chased most of the naysayers into the wings. She got involved in politics almost immediately, showing a serious aptitude for diplomatic enterprises.

While most Havenites remained curious about where she'd come from and why she was so driven to strengthen relations between humans and vampires, no one could refute her success. In a population where secrets came with the territory—no House was devoid of skeletons—in some ways, this made her fit in *more*.

For the next eighteen years, Tessa Hart would be the driving force behind the SpiderKing's push to bring the city-state of Haven closer to its sister city of Ashford. That extended to Ashford's "mothers," North Carolina and the United States. *And beyond that, the world,* Valeria mused.

In 1995, barely three years after joining Haven, Tessa became the Consort of External Affairs and Diplomacy, thus formalizing her role in Haven's legislature. Seven years later, in 2002, she accepted the position of Arbiter of Sanctuary, making her the youngest arbiter in Haven's history—and the next youngest was older by nearly a century. She had beaten Valeria's record for progression from initiate to arbiter by a full fifteen years.

This rapid ascent started all the tongues wagging again. Tessa Hart was powerful for such a young vampire, and to be named an arbiter at the age of *thirty-five*... Well, it ought to be no surprise that the old Houses erupted in murmured protest. After all, one did not argue with the king. Still, one could make one's displeasure known to the new arbiter via vague grumbles and curiously late invitations for all of Haven's top social events.

Valeria remembered these years. She had already been well entrenched as the Arbiter of Shadows by the time Tessa Hart emerged on the scene, and she had watched the young woman with deep curiosity. Tessa Hart was an enigma on the same level as her daughter. Where Valeria was privy to the circumstances of Elana's story—most of them, anyway—she had been barred from knowing Tessa's from the start.

This chafed, but Valeria respected the SpiderKing more than anyone else and trusted that he would tell her whatever she needed to know. If she was not on the need-to-know list for Tessa Hart's history, the next best thing she could do was become friends with her and find out as much as she could on her own.

Valeria hadn't expected to become friends with her. She typically limited the extent to which she became friends with anyone. Valeria firmly believed that connections were useful to a point. After that, they became liabilities. Therefore, she maintained relationships to the exact level that she needed them and no further.

Tessa Hart had blown that standard out of the water. The woman had been caring, kind, and motivated. She'd reminded Valeria of herself, but with a heart that wasn't guarded behind multiple layers of barbed wire and laser grids. Tessa Hart wore her heart on her sleeve and made no apology for it, and she leveraged that empathy in ways Valeria couldn't imagine would ever work…except they did.

Despite Tessa being a ray of sunshine to Valeria's dark side of the moon, she had never once indicated that she disapproved of Valeria's methods or attitude. She'd listened, discussed, asked questions, and listened more. They'd gone a few rounds in the sparring ring when Tessa had been particularly frustrated by one stonewalling old vampire or another. Tessa had held her own, but then again, Valeria had been holding back. By that time, she understood that Tessa's goal was working out emotions, not winning.

Valeria had been furious when Tessa got shot in the inter-House war. She'd been incandescent with rage when the wounds had proven fatal.

Most vampires considered gun violence passé, the unsophisticated, barbarian's way of escalating a conflict. Vampires were more clever and resourceful than that. It was *lazy*. Beyond the social faux pas of committing a drive-by shooting, gunshot wounds didn't usually *kill* vampires. At worst, you'd be stuck in the hospital for a few days while you healed.

Tessa had been on her way to an Arbiters' Council when she'd been shot. The incident had happened only blocks away from the Citadel, close enough to be heard through the open windows of the consulate on that hot, muggy summer day. Valeria had been out in Ashford earlier that morning on business and had rarely been so grateful for Haven's climate control.

As the Arbiter of Shadows, the gunfire had brought Valeria to her feet and out of the impending meeting before anyone had uttered a word. Scant minutes later, she'd skidded to a halt in front of her friend's silver AMG Mercedes, riddled with bullet holes and surrounded by shattered glass.

She'd pulled Tessa from the vehicle while barking orders on her earpiece. The first guardian car had pulled up not sixty seconds later, summoned by the hail of bullets more than Valeria's angry call, and the ambulance was on its tail...but it was too late.

Tessa had lived just long enough to smile at her friend.

Haven's surveillance system was extraordinary, especially in the Citadel's environs. Valeria had been able to watch the lethal event in her office minutes later after Tessa's body had been transported to the coroner.

Tessa's Mercedes glided up the broad avenue between Zevenda and Shestoi toward the Citadel ring road. A luxury SUV trailed her at a respectable distance. Another approached on the ring road and signaled to turn onto the avenue.

When Tessa stopped at the stop sign and the SUV turned, its back driver's side window rolled down and the barrel of an assault rifle poked out. Likewise, the sunroof on the trailing SUV rolled back and someone wearing all black emerged holding a similar weapon.

Both assailants opened fire. The windows of Tessa's Mercedes shattered, and pockmarks marred the silver sedan. Tessa jerked in her seat and slumped to the side. The car started forward as her foot doubtless slid from the brake, but the hail of gunfire apparently severed something important in the front end because the vehicle shuddered to a halt.

The two SUVs left rubber marks on the asphalt as they sped away.

The SUVs were found abandoned in Ashford. They were devoid of DNA evidence, and the guns were never found, but Valeria's relentless pursuit bore fruit. Within days, she had traced the SUVs' plates to human owners and from there to shell companies owned by vampires in two different Houses known to have a longstanding feud.

After getting that far, it was child's play to find the drivers and gunners. When the Arbiter of Shadows summoned the head of a House to her office, they showed up, and when they were greeted by the sight of Valeria in black from head to toe, they talked.

Valeria had executed the four personally. Three men, one woman. Double-tap pistol shots. It was one thing to be lazy in an inter-House war and another entirely to be efficient in cleanup.

She wore the blood-stained white suit jacket to the executions over her black dress shirt and slacks. She looked each vampire in the eyes as she killed them. She did not flinch.

They had not only murdered the Arbiter of Sanctuary but also Valeria Draven's best friend. Their Houses had the gall to claim that Tessa had been unfortunate collateral damage incurred during an unauthorized, opportunistic flare-up in an inter-House war that had contentedly contained itself to snide remarks at dinner parties for decades.

It had been obvious that the two Houses were using the story as an excuse to get rid of Tessa. Maybe they'd been pissed off about her pushing for more human involvement in Haven. Perhaps they didn't like her because they saw her as an uppity human claiming space that wasn't hers. Maybe it was a not-so-subtle "up yours" to the SpiderKing.

It didn't matter. There hadn't been evidence to contradict their version of events, no matter how deep Valeria dug, so she'd been forced to let the matter quietly slide into the annals of Haven's history.

Twenty years later, Tessa Hart's daughter hit a Runner

with her Ford F150 on her way home from work, setting off a chain of events that had led to Valeria Draven sleeping even less than usual.

Elana Bishop resembled her mother so strikingly that it had taken Valeria aback the moment she'd stepped out of her Mercedes. Combined with Elana's impressive takedown of the new vampire, Valeria had been suspicious enough to demand a blood test. Within hours, the proof that Tessa Hart had been hiding huge swaths of her life from Valeria was black and white on the page of lab results. Mere days after, Elana uncovered the first clues that Tessa had been investigating a conspiracy.

Valeria had access to Tessa's files. The Arbiter of Shadows had access to every arbiter's files, except in circumstances where they were locked by order of the king. Valeria had gone through them after Tessa's death, hunting for a sign that Tessa had known she was in danger, and she'd found nothing.

Valeria had opened Tessa's log. She hadn't made it very far. It felt too much like she was betraying her best friend. Besides, the first entries were only about her *feelings*. As much respect as Valeria had for how Tessa lived her life, she couldn't stomach reading about *feelings*.

Now she wished she'd struggled through. She'd like to think she would have noticed the typos that had led to so many discoveries. Matt certainly had, and thank goodness for that. Otherwise, they would likely still be in the dark regarding House Veridian's centuries-long shadow campaign of treason.

For treason it was, and Valeria was growing more certain of it by the day. Elana didn't have the in-depth familiarity with Haven's inner workings necessary to make the intuitive connections between the widely varied files referenced in Tessa's journal, but Valeria did.

House Veridian had built a shadow network hidden under so many layers of subterfuge that not even Valeria Draven had noticed. The extent of that network gave her pause, especially because she still couldn't figure out their precise endgame. Whether it was overthrowing the Spider-King or seizing control of industries or companies, there would eventually have to be a linchpin or a handful of key actors. *Someone* had to pull the trigger.

Normally, Valeria would presume it was the head of House Veridian, except the current head of House Veridian was the vampire equivalent of a "trust fund baby" daddy's girl. Terribly spoiled, whiny, and as useful as tits on a fish. Valeria considered herself a good judge of character, and Cherry Vino—yes, that *was* her real name—could not have held a centuries-old global conspiracy together even if it only related to her makeup drawer.

The power behind the throne would be the next place to look. However, on the surface, House Veridian had few branches to its tree, and none of them were significant. Either they weren't registering their kin, which was so uncommon as to be nearly inconceivable—illegal, in fact, in Haven. Or they were paying a great number of people large amounts of money to keep their lineage hidden.

But to what end? Valeria smacked her desk with an open palm in frustration. Hiding your lineage meant your scions had no standing, no clout, no *nothing*. None of this made *sense*. This investigation was going around in circles, and she hadn't even touched on the infuriating data point of *who turned Tessa Hart.*

Accessing Grace Memorial's security footage was a cakewalk, but their digital archives only went back ten years. It was *remotely* possible that there were hard copy VHS tapes from the nineties stored somewhere, but more likely they would have kept them until the statutory limitation ran out and recorded over them. It was a crapshoot whether they'd waited that long to begin with.

No records existed of a Haven-based doctor or medical specialist of any kind visiting Grace Memorial that day, neither in the human hospital's charts nor in those of any of Haven's medical clinics. Medical research boomed inside Haven's ring wall. Multiple clinics and facilities thrived in Etreta, Quarto, and Shestoi in particular, although they existed within every district of Haven. Each was required to open their archives to Valeria in her capacity as the Arbiter of Shadows, and each had responded to her request.

Still this doctor remained a mystery.

What had happened on that day in June of 1992? What vampire had visited Grace Memorial, and what had been their goal? Had they happened upon Tessa Bishop, or had they somehow known who they were searching for and why?

If they hadn't known ahead of time, why had they chosen to give this, for all intents and purposes, *random human woman* the Rights? What had they seen or heard that drove them to give a dying woman a sliver of a chance to live, and why had they *hidden her away* and allowed her family to believe she was dead?

Why, and how, had that woman gone on to become a central part of Haven's political landscape in such a short time? How had Tessa discovered House Veridian's plan, or why had she become suspicious enough to investigate them? Why had Tessa never told Valeria or anyone else the circumstances of her turning? She clearly remembered them well enough to find her daughter and turn *her*, so the question of Rights-induced amnesia was moot.

What had driven Tessa to give her daughter the Rights? How had she known that the little girl, barely a toddler, would have survived the grueling ordeal? Yes, children were resilient as a rule, but the process of becoming a vampire was unpleasant to say the least, and there were *reasons* most vampires were turned well after adolescence.

Valeria Draven loved puzzles more than anything else on the planet. She'd been the closest she could get to *gung-ho* about the prospect of figuring out the puzzle that was Elana Bishop. Then the puzzle exploded into multiple mysteries that threatened the foundation of her confidence in her ability to do her damn job.

If Valeria had missed all of this—Tessa's origins, Elana's existence, and the entire Veridian conspiracy—what else could she have missed? Did the SpiderKing know about all of this and was content to keep her in the dark and dealing with other threats?

It struck Valeria as likely that His Majesty knew about Tessa and Elana. Tessa could not have held the positions she had, otherwise—not without Valeria's entire understanding of the SpiderKing needing to be rewritten.

But the Veridian conspiracy... It was Valeria's job to uncover everything that happened within the confines of

Haven, and this had escaped her notice. Tessa had hidden her research so well that Valeria hadn't had a clue. Could it be that the king didn't know? Valeria had always believed that to be impossible. It might have been Valeria's job to *uncover* everything in Haven, but the SpiderKing *knew* everything in Haven. On multiple occasions, Valeria received tips from on high, as it were.

It was unconscionable that the king did not know. Therefore, if he knew, he was not concerned enough to bring it to her attention, and she did not need to worry about it.

Yet worry gnawed at her gut as it never had before. She felt like she'd eaten half an apple before discovering half a worm.

If it were only the puzzles she could not solve, that would be one thing. She would reapply herself, find a new angle, and figure it out. To her anger and dismay, those puzzles were rapidly bleeding into the real world in concrete ways, such as Elana Bishop's home being heavily vandalized. That meant someone in Valeria's domain was crooked, and the Arbiter of Shadows did not take kindly to being mocked in that fashion.

That might be the sole silver lining in the horrendous past weeks. If someone in the guardians was connected to House Veridian, Valeria could root that person out.

If she did so too soon, she didn't doubt the whole network would disappear into the void like so many mice into the walls. Valeria Draven was a patient woman when she needed to be. Patient until she was ready, then—*bang*. She would bring the hammer down on the ringleaders of this conspiracy. If she had the excuse to extradite Cherry

Vino from her decadent villa on the Italian coast, so much the better.

Valeria even knew what she would wear for the occasion.

She still had that suit jacket. It hung in the back of her closet. The blood had never entirely come out.

CHAPTER TWELVE

Elana slept in the next morning, and Matt could not blame her. He left a note on the kitchen island and slipped out of the condo, silent as a mouse.

Gone for brunch with my sister. Call me if anything happens.

He met Claudia at the same brunch joint he'd taken Elana to in those first few days of her introduction to Haven. Or to be more precise, he showed up at the restaurant and waited for Claudia. She was juggling a lot right now. Frankly, he was impressed when she managed to get anywhere on time. Unfortunately, today was not one of those days.

Claudia flopped into the chair across from him fifteen minutes after he arrived with a huge and forceful exhalation.

He hid a smirk. "Morning, little sis."

"*Buh.*"

"Assignment's that bad, eh?"

She scrubbed her hands over her face. It didn't look like she'd slept much last night. "No, it's not bad. It's the best opportunity I've had in, like, ever. But *oh, my God* I'm run off my feet. When do I stop needing sleep? What level is that?"

"You know I can't talk about that in public," Matt teased, then chuckled when she flipped him off half-heartedly. Claudia was only six years younger than him biologically, but *chronologically*, he had over a century more life experience—and vampire progression—than she did.

Claudia grumbled. "Since when is there not already coffee here by the time I show up?"

"Since Gerard's not the waiter today, and the new guy's catching up. I think I see him coming now."

Sure enough, the promised coffee arrived a moment later, and after the Richelieu siblings had ordered—more spinach crepes for Matt and a heaping platter of pancakes and sausages for Claudia—they sat back in their chairs and relaxed. Claudia cradled her coffee mug in both hands and inhaled its bitter aroma while Matt watched her with the analytical eye of a doting big brother.

"I'm a little worried about you, Claude," he confessed. "Every time I see you lately, you look more tired. I know Chimera training is beyond hard, obviously, but are you sure this is—"

"Can we please talk about *anything* other than my life?" Claudia implored him. "Like who you're spending all your time with? What's her name? Why's she important? I am dying to think about something other than how tired I am right now, so spill the tea."

Matt snorted. "Her name's Elana. I can't tell you why she's important any more than you can tell me what you're working on."

Claudia rolled her eyes. "Not like you couldn't find out if you wanted to. Hell, you probably already know." She narrowed her eyes when he wouldn't meet her gaze. "You *do* already know."

He shrugged but let her see the twinkle in his eye and his half-smirk. "Couldn't tell you if I did. Not my fault you *also* decided to go into special ops."

"When I decided to go into spec ops, you were a fucking social worker."

He clicked his tongue in mock disapproval. "*Language.* Also, I was in spec ops before you were born. I just needed a sabbatical."

"Oh, come off it." Claudia set her mug on the table and flicked a sugar packet at him. "Tell me about Elana. Do you *like* her? Is she *cute*? Are you finally gonna settle down like Mom and Dad have been after you to do for the entirety of my meager existence?"

Matt almost spat his mouthful of coffee. After managing to maintain his composure and the integrity of his light gray morning suit, he shook his head and grinned. "*No*, I don't like her. Not like *that*, anyway. It's primarily a business relationship, although I'd be lying if I said I didn't think we were also friends."

Claudia's answering grin was devilish. "I might have been born yesterday, but it wasn't in the dark. Methinks somebody doth protest too much."

It was Matt's turn to roll his eyes. "And I think *somebody's* grasping at straws because they haven't slept in a week."

Matt was entirely unsurprised to find Elana pacing holes in his living room carpet when he returned from brunch. "Have you eaten?"

She vaguely motioned at the frying pan on the stovetop. Upon closer inspection, he discovered omelet residue in the pan, and a glance at the French press showed she'd made coffee.

He nodded. "Good. Packed and ready to go?"

"If I wasn't packed, I wouldn't be pacing," she snapped, then winced. "Sorry. I'm more than a little anxious."

"Entirely reasonable. You *are* about to meet one of the most influential and impressive information brokers in the world."

Elana scowled. "Don't rub it in."

Matt chuckled and retreated down the hall to collect his bag. "She's actually really sweet once you get past the terrifying fact that she could know everything about you within a few hours if she wanted to. Really has that grandma vibe."

"I will believe it when I see it," Elana called.

When he returned to the living room, she was sitting on the couch and tightly gripping her hands. "Any word from Valeria?" she asked.

"About your house? No, I'm sorry. There should be by the time we get back, and it will be under constant surveillance while we're gone." He smiled reassuringly and put a hand on her shoulder. "If you want my advice, do your best to put all of that in a box for the next couple of days. Have you ever flown business class?"

Elana shook her head. "Not a chance. I've barely left

Ashford, and any time my dad and I went anywhere, we always flew economy. A penny saved is a penny earned."

Matt's smile grew to a grin. "Then you're in for a treat. Vampire transportation is even nicer than business class."

Elana pursed her lips. "Private jets are horrible for the environment."

"Not these. Come on."

He coaxed her off the couch and into the underground garage. They emerged on the road in his Audi under the overcast sky. This was the first cloudy day in some time, and while the break from the constant sun was nice, the resulting humidity verged on unpleasant even with Haven's climate control.

Elana fiddled with the zipper pull on her dimensional handbag all the way to the private airstrip outside the eastern edge of Haven. When they arrived, Matt parked in another underground parking lot like the one hidden below his condo complex. It was full to bursting with luxury cars.

"Why isn't there *more* vandalism?" she asked Matt as they strode through the aisles of sleek Lamborghinis and gleaming BMWs. "Is it because this is the *norm* for vampires?"

"More or less. It's generally considered a low blow to damage someone's property. Anyone can do *that*. It's much more impressive if you can outfox your competitors in whatever industry they're best at or outdo them at a social event. Wrecking someone's belongings is the little leagues. Why bother? They'll buy more."

Elana fell silent again. A flame of anger kindled in her gut. That meant House Veridian was attempting to send a message that *Elana* was in the little leagues—that she wasn't worth trying to outfox or outdo.

Well, she'd show *them*.

They rode a moving sidewalk through the underground level of Haven's private air terminal. It was quiet and extremely sophisticated, all steel and glass, with understated advertisements for various Houses' family companies. *Vetinar—Organizing the Unorganizable Since 1422. Wetherwac—Sensible Fashion for the Everyday Vampire; Not Dead Yet. Nanog—Genealogical Solutions for Every Tree, Even the Funny-Looking Ones.*

Elana counted fewer than six other people in the sprawling complex, including employees. "Not very busy in here," she commented under her breath to Matt.

Matt shook his head. "Vampires don't tend to travel en masse, but we *do* want convenient transport from one location to another. This hub includes the airstrip aboveground plus several other modes of private transportation on this level and the sub-levels. It's worth maintaining even at the low rate of use. Haven is world-renowned for being easy to reach. Great for business."

"I can imagine."

They ascended an escalator into the aboveground part of the terminal, which also heavily featured glass and steel. On a sunny day, the abstract stained glass patterns in the windows would throw sharp splashes of color onto the pristine white and gray tile floor. Those colors were muted today, giving the place a dreamy, surreal vibe.

Matt directed Elana to the Air Departures area, where a uniformed woman of average height with fair skin, a tight brown bun, and posture straight as an arrow took tiny blood samples from their fingertips, ran them through the interface on her desk, and bid them a good flight.

"No TSA?" Elana murmured as they strode through the empty terminal.

"No point," Matt answered. "A vampire could easily hijack a plane without a weapon. Like property damage, there isn't much *point*. It's considered small potatoes. Plus, like I said, we don't tend to travel in large groups. Why would you hijack a plane you chartered?"

Elana snorted. "I suppose that would be impressively stupid."

"I'm sure *someone's* done it. Humans certainly don't corner the market on idiots."

They strolled up to their gate. Other than the remarkable lack of people, the terminal resembled a standard airport terminal very closely, which made the entire experience doubly surreal. Elana felt like she was walking through an airport movie set before the film crew showed up.

Another employee in the dark gray uniform, this time with a thin blue stripe instead of a thin green stripe, waited behind the small desk. The dark-skinned man stood and politely smiled as they approached, and the glint of his perfect teeth matched the sparkle in his green eyes.

He greeted them in a warm, friendly voice. "Mister Richelieu, Miss Bishop. My name is Mamoru Ndawe, and I have the distinct pleasure of being the lead of your cabin crew today. Your jet is ready to fly at your convenience. Safeties were completed ten minutes ago and the crew is completing their preflight checks now. Will you want anything before you take off, or shall I inform the captain you'll be boarding right away?"

"Right away, thank you," Matt replied with an equally charming smile.

"Of course. Please, excuse me just one moment." Mamoru stepped back behind the desk and tapped the glowing interface a handful of times. With the final touch, it went dark, and he gestured for them to precede him through the door behind him. "Right this way."

Matt let Elana go first and winked at her as if to say, "Enjoy."

Elana didn't know what to expect as she walked down the perfectly normal corridor between the terminal and the plane. Would she be riding an uber-futuristic contraption, a supersonic jet like the Concorde on steroids? Or would it be more like a UFO, something Space Age in its glamor?

At first glance, the plane was almost disappointingly normal—except that its exterior was a matte dark blue, and flickers of light passed along its surface at random. Elana spied glowing interfaces on the interior walls with text too small for her to read before she turned right into the cabin and caught her breath in surprise.

Elana had seen pictures of early commercial flights and modern super-rich private jets in magazines and online retrospectives. The walk-up bars, lounge seating, pools where there shouldn't be pools... This managed to tick all those boxes, plus more she never would have dreamed of.

The cabin only held six seats, each a self-contained pod that reclined fully and included a retractable canopy for extra privacy. Their navy cushions looked plush enough that she would sink into them at the slightest touch, and she couldn't wait to try. The pods included foldout trays that had to be interfaces, and Elana spotted a Swiss-cheese-esque array of jacks on the arm of the pod nearest her. You could plug anything in and watch anything you wanted. It probably had free Wi-fi that didn't suck.

Past the seating area, which held three seats on each wall with a sizable window apiece, a full-service bar stretched down one side of the plane. A well-appointed kitchenette occupied the other. These were set up as counters with gates at one end, evidently meant to be manned by Mamoru or another crewmember. Elana suspected she could ask for a five-course meal, no matter how long the flight, and they would serve her without a blink.

Beyond the dining section were two washrooms on either side of the cabin. From here, they appeared to be twice the size of standard airplane lavatories, but Elana wouldn't have been surprised to discover they were bigger than they appeared.

Beyond *that*, a pool inset into the cabin floor glowed from within, sending refracted light over the ceiling and walls. She glimpsed the corners of lounge chairs on each side of the narrow pool and was reasonably certain a *second* bar stood at the very back of the plane.

Matt nudged her elbow, and she started. She hadn't realized she'd been standing stock-still and staring at the amenities.

Elana cleared her throat and swallowed. "Ah…which one is mine?" She endeavored to sound as calm, collected, and high society as possible, but from the twitch she spotted at the corner of Matt's lips, she'd only *partially* succeeded.

Mamoru was the picture of professionalism and graciously indicated the entire cabin. "Whichever one suits you best, Miss Bishop. You're welcome to move about the cabin as you please, as long as the seatbelt signs are off."

"Oh! Thank you." She ignored the faint blush rising on her cheeks and picked the middle starboard seat. She tucked her dimensional handbag into a compartment with a latch on the side of the pod, then sat and promptly sank two inches into the most comfortable foam she'd ever experienced. It was all she could do not to exclaim in wonder.

Matt grinned at her from across the aisle, obviously noticing—and delighting in—her astonishment. She refrained from flipping him off only because the ever-attentive Mamoru was still with her, ensuring she was settled. "Can I offer you anything to drink?"

Elana's mouth hung open awkwardly for several long seconds until she managed to stutter the first thing that came to mind. "Red wine?"

"Certainly. Do you have a preferred vintage?"

She silently groaned, but she'd set herself up for that one, and she knew it. "I trust your judgment."

Mamoru smiled brightly. "Of course. Right away." He turned to Matt. "And yourself, sir?"

"The oldest whiskey you have, neat, if you please."

"Coming right up, Mister Richelieu."

Mamoru clicked the bar gate closed behind him at the same time as the cockpit door slid aside ahead of them. A short man with square shoulders, a salt and pepper beard, and a brimmed hat to match the dark gray and blue uniform stepped out and nodded politely at Matt and Elana.

"My name is Barry Lutes, and I have the honor of being your captain today." His voice was sonorous and deep. Elana wondered if he sang. "The weather looks good all the way across the Atlantic today. We'll catch a tailwind that will reduce our flight time to the Highlands to a hair over four hours."

Elana's eyebrows shot up. *Four hours?* She glanced at Matt, who nodded subtly.

"Mamoru will see to everything you need while on board, so don't hesitate to ask. Thank you for flying Haven Air, and I hope you enjoy your flight."

"Much obliged, Captain Lutes." Matt grinned. "It's Elana's first time on a Haven jet."

Lutes' face brightened. "Is that so? Then it's even more of an honor. Kick back and relax, Miss Bishop. There's nothing like traveling in Haven style."

"I'm getting that impression," Elana sheepishly admitted.

Something buzzed in the captain's earpiece, and he tilted his head to listen before clasping his hands and nodding again at each of them. "My copilot has informed me that we're waiting on my final go-ahead. If you're both ready, we'll take to the skies."

Matt tilted his head toward Elana. "Miss Bishop?"

Feeling like she was deciding something much more monumental, Elana replied, "Take us up, Captain."

Captain Lutes saluted and disappeared back into the cabin.

A moment later, Mamoru walked them through the safety features. They were similar to a standard commercial jet but without the unspoken suspicions that none of the life jackets had been refurbished since the seventies and the oxygen masks seemed flimsier than dollar-store Halloween masks. Instead, they each had slim-fitting, self-inflating vests tucked under their chairs and a personal oxygen canister and rebreather.

Mamoru assured them that in the extremely unlikely event they went down, the jet could withstand collision damage and was equipped with engines that could swap to functioning underwater.

"By air or land, we'll get where you need to go," Mamoru affirmed with a stunning smile. "Now, whiskey for the gentleman and wine for the lady."

Four hours passed in a flash. They hit no turbulence, or if they did, Elana didn't feel a thing. They ate a delectable boeuf bourguignon for lunch, which they smelled cooking for a solid hour before Mamoru served it with roast potatoes and tender-crisp green beans and baby carrots lightly tossed with balsamic vinegar and olive oil.

While eating, Elana watched the two newest episodes of her favorite crime drama. They had aired within the last couple of weeks, and she'd forgotten to record them in all the excitement. She'd resigned herself to waiting for them to be released on one of her streaming services and had been happily surprised to find them on the interface in her pod. The lifestyles of the rich and famous were *nice*.

She'd also brushed up one more time on her notes for the meeting that day with Madame Lucia. They'd be landing at another private airstrip relatively close to the manor—no multi-hour drive to gather her thoughts *or* let her nerves get away with her. Small mercies.

They landed without a bump and taxied to a small terminal while rain pattered against the windows. It was a gray and misty day in the Scottish Highlands, drizzly and dull, but the moors beyond the asphalt strip enchanted Elana. The coarse bushes of heather and the far-off hazy shadows of the hills put her in mind of all the Regency novels she'd ever read *and* such cinematic classics as *Outlander, Highlander,* and *Braveheart.* Elana might have had a thing for Scotsmen. She'd never tell.

"An umbrella for madam?" Mamoru inquired as they stopped. "Your car is waiting on the tarmac, but unfortunately, this terminal does not include a gate tunnel." He extended a long black umbrella with a polished wooden handle toward her, handle first. The crescent moons of his manicured nails gleamed.

Elana accepted it and stood. "Thank you. How do I get it back to you afterward? Do I leave it in the car?"

Mamoru laughed. "Oh, no, Miss Bishop, not at all. It's yours to keep. Consider it a memento from your first trip with us and a promise of many more."

Elana blushed, but this time it was happily instead of awkwardly. "That's very kind of you. I hope I get to fly with you again, too. I never did get to try out the pool."

The flight attendant beamed. "It's *excellent* for long-haul flights."

"Wholeheartedly seconded," Matt chimed in. "Shall we, Elana? The matriarch awaits."

Elana nodded and preceded Matt out the door, unfurling her umbrella as she exited onto the steps. He did the same behind her, having also accepted an umbrella from Mamoru. The two descended to the tarmac where a sleek black Rolls-Royce waited, its windshield wipers swishing the rain away.

"You ready?" Matt quietly inquired after they were inside the vehicle.

Elana wiggled her foot to shake the water off her boots. "Yes? No? How can I ever tell? Every time I feel like I'm ready, I stick my foot in my mouth, but actively choosing to fly by the seat of my pants is a stupid idea."

Matt let out a short laugh. "You're right about that. Let me put it to you this way. Have you checked all your notes?"

"More times than I can count. I think I have them memorized."

"Are they thorough?"

"*Beyond* thorough."

He smiled, put a hand on her knee, and squeezed it. "Then you're as ready as you can be. You know who you're talking to and you know what she likes and doesn't like. You know your facts. All you gotta do now is charm her pants off like I know you can."

"What if she's not wearing pants?"

"I highly doubt Madame Lucia of Stormhaven greets visitors in the nude."

"Would anyone *argue with her?*"

"You have a point."

CHAPTER THIRTEEN

Neither Matt nor Elana spoke much on the way to Castle Stormhaven. Elana was too preoccupied with looking out the window at the Scottish countryside, and Matt was busy reading something on his phone. Judging by the set of his jaw, it was important. Elana was curious, but she had too much on her mind already to add more to her pondering plate.

Their driver was a gruff older man with a short, black, bushy beard and a cap settled low over his brow. He was taciturn in the way of every vampire chauffeur Elana had met to date, so much so that she wondered whether it was a job requirement. *Wanted: Chauffeur. Needs to be trained as a professional driver. Must pass stringent background check and must maintain air of mystery on the job at all times.*

She spotted Castle Stormhaven several minutes before they arrived. It loomed out of the coastal fog like something out of a period horror movie. A few lightning strikes flashing across the ramparts wouldn't have gone amiss. Elana kept waiting for ghostly horsemen in kilts to emerge from the mist on a battle charge with claymores held high, faces painted, yelling their challenges to the unforgiving rocks and their even less forgiving foes.

No undead cavalry appeared on their final approach to the multi-story medieval castle, and the mossy stone towers, glistening with rain, quickly caught Elana's attention. Blue and white banners with a tower crossed by a lightning bolt hung from the ramparts and flapped in the lethargic wind. Two huge lightning bolts formed the arch under which they drove across the thick, solid boards of the drawbridge. Water roiled in the moat below. Elana assumed it led out to the open water and its myriad rocks.

Castle Stormhaven stood on the coast like a majestic warrior with their feet firmly planted and their hand on their sword. A dozen towers rose from its stout base within the wall between the moat and the keep. Some towers were short and squat, others tall and thin, but they all loomed like so many guards watching the approaching car with hawk eyes and drawn bows.

"I take it Castle Stormhaven has never fallen," Elana murmured.

Their driver snorted. "T'would be the day hell itself froze over, lass."

He drove under an arch set in the middle of the keep's eight-foot-thick stone wall. Steel points glinted in the darkness above, hinting at the gate that would keep intruders out and the castle's denizens safely inside. Then he crossed the cobblestone courtyard to the keep's main entrance, a set of oaken double doors easily eighteen feet high and twelve feet across, banded in black metal in the shape of more crossed lightning bolts.

The Rolls-Royce stopped beside the wide, deep steps that led to the doors. The driver put it in Park but did not kill the engine nor move to exit the vehicle. Instead, a boy Elana guessed to be in his mid-teens bounded down from a niche in one of the two towers beside the doors and opened first Elana's door, then trotted around the car to open Matt's. He wore bright blue livery and could have walked out of a Renaissance Faire, pageboy cut and all.

He was back on the first step by the time Matt and Elana climbed out of the car. He tapped his heels together and sang out in a high tenor of a Scottish lilt, "Madame Lucia Lambra Mor of Stormhaven welcomes the Master Richelieu and the Missus Bishop to her ancestral domain! Please, if you would be so kind as to follow me!"

He trotted up the stairs and rapped on the door four times, smart and sharp, then scrambled back and stood at attention while the pair of massive oak slabs smoothly swung inward to reveal the entrance hall of Castle Stormhaven.

If the Haven Air jet had been the Space Age for vampires, Castle Stormhaven was a fantasy writer's dream. Heavy tapestries in brilliant colors depicting the many and varied escapades and adventures of House Stormhaven hung on the walls, which were stacked stones bigger than Elana's chest. The floor was made of the same but in a pale beige rather than the iron gray of the castle walls. A deep blue carpet stretched from the threshold to the base of a fireplace the same size as the doors.

Narrow windows sliced through the thick stone between the woven artwork. As Elana advanced toward the woman standing in front of the roaring fire, she glanced aside to see those thin windows filled with what appeared to be melted glass—or perhaps that was a trick of the light coming through the rain.

The fire was not the only light in the entrance hall. Wrought iron torches as long as a man's leg stuck out of the columns that bordered the long carpet in pairs, creating a single aisle and two wings where the windows and tapestries hung. Their flickering light made the images on the tapestries appear to move in Elana's peripheral vision.

Elana stopped half a dozen paces shy of Madame Lucia. The head of House Stormhaven embraced the traditions of her clan without becoming a stereotype. She wore no overwrought costume of tartan, and her hair was not a mess of piled red curls. A thin tartan belt tied her long, simple, navy gown at the waist, and her auburn hair hung down her back in an equally simple ponytail.

She had a round, heart-shaped face with eyes that glittered like dark emeralds in the torchlight. She wore a necklace of the same color. Its teardrop pendant sat in the hollow of her collarbone. Simple silver rings adorned her fingers, and a single silver clip pinned her bangs back over one ear. Her skin was smooth and unwrinkled, but Elana knew Lucia was centuries old even if she didn't look it.

Those gemstone eyes pinned Elana the moment she walked into the room. Lucia's hard gaze did not waver once, not even to glance at Matt walking beside her. Elana felt underdressed in her understated charcoal pantsuit and black pocket heels. She'd picked the outfit because to her, it radiated authority. Compared to Lucia's quiet, royal presence, Elana felt like a jumped-up scullery maid.

"Elana Bishop." Lucia's voice was musical. Her accent was less broad than the pageboy's, having a softer edge but no less presence. "How come ye to be added to the House of the SpiderKing?"

Elana drew a deep breath and let it out as unobtrusively as possible. While House Stormhaven trafficked in secrets, they were renowned for their commitment to honesty and candor. A Stormhaven would never lie to you. They would say nothing if they could not speak the truth without betraying a confidence. These halls did not echo with whispers. They echoed not at all.

"My mother was Tessa Hart," Elana stated. "She was inducted into the House of the SpiderKing for reasons I am not privy to. She gave me the Rights before I could form memories. I discovered I was a vampire weeks ago. When my lineage came to light, my mother's line was reinstated as an active branch of the House of the SpiderKing, of which I am the only scion."

Madame Lucia regarded Elana calmly while she spoke, then nodded solemnly. "I had occasion to do business with Arbiter Hart during her tenure. She was a capable and determined woman, and I was sorry to hear of her loss to senseless violence. Am I to understand that you did not know her at all? Or were you simply unaware of your status as a vampire?"

Elana swallowed again. Valeria's injunction against telling too much, too fast echoed in her mind. However, you couldn't hide anything from a Stormhaven if you wanted them to trust you—and Elana *really* wanted Madame Lucia to trust her. Finding out that her mother had already established a connection with the powerful

House further cemented her conviction that this was an alliance she *needed*.

"I did not know her," Elana confirmed. "I believed she had died soon after I was born. Discovering she had lived for almost thirty years as a vampire was a complete shock to me."

"I can imagine." Her green eyes tracked Elana's subtle movements without betraying any emotion. "Do you come to follow in her footsteps, or do you mean to create your own path?"

Elana briefly considered her words before replying, "Some of both. While I admire, respect, and share her goals of deepening human-vampire relations, I have no intention of becoming a carbon copy of my mother. I will pursue those values in my way, which I've yet to determine.

"The reason I've yet to determine that course of action is twofold," she continued. "First, I've been a vampire for only a few weeks, and I'm still learning where and how I want to fit into this global society. The second reason is far more pressing."

Elana straightened and pitched her voice a touch deeper. "My mother left me archives of documents concerning a conspiracy she was tracking. I believe her investigation into this conspiracy led to her murder. It has certainly led to multiple attempts on my life in the last few weeks.

"I intend to follow that conspiracy to its source and uproot it. I believe it is a danger not only to Haven and its monarch but to the balance and power of vampire communities across the globe. Uncovering and combating that conspiracy is why I've come to you seeking alliance."

Elana exhaled as unobtrusively as she could, bit the inside of her lip, and waited. She'd swear she could feel Matt holding his breath next to her.

"A conspiracy," Lucia repeated. A gleam appeared in her deep green eyes. Stormhavens hungered for knowledge above all. They were information brokers not because it gave them power or leverage, although those certainly didn't hurt, but because they wanted to know *everything*. Dangling secret knowledge in front of Lucia was like tempting a dog with the juiciest steak straight from the butcher block.

"A *centuries-old* conspiracy," Elana added. Now was the time to sweeten the pot.

Lucia raised an eyebrow. "A centuries-old conspiracy of which the SpiderKing is unaware? That is…unlike him."

"Ah. I should clarify. I have no proof one way or the other that he knows about it," Elana admitted. "If he does, he hasn't acted on it, at least not in ways I've seen. It's certainly flown under the radar of everyone else in Haven. Its organization and spread have been extremely well-orchestrated."

Lucia tilted her head. "Who do you believe is at the heart of the conspiracy, and what is their goal?"

"House Veridian," Elana replied. "I am not fully convinced of their goal yet, but my belief is that they eventually want to overthrow the SpiderKing. I suspect they want to slowly stack the Council of Arbiters with vampires sympathetic to their cause, then strip the king's powers either gradually or in a coup. After that, I imagine they want to use Haven's clout and position to do the same to other vampire city-states or simply to other Houses."

Lucia hummed thoughtfully and drummed her fingers once on her thigh. While she thought, Elana resisted the urge to shift in place. She'd hoped that after exchanging pleasantries, Madame Lucia might have brought them to a sitting room or a study, somewhere they could sit and talk comfortably. Alas, the statuesque head of Stormhaven showed no signs of moving and seemed entirely content to discuss their business in the silent entrance hall.

"Why should I care?" Lucia finally asked.

Elana was not thrown by the question's nonchalance. She had expected this. By all accounts, Lucia Lambra Mor was a canny negotiator and a clever conversationalist. She would divulge only as much as needed to get what she wanted, and many would-be business partners left believing they'd come away much richer in information than they had. Meanwhile, Madame Lucia contentedly added to her stocks of knowledge without her informants realizing they'd shared anything at all.

"The biggest reason you should care is because this conspiracy could prove to be the biggest secret in vampire politics of the last millennium," Elana offered first. "House Veridian has been hiding its connections to innumerable other Houses for centuries. The leverage potential inherent in researching those connections could be *huge*."

"It could also result in nothing at all," Lucia countered.

Elana shook her head. "I find that very unlikely. If there was nothing to gain, there would be nothing to hide. Houses that try to keep useless secrets usually don't hide them very well, and no one would know that better than yourself. They're too arrogant and too busy making shows of power to impress their competitors and allies on the same level of the playing field.

"House Stormhaven doesn't play on that level," Elana continued. "House Stormhaven plays on the same level as the House of the SpiderKing. We play the long game, and we play for keeps. House Veridian has been pretending to play on the lower level for centuries while building a team in the background on *this* level.

"They've even proven *good enough* at it that they managed to pass off my mother's death as collateral damage in an inter-House war where neither House had any visible connections to House Veridian. They got that one past *Haven's guardians*. They're *good*…but you're better, and so are we."

"Arbiter Draven can't be happy about that." Lucia's statement was mild, but she crossed her arms. The first red flag.

Elana hid the automatic tensing of her jaw. She wasn't sunk yet. One suspicion wouldn't capsize the ship. "She's not," Elana admitted. "Which I'm certain you know means that her efforts are redoubling, to say the *least*, to root out this conspiracy. Allying with me means allying with her. It's not hard to see the possible return on investment when it comes to allying with the Arbiter of Shadows when she's on the warpath."

"Are you authorized to guarantee her cooperation?"

"No, but I can personally vouch for her determination to get to the bottom of this. Also, she recommended I speak to you. I think that carries significant weight when it comes to estimating her willingness to play ball."

Lucia remained silent for several breaths. She did not

uncross her arms, nor did she drop Elana's gaze. Elana maintained steady eye contact and refused to flinch or give anything away in her face. She couldn't tell if Lucia's intensity was a tactic to get Elana to spill more or just her "thinking face." It wouldn't have surprised her if it was both.

At length, the head of House Stormhaven spoke again. "I know when to trust Valeria Draven." Her tone did not give any hints as to when that was. Lucia might have been suggesting that the proper time to trust Valeria Draven was *never*, for all Elana could tell. "But tell me, Elana Bishop. Why should I trust you?"

"Because I'm not stupid," Elana readily replied. "I know that to play ball with House Stormhaven, you have to be honest. It's not about tactics and strategies. It's about truth. I have made a point of telling you the truth in everything I've said today, and I am willing to share more.

"I respect the hell out of you and what your House has built and accomplished. I can't think of a better ally than you when it comes to information and networking. I'd be surprised if House Veridian didn't intend to take you on at some point down the line, but as far as I've been able to tell, they're steering clear of you. They know you're not to be trifled with. So do I."

Elana rolled her shoulders to release the building tension between her shoulder blades but kept eye contact with Lucia. "My dad passed away several months ago. Until he died, I worked with him in his small business. He treated his employees and his customers fairly and always told them the truth. He did so even when it might hurt him, whether it was telling a client that the machine they'd brought in to repair was irreparable or telling his crew that a project would take longer than expected.

"He taught me that honesty was the best policy, bar none, and that your word was your bond and solemn promise. If Jeremiah Bishop said he'd get the job done, he would, and he'd seal it with a handshake that meant more than any signature. To him, a handshake contract was worth more than anything on paper. If you had to put something on paper, it meant you didn't trust each other, and you weren't trustworthy yourself. He lived his integrity, and so do I."

The gleam was back in Lucia's eyes. Her arms remained crossed, but her eyebrow rose another fraction of a degree. She looked interested or maybe intrigued.

Elana's heart picked up speed. She was close to landing this deal. She could *feel* it.

"*That's* what I bring to the table," Elana concluded. "I'm not someone who's spent decades or centuries learning how to skirt the edges of agreements and find loopholes that someone forgot to close ages ago. I'm a woman of my word, and I'll stake my reputation on this being worth your time and attention. If it's not, then I take responsibility."

Elana half-chuckled. "What that would look like, I have to admit I don't know, but I'm sure it wouldn't be pretty. I'll also admit I'm new at this and finding my way."

She sobered. "Neither of those admissions make a difference in how committed I am to my word. I'm ready to take the fall if I'm wrong, but I'm confident I'm not.

"This is likely to be the biggest treasure trove of information of the millennium. House Veridian has been successfully building and nurturing a network of informants and connections under the nose of one of the most influential city-state monarchs in the world for centuries. Whatever they're doing, they're patient about it, which means it's valuable to them. Haven is world-renowned for being what it is—a hub of vampire commerce and society with more human interaction than any other comparable community in the world.

"That's not a game House Stormhaven can *afford* to pass up on," Elana finished. She finally allowed a spark of challenge to light her expression. "Allying with me is a fantastic move for you, politically *and* industrially. *Not* allying with me is likely to be equally disastrous in the other direction.

"My offer's on the table. I'm happy to provide more information. What do you say, Madame Lambra Mor? Will you join me in discovering what House Veridian's been trying to hide for the better part of a thousand years?"

Elana stuck out her hand to shake, then patiently waited. The solemn redhead regarded her for several long breaths with an unreadable expression, then uncrossed her arms and firmly shook Elana's hand.

"Your sincerity is impressive," Lucia remarked. "You speak well for someone so young."

Elana inclined her head and released Lucia's hand. "Thank you. That means a lot, coming from you. Whatever happens now, I promise you won't be disappointed."

In the first display of true emotion since Elana and Matt had walked in, the unflappable head of House Stormhaven chuckled. "Oh, I've no doubt of that."

CHAPTER FOURTEEN

Across the Atlantic, a hatch hidden in a field of waist-high wheat in Senkyem slid open. Valeria Draven rose on a floating platform until she was half-hidden in the golden stalks.

She went to take a step, paused mid-stride, and sniffed the air. With a slight frown, she turned side to side, searching for the source of the sickly sweet stench until she found it off to her right.

Valeria stepped off the platform. It sank into its shaft and the hatch slid across to hide the entrance, another patch of tall grass nearly ready to be harvested and brought to Shestoi's processing plants.

The Arbiter of Shadows followed her nose as she picked her way through the field, testing each step before putting her weight down. She knew that smell better than most, and while she suspected the intent behind its origin, she refused to make assumptions.

Ten yards from the hidden access to her subterranean network of bunkers, offices, and training rooms, the smell became overpowering even for her accustomed sensibilities. She covered her nose and mouth with the sleeve of her suit jacket and nudged stalks of wheat aside with her toe until she found its provenance.

A dead body, as she'd expected. Bludgeoned postmortem, but the cause of death was likely poison based on the color of the skin and pustules rising from it, not to mention the swollen tongue poking out of the mouth. Gender was near impossible to tell with the severe edema and advanced state of decomposition. They had been shaved bald before their death, which made her *guess* female—the person's murderers having shorn her locks to help avoid identification—but that was not a guarantee.

They would have injected her with a serum to scramble the DNA profile of any blood sample taken. Hell, the poison they used to kill her might have done the same. Determining her identity would be difficult at best and impossible at worst.

There was no mistaking the message being sent. They'd missed the entrance by thirty feet, but that was uncomfortably close to a bull's-eye by Valeria's reckoning. No one should have been able to target any of her secret entrances by fewer than a hundred feet, and that was pushing it.

No, this was as clear as you could get. This had to be the House Veridian informant Matt Richelieu had contacted without telling her, being dropped on her figurative doorstep as a warning to say that House Veridian didn't suffer traitors and wasn't afraid of the Arbiter of Shadows. In other words, "We know what you're doing and who you're tracking, so back the fuck off."

Valeria grimaced and retrieved her phone from her

pocket to call in her guard to deal with the body. She disliked using them as frequently and openly as she had to these days. The sight of the black-suited guardians made everyone in Haven nervous, and when Havenites were nervous, they had a nasty tendency to start getting *dramatic*. Valeria Draven could handle drama, but she preferred Haven's social life at its normal pace and level of intrigue.

Unfortunately, until she smoked out the mole within the rank-and-file guardians, she had no choice but to continue calling in her Shadowguard and the Chimeras in last-ditch situations. She hoped it would communicate to House Veridian that she wasn't intimidated by them—because she wasn't—and she would *not* let them get away with this.

She let the wheat stalks sway upright to hide the body from view. The Bishop-Veridian situation escalated daily, and it was only a matter of time before something momentous went down. Valeria had to ensure it happened on *her* terms, not House Veridian's.

The hatch behind her slid open, and she heard quiet footsteps *swishing* through the wheat.

Her Shadowguard quietly greeted her. "Ma'am." When she nodded, he added, "Richelieu and Bishop are touching down at the airfield within the hour."

"Understood. Get this body to our morgue and send me the postmortem as soon as it's complete."

The plane ride back from Scotland was even more relaxing than the flight to the Highlands. They had a late supper of pasta carbonara paired with dry white wine on the flight. Elana decompressed with a movie that she barely paid attention to in favor of letting its background noise wash over her while she watched the clouds roll by outside.

She felt wrung out but in a good way. She'd successfully parlayed her way into three alliances with extremely powerful Houses, each with Old World connections. Her position against House Veridian strengthened with every passing day. Elana needed more training, and there was always more to learn, but for a vampire barely two months into Haven society, she thought she was acquitting herself admirably.

Elana was beyond ready to fall into the spare bed at Matt's place the moment they returned to Haven, but his phone chimed five minutes after they got on the road. She moved to grab it from the cupholder and offer to hold it up for him, or if he was okay with it, to read the message aloud. Before she could, he blinked, and tiny squiggles of blue light flickered across his eyes.

"Did you just—" she began.

At the same time, he said, "Change of plans, we're—"

They both snorted at each other and in unison, said, "After you," which caused a fountain of fatigue-fueled giggling.

Elana motioned for him to go ahead. Her curiosity about what the hell he'd done could wait thirty seconds, especially if there was a change of plans involved.

"Valeria says to meet her at your house," he explained. "What were you saying?"

"I was gonna ask if you'd read that message on your *eyes* somehow. All the tech in Haven is mildly *Minority Report* flavored, but *that's* a new one to me."

Matt chuckled. "Essentially, yeah, I did. I don't use it much, but when a priority message from Valeria comes through, time is usually short. If she was telling us to stay away from Haven, for instance, I didn't want to get too far down the road."

"Fair enough." A shiver ran down Elana's spine at the thought of a situation where Valeria would tell them to avoid Haven. A wave of dread rapidly followed on its heels when she realized what Valeria's message had been. "She wants us to meet at my place? I wonder if she found something about the vandals."

"It's possible. We'll just have to find out."

Elana wished the rain had followed them from Scotland. It would suit her renewed glum mood. Instead, North Carolina was as hot and humid as ever.

Elana frowned as they pulled up in front of her house. No trace of vandalism remained from the night before. The property was so pristine she would have believed it had been rolled back in time if not for the new flowers in the front beds.

Valeria was waiting for them on the front step, clad as always in white. Today's outfit was a crisp pencil skirt and blouse with stiletto heels that easily doubled as stiletto knives. In the fading sunset, Elana noticed swirling tattoos on Valeria's arms that disappeared into the short sleeves of the blouse.

She'd seen them before in the training room but had always been too preoccupied trying not to fall flat on her face or be pummelled into a wall to pay much attention. Tonight, the tattoos appeared to move on Valeria's porcelain skin. Elana shook her head. It had to be a trick of the light.

"Arbiter Draven," Matt greeted her as he exited the car and crossed the lawn with Elana a step behind him. "Your crews work fast."

"I only employ the best of the best." It wasn't a boast but the plain truth. She turned her full attention to Elana, and her ice-blue gaze bore into Elana's soul. "Your meeting with House Stormhaven went well." The statement was as much a question as the first had been prideful—that was to say, not at all.

Elana nodded. "Madame Lucia is behind us a hundred percent, and I didn't promise her anything but the truth in every conversation we'd have. You're under no obligations or expectations that you weren't this morning."

"I heard as much. Well done."

Validation bloomed in Elana's chest like tea in hot water. "Thank you."

Valeria motioned to the house. "Everything is back in order. We've completed our investigation and put further security measures in place. You're safe to move back in."

Elana's eyebrows rose. "*Wow.* Already?"

"Yes." Valeria's tone brooked no argument. "You need to be seen as independent. Staying with Mister Richelieu, while safe and convenient for your combined work, has the unfortunate side effect of creating rumors you do *not* want to have to deal with. It also undermines your status as a member of the House of the SpiderKing. You are Havenite royalty. You *must* act like it."

The sensation of warming tea curdled in Elana's stomach, and she blushed. "Oh. I didn't think of that. I'm sorry."

Valeria shrugged a shoulder. "You are still learning and under incredibly fraught circumstances. I'm not saying this to *scold* you, Elana, only to inform you. Staying at Mister Richelieu's was the best call you could have made in that situation, but it was important that we use all available resources to remedy it as soon as possible. I've done so, and now you know."

Elana swallowed hard. "Of course. Thank you."

The arbiter nodded. "It is my job to maintain the security of the royal House, among other things. On that note, I have news that needs to be shared in a secure location."

Elana glanced at the house. "Does this count as secure? I can make us all something to drink. No offense, Arbiter, but with the week you've had you could probably use one."

Valeria's lips twitched toward a smile. "I'd take a cup of coffee. And yes, your house is now as secure as it can be."

Elana led them into the kitchen, where she busied herself making coffee. The house was back exactly as it had been before being trashed, down to the cardboard boxes stacked along her living room wall. She had no idea when she'd find the time to unpack and settle in. "What kind of security measures are in here now?"

"Multiple sensor and surveillance systems connected to my personal guard corps," Valeria responded. "The control panel is in your ensuite mirror. Before I leave tonight, I'll show you how to use it. Your informant was killed sometime in the last twenty-four hours."

Elana's grip on the scoop of coffee beans faltered, and several beans skittered across the counter. "*What?*"

"Which informant?" Matt grimly inquired.

"The one from House Veridian you thought I didn't know about," Valeria tartly replied. "I'm honestly shocked they didn't use her to lead straight to you. You *must* tell me when you arrange meetings with informants. When you don't, I can't protect you or them sufficiently."

Elana heard Matt exhale unhappily, but she did not turn around. She kept her gaze on the white and gray tile backsplash while she picked up the stray coffee beans. "I thought you had to be hands-off from this. We didn't want to implicate you. You've left meetings so you can maintain plausible deniability. What am I missing?"

Elana could feel the withering look Valeria gave her like a laser between her shoulder blades. "I've been helping you the entire time. I just can't be seen doing so *publicly*. This was a serious mistake on both of your parts. I expect better of you, Mister Richelieu."

Matt sighed again, more quietly this time. "My apologies, Arbiter Draven. I certainly didn't intend to keep you out of the loop in such a fashion that it would cause more problems than it solved. The turnaround on that contact was less than an hour in total. Given that you were dealing with the situation in Ashford at the time..."

He shifted his chair with a *squeak*. "Regardless, that judgment call was mine, and I recognize it was a bad one. It won't happen again. How do you know she's dead?"

"Because she was dropped almost on my doorstep two hours ago."

"Almost?"

"A couple dozen feet away from one of the hidden entrances to the Senkyem complex."

Elana poured hot water into the French press while Matt hissed between his teeth. "Oh, that's bad," he muttered. "That's *very* bad."

"Yes. They're moving fast and getting far too close for my liking. We need to get back on *our* terms. I have a few ideas, but they all revolve around forcing House Veridian to slow down."

Elana took mugs from the cupboard and set them on the table. Valeria's mouth was as thin a line as she'd ever seen it, and Matt's face looked like the calm before the storm. "Does that mean you've figured out their end goal?"

The corner of Valeria's mouth curled down in a tiny scowl. "Yes and no. It's clear that they intend to nurture their clandestine connections in Haven until they have the clout to make a big move, but what that big move is, I can't tell. It could be as simple as, and as *stupid* as, angling to overthrow the SpiderKing himself."

"They'd never get away with it," Matt argued. "They *must* know that. No one's *that* stupid."

Valeria shrugged. "It is a paradox, I'll grant you that. To be smart enough to hide a conspiracy of this size for this long but stupid enough not to realize that your target is several leagues beyond you defies comprehension. Regardless, it suits His Majesty to keep them where he can see them until the right time to strike arrives."

Elana depressed the plunger on the French press, then

poured coffee into each mug. After she replaced the pitcher on the counter, she returned with a sugar bowl, a small carton of cream, and three spoons. She knew Valeria typically took her coffee black, but there was always a first time, and it wouldn't do to be rude. "How do we know when it's the right time?"

"We decide. Until then, you need to be distracting so we can continue digging without them causing even more trouble."

Elana stirred sugar into her coffee. "That sounds ominous."

CHAPTER FIFTEEN

Valeria stayed long enough to outline her goal. It was for Elana to increase her involvement in vampire society to the point that continuing to attack her openly would cause the public to want to investigate. "You need to become Haven's golden girl, in short, and you need to do it fast," was the arbiter's conclusion.

Then she left to tend to other business. When the door closed behind her, Elana refilled her coffee and offered Matt a second cup, which he declined.

"Does she ever sleep?" she asked as she returned to her seat.

Matt chuckled ruefully and shook his head. "She's honed her vampire powers so she needs much less sleep than most. I think she sleeps once a week, if that. Comes in handy for her job, I'll say that much. Hard to sneak anything by a spymaster who doesn't sleep."

Elana hummed in agreement. "Madame Lucia was right about that much. Valeria must be pissed beyond measure that this conspiracy's been growing under her nose for centuries."

Matt grimaced. "Especially since she and your mother were friends."

Elana blinked. "Run that by me again?"

Matt raised his eyebrows. "Didn't you know?"

"That my mother and Valeria Draven were friends? I definitely did *not* know. My impression was that the closest thing to a friend Valeria had was, well, you."

Matt laughed again, but the sound had a sad edge. "I'm a trusted employee, no more than that. You're not wrong, though. Your mom was pretty much the *only* friend Valeria had.

"She hasn't said anything to me, but finding out that Tessa hid all of this from her probably makes her even angrier. This, on top of the fact that yes, she somehow missed a massive conspiracy budding right here in Haven. The minute she figures out whose heads need to roll, they're done for."

Elana stared at the reflection of the ceiling light in her coffee. "I wonder *why* my mom hid it from her. Maybe she thought Valeria was crooked?"

Matt grimaced. "I suppose that's possible, but I figure it's more likely that your mom didn't think she had enough to go on to bother sharing it yet. As we've discovered, very little of the information in Tessa's journal is actionable. It's evidence of a widespread net of unofficial connections that *looks* sketchy. Until House Veridian decided she was getting too close to whatever they're hiding and had Tessa killed, there was no evidence of any illegal activity."

"Maybe Mom knew they'd come after her."

"I wouldn't be surprised if she did." Matt stretched his legs under the table and sipped his coffee. "So, what's your plan?"

"For what?"

"What Valeria said. Becoming vampire society's golden girl. The next big thing."

Elana grumbled and heaved a sigh. "I don't know. I'll probably ask Cathy to hook me up with some big names or whatever. Buy a few more outfits from Zizi. Get some tips on the proper deportment of a celebrity from Vicky. I've spent my life fixing VCRs and moving office furniture, not walking the red carpet. I am *hardly* qualified for this shit."

Matt swirled the remaining liquid in his cup thoughtfully and contemplated for several seconds. "What's your endgame?"

Elana blinked. "Uh. I thought we just talked about that. My endgame is becoming the next vampire It Girl so House Veridian can't touch me without all of Haven's socialites hunting them down."

"No, that's our current battle plan. What about *your* goals? You're a vampire now. What do *you* want?"

"Does it matter? Is there any point in planning for the future until we handle House Veridian?"

"Of course there is! Come on, Elana. I know you read *Twilight*, so I refuse to believe you didn't also read your pick of the litter of YA dystopian novels that came out in the years after. Without something to work for, something to *want*, all that drive turns into bitterness and resentment against the system that used you."

Elana raised an eyebrow. "Are you seriously telling me I need to be the next Katniss Everdeen?"

Matt snorted. "Not the best example you could have picked, but it works. If you don't have something to work toward, you'll end up pissed off that Valeria used you to deal with whatever House Veridian is planning, regardless of how good you believe her intentions are. That's *not* a good foundation for the rest of your life as a vampire."

"Why, because I might try to unseat Valeria?"

"I'd like to see you try, but essentially, yes."

She narrowed her eyes. "So...you're telling me to come up with a reason of my own to want to fit into vampire society so I don't try to bring it to the ground after the current crisis is over. You are more or less telling me to find a reason to be happy with the current state of political affairs so I don't want to burn it down."

Matt stared at her for several seconds, then chuckled, and soon laughed hard enough that he had to put his coffee down before spilling it.

Elana did the same and glared at him. "What?"

He wiped a tear from his eye and leaned back in his chair. "I swear, for a second there you channeled your mother down to a T. Righteous anger and all." He held up a hand to stall Elana's incoming retort. "In a good way, I promise."

Matt sat up, put his elbows on the table, and gestured with an open palm toward Elana. "You're not wrong. *But*, in my defense, like I've told you before, I think the current state of political affairs—Veridian conspiracy notwithstanding—is a good one to uphold. You're free to decide otherwise at your leisure, naturally. Neither I nor Valeria would force you to act against your will, at least not in a personal capacity."

"Don't piss off the Arbiter of Shadows and she won't wreck your day," Elana wryly commented.

"Precisely." He smiled knowingly, then went on. "I wasn't asking in some jaded attempt to influence your beliefs. I was serious. You're joining a society that you studied from the outside for a long time, and you're doing it in a time of crisis. You'll have a better time fitting in if you do so authentically rather than out of any sense of obligation toward solving that crisis."

Elana mulled this over while finishing the last gulp of coffee. "Sometimes I forget you have social worker training." He winked, and she rolled her eyes good-naturedly. "You have a point. I'll always feel like I'm champing at the bit if I don't do this for my own reasons."

"Exactly. Which brings us back to my original question. What are *your* goals?"

She drew a deep breath and contemplated the patterns in the popcorn ceiling. "Stay alive? Figure out what my mother left me?"

"Staying alive is a decent threshold, I'll give you that," Matt agreed with mild amusement. "I'll caution you that plenty of people give parental legacy *way* more weight than it's worth, however."

"Mm. Fair enough." She frowned at an outcropping of plaster that reminded her of Jesse's nose. What an ill-fated fling *that* had been. "I think my mom was on the right track, trying to get humans and vampires working together more closely.

"In my opinion, Haven and vampires in general have so much more to offer humanity than they currently do. While I get that technology can be dangerous if it falls into the wrong hands, I think more harm is ultimately done by cultivating the superiority complex. To be quite honest with you, I think most vampires believe it more than they say they do."

Matt raised his empty mug. "I would readily agree with that."

Elana hesitated at the door to the walk-up apartments. She'd picked Cathy up here before but had never gone inside. It was hard to believe this quiet, unassuming Thani neighborhood of apartment buildings and townhouses, which reminded Elana of pictures of Georgetown in Washington, DC, would be where Cathy Smith of House Lucciola would choose to live.

She'd done more reading on House Lucciola while procrastinating about getting a move on in the Veridian conspiracy. It turned out that House Lucciola counted itself among the world's longest-lived, most prestigious Houses. Its current name came from the House's time as one of the most powerful *famiglia* in the city-states of Italy, namely Venice. Elana couldn't help drawing mental parallels between the Lucciole and the Medici. She only hoped they weren't more closely aligned with the Borgia.

House Lucciola had been powerful long before its time in Venezia, however. Its lineage could be traced back well into antiquity—into the annals still out of Elana's reach as an initiate despite having her mother's access. Elana was beginning to chafe at the restrictions. She wanted to know more.

That was one reason she was here to see Cathy. Not to pick her brain, although she was certain Cathy could tell her reams of stories beyond anything available in even the King's Archives. Rather, it was to take action on another aspect of Elana's advancement as a vampire. *Connections.*

As Elana had learned in her studies, advancing ranks in the Sanguine Nexus was not limited to physical training. While those aspects were important, it was equally important to forge links within the vampiric social structure of whatever community you lived in. Something about mental and emotional acuity.

Elana was still waiting for someone to talk to her about the mystical side of the Sanguine Nexus. She'd walked past the Sanguine Hall in the Citadel a few times now, and its shining jet black marble exterior never failed to make a shiver run down her spine. Nobody talked about what happened in there. She wasn't allowed to read books about it in the archives. Matt had dodged her questions about it so far. She hadn't dared ask Cathy yet, much less Valeria.

Elana's best guess was that she needed to prove she was ready to advance before someone would open the door, and she knew the area in which she lacked most was social graces. Therefore, it was time to call in the big guns.

She reached for the doorbell and started violently when a small interface popped up in glowing blue next to it and buzzed loudly.

"I wondered if you were going to stand there all day," Cathy teased through the intercom. "Bat got your tongue?"

"Very funny." Elana put a hand over her pounding heart. "Can I come in?"

"Of course." Another *buzz*, then a *click*, and Elana opened the lobby door.

The lobby was as unassuming as the outside of the building had been. This could have stood in for any middle-class apartment building in Ashford. Large granite-style tiles in dark pink and gray covered the floor, and long benches with black leather cushions lined the walls. One wall consisted entirely of mailboxes marked with the Haven Mail crest.

The only hints that this wasn't your standard apartment building were the lack of security or management office and the impressive lack of obviously needed maintenance. Elana knew Cathy owned the building and occupied the penthouse while other members of House Lucciola and its favored client Houses occupied the other suites. Elana had never been inside an apartment building this well-kept. Nothing needed to be fixed, nothing was marked out of service, and she didn't see a speck of dust on the floor.

Maybe once you were an old enough vampire, you stopped caring about whether you *looked* wealthy. Or maybe Cathy was an outlier that way. Elana didn't know.

She pressed the up button on the elevator. A melodic *ding* rang out a moment later as the doors slid open. Elana stepped in, selected the top floor, and felt the sharp prick on her fingertip. It meant the interface was checking who she was and whether she was allowed in the penthouse.

The doors closed, and the elevator car glided to the sixth floor. Elana barely felt the movement, and the ride was over as soon as it had begun. Elana exited into a small foyer with a comfortable loveseat and armchair, a coffee table, and a lovely view of the street outside, complete with trees on either side of the large window.

Cathy's apartment door stood in the corner of the vestibule, and Cathy opened it as Elana approached. The eccentric vampire matriarch wearing a khaki pantsuit with more angled hems than an Escher painting beckoned her in.

Elana inhaled slowly in wonder as she entered Cathy's apartment. The open-concept penthouse reminded her of a Bohemian artist collective's loft. Abstract art installations hung from exposed girders and pipes on the ceiling, all of which were painted in myriad colors and patterns.

An equally dizzying array of fabrics adorned the upholstered furniture, which was also covered in throw pillows and blankets. Sculptures and artwork of varying sizes sat or hung on every surface with no visible theme or unifying style.

The effect was kaleidoscopic but somehow not overwhelming. A sense of flow emerged after the eye adjusted to the explosion of color and shape. No surface was crowded, although each was decorated. The space was busy but not cluttered.

As Elana paid more attention to the items on display, she realized the apartment was a deeply personal expression of Cathy's taste and a stunning collection of priceless work from easily the last two millennia.

"I *really* don't want to know how old you are, do I?" Elana muttered. "There's no way your name is *Cathy Smith*."

Cathy chuckled and patted the wide-eyed, slack-jawed Elana on the forearm. "I'm from a time and place when surnames weren't a thing, and I speak languages that have otherwise been forgotten. My name became Katharà at some point and evolved over the ages to Cathy. I take whatever surname is most common wherever I settle down. Have a seat before you faint, dear."

Elana did so, sinking into an armchair that felt like a hug. She gathered her wits while Cathy bustled around the open kitchen and made tea. "I came to ask for your help."

"I expected as much. What with?"

"Connections." Cathy raised an eyebrow over her shoulder, and Elana hastened to elaborate. "I don't want to get anywhere on *your* merits, that's not what I'm saying, but I need some advice on how to start making friends and influencing people in Haven's social circles. I'm used to water cooler talk, not high society."

Cathy chuckled. "Evidently."

Before Elana could ask what that meant, Cathy swooped into the sitting area with a pair of stoneware mugs that could have come from ancient Greece for all Elana knew. She handed one to Elana, then curled, catlike, into a hoop chair.

The aroma from the steaming mug was pleasant and spicy, perhaps a variety of chai. Elana sipped it and tasted cinnamon, cloves, and other warmer spices that put her in mind of desert tents and mournful horn calls.

Cathy had closed her eyes and appeared to be taking time to enjoy the beverage without discussion. Elana followed her lead and waited patiently, although she itched to interrogate the ancient vampire about an increasing number of topics. Top of her mind at the moment was whether *Cathy* had met the SpiderKing—or, even more daring, whether she was *older* than him.

At last, the venerable matriarch nonchalantly lowered her mug from her lips and opened her dark hazel eyes. "Making connections in society *cannot* be an individualistic affair, Elana. You cannot 'American Dream' your way out of this one, although believe you me, many of your countrymen and women have tried their damnedest to haul themselves up by their bootstraps.

"In this, you *must* rely on who you already know. By parlaying your way into the right social circles on your friends' merits, you can *then* use your talents and abilities as currency to increase your social standing.

"However, be attentive not to make it a matter of one-upmanship. Again, it is not about *what* you know, but *who* you know and whether they like you—which is almost always a factor of whether you can be *useful* to them. Society life is a multidimensional game of chess, Monopoly, and poker, all happening simultaneously. You must forge alliances, make concessions, and build relationships on as many levels as there are people."

Elana felt woozy. "That sounds impossible."

"Not at all. At its simplest, it's about making conversation." Cathy savored a sip of tea, then smiled. "My cohort has been after me for ages to host tea. I'll indulge them for once and invite you. Give you a taste and let you meet some of my people. How does *that* sound?"

"Terrifying, but I'd appreciate it nevertheless."

CHAPTER SIXTEEN

Elana consciously kept her hands out of her pockets as she walked down the street toward her car. She'd left Cathy's with a formal invitation to tea two days from today, handwritten on cardstock with a wax seal in the shape of a firefly. Cathy had assured her that the rest of the invitations would go out later that afternoon, and she'd be stunned if a single one of her invitees would turn down the request.

"It's a rare occasion that Cathy Smith hosts a salon," the timeless vampire had said with a wink and a finger on the side of her nose. "Dress accordingly and bring your best small talk."

No pressure, Elana mused. She caught her reflection in the windowed façade of a tall apartment building and straightened. *I need an etiquette manual. There must be one in the archives.*

She settled into the driver's seat of her Emeya, already planning a late afternoon visit to Quarto, and her phone went off. Grumbling, she fished it out of her handbag and saw a message from Valeria.

Meet me in the consulate in fifteen minutes if you can manage it. Thirty at the most.

Elana sighed. You didn't keep the Arbiter of Shadows waiting. She texted a confirmation, then started the electric vehicle and headed to the Citadel. After parking outside the wall, she slipped the key fob into her bag and headed through the courtyard to the consulate, giving Sarah Goldin a wide berth and doing her best to walk silently on the flagstones.

Elana exhaled in relief when she reached the consulate without alerting the mysterious and awful woman to her presence. Valeria was not in the atrium, so Elana hurried up the stairs under the New Moon sigil and hoped she'd run into the arbiter before she had to guess at doors.

She was not so lucky, but she discovered the door to the Mirabilis room was slightly ajar. Elana knocked politely and slipped inside when she heard Valeria's curt, "Enter."

Elana slid into a seat at the table and nodded. "Arbiter. What do you need from me?"

Valeria's outfit today was far more formal than yesterday's. The angles of her snow-white suit were so sharp Elana honestly wondered if the hem of the jacket might cut her if she touched it. The opal cufflinks and matching stud earrings that glimmered behind her hair did not remind Elana so much of hazy, dreamy clouds as they did the milky white eyes of a drowned corpse.

The arbiter's ice-blue eyes flashed as she looked Elana over. "You are nervous."

Elana blinked and straightened again. Lying to Valeria was next to impossible, so she didn't even try. "I came from

Cathy Smith's. She's hosting a tea on my behalf the day after tomorrow to help me increase my social standing in Haven. Yeah, I'm nervous about it. My next stop is the archives to find some etiquette guides so I don't choke on my foot."

Valeria nodded once. "Wise. Hold yourself with confidence and the rest will come."

"Thank you for the advice."

The arbiter turned her attention to the interface in front of her. She double-tapped something, then flicked it across the table to Elana. The glowing blue square slid smoothly along the sleek tabletop and stopped before her.

Elana scanned it. "This is a Domain of Shadows file on my mother. Is this—are these the results of your investigation?" Her heart pounded.

"They are *some* of the *interim* results of my investigation," Valeria clarified. "I have added that to your personal files. You may access it from any secure terminal. I suggest limiting your exploration of it to the sub-basement of the King's Archives."

"Of course."

"Before you read it on your own, however, I wanted to explain certain details in person."

Elana redirected her focus to Valeria. "I'm all ears."

Valeria swiveled to face the blank wall at the head of the table. With a flick of her fingers across the table, the blue glow transferred from the flat surface to hang in the air a foot or two in front of the wall. More casual manipulation of the interface, done without looking, opened several sub-files and turned the projection from regular blue to full color. From the top-right corner,

Tessa Hart stared at her daughter with the too-lively sparkle Elana had come to associate with vampire photographs.

Elana tore her gaze from her mother's face to skim the other projected windows. One showed a brief chronology of Tessa Hart's life. One showed a list of major legislative decisions and political events she was involved in as Consort of External Affairs and Diplomacy or the Arbiter of Sanctuary, and the last showed a short list of names. Elana recognized several from the research she and Matt had done, but others were unfamiliar.

The last was a blurry picture of…someone. They were on the shorter side, maybe a couple of inches shorter than Elana, although the camera angle was from above and behind them, so it was hard to tell. They wore dark blue, perhaps a suit. Lighter skin, unless the single visible hand was gloved, and darker hair tied back in a ponytail. Their frame was blocky, with broad shoulders and a square silhouette, which made Elana think masculine despite the ponytail.

Elana indicated the picture. "Who's that?"

Valeria's lips pressed together in a thin line. "That, as far as I can tell, is the vampire who gave your mother the Rights."

Elana's eyebrows drew together. "You don't sound very happy about that."

"I am the Arbiter of Shadows. It is not my job to be happy about my job."

Elana decided not to push. After Matt's revelation that Valeria and her mother had been friends, she didn't think it wise to pry. "Fair enough. Do you know who they are?"

"No. This is the only image I could find, and doing so required significant forensic datamining."

She still sounded like she'd swallowed an entire lemon. Elana did not want to be anyone who might have been between Valeria and this bit of intel.

Valeria expanded the image so it took up most of the projected screen. "This person, as far as I can tell, visited the Citadel Center for Health several times around your date of birth. Their name was not recorded in the visitors' log, but I spoke with as many staff members and patients as I could find who were working or in care at that time, and many remembered a visiting healer."

"But no one remembered their name?" Elana frowned. "That seems unlikely."

If Elana didn't know better, she'd have thought Valeria *grumbled* under her breath before replying. "Each vampire's powers are slightly different. I can't divulge more detail to you as an initiate, but suffice it to say that there *are* those who can influence even higher-level vampires when it comes to memory."

"Like how vampires can influence humans' memories," Elana mused. "Right. That makes sense. It seems sketchy as hell, though. Wouldn't the…" She bit her tongue.

Valeria looked over her shoulder at Elana and raised an eyebrow. "Wouldn't the what?"

"Um." Elana glanced from side to side. "How much trouble would I get in for questioning, uh…the king's abilities? Is Haven like an old monarchy where I'd get hauled off and beheaded?"

Valeria snorted. "No. You're wondering if the Spider-King knows who this person is."

"Well... Yeah." It seemed like an obvious line of questioning.

The arbiter nodded. "He likely does. He has not answered me. That means he does not wish to tell me, or he wishes me to discover more first. It is impossible to tell."

Elana squinted in thought. "Seems like you have to take a lot of stuff on faith when it comes to His Majesty. Everyone thinks of him as a benevolent dictator, but... man, he's really not around much, is he? I always thought the rumors of him being this mysterious shadow figure were mostly to keep humans out of Haven's business."

"Those rumors are true, unlike many that swirl around Haven," Valeria admitted. "He speaks when he deems it relevant. Otherwise, it is our job as the arbiters to ensure his will is done and his interests furthered."

Elana shook her head. "That's a tough job."

"You have no idea," Valeria muttered, then shook herself and returned to the image. "I will continue digging, but I am convinced this is the person who turned your mother. *Why*, I don't know yet."

Elana drummed her fingers on the table. "Can you give me the names of anyone you spoke to? Maybe I can make friends."

Valeria considered this in silence for several seconds, then nodded. "I will send you several names. Proceed with caution."

"Absolutely."

The arbiter minimized the picture of the unknown vampire and brought up the list of names and the timeline. "Your mother was a very cunning individual."

"Thank you?"

Valeria chuckled. "Yes, I suppose that *would* be a compliment. At first, I will admit I was dismayed by the apparent ease with which she hid this investigation from me. The more I uncovered, however, the more my dismay turned to pride."

The woman in white turned to face Elana, and the intensity in her eyes froze Elana to the spot. "If you learn nothing else from your mother, learn this. In Haven, you must at once trust no one and everyone. When each person you meet might have already lived a hundred lifetimes and may well live a hundred more, you have no way of knowing their intentions or capabilities.

"Your mother was my friend." A hint of amusement appeared at the corner of Valeria's mouth, and Elana acknowledged it with a tiny smile but said nothing. "My single mistake, in approaching this case after the fact as I have, was to believe that being a recently turned vampire, she could not have grasped this intrinsic fact about vampire society. Older and wiser vampires than she have fallen victim to that strain of naïveté.

"But grasp it she did, and better than anyone I know—and here I begrudgingly include myself." Valeria returned to the projections. Elana deflated in relief. "I haven't pinned yet how your mother became suspicious of House Veridian, or indeed, where the hell she picked up their name to *begin* with. But I *have* figured out that she knew, decades before I did, that someone in my corps is connected to that web of lies, so she did not so much as *breathe* in my direction.

"I have no idea whether she thought *I* was corrupt. I choose to think she did not because I believe she knew me well enough to know that my loyalty to the SpiderKing is dyed in every cell in my body. But she knew there would be a chance, no matter how good my security was, that whoever was corrupt in my organization would find out what she knew."

Elana spoke up. "I noticed when Matt and I were researching that none of the names my mother found were guardians."

"I noticed the same. A conspicuous omission and one I looked into. I won't tell you more yet for reasons of operational security, but rest assured that I will not tolerate rot in my house."

"I wouldn't have doubted it for a second." Elana shifted in her chair and bit the inside of her lip. "So…what's the next step?"

"We need yet more information," Valeria grimly replied. "I believe I have come to a conclusion regarding your mother's activities, but it only leads to more questions."

"Oh?"

"Your mother was either acting under orders from the SpiderKing, or he was directing her. She was cunning and clever, and her natural talents lent themselves very well to the work she found herself in, but her accesses and *extremely* rapid rise in power cannot be explained otherwise.

"In the Old World, I would have assumed she was a sleeper agent for another House," Valeria added with a mild scowl. "I pursued that angle for several days, testing every link in Tessa Hart's family tree for any connection to Houses across the Atlantic or elsewhere in the world. In *theory*, a House with enough clout could have falsified her documents.

"But she was part of the House of the SpiderKing," Valeria firmly concluded. "His Majesty does not tolerate impostors. If your mother was a plant from another House, either this person has power beyond imagination." She brought up the image of the unknown figure. "Or the king is not as unassailable as the history of Haven would have us believe."

Valeria brought her hand down on the table. Elana jumped, but the arbiter's laser focus remained on the projected images. "I have witnessed the SpiderKing's power personally. The latter is not an option. Tessa Hart would not have advanced as she did without the king's approval. Therefore, this person must be an associate of the king's, and Tessa was acting under his banner."

Elana cleared her throat. "Are you sure that person *isn't* the king? If he's so reclusive…"

"That is not the SpiderKing."

Elana swallowed. "Gotcha. Um…is there anything else you wanted to tell me?"

Valeria was still staring at the image as though she could burn a hole in it with her eyes. For all Elana knew, maybe she could if she tried hard enough.

"Not at this time. I will see you in three days on the training grounds. I look forward to hearing about the results of your…tea."

"Of course, Arbiter." Elana stood as hastily as she dared and booked it since being in a room with a grumpy Arbiter of Shadows was generally considered a Bad Idea.

Back in her car on the other side of the Citadel wall, Elana rested her head on her driver's seat headrest and stared at the car's roof. She'd intended to visit the King's Archives after her meeting with Valeria, but now her head was awash with doubts she couldn't shake.

"I wish I could *talk* to you, Mom," she murmured. It wasn't the first time she'd wished that, and it wouldn't be the last. "What were you *doing?*"

She bit her lip, sat up, and started the car, but instead of driving to the archives, she headed to the gallery where Valeria had dropped the bombshell that her mother hadn't died when Elana was born. Elana hoped she could get in without the arbiter's assistance. If not, she'd find somewhere else to sort out her head before she dove into the minutiae of vampire etiquette.

Her hunch proved correct. While the exterior entrance to the building housing the Consorts' Gallery was open to the public, the private portrait gallery was not. A tiny prick of the finger admitted Elana.

Without Valeria here to direct her, Elana took the opportunity to admire the portraits and artifacts before finding her mother. Most of the portraits were between four and six feet tall, meaning their subjects were either life-size or slightly larger. Elana let her gaze drift across the piercing gaze of each consort immortalized in paint and noted their distinguishing features. Here a hooked nose, there a thick brow, one with curly red hair, another without a single lock of hair.

The arbiters' portraits, few as they were, hung higher

up, under the rafters of the high cathedral ceiling. The portraits on the lower levels were all consorts, men and women who had wielded power over smaller areas of influence. Her mother's portrait hung halfway up the wall, on the edge between the two unofficial sections. Elana wondered who decided which portrait hung where. There had to be a curator.

In niches on the walls between the portraits sat artifacts from throughout vampire history. Elana hadn't had time or focus to explore them on her last visit, although she'd noted that some seemed beyond the limits of current human technology despite being in a museum. Unlike the portraits, none of the items on the small plinths were labeled, so Elana remained at a loss as to the function of the strange blocky thing that looked like a cross between a universal remote, a theremin, and a jar of glowing gumballs.

She couldn't help it. She cracked a smile. Sometimes, being a vampire was just plain *weird.* Suddenly you got the ability to live forever, plus weird powers that nobody *really* told you anything about, and you were inducted into a super-secret society full of intrigue. It was like James Bond meets *Crazy Rich Asians* with a side of magic—except magic wasn't real. If you suggested such to a vampire, they'd look at you like you'd crawled out from under a rock and were about as evolved as a slug.

Elana wondered if she'd ever attain a high enough level in the Sanguine Nexus to be allowed to understand how vampires had advanced so much farther than humans. At least it wasn't like Scientology, where you had to pay to learn the secrets. For all their mystery, vampires mostly seemed to have everyone's best interests in mind…or the overarching interest of "Let's not blow the world to smithereens just yet since we still live here." She could respect that.

Elana let out a long breath, rolled her shoulders, then found the inset platform she and Valeria had used to view her mother's portrait. It had no visible interface. Elana hoped stepping on it would be enough to trigger it to rise.

It wasn't. She stayed firmly on the ground.

Elana groaned and made a face. "God, I wish being a vampire came with an instruction manual," she muttered under her breath.

She tried tapping the platform with her toe, but nothing happened. She eyed the wall in front of her. Portraits hung to her left and right, but the space directly in front of her was blank.

Elana stretched out a palm and hovered it over the wall. Most systems in Haven were remarkably intuitive and responded exactly how you thought they should. With any luck…

A blue panel glowed under her hand, and the platform lifted a few inches from the floor. The glow disappeared from the wall and transferred to the disc under Elana's feet. When Elana lowered her hand and looked up, the platform rose—quickly at first, then more slowly when Elana adjusted her gaze lower. The last thing she needed today was to give herself motion sickness by swooping around.

Elana drifted up the wall until she came face-to-face with her mother. The portrait looked exactly as it had the first time she'd seen it, which struck her as an odd thought.

Had part of her expected the painting to look different because she understood more about Haven and vampires?

No, she'd expected it to look different because she thought differently about her mother.

"Who *were* you?" Elana quietly asked the portrait.

Her mother's painted face did not move, and no magical voice echoed in her head. Elana hadn't expected anything to happen, but a tiny part had hoped for something strange and monumental. Her mother's ghost emerging from the portrait to give her all the answers, maybe. That would have been handy.

Alas, it was only Elana and the silent oils.

She heaved a sigh and crossed her arms. "It'd be nice if this thing had a rail," she grumbled.

Elana watched her mother's face for several seconds, then sighed again. "Would you be proud of me if you were here? Is this what you wanted for me? When did you want me to find out I was a vampire? Were you planning to tell me at some point? Some momentous occasion? I know that kind of thing only happens in books, but everything else feels like it's straight out of a fantasy novel, so…"

She rubbed her temples and re-crossed her arms. "You missed all the big milestones. Didn't tell me on my eighteenth birthday or even my twenty-first. You only died a few years ago, Mom. Why were you waiting? Was it something here? Something with the conspiracy?"

It occurred to Elana that it might be wise to keep her voice down. She'd never seen anyone else in this building, but she had no idea what the surveillance situation might be.

She pitched her voice lower and kept talking to the

portrait. If Cathy Smith could live forever in a cross between a Bohemian loft and an art museum, Elana Bishop could talk to paintings. "Were you waiting for someone to make a move? Slip up? Show their hand? Did you know they were planning to kill you? What was *your* plan, Mom? Survive long enough to pass it off to me? Gather enough information to tell Valeria?

"I can't believe you were *friends* with the *Arbiter of Shadows*," Elana whispered. "Somehow, I think that's the weirdest thing of all right now. I'm sure that'll pass and I'll find something even weirder, but hey. Gotta cling to the normal things, right? Otherwise, I'll go insane."

She gazed into her mother's eyes for a long moment before continuing. "I can't help but wonder if you hid an even more secret journal somewhere. Something with the *whole* truth, nothing left out, nothing coded. What you *really* thought. Were you scared? When you woke up in Haven and everything was different, did that scare you, or did you jump in with both feet and no fear at all?

"Because I'm terrified," Elana confessed. "I'm fucking *terrified*, and I feel like I have to hide it every second of every day. I think Valeria expects me to fill your shoes in a fraction of the time you had to do the same…or maybe the SpiderKing does, I don't know. That's even scarier.

"I have *no idea* what I'm doing!" she exclaimed. "I am one hundred percent flying by the seat of my pants here, Mom! If you knew you were leaving me this huge mystery to solve, couldn't you *also* have left me an instruction manual on how to become a vampire?

"Maybe you meant to be here to guide me through it all. Or maybe…" Elana groaned, dragged her hands down her face, then let her shoulders slump and her head fall to her chest.

"Maybe you turned me so I'd have the best chance at a good life, but you never intended me to get involved in this. That's really hard for me to believe because everything in your files tells me you made your decisions with a *lot* of planning and foresight. But you turned me so early…

"I just don't know, Mom. I don't know. I feel so lost." She looked back up at the portrait, seeking solace in the paint, but she found only the reflections of the soft, indirect light of the gallery that made her mother's eyes appear to twinkle.

Elana sighed one more time. "Thanks for the chat. I'm sure I'll be back the next time I get the stupid idea that talking to a painting will help."

She couldn't bring herself to look away for what felt like an eternity. Finally, she whispered, "Love you, Mom," and tried to ignore the pang in her heart as she turned her gaze to the floor and the platform sank.

CHAPTER SEVENTEEN

Elana woke up the morning of The Tea, as she'd come to think of it, *far* earlier than her alarm went off. She rolled over in bed and glared at the alarm clock that read 5:30 AM in big red LED numbers. "Fuck you," she accused it.

Its numbers did not waver, and she was well and truly awake.

Elana sighed and got up. The tea wasn't until three in the afternoon. If she needed a nap, she'd take a nap.

She wasn't hungry yet, so she made coffee and worked on unpacking the kitchen while drinking it. By the time her alarm went off two hours later, the room was unpacked, and she'd even tidied the cardboard, packing paper, and tape.

Elana cracked her neck and refilled her mug. "Take that," she told the universe. "You think you can throw me off? Elana Bishop is unfazeable...and do *not* make me eat those words."

Breakfast time. She tossed a little oil into her newly unpacked frying pan, cracked two eggs into the sizzling oil, and made rye toast while the whites set. She slid the sunny-side-up eggs onto the buttered toast and topped it with a sprinkling of grated cheese, salt, and pepper. Simple, hearty, and well accompanied by her third cup of coffee. The caffeine buzz had settled in between her eyes, and she was stolidly ignoring it.

After cleaning her plate, she went downstairs to argue with herself further about what to wear that day. She'd initially picked an elegant brown slacks and blue blouse combo that she thought would announce her as friendly but not ostentatious. Vicky had given it a skeptical once-over and an "I suppose that'll do," which did not inspire confidence.

The early morning headache set in with a vengeance at 8:30 AM, and Elana was nowhere near picking an outfit. She gave up and headed for the backyard, where she'd set up a training circuit. She threw herself headfirst into the exercise regimen, running between deadlifts and chucking cinder blocks across the lawn, then dropping into a series of aerobic exercises and finishing with three rounds of quarterstaff drills she did with two broom handles duct-taped together.

When she finished, she flopped in the grass and panted. The headache was gone—or disguised by the exhaustion in every other part of her. She also *really* needed to pee. Funny what three cups of coffee would do to you.

Elana hauled herself to her feet, stumbled back into the house, and relieved herself. She turned the shower on as hot as she could bear and stood under the streaming water for long enough that she might have fallen asleep.

She rested her forehead against the slick tile and stared

at a droplet making its way down the expanse of white. The hot water eased her physical aches, and the exercise had shaken the early morning and caffeine headache, but doubt still ate at her heart like a worm in an apple.

Elana wasn't ready for this. No *way* was she ready for this. She could live in Haven for a million years and not be ready to face down an afternoon tea of society mavens.

Cathy hadn't given her any idea of what to expect. Elana had spent every spare moment yesterday devouring etiquette guides and society magazines, memorizing the tips and tricks—and rules and regulations—until she could have spat them out verbatim. Nevertheless, the concepts felt foreign to her, like a second language she'd only had a few lessons in and was still fumbling through the phrasebook. *¿Donde esta el baño?* would only get her so far.

She finally grabbed the bottle of shampoo. She couldn't very well cancel. She'd have to do her best and hope it was enough.

It was nowhere *close* to enough.

Elana had resisted the urge to run screaming for the elevator more times than she could count. She kept her sweating hands flat on the smooth fabric of her navy pencil skirt when she wasn't daintily drinking from her teacup, or God forbid, the earthenware goblet that held *straight-up blood.*

This was the first time Elana had encountered actual consumption of blood in Haven. From what she'd read, the practice was relatively uncommon in modern vampire society, at least in public. You did what you wanted in the privacy of your home, but the consensus was that vampires had evolved past the need to openly *consume* that which fed their powers.

"How do we enhance our powers if we don't drink blood?" Elana had asked Matt. "None of the books I'm reading say *anything* about that. It's all just, 'We don't drink blood anymore, that's old-fashioned,' but nobody spills the beans on what we do *instead*."

Matt's only response had been, "When you're in the lower levels of the Nexus, your power needs are taken care of by the systems the higher levels have put in place around you. In Haven, no one except the highest-powered vampires needs to drink blood. If you lived outside Haven, you'd have problems. That's one of the reasons we track down Runners as quickly as we do."

It had not escaped Elana's notice that Matt had not answered the question in the slightest.

It was still considered *en vogue* to provide your high society guests with their choice of room temperature or—ew—*warm* blood. Too cold and it would congeal, Elana guessed, and too hot and the whole room would smell like a murder scene.

Cathy had also offered each guest their choice of blood *type*, which had made Elana's stomach curl even tighter. Since this hadn't been mentioned in any of the books Elana had read, she'd opted for O negative. The one *good* choice she'd made so far if the tiny smile Cathy had given her was any indication.

Otherwise, Elana was dreadfully certain her comportment through the rest of the tea had been stunningly poor.

She'd brushed up on the guest list ahead of time, thanks to Cathy graciously providing it to her. It turned out that knowing who was sitting next to you and what their House specialized in didn't mean you knew what Mistress Elvira of House Noctis enjoyed doing in her spare time. Elana's cheeks were still red after that faux pas.

She'd held her own in the discussions about Haven politics, thank *God*. Elana had noticed impressed nods from Cynthia Redding of House Vulicia and Miriam al-Ghayb of House Almutlak, both of which she'd have happily taken to the bank if she hadn't *also* noticed mild scowls from Isolde Ferrand of House Nyctiel and Helena Kartilova of House Misticet.

You can't win them all in one day. Slow and steady wins the race.

They were halfway through the tea, as far as Elana could tell. The only visible clock in Cathy's penthouse loft apartment was a tall, slim hourglass shaped like an infinity symbol mounted on the wall above the elevator door. It was a gorgeous work of art.

The chamber was blown glass with a faint iridescent sheen. Its frame was a brass ouroboros that went from polished head to tarnished tail, and the sand within glimmered when the light caught it as though it were metal flakes. Elana hadn't realized it told time until she noticed the marked scales on the ouroboros' body. Two hours in, two more to go.

Two *excruciating* hours to go.

Cathy had told her to expect that at some point during the afternoon, the talk would naturally turn to a full interrogation of Elana. "Until they feel they have the right of you, it'll be business as usual," she'd explained. "But after they've sounded you out on however many topics they feel like discussing, they'll grill you within an inch of your life."

"About what?"

"Everything."

The conversation had petered out again, one of those moments where everyone happened to fall silent at the same time. Elana caught a couple of the ladies tossing glances between themselves and her heart fluttered.

Did they like her? Did they hate her? Were they agreeing to significant business deals with only a twitch of an eyebrow and the clink of a teacup on a saucer? Did it matter what kind of blood you chose to drink? If you didn't drink any, would they think you were a wimp?

For that matter, did vampire *men* have hazing rituals this bad? Elana would take the most grueling training sessions with Gustav over this torture any day.

"Where do you see yourself in five years, Elana?" Isolde casually asked.

So much tiny embroidery covered the House Nyctiel socialite's olive green dress that Elana had thought it was honest-to-God moss when she'd walked in. After the fiasco resulting from Elana's assumption that Carla Bryden's blouse had fiber-optic threads sewn in to allow for the shifting images of flying birds, she didn't dare ask. She was also no closer to knowing what created the effect since the look Carla had given her could have turned milk into yogurt on the spot.

Elana swallowed. Her mouth was dry, but sipping tea— or, God forbid, the blood—would have looked like she was stalling since she didn't already have the cup on the way to her mouth when the question was asked. "Building my place in Haven society," she carefully replied. "Before I moved here, I worked in construction and electronics. I'm considering looking into work in the latter, perhaps with an Etretan firm or a research lab in Quarto."

"You don't intend to follow in your mother's footsteps?" The deceptively light question came from someone who had barely spoken that afternoon, Sonal Paramartha of House Karapak, a woman with dark honey-colored skin wearing an orange sari that dripped with garnets, tiger's-eyes, and citrines. She had not touched her tea but had refilled her goblet twice.

Elana politely met Sonal's gaze and folded her hands in her lap, ignoring the thin film of sweat making them sticky. *Thank God I wore black.* "I wouldn't presume to ride my mother's coattails. She did incredible work, and I'm very proud of her. Of course I would love to continue that work since I share the principles she fought for, but I intend to advance on my own merits, not just my name."

The temperature in the room dropped by several metaphorical degrees, and with it went Elana's stomach. She caught the faint tightening around Cathy's eyes that told Elana she'd screwed up *again*, and she resisted the urge to backpedal madly. The only thing worse than making a conversational faux pas in the first place was pretending you hadn't meant it because *that* showed you were wishy-washy and easily manipulated. Not a good look for anyone, but an even worse look for someone in the House of the SpiderKing.

"Do you think so little of the House you were born to?" Elizabeth Dromenkopf of House Waldenfell inquired. Her tone was equally casual, but she flashed a fang when she spoke. In a room of well-bred society ladies who'd practiced their social skills for centuries, that was as good as an open threat.

Elana's stomach dropped past her seat and into her toes. *Right.* She kept forgetting that in Haven, you couldn't divorce anything you said about yourself from your family, much less your House. She'd as good as said that she thought she was better than the SpiderKing. House Waldenfell was a staunch supporter of the monarchy. Making enemies there was a poor plan.

"No, certainly not," Elana firmly stated. "I'm beyond honored to have joined the House of the SpiderKing. I only mean to ensure that my actions reflect positively on the reputation of that great House. I have big shoes to fill, and I don't take my new position or its responsibilities lightly."

A chorus of muttered "hmm"s and "I see"s followed that pronouncement. The tightness around Cathy's eyes hadn't lessened, but it hadn't deepened. Elana might not have been actively digging her grave, but she remained on shaky ground.

"Do you intend to avenge your mother's death?"

The question, innocent but for the faintest spark of malintent in the speaker's eyes, brought every whisper to a sudden halt. Elana locked gazes with Mary Reynolds of House Mericia across the circle of pouffes and armchairs and let the words hang in the air while she observed the other woman and considered her response.

House Mericia was a quiet but powerful House with New World roots. It was founded in the 1950s. Mericia specialized in agricultural work and was quartered in

Senkyem, as you'd expect. It owned and worked land across the Midwest and into the Canadian prairies.

Elana hadn't given it nor its head, Mary's mother Olga, a second thought since Mericia hadn't shown up in her mother's files. She might have posited that Mericia would be friendly to her cause since they employed thousands of humans to work their fields and shipping lines to the production facilities run by their allies in Shestoi. Based on the cool condescension and mild distaste on Mary Reynolds' face, Elana's hypothesis would have been wholly incorrect.

Mary Reynolds was a slight woman with small bones and a petite frame. Her face was heart-shaped with a button nose and a weak jawline. Her hair was mousy brown and tied in a chignon at the nape of her neck with wisps floating around her face. Her brown eyes were cold, and her lips were thin.

She wore a tea-length dress in beige, which did nothing for her skin tone. The strings of pearls and diamonds at her neck and on her wrist announced her status as the heir apparent to one of the wealthiest New World Houses to anyone with eyes.

Elana hadn't expected anyone to bring up her mother's death, and certainly not this brazenly. She made a mental note to investigate House Mericia more closely, then broke the tense silence by responding, "The Arbiter of Shadows personally executed those convicted of my mother's death. As far as the file currently stands, the case is closed."

She was careful not to add too much emphasis on "currently," but she gave it a tiny verbal underline. She also didn't bother answering the question. Nothing in what

Elana said indicated whether she agreed with the case's closure nor whether she intended to seek further punitive action.

"How...polite of you," Mary murmured. Then she added more loudly, "Will that courtesy extend to the House of those guilty of your mother's death? Will you do business with House Ateles?"

Mild surprise rippled through the salon. Cathy's eyebrows lifted a degree. Despite House Ateles being on record as the House Tessa Hart's killers belonged to, this was not considered average teatime conversation.

Elana mustered every ounce of the calm, collected aura she'd witnessed her mother use in C-PAN videos. "I have no dealings with House Ateles at present, but I would not automatically exclude them from business in the future, just as I would not favor or dismiss any other House out of hand. Fair is fair."

"You are truly your mother's daughter." Mary set her teacup on its saucer with a tiny *clink*, then delicately picked up the goblet she hadn't yet touched and raised it to the group. "To her legacy. To the legacy of Tessa Hart, Arbiter of Sanctuary, cut down so *unfairly* in her prime."

Elana still hadn't dropped Mary's gaze, and the other woman seemed equally unwilling to end the quasi-staring contest. Elana didn't flinch from the challenge and met Mary's toast with her goblet. "To the memory of Tessa Hart and everything she stood for."

"To Tessa Hart," the assembled echoed in murmurs, and the circle of women toasted and drank.

Elana briefly considered faking the sip—she did *not* particularly want to consume blood—but something told her the others would be able to tell. This was one of those social compacts you didn't mess with. She steeled her stomach and dutifully sipped the liquid within the earthenware cup.

The taste that erupted across her tongue was as she'd expected: iron-forward, cloying, and heady. It wasn't as though Elana had never tasted blood before. She'd stuck her fair share of papercuts and scraped knuckles into her mouth before on instinct, just like everyone else. That didn't even touch bloody lips or bitten cheeks or tongues. Drinking it straight, even a sip, was a very different experience. The scent rose into her sinuses and lodged there like she had a nosebleed, and the back of her mouth felt sticky.

She swallowed and immediately wished it were kosher to follow the blood with a huge gulp of tea. Unfortunately, everyone in the circle politely swirled their goblets and replaced them on the low table in the center, then looked at her expectantly.

Oh, shit. What do they want now?

Elana wracked her brain for anything she could remember from the dozens of etiquette guides she'd read the day before. Toasts, toasts, what had they said about toasts?

She was at a loss. She couldn't remember anything about the proper post-toast response. Elana cast a despairing, Hail Mary glance at Cathy.

Cathy caught the look and smiled faintly. "Did you want to speak in your mother's memory, Elana? Now would be the time. You have our attention."

"*Oh*—um… Yes, of course. Of course." Elana awkwardly smoothed her hands over her skirt again and frantically dredged up memories of her mother...which were all secondhand, gleaned from the endless hours of C-PAN footage she'd consumed and the pages of her mother's journal.

She swallowed again. The taste of blood surged through her sinuses anew, and she fought the urge to retch.

"My mother..." Her voice trailed off. What could she say about Tessa Hart that wouldn't either play Elana's hand too early or else be so milquetoast that these terribly powerful women would write Elana off even more than they already had?

There was nothing for it. She had to say *something*, or they'd ridicule her for the rest of eternity for sitting there gaping like a fish out of water.

"My mother was a force to be reckoned with," Elana finally said. "She knew what she wanted, and she fearlessly went for it. She fought for justice, equality, and sanctuary for all. I believe those are honorable pursuits. I'm proud to be her daughter and to carry on her work in whatever way I can. I can only hope I honor her memory by my actions."

The words were true enough, and Elana meant them, but they fell flatter than the lace doilies on the table below the painted china saucers. The gazes of the women around her remained cool and unmoved, some even going so far as to be disappointed, or worse, bored.

"Hear, hear," Cathy chimed in, coming to Elana's rescue in the awkward silence and raising her goblet again. "To Tessa Hart, and to her daughter's future."

"Hear, hear," the other women chorused in varying degrees of confidence, and they drank again.

Elana did too, reluctant as she was. This time, the iron

tang felt like a hammer blow to her skull. Was it just her, or was her heart rate rising? She felt warm, and she couldn't tell if it was because she'd deeply embarrassed herself for the *nth* time in four hours or if something in the blood made her feel that way. Vampires *could* drink blood to increase their powers, couldn't they? Should Elana have been taking blood supplements before all her training sessions? Would that have made her less of a wimp?

She set the goblet down on the table with slightly more of a *thump* than she'd intended and smiled apologetically at a couple of unimpressed eyebrow flickers she received. "Thank you for the invitation to speak in my mother's memory," she offered to Mary across the table. "I never knew her as a child, so learning about her has been very interesting."

Hushed breaths fluttered around the circle, and Elana's eyes widened in sudden alarm. What had she said wrong *that* time?

"It's terrible when a child doesn't know their parent," Mary all but whispered. Her brown eyes gleamed like a cat in the dark, waiting to strike. "Truly heartbreaking. Not knowing where you come from…"

Cathy cleared her throat pointedly. "My deepest apologies, ladies, but I'm afraid I have to call a slightly early end to this afternoon's salon. I've just remembered I double-booked myself to speak with the Arbiter of Vision about a new installation featuring some of my extensive collection of artifacts from the Densorin dynasty. I'll have to tidy up here before I head to that appointment."

She delicately chivvied the society ladies out of their seats toward the vestibule door and from there the elevator, exchanging pleasantries and nonsense until, in surprisingly short order, only she and Elana remained in the grand loft apartment.

"It's a damn good thing none of them have the balls to argue with me," Cathy grumbled as she gathered teacups and saucers with distinctly *indelicate* clamor. "Helps when you have a millennium or three on all of them…"

Elana was too stunned by the abrupt end to the salon that she barely noticed the reference to Cathy's age. "What did I do? I knew I wasn't doing great—God, I did *so* badly, I want to crawl under a rock and die—but what the hell did I *do?*"

Cathy sighed as she dumped half-empty teacups into her sink. "Elana, my dear… You told them you didn't know your mother."

Elana blinked in confusion. "But it's *true*. I didn't know her. She died almost four years ago, and I *thought* she was dead from the time I was old enough to form memories."

Cathy downed the remainder of her goblet of blood, rinsed it, and set it on the counter with a hard *thud*. "Yes, Elana, but *they didn't know that.*"

Elana was still lost. "So? What's the big deal? I'm sure I'm not the only vampire who grew up not knowing a parent. It happens more often than you'd think, for one reason or another. Somebody dies, somebody leaves, your dad wasn't really your dad…"

"*Elana.*" Cathy gripped the counter's edge, caught Elana's gaze, and held it fast. "I love you dearly, and I know you are so far behind the eight ball in this game that it isn't even funny, which is why I'm holding your hand through the absolute clusterfuck that is Haven high society. But for Inanna's sake, *use your brain.*

"Your mother showed up out of nowhere in the early nineties and was already attached to the royal House before she did *anything.* Nobody knew where she came from, and nobody was allowed to ask. She died less than thirty years later after a *skyrocketing* political career that most vampires could only *dream* of.

"She died in mysterious circumstances. A thoroughly disappointing murder investigation ends with the Arbiter of Shadows—*her personal friend*—executing four low-level goons. Four years later, her adult daughter shows up and is also *immediately* inducted into the royal House.

"It would have been one thing if you'd let the mystery lie," Cathy lamented. "They would have believed intrigue upon intrigue and made up rumors about why you'd grown up as a human outside the Wall. But now they know that you *didn't* know anything. Giving those vultures *any* scrap of information is playing a dangerous game, but giving them personal information about yourself that reveals weakness?"

Cathy shook her head. "Oh, Elana, you already had a long way to go, and you've just made it a whole lot longer."

CHAPTER EIGHTEEN

Elana slammed her fists into the punching bag and imagined it was Mary Reynolds' face. Uppercut. Right hook. Left jab. Sucker punch.

She tucked her chin and battered the sand-filled bag until she couldn't feel her knuckles anymore, which wasn't hard because she was so deeply in her thoughts that she almost nailed Gustav in the jaw when he appeared in her peripheral vision.

The sturdy Russian trainer caught Elana's fist and twisted it aside. When he let go, Elana shook out her hand and hissed in slight pain as her mind reconnected to her body and she realized how hard she'd been hitting the training apparatus.

"Sorry." She blushed and averted her eyes. "Thought you were someone else."

Gustav arched an eyebrow. "Do you make a habit of attacking colleagues outside of the sparring ring?"

"Well, no…"

"Then who were you expecting?"

The blush on Elana's cheeks deepened. "No one."

Gustav narrowed his eyes. "You are not a good liar, Miss Bishop."

Elana huffed and stalked over to the wall, where she unwrapped her hands and stretched her fingers. When Gustav followed, she pursed her lips. "It's dumb. I need to get my head in the game, that's all. I'll do better."

Gustav leaned on the wall. "I agree you need to get your head in the game, but dismissing your troubles out of hand will not fix them."

Elana threw him a look. "You gonna tell me your last career was in psychotherapy?"

The trainer chuckled. "No. I have been fighting all my life. I am glad I get to do it in a gym now instead of on a battlefield fighting *for* my life. The safety allows me to appreciate the art of battle far more effectively. Also, I like teaching."

"Because you can pound your students into the dirt?"

Gustav sighed and shook his head. "You are in a *mood* today. No, Elana. You know me better than that. Training comes with discomfort and occasionally pain, yes, but a sadist conditions their victims. A trainer builds their students."

He snagged a pair of badminton rackets from the wall—which Elana had honestly thought were decorative until that moment—then foraged in the cupboards in front of them until he came out with a solid metal birdie. "Come with me. We do something different today."

Gustav led Elana out of the main training room and down the hall to a set of closed-in courts with lines on the floor and rails for nets in the center of the walls. After he closed the door behind them, he offered her a racket. "Do you know the rules?"

"Yeah. I played badminton in high school." She eyed the birdie. "That looks like a lethal weapon."

Gustav grinned. "That's the idea. Sometimes it shoots lasers."

"I cannot tell if you're joking."

"You will find out."

He jogged across the room, pausing to tap the rail holding the nets. The net completed its descent to the correct height as he reached the other side of the court, and he bounced on the balls of his feet while Elana took her place diagonal to him.

Elana watched him carefully, her gaze flicking between his feet and the birdie in his hand. "Why are we doing this?"

"Something different. It is important not only to train your powers in combat but also in simple reaction time and situational awareness."

He made his serve. The birdie soared through the air on a deceptively lazy arc, then plummeted, and Elana dashed forward to smack the projectile back.

She grimaced. *Should have seen that coming.* Her grasp of basic physics was better than *that*. Obviously, a solid metal birdie wouldn't fly like a normal—

Elana gasped and sprinted across the court to catch the veritable comet Gustav sent her. Not focusing was *not* an option here.

They batted the birdie back and forth several times. Gustav gave Elana no quarter, sending her scrambling to every corner of the court in quick succession. By the time the birdie let out its first blast of laser fire, Elana was panting so hard she could barely breathe, and she instinctively threw herself into a forward somersault to miss the scorching beam.

The birdie hit the wooden floor with a low-pitched *ding* that echoed off the walls, and for several seconds after that all Elana could hear was her heavy breathing. The cool surface of the planks felt like a feather bed. Her head spun.

"Holy shit," she hoarsely muttered.

Then, all too aware of Gustav's black and white shoes across the room from her vantage point of hugging the floor, she hauled in two breaths deep enough to clear her head and shoved herself upright. The only reason he hadn't immediately launched another volley was because the birdie was on her side of the court.

Elana cracked her neck and retrieved the birdie. "I thought you were kidding about the lasers."

"Do I look like a man who kids?" He winked.

She snorted. "Fair point. Am I supposed to dodge them?"

Gustav shook his head. "See the button on your racket?"

Elana frowned and examined the handle. A small depression sat just above where her thumb rested. She pressed it until it clicked, and the surface of her racket smoothed over like a mirror.

"Hit the laser, then the birdie," Gustav explained. "Later, we will play in the mirrored courts."

Elana stared at him. "Meaning every time the laser fires..."

"You have more things to hit."

"Do they ever stop?"

"If they hit you."

Elana held up the birdie. "This just seems mean."

He grinned unapologetically. "You will have a difficult time dwelling on whatever is bothering you when you are avoiding lasers *and* solid metal projectiles the size of your fist."

She had to admit he had a point.

Forty-five minutes later, Gustav caught the birdie one-handed and flipped his racket around so the handle pointed to Elana. "We are finished for today."

Elana unceremoniously stumbled across the court, slumped against the wall, and groaned as she slid down it to flop on the floor. "Oh my *God*, kill me now. I don't think I'm gonna be able to move for a week."

Gustav chuckled and raised the net to the ceiling. "You will be fine. You rose to the challenge today, Elana, and your body will reward you for it. I am consistently impressed with your progress."

She cracked an eye open and peered up at him. Every muscle ached. She'd lost count of the thin burns she'd accumulated from the laser fire. She had also taken more than a few birdies to parts of her body that did *not* appreciate being hit with half a pound of solid metal, or however much the stupid fucking piece of shit weighed. "Seriously?"

"Seriously," he echoed and punctuated the pronouncement with a decisive nod. He held the birdie and racket in one hand and offered the other to help her up.

Elana took it and pulled herself to her feet with his

welcome assistance. A smile bloomed on her face when she realized that although she'd collapsed in a heap only moments before, she already felt like she was bouncing back.

Gustav matched her smile. "You feel it. Good. That is a good sign."

A familiar female voice interrupted before Elana could say thank you. "What is?"

Valeria stood on the court's threshold. She hadn't arrived to work out since she wore low-profile combat armor in pure white and a long leather cloak hung over her shoulder. Elana hadn't seen Valeria in combat gear before, and it took her a second to recognize what it was.

"Expecting trouble?" Elana blurted, then grimaced. "Sorry, you probably can't tell me."

The Arbiter of Shadows flicked her eyebrows upward once in acknowledgment, then settled her gaze on Gustav again. "A good sign of what, Gustav?"

Gustav straightened and motioned at Elana with his racket. "I believe she is ready, Arbiter."

Elana opened her mouth to ask, "Ready for what?" but Valeria spoke first.

"What makes you say that?"

"We just played nearly an hour of Chimera badminton," Gustav explained. "Miss Bishop had never played before, but she learned how to handle the birdie and mirror the laser fire within two exchanges. I fully expect she will quickly adapt to the extra difficulty when we train in the mirror hall later today.

"She was extremely fatigued upon finishing our game, but as you can see, she is recovering nicely," Gustav finished. "She has learned her body's capabilities and is able to push her limits. We left a punching bag in the main room that will need to be recalibrated because she nearly knocked it off its hook."

Elana blushed. She hadn't noticed that. Now that Gustav mentioned it, she felt almost ready to get back on the court and eager to up the ante. She'd always liked a challenge.

It helped that she could *succeed* in the training rooms. Maybe she should invite Mary Reynolds to a game of badminton...or rather, *Chimera* badminton.

Valeria tilted her head and looked Elana up and down. "I leave Haven for two days this evening. Come find me when you are finished with Gustav this afternoon."

Elana nodded. "Yes, ma'am. Um...where can I find you?"

Valeria smiled. "Wherever I am to be found."

Oh. It was a *test*, then. Great.

Elana hid a sigh, nodded again, and shifted her grip on her badminton racket. "Okay, Gustav, where's the mirror court?"

Elana stared at herself in the full-length mirror. More specifically, she stared at the rapidly disappearing red lines on her skin. When the evidence of her epic mirror-laser battle with Gustav had fully vanished—Chimera badminton was officially her favorite sport in the world, and she had *plans*—her attention shifted to her body in general.

She'd been so busy over the last several weeks trying to find her "vampire legs," as Matt called them, that she hadn't taken many opportunities to appreciate the results. Now, though...

Elana had already been strong, thanks to her work in her father's hauling business. While she hadn't *needed* to work much harder than the men around her thanks to her vampire blood, she'd enjoyed pushing herself to do more. Therefore, she'd always maintained a respectably muscled figure with toned calves and biceps that strained a T-shirt sleeve if she bought them tight.

Her abs had been nothing to sneeze at either, although she hadn't kept herself ridiculously dehydrated so you could *see* them. That was dumb. Anyone on the Bishop's crew who showed up with washboard abs got sent home to hydrate for three days before being allowed back on a job site.

Secret vampire Elana had looked like a hobbyist bodybuilder, someone who focused on lifting weights, eating right, and taking care of themselves to a higher degree than most folks.

Fully trained initiate vampire Elana, on the other hand...

She hadn't lost the biceps—if anything, they were a touch bigger—but she'd gained definition in her back and shoulders. Her posture was better, too. She would swear she'd gained an inch, and she wasn't wearing heels.

Elana's thighs, waist, and hips had slimmed slightly. It wasn't so much that she'd noticed a significant difference in her clothes. She'd glimpsed the mirror on the other side of the room between her legs when she'd been drying off after a seriously luxurious shower and realized with a start that her *ass* had definition. *Did* gluteal muscles gain definition?

Whatever, she didn't know the specific terminology, and it didn't matter. The point was Elana's body had changed shape thanks to her hard work, and the results were visible. They were also sexy as hell.

Correction. *She* was sexy as hell.

Elana grinned at her reflection and left the locker room humming Shania Twain's *Man, I Feel Like a Woman*.

Elana stood in the middle of a silent field in Senkyem, closed her eyes, and listened.

She'd started her hunt for the Arbiter of Shadows in the Citadel, wandering the corridors of the consulate until her calves ached from the stairs. Having found neither hide nor snow-white hair of Valeria, she'd slipped into an empty room and texted Matt. It wasn't cheating if you were using your resources wisely.

Hey. Any idea where Valeria is?

He hadn't been far from his phone. His return text was seconds later.

No. Why?

She told me to find her after I was done with Gustav, but she didn't say where. I've scoured the consulate. She

doesn't post anything on social media so I don't know where she likes to hang out.

Elana snorted as she read her text and sent another on its heels.

I just realized how unlikely it is that the Arbiter of Shadows, Valeria Draven, the king's consort... HANGS OUT.

Again, Matt texted right back—first with a laughing emoji, then with something that made Elana's brow furrow in deep confusion.

Can't make any promises, but you might try going to Senkyem and standing in the fields.

She blinked several times at her phone before answering him.

Uh. What?

Unhelpfully, all he wrote back was:

You heard me.

Here she was in the middle of a field in Senkyem, pretending she could *sense* Valeria through some arcane means of—

"Hello, Elana."

Elana jumped a foot, whirled, and brought up her fists

before her brain caught up with her reflexes and she stopped herself from attempting to deck the Arbiter of Shadows with a haymaker.

"*Jesus Christ on a roller skating pogo stick,*" Elana exclaimed as she brought a hand to her racing heart. "How the *fuck* did you do that?"

The corner of Valeria's mouth twitched toward a smile that was closer to a smirk. "Vampires are very good at moving silently."

Elana had noticed her footsteps getting lighter, but not *that* much. She raised an eyebrow. "We're standing in a field of wheat. There's no wind. Wheat makes noise when you move through it, no matter how quietly you tiptoe. What, did you teleport?"

This time, Valeria smiled. "Not quite. Did you ask Mister Richelieu how to find me?"

Elana's heart, which had calmed down by a couple of dozen beats per minute, ratcheted right back up to *oh shit* territory. "Sort of? I tried the consulate but couldn't find you anywhere, so I asked him if he had any ideas. I thought that would be a wiser use of resources than wandering the entire city and hoping I caught sight of a white shoe disappearing around a corner."

"What did he tell you?"

Elana noticed that Valeria hadn't confirmed *or* denied whether Elana had wisely used her resources. She swallowed. "He told me to go stand in the fields in Senkyem. I, uh, definitely thought he was off his rocker, but again, I didn't have any better ideas, so…"

"He did not tell you which field?"

"No?"

Valeria nodded. Maybe it was the summer sunset, but Elana thought she spotted satisfaction in Valeria's ice-blue eyes…perhaps even pride.

"Very good," the arbiter proclaimed. "Walk with me, Elana."

Elana fell into step beside the white specter of a woman. The sun cast golden rays over the rustling wheat as they swished through it, and nothing sounded but the quiet susurrations of crickets and wheat stalks. It felt like a bridge between the real world and something beyond, a space on the edge where something was about to change.

Valeria's voice was barely audible through the whispering wheat. Luckily, both women were vampires, and such mundane obstacles posed them no trouble. "You are nearly ready to progress to adept."

Elana's step faltered when she processed what Valeria had said. "Wait—you mean—I'm already done being an initiate?"

Valeria chuckled. "You have been an initiate for quite some time now, you know."

Elana blushed. "Right. I suppose that's been since I was two or so. It just feels…quick. I only *feel* like I've been a vampire for a couple of months."

"Understandable. You've made impressive strides since coming here. Your determination is commendable. Do you want to advance?"

"I have a choice?"

"Of course. It is not a requirement that you advance through the Sanguine Nexus as you age. Many vampires settle in quite happily at adept and savant."

Elana didn't respond. She remembered what she'd read about adepts in the medical textbook Matt had shown her.

Adepts have mastered their basic abilities and are integrating into vampire society. They begin to differentiate their skills into unique specializations and take on roles within their communities that match their interests. Speed, strength, and regeneration improve.

She would become even stronger and faster. Her regenerative ability would improve beyond the miraculous healing she'd witnessed that day in the locker room after Chimera badminton. She'd develop her unique specialization...whatever talent her genes possessed, crossed with the vampire blood gifted to her by her mother.

Elana lifted her gaze from the flowing golden stalks to the high horizon of the Wall. "What do I have to do to advance, and what happens after that?"

"You'll undergo a ceremony in the royal temple in a week if you choose to advance. You'll need to spend the week in between learning your part in that ceremony...and finding a sponsor. Mister Richelieu could assist, or you could ask Cathy Smith if you felt brave."

"A sponsor?"

"Do your research. Part of being a vampire is taking initiative. Another part is knowing when to rely on your allies. You must learn the difference to succeed."

"I will," Elana promised. When Valeria said nothing, Elana frowned and checked to see if she'd managed to piss off the arbiter without trying.

She was alone again. "God*dammit*," she muttered, then laughed and shook her head. "What level do you learn *that* trick?"

CHAPTER NINETEEN

Elana woke the next morning feeling fit as a fiddle. She bounced out of bed, stretched, and several vertebrae popped in a deeply satisfying fashion.

She brushed and braided her hair, then put on light makeup and selected a simple outfit of loose slacks, strappy sandals, and a flowy blouse. All were in varying neutral tones. She aimed for something comfortable that she could move in if push came to shove but was still elegant. She figured the designer monograms on the cuffs of the blouse and embossed in the leather thongs of the sandals would go a long way in that respect.

The diamond tennis bracelet and earrings didn't hurt, either. Elana added a diamond-encrusted comb to her hair as a final touch, then nodded at her reflection. Perfect for a day in the library and the archives.

She opted for a simple breakfast of avocado toast while she waited for her coffee to brew and pondered her plan of attack.

Elana hadn't done any research into the esoteric aspects

of vampirism. One, she'd been too damn busy, and two, she'd figured—probably rightly—that she wouldn't have access until she was allowed. She had walked by the royal temple every time she went to the consulate but never dared to go in. She had no reason to.

Now she did.

She needed a sponsor, and she needed to learn her part in the ceremony. Valeria entrusted her with the responsibility of doing her research ahead of time. Elana had no doubt that initiates who didn't adequately know their shit when they walked into the temple would be summarily thrown out.

Would they kill me? Or would I get a second chance?

Elana shivered and decided she didn't want to risk it. She would be ready.

After yesterday's grueling match of Chimera badminton, she felt a hell of a lot more ready for every other aspect of vampire society, too. She would also put *those* plans in motion today, and Elana *couldn't wait*.

She grinned at her reflection in the kitchen window while mixing her coffee in her travel mug of choice, a thoroughly ironic *Twilight*-themed vacuum canister Vicky had shipped her as a joke gift.

Elana Bishop was done joking around.

She sipped the coffee as she climbed into her Emeya. Today would be a *good* day. She could feel it in her fangs, as the saying went.

Elana approached the main desk in the atrium of the King's Archives with a spring in her step. The head librarian was not on duty today. Instead, Elana walked up to a man who appeared to be in his late forties with a touch of salt and pepper in his neatly groomed sideburns and short, styled black hair. A handful of laugh lines creased his tanned olive skin.

His nameplate read Alberto Esperanza, Senior Librarian. Currently, Alberto was occupied with the interface in his desk. His long fingers with short, perfect crescent-moon nails flew over the glowing blue text as though he were playing the piano. Elana wondered whether he did.

She also wondered how frequently vampires changed careers or whether Matt was an anomaly that way. Did most vampires pick a vocation and stick to it for centuries, or was it more common to change it up?

Elana politely cleared her throat and smiled when Alberto's hazel eyes met hers. "Good morning. I'm looking for books on a particular subject, but I'm not sure what keywords to search for in the interface or which wing to browse. Could you help me?"

Alberto's smile was as sunny as the beaches she imagined him strolling. "Of course." He had a very light European accent. She guessed Spanish based on his name. "What topic?"

"I found out yesterday that I'm…eligible, I guess? To become an adept," Elana explained. "I was told I needed to do my own research to prepare. Would books about that be listed under religion or something else?"

Alberto's eyebrows rose, and his smile warmed. Without breaking his gaze, he typed anew on the interface.

"Congratulations! That's wonderful. Always an honor to help an eager initiate. If you ask me, too many initiates spend their time hunting for the sanguine panacea. It doesn't exist. The only way to progress in the Sanguine Nexus is hard work and persistence."

"So I'm learning. Nothing about this has been easy so far." She glanced at the desk but couldn't read much upside down. Alberto kept his text size impressively small. "Where would you recommend I start? Like I said, I wasn't sure if I should look in the religion section or if somewhere else would be better."

Alberto nodded. "You were on the right track. The books on the ceremonial and traditional aspects of Nexus progression are found in a subsection of the religion wing. Do you have a sponsor yet?"

"No. I know I need one, but I didn't want to ask someone until I understood what being a sponsor meant. I don't want to be rude and ask someone for something they can't do."

"Very sensible of you. Again, too many initiates don't consider all the facets of the decision. You seem to have a good head on your shoulders." Alberto tapped with authority on the interface, and Elana's phone buzzed in her pocket. "I've sent you a list of suggested reading. All the listed titles are in the southeast corner wing on the top floor."

Elana briefly wondered how he'd done that, then remembered the Haven app included proximity connections for public services, like the gliders. Library books must fall under the same umbrella. "Thank you very much."

"You're most welcome. Good luck!"

She smiled and headed for the southeast corner, where she ascended the tall spiral staircase to the top floor. The stairs functioned much like an escalator, but she still felt her body moving faster than ever before, and she reached her destination without being the slightest bit out of breath.

"Being a vampire *rules*," Elana muttered—although she needn't have kept quiet because this wing of the King's Archives appeared to be deserted apart from her.

Elana retrieved her phone and tapped the Haven app notification on the screen. Alberto's list of recommended reading popped up. *An Initiate's Guide to the Rituals of the Sanguine Nexus. Vampyre Eſoterica. Sponsoring Initiates in Temple Rituals. Ceremonies, Vestments, and Chants—A Primer...*

"Okay, well, I'm not sure I'll be able to decipher anything that uses a *long s* in its title, so let's cross off *Vampyre Eſoterica* right now. These three, though..." Elana selected the other three books at the top of the list and requested them. A library cart parked beside the staircase hummed to life, lifted an inch off the floor, and moved into the stacks.

Elana wandered until she found a reading nook she liked the look of. Two poofy maroon armchairs with dark curls of wood at the ends of their arms and legs sat tucked away in a corner with a matching table between them. A small lamp with a fringed shade in the same color as the upholstery stood on the table.

When she sat, a small holographic "plaque" appeared on the table's edge. **In Memory of C. Deloraine.** Nothing else.

No dates nor any mention of who had made the memorial donation. Elana tried waving a hand over the inscription, then hovering her hand over it, but no extra information appeared.

She vaguely wondered whether it was worth looking up C. Deloraine, then dismissed the idea. Chances were good it wouldn't lead to anything. A random memorial plaque in a dusty corner of the library would be a red herring in any self-respecting mystery novel.

The library cart's arrival forestalled any further contemplation. Two of the three books it had brought were thin and appeared new. The third was bound in fraying red cloth, and its pages were well-thumbed.

Elana tried to lift them off the cart but was surprised when she could not move them. She frowned until she spotted the blue text glowing beside the books.

These books contain information that may not leave the archives. Please place your personal belongings in this cart's secure containment area before retrieving your manuscripts.

"Wow." She shook her head in wonder and deposited her phone into the drawer on the side of the cart. She tried to move the books again, but they didn't budge. "Seriously? You want my purse too? Geez…"

The moment her dimensional handbag was safely in the drawer, it slid shut, the cart *beeped*, and Elana could remove the books from the cart.

"They *really* don't want people learning about this without permission," she mused as she sat back in the armchair. "I guess it makes sense—this is the super-secret stuff."

Elana cracked open the first book, *An Initiate's Guide to the Rituals of the Sanguine Nexus*, and proceeded to lose herself down the rabbit hole of esoterica.

An insistent growl from her stomach tore Elana's attention from the middle of the third book—*Ceremonies, Vestments, and Chants—A Primer*—and she realized with a start that she'd missed lunch.

She stretched, put the book on the table, and rubbed her sandy eyes. No way would these books be allowed to leave the archives, so she'd have to come back and finish reading later. Luckily, she was pretty sure she'd covered enough of the basics to talk to Cathy.

Elana replaced the books on the cart. The text on the side changed.

Have you completed your session?

Not seeing any text input, even when she hovered her hand over where it would normally be, Elana awkwardly announced, "Yes," to the air.

The side drawer unlocked with a *shunk* and slid open to allow her access to her phone and bag. The moment she removed them from the drawer, it shut again, and the cart glided away to return its precious cargo to the shelves.

Elana stood and stretched again. Much like the last time she'd spent hours in the archives devouring information about her new life, she felt invigorated and ready to take on the world—if a little sore from impersonating a shrimp for hours on end.

She texted Cathy, asking if she was free for tea, then reviewed everything she'd read while walking through the stacks to the atrium and outside, where her car awaited.

The two thin books had only covered the earliest, most basic rituals in an initiate's life, the reception of Rights and the progression to adept. Their authors were Havenites who had written from the perspective of a Haven initiate, for which Elana was grateful.

From the sounds of it, while the ritual *content* was largely the same worldwide, the minutiae and language used in the ceremonies varied...to say nothing of the vestments and accessories. The books included example illustrations of ceremonial outfits from around the world, and those were as varied as you could get.

Progressing to adept was relatively simple, at least from where Elana stood. She needed a set of ceremonial robes and a sponsor, and she needed to memorize a handful of phrases. Memorizing lines had never been her forte in high school English, but she figured she could handle that.

It was convenient that Cathy stood out as Elana's best option for a sponsor. Elana wanted her help with her new plans after the tea party fiasco.

"I should have expected I'd see you soon," Cathy commented while making tea at her kitchen island. "You're not one to shy away from a challenge or a failure. What's your plan?"

Elana snagged her favorite blue and red afghan from the back of her chosen couch—olive green and violet paisley—and snuggled in. Cathy's loft was chilly compared to the late summer-slash-early fall heat and humidity, even in Haven. "I'll get to that in a second," she promised. "But first, would you consent to being my sponsor?"

Cathy's head snapped up from her tea preparations and a grin spread across her face. "You're kidding. Already?"

Elana blushed and ducked her head. "I *knew* I wasn't crazy thinking it was early… But you seem happy about it. Will you do it? Do you think it's too early?"

Cathy rushed from the kitchen, sat beside Elana, and grabbed her hands. "*No*, it's not too early, and *yes*, I'll do it. I'd be honored."

"Oh, thank God." Elana let out a breath she hadn't realized she was holding and pitched forward to lean on the other woman's shoulder. "I thought you were about to tell me I should go back to vampire kindergarten until I learned my social ABCs."

Cathy laughed, let go of one of Elana's hands, and wrapped her in a one-armed hug. "No, no. I merely thought your mentors might insist on seeing more progress than they'd expect from a more common initiate."

"Holding me to a higher standard because of my House?"

"In part. More likely the higher standard would be thanks to your precarious political situation and abnormal development stage. Most vampires who spend thirty years as an initiate work toward progression *constantly.* Technically, you've only been at it for a couple of months."

Elana nodded against Cathy's shoulder. "That's about what I thought, which was why it surprised me when Valeria told me I was ready."

"When is the ceremony?"

"A week from yesterday."

Cathy held her tight and nodded once. "Okay. I assume you've spent the day reading."

"Is it that obvious?"

"You're assiduous. The moment you know you need to do something, you figure out how to do it. So, you spent the morning and most of the afternoon reading up, then came to find me. You need a set of robes, of course…"

"Yeah." Elana straightened and smiled when Cathy patted her on the head and got up to finish the tea. "I figure there's no way I can smuggle a pattern to my preferred tailor."

Cathy trilled with laughter. "Definitely not. *But…* I think this calls for you to finally meet Arturo."

Elana blinked as she tried to remember where she knew that name from. "Arturo…"

"*My* tailor. Also my partner for most of the last several centuries, as a side note."

Elana's eyes widened. "*Oh.* Does he not—" She looked around.

"No, he doesn't live here. We go through phases every century or so where we do, then we don't, then we do again…" She waved dismissively. "Anyway. You said you had something else you wanted to talk to me about?"

Elana's grin grew, and when Cathy spotted it, she raised

an eyebrow. "I sure do. I'm not giving up on joining Haven's elite society…but I think I need to do it *my* way. Am I right in thinking everyone at the salon the other day is as strong and fast as I am?"

Cathy shrugged. "With varying degrees of accuracy, yes. Some choose to develop their physical attributes more than others, but we all have the strength and speed vampirism endows us with. Oh, that's an *evil* grin. What *are* you thinking?"

"Have you ever played Chimera badminton?"

Cathy's grin rapidly matched Elana's. "It's been a while, but I have a set of rackets."

CHAPTER TWENTY

Three days later, Elana stood on her brand-new deck with a mimosa in hand and smiled in satisfaction at her newly landscaped backyard, complete with an in-ground pool and outdoor kitchen-slash-BBQ patio.

She hadn't been convinced the contractors would come through on such short notice. It turned out that vampire contractors could work significantly longer hours than human ones and had the advantage of multiple decades of experience under their belts. The pool guys had been installing in-ground water features for longer than humans had understood how to chlorinate pools, for God's sake.

Elana sipped her mimosa and wished, not for the first time nor the last, that Vicky could attend tomorrow's festivities. She'd gotten her best friend's input on the design and the menu, but the travel writer was off on assignment in Maui—what hardship!—and couldn't make it back.

Plus, there was the minor detail that initiates weren't technically allowed to bring humans into Haven without consent. Elana was a member of the royal House, but she didn't think flaunting that particular advantage was a good idea.

The guest list comprised each woman who'd attended Cathy's salon. It also included several younger, less well-connected vampires who had piqued Elana's interest over her couple of months in Haven and people Matt had recommended to her. Elana was throwing a smasher of a late housewarming party, and while she wasn't *indiscriminate* with the invitations, she was certainly less openly snobbish about it. There were even *men* on the list. *Shocking.*

Today, the main event was her meeting with Arturo, where he would fit her for her ceremonial robes. Elana had been practicing her lines repeatedly in the mirror each night and almost had them memorized.

This morning, she had specifically asked to warm up with some Chimera badminton with Gustav, after which they were running the initiate training courses until Elana crumpled from exhaustion. Then she would meet Cathy and Arturo for supper at their favorite restaurant in Shestoi before retiring to Arturo's atelier in Octava for the fitting.

"But I'll be bloated from dinner!" Elana had protested.

Cathy had snorted. "They're *robes,* dear. You could be nine months pregnant and you'd barely be able to tell."

So, Elana would be wearing a tent. A fancy tent, but a tent nonetheless. Oh, well. She would be the only initiate in a thousand years with the privilege of wearing Arturo Carini to her adept progression rites.

Elana did a little dance as she went back inside. House

Veridian hadn't tried anything since their last bullshit, and Elana felt like she was on *fire*. In half a week, she'd be an adept and one step closer to bringing down those sons of bitches who killed her mother.

She downed the rest of her mimosa and smacked her lips. Life was good.

Elana arrived at the sushi restaurant five minutes early, which was three minutes before Cathy arrived and fifteen before Arturo.

"He's always late," Cathy told her with fondness and exasperation. "It's one of the reasons we *don't* live together. I can only stand his *creative punctuality* for so long at a time."

Elana stifled a snicker as she followed Cathy into the restaurant's lobby. Ryuusei was a high-scale sushi restaurant decorated largely in black and red with a huge fish tank that took up an entire wall. The dozen or so booths' glossy black tables and red leather seats shone with the faint blue glow from the fish tank's lights.

Elana morbidly wondered whether the tank was regularly stocked with fish that were then served. Since the fish in the tank were largely small and colorful, and the fish on marble slabs visible through the pass-through kitchen windows were considerably bigger and mostly gray or silver, she figured probably not.

Cathy led her to the booth in the farthest corner. They'd barely sat before a waitress in a tight black wrap dress with a high collar—continuing the mildly Japanese-themed décor—approached with a bamboo tray with a clay teapot on top and a calm smile. Her dark brown hair fell in a sharp bob to her chin, framing her light brown face and mahogany eyes in a perfect circle. A single gemstone stud glittered pink in her nose.

"Good evening, Madam Smith." Her voice was as smooth as her hair, a light alto with a hint of an accent Elana couldn't place. She placed the bamboo tray in the center of the table and backed up a step. "Your tea. Will you be waiting to order?"

Cathy beamed at her. "No, Kat, not tonight. The usual, if you please, but for three. Arturo will be along whenever he arrives. Would you show him over?"

"Of course." Kat bowed and swept away, her low slingback heels tapping on the gleaming black floor. Elana hoped she was allowed to sit in between her rounds of the dining floor. She'd waitressed for a while when she'd briefly entertained the idea of not following in her father's footsteps, so she knew how sore your feet were after a shift.

"Feeling ready for today?"

Cathy's question roused Elana from contemplating the fish tank, which sat immediately above them and to her right. She'd been watching a blue and yellow fish with long, pointed fins weaving between strands of kelp that appeared almost black in the bright blue glow of the water.

"For the party or the fitting?"

"Both."

The blue and yellow fish disappeared behind a rock twice its size. Elana's gaze shifted to a bright pink fish that wobbled when it swam.

"Yes and no. Mostly yes. Everything's as ready as it can be. The backyard and pool are done, the caterers are booked, everyone's RSVPed... I remembered to reserve the badminton courts for the afternoon..."

"That's all well and good, but are *you* ready?"

The bright pink fish darted in a circle around a smaller black and silver fish. Half a dozen more of the small fish surged from a spray of seaweed and the bright pink fish took off toward the other end of the tank.

"Yes," Elana firmly stated. "Training's been excellent the last few days, and I've fully memorized my lines for the ritual. I'm *nervous*, but I'm ready."

Cathy nodded. "Good. Keep those nerves. Use them. Tea?"

"Sure."

Cathy proceeded to make tea in the most ceremonial manner Elana had ever witnessed. First, she tapped the wall beside them, below the fish tank. A square glowed blue, then slid into the wall, revealing a clay pitcher with a lid and four clay cups no bigger than the palm of Elana's hand. Both matched the teapot on the tray in front of them.

The older woman removed the pitcher, and without opening the teapot, poured steaming water over in a gentle figure-eight stream until it thoroughly soaked the pot. It changed color as she did so, signaling to Elana that the clay was unsealed. The hot water sluiced off the teapot and disappeared between the open slats in the bamboo tray.

Then Cathy replaced the pitcher in the wall cubby, where a spigot in the top refilled it with more steaming water. She removed the teapot's lid, leaned in, sniffed, and hummed in appreciation. *"Baihao yinzhen,"* she told Elana and tilted the teapot so she could see the slim, light-colored, rolled-up leaves within. "White Hair Silver Needle."

Elana raised her eyebrows. "I regret to report that I have no idea what it means."

Cathy chuckled, took the pitcher from the cubby, and set it on the tray beside the teapot. "It's a white tea from Fujian province in China. Highly prized, quite expensive, and absolutely delicious. My favorite, as Kat knows well."

She held an open palm over the steaming pitcher for a couple of seconds, then nodded in satisfaction. "Just below boiling," she announced, then filled the teapot and closed the lid. "Now we wait."

While they waited, Cathy soaked three teacups in the same manner as she had the teapot. Five minutes passed before she filled two cups with a pale yellow tea that smelled a bit like Elana imagined fresh-cut hay would smell.

Cathy passed Elana a cup at the same time that Kat arrived with a short man who had to be Arturo. The waitress bowed politely and left again while Arturo slipped into the booth beside Cathy. Cathy fondly smiled as she filled the third cup.

Elana cradled her teacup and took in the new arrival.

Arturo Carini was short, maybe five-three if he stood straight. He didn't appear at first glance to share his partner's eclectic taste in fashion despite his purported career as a master fashion designer. A closer look revealed subtle personal details about his impeccably tailored jet black suit.

For one, his pocket square was embroidered so thickly you couldn't see the fabric, and the pattern was dizzying. His necktie was the same and tied in a complex knot that resembled a herringbone. The gentle blue glow of the fish tank further revealed that the jet black fabric was not solid but also featured the complex knotted embroidery pattern.

When he slid into the booth, he turned and kissed Cathy's cheeks European-style. Elana spotted subtle silver-gray tattooing on the sides of his head and neck, a fractal pattern that rose to his ears. It surrounded a series of tiny metal studs that lined the edge of his ear. Elana caught the glint of light when he turned back, which meant both ears matched.

His hair was almost the same color as the tattooing. A very short fade rose from the nape of his neck to the crown of his head, where a couple of inches of silver hair stood almost straight up. He sported a prim mustache and goatee, which were pure white and neatly groomed. His eyes were sky blue, his skin was pockmarked and pale, and his eyebrows were so thick they could have been mistaken for an ermine.

Arturo stuck a hand out across the table to shake. "You must be Elana Bishop. *Cara* speaks highly of you."

Elana shifted her teacup to one hand and shook his. His grip was solid, and his hand was warm and smooth. "That's me. I'm glad to hear it. Cathy's been an amazing friend, and I'm incredibly grateful for everything she's done for me."

"Including sponsoring you to become an adept, I hear." He picked up his tea and delicately sipped it. "Delicious as always. You brew it perfectly."

"I've had practice," Cathy replied, but the continued fondness in her eyes belied the mild barb.

"Yes," Elana confirmed. "Speaking of, thank you very much for agreeing to make my robes—and on such short notice, too."

"Pah." His eyes glittered with intensity as he waved in dismissal. "I only take clients who are *interesting*. That's why I've barely made anything for anyone other than *la mia dolcina* for so many years. The world is boring these days."

If this was what Arturo called boring, Elana didn't want to see the kind of world he found interesting. "I think that's a compliment?"

He smiled. "Oh, yes. *Catarina* dearest has told me all about you, and I am entranced. It will be an honor to robe you for the ceremony. Now, I need a few details about your life so I get the embroidery right. If you wouldn't mind a little game of twenty questions, I'd appreciate your patience. Let's start with the basics. What is your favorite color?"

Elana rolled her neck and enjoyed the stretch as she watched the other "competitors" warming up. Everyone she'd invited had shown up, although not all had chosen to compete. As a result, her little Chimera badminton tournament had a respectable audience in the upper level of the training facility. The area was normally used as an observation deck for grading guardian and Chimera recruits. It served perfectly well as a spectator area for a friendly tournament.

Only it was setting up to be anything but friendly, exactly as Elana had planned.

Twenty-four competitors would face off on the four badminton courts below over the next couple of hours. The winner would receive an engraved custom trophy Elana had procured the day before and a seriously expensive bottle of wine at the barbecue afterward. It wasn't anywhere near as impressive as some of the prizes for other competitions Elana had heard of in the last several days as people called her to RSVP. Then again, she had made the point that *this* tournament wasn't high-stakes.

Naturally, that had only fanned the competitive flames. If there was one thing you could count on a bunch of vampires for, it was being the most competitive little shits on the planet. Elana had figured that out *damn* fast. Instead of bemoaning that she was starting at a serious disadvantage, she'd decided to leverage it in her favor. Although the prize wasn't huge, the bragging rights that you'd won a tournament hosted by a member of the royal House *were*.

"Getting us all to play Chimera badminton was genius," Cathy murmured in her ear.

She had sidled up to Elana in the locker room, wearing the gaudiest tracksuit Elana had ever seen. It came straight out of the '80s, complete with swishy nylon and fluorescent-bright colors. Elana had to blink every time she looked at it for longer than a second. It would be dizzying in the mirrored court, which Cathy would no doubt be counting on. Chimera badminton had few rules, and there *wasn't* one against confusing your opponent.

"Well, when every other tournament at this level of

Haven society involves no personal involvement but your pocketbook, I figured it was an obvious choice," Elana replied with a sly smile. "Nothing like a physical challenge to raise the stakes and shake things up a little."

The smile Cathy returned was devilish in the extreme. "I look forward to wiping the floor with Mary Reynolds' blood, sweat, *and* tears. Preferably in that order."

Elana was playing too, naturally. That would allow her to see the capabilities of some of the society elites she needed to make friends with. It would equally give those she played with and those watching the chance to see *her* in action.

Her first match was against Belinda Leclerc of House Befonius. Belinda was one of the up-and-comers Elana had identified in her careful perusal of the Haven gossip rags. She was a socialite who *appeared* to have more money than sense and was more interested in living it up than upholding her House's legacy of supporting the arts. Except Elana suspected Belinda had more of a finger on the pulse of *current* artistic pursuits, and the Befonius leadership didn't want to admit their taste was out of date.

Belinda *also* regularly made appearances at several of Haven's top non-military gyms. While she frequently appeared in social media posts as though she was there to appreciate the eye candy on display, Elana again suspected otherwise. This match would show her whether her intuition was correct.

The tall, curvy woman with skin the color of teakwood

and dreadlocks dripping with beads tied back in a ponytail faced off against Elana on the other side of the court. She wore a no-nonsense track shorts and tank top combo that highlighted her impressive cleavage...and her equally impressive biceps.

Elana hid a grimace. *Yeah, I was* super *right.* She only hoped she'd manage to win this one. While she was under no illusions that she was likely to win the tournament, she hoped to make it past the first round.

Elana made the first serve, and the game was on.

Belinda dashed across the court and batted the birdie back deceptively casually. Elana had to scramble forward to catch it before it hit the floor.

Tournament rules stated that the first person to score twenty points won the match, and any missed lasers or birdies counted as a point. This became exactly as insane as you would think if a volley went on long enough to have multiple laser beams in play at once.

Belinda's next return was another clever hit. The birdie flew straight, true, and *high* until it reached the far corner of Elana's court and dropped like a rock.

Elana backpedaled as fast as she dared and managed to smack it back, but it was hardly a stunning shot. The birdie wobbled through the air and completed its downward arc far too close to the net for Elana's liking.

Belinda was right there to catch it. Luckily, Elana guessed right and was already sprinting forward when Belinda *barely* tipped the birdie back over the net.

Elana hit the birdie as hard as she could, spiking it down and to the right. Belinda dove, but the birdie hit the floor a couple of inches beyond the edge of her racket, and the buzzer sounded. One-zero to Elana.

Elana caught her breath and locked eyes with her opponent. She'd expected Belinda to level a snarly, smarmy look at her the way most of the socialites at Cathy's salon had. Instead, she was pleasantly surprised to find a small, excited smile tweaking the corners of the woman's mouth.

"Nice shot," Belinda told her.

"Thanks," Elana replied. "You play nasty."

Belinda's smile turned into a grin. "I do. Complaining?"

"Fuck, no."

"*Good.*"

She grabbed the birdie and jogged back to her corner. As Elana did the same, she didn't bother hiding her smile from the couple of dozen people watching her from above.

The point of this endeavor was to find a way into Haven's society that didn't require Elana to be someone she wasn't. So far, that was working out *very nicely.*

Elana collapsed onto a bench in the spectators' area an hour and a half later, drenched in sweat and sore all over. She gratefully accepted the bottle of water Matt offered her, drank half of it in one go, then swiped a towel over her dripping face.

"You did well." He sat beside her and handed her a second bottle after she finished the first in another gulp. "Quarterfinals is *very* good for an initiate."

"Almost adept," she teased. "It's not like I was turned yesterday."

Matt chuckled in agreement. Elana was relieved that after the initial hubbub she'd been greeted with upon her loss to Clarke Coballon of House Milini, everyone in the observation deck had been too excited about the semifinal that was about to start to pay her any mind. It meant she and Matt could chat without much fear of being overheard. Anyone *could* hear them, but they were all too preoccupied to care.

"Who's playing now?" she asked. "I haven't been able to keep up with the bracket. Although if I *had* been, I would have known I was going up against Ebony two matches ago and I would have psyched myself out big time."

"For being such an overdramatic example of an ultra-Gothic vampire, she is fiendishly good at Chimera badminton," Matt mused. "I must admit I'd pegged her as a Dracula's bride type. You picked your guest list well. I wouldn't have expected you to invite her in the first place."

"I wanted to see the other side of everyone," Elana explained. "So many of Haven's high society circles and events focus on the cerebral. You don't do things like this if you're not a guardian or personally interested in physical or athletic challenges. I think that's a shame. Everybody needs to get their blood pumping once in a while. Now answer my question."

"What? Oh—Valeria and Mary Reynolds."

Elana almost spat her mouthful of water at him. *"What?"*

"Valeria and Mary—"

"I heard you! I just—I didn't think Valeria was coming! She told me she was busy! I didn't even think she was in the *city* today!"

Matt put a hand on Elana's shoulder to stall her panic.

"Relax. Yes, she's coming to the barbecue. She messaged me an hour before the tournament started and asked if I'd convey a request to David Marlowe that she take his place."

Elana snorted. "As if someone from House Jameson could say no to the House of the SpiderKing."

"True, but it's polite to ask."

"Sure. Yeah." Elana stood on exhausted legs and wobbled over to the windows. She was not missing this match for the world.

The excited murmuring of those gathered died to nothing as the two women on the court below politely bowed to one another. Valeria wore white as always, an outfit similar to the tennis skirt Elana had seen her wear the week before. Mary Reynolds looked as dour as ever in pure black knee-length shorts and a three-quarter-sleeve T-shirt.

"She really shouldn't wear black," Cathy's familiar voice muttered in Elana's ear. "It makes her look like death warmed over."

Elana stifled a snort. "I mean, she *is* a vampire."

Cathy snickered. "We're only classed as undead in the fantasy sense, dear."

"I know, but it's still funny. Think a stake would do her in?"

"As much as it would any of us."

That wasn't a yes or a no, but the eruption of movement below forestalled further chit-chat. For all Mary resembled a dowager more interested in the goings-on of Goody Proctor than a fangs-and-blood vampire, she *was* good on the badminton court. Her spindly limbs moved like willow branches, whipping this way and that to return her opponents' serves.

Valeria Draven was only a step away from death incarnate.

The match was a given, and everyone knew as much—including Mary, to be sure—but that didn't mean it wasn't a good show. Valeria barely appeared to move from her position on the court while Mary was a blur. That only meant Valeria was moving faster than most of those assembled could see.

The first volley lasted long enough that the laser fire began before either scored a point, but this was the turning point in the match. Mary quickly proved that while she could match Valeria in strength and speed, if only just, she could not match the Arbiter of Shadows when it came to *attention*. The birdie never hit the floor, but Valeria scored twenty points within five minutes because Mary missed every other laser shot.

When the final buzzer sounded, Elana realized she hadn't taken a breath in several minutes. Judging by the explosive exhalations of those around her, she wasn't the only one.

While the two opponents frigidly bid each other a good game—Mary Reynolds' back barely inclined, while Valeria swept an arm out in a monumental gesture of goodwill—Cathy hummed. "Oh, this *will* be fun."

Elana looked over and raised an eyebrow. "Oh?"

The matriarchal vampire rolled her shoulders and stretched her neck. "Well, yes. That was the last semifinal. Time for the last match of the day."

"You look like you're gearing up."

"Naturally. I'm playing in it."

Elana's second eyebrow joined her first in approaching her hairline. "*You* won the other bracket?" The next time she ran this tournament, paying attention to the standings was *necessary*.

Cathy smirked. "Don't look so surprised, dearie. I have a *wicked* backhand."

Cathy left Elana and drifted down the stairs to the main concourse. Mary Reynolds had disappeared from the court, and Valeria was doing a few simple stretches to prepare for the final game, which would start when Cathy joined her.

Matt came to stand beside Elana and offered her another bottle. This one's contents were bright green. "You look like you could use some electrolytes."

She accepted the bottle and cracked the seal. "If you were anyone else, I'd suspect you of trying to poison me. This looks like nuclear waste."

He chuckled. "Ready for the last game?"

Elana shook her head in wonder. "I had no idea Cathy had progressed so far. I expected her to play well, but isn't she, like, a couple thousand years old?"

"More like three or four thousand, I think. But it's not polite to speculate about a lady's age. About any vampire's age, actually."

"Doesn't stop anyone from doing it," Elana retorted.

Matt stuck his nose in the air. "It still *behooves* me to instruct an initiate on the cusp of becoming an adept in the proper social niceties."

Elana narrowed her eyes at him until she detected the

faint twitch of his lips that meant he was holding in laughter. "You *are* pulling my leg."

He dropped the posh act and grinned. "Had you going there, didn't I."

She gently hip-checked him and chuckled. "You did. What was that for?"

"Just harking back to my ceremony." Matt got a distant look in his eyes and shook his head. "My sponsor was incredibly knowledgeable and an excellent mentor, but oh, my *God,* he could be the stuffiest, most ostentatious windbag if you got him wound up."

"Let me guess. You frequently got him wound up."

"Every chance I could. It was *hilarious.*" He leaned toward the window. "Cathy's coming. This will be *epic.*"

Elana gulped down a quarter of her bottle before stepping closer to watch. Mary Reynolds entered the room with a huff, but no one paid her any mind. Everyone was *far* too engaged in the impending spectacle.

Cathy and Valeria met at the net and shook hands amicably. Valeria said something inaudible through the observation glass, and Cathy presumably responded, but Elana couldn't even try to read her lips.

"Valeria asked if Cathy wanted to give us a show," Matt murmured.

"Oh boy. That means…"

"Buckle up."

The two women moved to their respective corners. Valeria lifted the birdie to ask if Cathy was ready, Cathy nodded, and Valeria served it so fast that Elana couldn't *blink* before it was across the court.

Cathy was there to meet it, although Elana couldn't tell

how she could have seen it move. Then it was back on Valeria's side, then Cathy's, then Valeria's…

She pressed her hands to her temples. "I'm getting dizzy."

"Just wait until the lasers start," Matt promised.

The match appeared to the spectators like a sped-up film, with one white figure and one in neon green and pink blurring around their sides of the court. They could have written messages like fire-writing in delayed shutter photography. Elana was surprised the birdie wasn't trailing flames because surely, it was traveling fast enough to simulate re-entry into atmosphere.

Cathy took the first point ten minutes in. A gasp went up around the room, and Matt hissed between his teeth.

Elana tugged on Matt's sleeve. "What *happened*? I saw *nothing*."

"Cathy stuck Valeria between a rock and a hard place by forcing her to fend off multiple laser blasts while she sent the birdie to the opposite corner. Tough gambit, but when you're playing Chimera badminton at this level, it's more like chess than a racket sport," Matt explained.

"Jesus Christ. I couldn't even tell the birdie had hit the floor."

Elana hadn't been watching the lasers. She'd been too busy trying to follow even ten percent of the movement on the court. Now she attempted to watch the court as a whole, allowing the lasers and the general directional flow of the players, which indicated where the birdie was at any given point in time, to drift across her vision.

Stepping back from the intense focus allowed her to see

the movement patterns. Within a few minutes, she could tell that Valeria and Cathy were attempting to reflect the laser blasts in play, of which there were dozens, into disadvantageous positions for their opponent. Their other method was to aim them into patterns that would effectively take them *out* of play. Bouncing them back and forth along the ceiling at such an angle that neither player would have to worry about them for a minute or two was preferred.

The next tactic was to break the patterns you had established at an inopportune time for your opponent. This was how Valeria scored her first points. She popped the birdie into a high arc that forced Cathy to pause for half a second, then leaped six feet in the air and redirected a barrage of laser blasts toward Cathy in a wide semi-circle. She scored four points in quick succession since Cathy only caught a hair over half of the lasers, plus the birdie.

"Is Chimera badminton a Haven-only sport?" Elana asked Matt under her breath. Everyone in the observation area was glued to the windows. She hadn't heard a peep in almost half an hour.

"It started here, but it's spread," he replied equally quietly. "Tournaments happen all over the world now."

"Would Cathy or Valeria stand a chance in any of them?"

"Oh, yes."

Cathy took the next set of points by interrupting Valeria's flow with a quite frankly *rude* laser blast directly to her torso, followed by an array of lasers in a spiral around her. Valeria avoided the first laser but missed the subsequent spiral by doing so and lost half a dozen points before catching the second half of the volley. Seven-four for Cathy.

That became ten-seven for Valeria eight minutes later when Cathy was surprised by a row of lasers that snuck down behind her. Valeria had cleverly angled them in that direction over fifteen minutes before.

The Arbiter of Shadows played a long game, but it turned out that Cathy Smith of House Lucciola was equally adept at doing the same. Ten minutes after that exchange, Valeria was forced to twist, leap, and dodge a veritable hailstorm of laser blasts. As far as Elana could tell, they had materialized out of nowhere. Cathy scored ten points in thirty seconds.

"She's been setting those up from the beginning of the match," Matt softly told her. "She directed every third or fourth laser to a specific corner. Hit the mark every time."

Elana gaped. She'd set this tournament up as a clever way to suss out potential alliances and opposition alike. While she'd certainly succeeded in that—she had a list of names and Houses in each column—she'd also been treated to a spectacular display of vampire prowess.

Seventeen-ten for Cathy. Valeria upped her game *somehow*, but the result was an excruciatingly slow series of birdie volleys that ended with five more points in the arbiter's favor. Seventeen-fifteen.

Matt raised his hands in protest when Elana glanced at him for the latest play-by-play. "I'm a sentinel, and not even *I* saw how that happened. They're going too fast for me."

Elana frowned. "But I can *see the birdie* again. They're going *slow.*"

He shook his head. "They're moving so fast that it *looks* slow. Watch the lasers."

Elana did. Matt was right. The birdie gracefully soared through the air while a kaleidoscopic laser show erupted around it. Elana wanted to cover her eyes but didn't dare.

Seventeen-sixteen. Eighteen-sixteen. Eighteen-seventeen. Eighteen-eighteen. Nineteen-eighteen.

Nineteen-nineteen.

The tension in the observation room had thickened to the consistency of congealed blood. Elana hadn't heard anyone breathe in recent memory, and the match was approaching a full hour. The next point would take the game.

She stared transfixed at the dance in the room below. Valeria and Cathy had not stopped moving for the past hour, twirling, jumping, and ducking innumerable lasers while batting the half-pound metal projectile back and forth, mostly faster than any human eye could see.

The sheer number of laser blasts rocketing around the mirrored room was mesmerizing. It had been hard enough for Elana to track a handful of lasers when she'd played with Gustav or the matches she'd played today. How did either woman tell which lights were the actual lasers and which were only reflections?

Valeria was trained for this kind of deadly dance. As far as Elana had known, Cathy was not. She'd invited Cathy to participate out of respect. She hadn't expected Cathy to take her up on it any more than she'd expected Valeria to take time out of her packed arbiter's schedule to do the same.

Elana realized with a slow intake of breath that this was as perfect an opportunity for both women to reinforce their social status within Haven in an unconventional way as it was for Elana.

Cathy was multiple millennia old. She mostly kept to herself, enjoying her hobbies, her long partnership with Arturo, and her circle of friends—who were not the same people as her salon circle, to be clear. She didn't involve herself in politics, although she was the head of House Lucciola. She made decisions, but only on the advice of her senior House members.

Valeria was possibly the most powerful person in Haven, barring the SpiderKing. Her daily decisions frequently determined life or death for any number of people. The amount of information that flowed through her office was immeasurable. She wielded ultimate power and held ultimate responsibility in ways most Havenites couldn't properly conceive of.

Participating in a silly Chimera badminton tournament hosted by a relatively no-name initiate was a *great* way to introduce something entirely new, and mainly harmless, to the Haven gossip mill. It also showed the city that Cathy Smith was no retiring grandmother, and Valeria Draven wasn't a workaholic.

Elana's gaze caught on a laser coming directly at Cathy. Even from behind, she could tell that Cathy saw it coming. Her head twitched up toward it...and she stepped aside and let it hit the floor.

The buzzer sounded as the observation deck erupted in

raucous cheers and applause. Final score twenty to nineteen for the Arbiter of Shadows.

Valeria and Cathy were the epitome of professionalism as they shook hands again. As far as Elana could tell from here, neither had broken a sweat. *Show-offs.*

When they turned toward the observation windows to head for the locker rooms, Elana caught Cathy's gaze. The corner of Cathy's mouth twisted up in a tiny smile, and she winked. Then they were out of sight.

Elana frowned faintly as the rest of the room celebrated the impressive game. Why had Cathy winked? What had she meant?

The answer hit her like a birdie to the chest.

Cathy had let Valeria win in the least obvious way possible. Elana doubted many people would have noticed the specific set of movements she had been lucky enough to spy. If they had, they likely would have chalked it up to good planning on Valeria's part...which was the point.

Cathy didn't need to win. She was comfortable in her position, and there was no shame in losing a friendly badminton match to the Arbiter of Shadows. Valeria would have suffered serious social loss if she hadn't come out on top in any tournament she entered. Therefore, they'd both played brilliantly to showcase their skill, but Elana suspected they'd known how the match would end from the first serve.

Everything in Haven was moves and countermoves, with no exceptions.

Elana drew a deep breath, then put on her celebration face and went to greet the newest arrivals, who were being lauded and congratulated on their spectacular game. She'd blown all her goals for the day out of the water so far. She couldn't detect the slightest hint of animosity anywhere in the room. Even Mary Reynolds looked impressed. Since she always looked like she'd eaten a rotten lemon, that was one hell of a win.

Next up, barbecue and pool party. Elana wasn't through the gauntlet yet.

CHAPTER TWENTY-ONE

Elana slipped away from the end-of-tournament celebrations to run home and ensure everything was prepared. She was relieved to arrive to the aroma of roasting pork. That meant the caterers had arrived on time and nothing had gone amiss. She would have received notifications if something *had* gone amiss, but it was always reassuring to see or *smell* proof.

She popped out the back door to wave at the caterers, who greeted her with nods and a couple of friendly salutes. The company she'd booked was based in Shestoi and prided themselves on delivering a spread that would please any palate. Elana had opted for the whole roast pig with a full buffet of sides, including vegetarian options. Vegetarian and vegan vampires were rare. Elana had never met one, but they existed, and she had no intention of being a less-than-accommodating host.

Elana left them turning the pig on a spit above their portable firepit. It was easier to clean than trying to use the stone oven she'd had built, and besides, that would be used for wood-fired pizzas. She ducked back into the house and ran through the fastest shower known to humankind. She was about to jump in a pool but wanted to get rid of the sheen of sweat and grime from the tournament.

She rebraided her hair and donned her new swimsuit, a gorgeous bright green and blue bikini set with a leaf pattern that made her think of Vicky in Maui. She threw on a white beach wrap, which she knotted around her waist, and slipped into white flip-flops before returning to the backyard. The other guests would arrive any minute after showering and preparing at the training grounds.

Elana completed a quick once-over of the preparations and found them to her satisfaction. The pig smelled divine, and her stomach rumbled at the delicious array of side dishes spread out on the long tables the caterers had brought.

The pool was crystal clear. She fetched a dozen pool noodles and inflatables from her brand-new shed and tossed them into the shallow end. Tonight was for relaxing and having fun, not showing off how many lengths of the pool you could do.

The first guest arrived through the door in the back fence. It was Belinda, the House Befonius socialite whom Elana beat in the tournament's first round. She'd changed into a tankini in a dusky sunset orange that matched the color of several strands of beads in her hair, and she had a woven cream tote bag over her shoulder.

She smiled appreciatively as she surveyed the yard. "You know how to throw a party."

Elana turned to stand beside Belinda and nodded. "I try.

I've done enough of the standard high society gigs here that I knew I needed to do something more my speed."

"Amen to that." Belinda pulled a red and yellow beach towel from her tote bag and tossed it over her shoulder. "Mind if I christen the pool?"

"Be my guest."

Belinda hummed in acknowledgment and strolled toward the pool. She dropped her bag and towel on a lounge chair, along with the dark brown shawl she'd had tied around her shoulders, then stepped up to the deep end and gracefully dove in.

Footsteps behind Elana made her turn, and she promptly half-bowed in polite greeting to Lord Aldric of Rothschilde. "Glad you could make it, Lord Aldric."

"My pleasure. Thank you for inviting me. It's rare I get to attend anything but formal dinners and business lunches. Today has been much more fun." Lord Aldric was dressed semi-formally in a light blue polo and beige trousers. He hadn't participated in the tournament, but he'd been pleased as punch to be put in charge of the statistics and standings.

He eyed the roasting pig dubiously. "Anything non-pork-related on the menu tonight, my dear?"

"Oh!" Elana blushed. "Of course, yes, there's plenty. I'm so sorry, I was so busy thinking about dietary requirements that I didn't think about—"

He waved her off with a smile. "Not a problem. You're certainly not the first to have forgotten, nor will you be the last. I appreciate that other options are available."

"Honestly, I didn't want to assume that *every* Rothschild was Jewish. That seems like stereotyping all on its own."

Elana cocked her head as a thought struck her. "Can I ask a *really* dumb question?"

Aldric snorted. "Only if I'm allowed to respond with an equally idiotic answer."

"Seems only fair."

"Then go ahead."

"Is blood kosher?"

Aldric chuckled. "I figured that was where you were going. If you're truly interested, I can point you to some terrifically interesting rabbinical discussions over the millennia, but suffice it to say that I'm managing just fine, and you needn't worry yourself."

Elana rubbed the back of her neck. Her cheeks retained their crimson flush. "I can't deny that I'm curious, but maybe another time?"

Aldric's eyes twinkled. "Over a slab of roast pork and a side of macaroni salad?"

Elana groaned. "You're never gonna let me live this down, are you? Don't get me wrong, I deserve it."

He winked. "Maybe in a few centuries. Look on the bright side. At least I'm not your only guest. Now *that* would be embarrassing."

Aldric graciously excused himself to peruse the buffet, and Elana was free to greet the rest of her guests, who were arriving in greater numbers by the minute. Soon the yard, patio, and deck were bustling, and the quiet late-summer evening was alive with engaging conversations and laughter.

Lady Vivian was in attendance with her youngest daughter, Ophelia. The head of House Ravenwood had taken up residence in a corner of Elana's deck, where she'd settled in a comfortable chair with a glass of red wine and a plate of snacks. She quickly attracted half a dozen other guests, and Elana heard snippets of conversation about renewable natural resources and greenhouse management every time she wandered by.

Ophelia Ravenwood was in the pool with Belinda, Clarke, and a handful more of the younger crowd. Belinda and Clarke were batting a beach ball back and forth while discussing the artistic merit of a band from South Korea, while Ophelia was floating in an inflatable ring with a vodka spritzer in its cupholder and staring contentedly at the early evening sky.

Matt had arrived with his sister Claudia in tow. Claudia was devouring a huge portion of roast pork and a mountain of potato salad in between complaints about work. She'd just finished one hell of an assignment and was grumpy and ecstatic about it. Matt built roast pork sandwiches and reassured his little sister with encouragement about her skills and work ethic. The exchange made Elana smile. Matt was a good guy.

Cathy arrived last with Valeria. Cathy mouthed, "Later," to Elana, which intrigued her to no end. She took the opportunity to present Valeria with the small golden cup she'd had engraved with *Bishop's Annual Chimera Badminton Tournament* and the bottle of wine. The trophy would have been kitschy if it wasn't real gold.

"I'll have your name put on it tomorrow, then give it to you the next time we see each other," Elana offered while the other party guests clapped and cheered. The difference between this party and the gathering at Cathy's was night and day.

Valeria smiled faintly, but for once it was a real smile, not one of amusement or anticipation. "I'd appreciate that."

Cathy nudged Valeria's elbow. "You and I will have to sit out next year to give the rest of the city a chance," she teased.

"We certainly will." Valeria chuckled. "Good game, Catherine."

"Always a pleasure, my dear."

Valeria's phone buzzed in her pocket. She pursed her lips, handed Elana the trophy, then disappeared around the side of the house to take the call. Elana encouraged the rest of the guests to eat, drink, and be merry since there were no more definitive plans for the evening otherwise. When Belinda asked if she could get some music going, Elana agreed as long as everyone could still hear themselves think.

Belinda grinned. "Aw, where's the fun in that?"

Elana snickered. "When I throw one of these just for our generation, we can crank the bass as loud as we want."

"*Now* you're speaking my language."

Cathy tapped Elana's shoulder as Belinda rooted around in her tote bag, presumably hunting for portable speakers. "Could I speak with you inside for a moment, Elana dear?"

"Sure." Elana brought Cathy up the deck, past Lady Vivian's miniature court, and into the kitchen. "Is something wrong?"

Cathy smiled brightly and took Elana's hands. "No, no, nothing's wrong. I only wanted to tell you privately how *proud* I am of you. Today has been a *marvelous* success beyond anything I could have hoped. You are doing *wonderfully.*"

Elana's chest swelled with warmth. "Oh, my God, Cathy, you have no idea how happy I am to hear that. Thank you *so* much. I was nervous this morning, and to tell you the truth I haven't *stopped* being nervous, but everyone seems like they're genuinely enjoying themselves. That's really all I could ask for. That's all I *wanted.*"

Cathy patted the back of Elana's hand. "You're reminding all of us that vampires don't have to be tied to the traditions we've held for thousands of years. This is a breath of fresh air not even *I* realized Haven needed as badly as it obviously does.

"You'll make a huge difference in this city," Cathy promised. "I can feel it. You'd make your mother proud."

Valeria tucked herself around the corner of Elana's house, out of the way from prying eyes, and put her phone to her ear. "Captain Winchester, I trust this is extremely important *and* bad news if you are contacting me on my priority line during a time when I have designated myself as unavailable."

The voice on the other end of the line was gruff, unapologetic, and firm. All excellent qualities for the head of Valeria's guard. "Unfortunately, ma'am, it is indeed both those things. Kappa Squad has located one of your listed cold case targets."

Valeria's lips tensed to a thin line. "Case number?"

"60572, ma'am."

Valeria raised an eyebrow. She honestly hadn't expected to *ever* find that particular target. "Is the target still on location?"

"Yes, ma'am. Kappa Squad will remain until you arrive or until ordered otherwise."

Of course, they would. The Shadowguard were the best-trained, most professional guardians in Haven. The day they abandoned their orders would be the day hell froze over.

"Very well. Inform Kappa Squad leader that I am on my way and send the coordinates via secure line."

"Yes, ma'am. Will you want your detail?"

"That depends, Captain Winchester. Do I need one?" Captain Winchester had worked for Valeria for over seven decades. He had more than earned his place at the top of the Shadowguard. If he told her, in the oblique way that was required on an unsecured line, that she needed extra protection, she would trust that it was a legitimate threat assessment.

Captain Winchester gave the question several seconds of consideration. "Unlikely, ma'am. Kappa Squad reports that the target is, let's say, *cold*."

"Understood. Thank you, Captain Winchester. Anything else to report?"

"No, Ma'am. I do have a question if you'll allow."

"Speak freely."

"Did you win the tournament, ma'am?"

Valeria smirked. "I don't think I ought to dignify that with a response, Captain."

Winchester chuckled. "Message received loud and clear, ma'am. I'll tell the boys to expect you. Winchester out."

Valeria ended the call and texted Elana on her way to her Mercedes.

Apologies for the disappearance. Duty calls.

She didn't receive a reply text until she was in the car and headed up the road. No surprise there. Miss Bishop had her hands full with a very successful social gathering.

Of course. Good luck. Try to make sure everybody else dies instead of you.

Valeria snorted. Miss Bishop certainly had a way with words… just like her mother.

The coordinates Captain Winchester sent led Valeria to the King's Archives, much to her puzzlement. While it was after regular business hours, the archives never technically closed—or not to those with sufficient clearance. She nodded at the night librarian on her way to the basement entrance. The y-axis on the coordinate set was deep underground, which made her suspicious.

A member of Kappa Squad in the subtle black-on-black, low-profile armored uniform of the Shadowguard stood at the entrance to the confidential archives. They wore their helmet, so Valeria didn't know their name until a soft blue ID number luminesced on their breastplate at her approach. Service number 8323-67, Corporal Moira Richards.

Before Valeria could open the door, Corporal Richards cleared her throat. "Ma'am, there's a possibility of biological contamination present at the scene. Sergeant Li recommends you take the appropriate precautions."

Valeria tilted her head. "This wasn't conveyed to me by Captain Winchester."

Corporal Richards was unfazed. "No, ma'am. Sergeant Li only discovered the possibility five minutes ago after making his initial report to Captain Winchester. I expect he's on the horn with the captain now, ma'am. He let me know in case you got here first."

"Understood. I take it he considers this at least a level seven threat?"

"Level unconfirmed at this time, ma'am, so maximum protection level recommended."

"Is the entire sub-archive affected?"

"Again, ma'am, unknown at this time."

Valeria sighed. "Very well. Please inform Sergeant Li that I am entering with full recognizance of the potential danger."

"Yes, ma'am."

Valeria pressed her palm to the handle of the sub-archive door and waited for it to prick her skin and log her entry. She headed to her private archive in the third sub-basement, where she kept two old combat suits. Haven's combat suit technology had progressed past what was in these suits. They were still sufficiently advanced compared to human technology that they had to be kept under several levels of lock and key.

She donned the pure white full bodysuit with helmet, felt the warm rush of recognition that started in her arms and spread to the rest of her body, then left her office and continued into the depths of the sub-archives.

Only those with guardian clearance and above could access the third sub-basement. Access to the lower levels required successively higher levels of clearance. Valeria could access all levels except the lowest, which was reserved for the SpiderKing. By her estimation, Sergeant Li's specified location was at least in sub-basement five, if not sub-basement six. In other words, either this was a glaring security breach, or something was very rotten in the state of Haven. Valeria was unsure which hypothesis she preferred.

She encountered more members of Kappa Squad on each level, guarding the entrances and exits. None spoke to her, signifying they had no further information from their sergeant or captain. At last, in a back corner of sub-basement seven, she encountered two Shadowguard sentries blocking a door. All three breastplates glowed with ID numbers as the suits recognized their ally, and the two guards stepped aside to allow Valeria entry.

Valeria had seen so many dead bodies over her long career that it was difficult to imagine a situation that would shock her or give her pause. The potential addition of a biological contaminant created frustration but not alarm. She had dealt with all manner of those before without breaking a sweat. Very little in the world could faze an archon-level vampire.

She was almost disappointed when the dead body in the otherwise bare room did not appear dangerous. However, she was more than smart enough to know that appearances could be deeply deceiving.

Valeria knelt beside the body. At a glance, she could tell it was a white male with an apparent chronological age of mid-fifties. The man wore clothes he could have bought anywhere—a white polo shirt, gray trousers, and a brown leather belt. He wore glasses, which was an uncommon affectation in Haven. It was not unheard of in vampires who'd been turned later in life and who had gotten used to requiring assistive devices for myopia.

His hair was short and medium brown with a smattering of gray. Nominally clean-shaven, but a day's worth of stubble. No visible lividity in the hands or face. She'd have to scan more thoroughly or remove clothing for better data on that. She *could* guess based on visible evidence that he'd been in control of his faculties until a day before his death, if he'd had the chance to shave.

The most interesting thing about him, and therefore the most dangerous, was the faint blue pattern on his skin. Valeria only saw it if she turned her head slightly. It was as though he had reflective lines lightly tattooed on his skin in tiny hexagons.

That had to be the reason Sergeant Li had called in the potential biological hazard. Valeria agreed with the assessment. Theoretically, it *could* be a tattoo, but most people didn't get tattoos done over their corneas. It tended to fuck with your vision.

She exhaled slowly, considered the wisdom of personally performing a scan, and decided it wasn't worth the risk. This could be the first sign of what House Veridian was *really* playing at. Chancing incapacitation, even if only temporarily, would only slow her progress.

Valeria stood and faced Sergeant Li, who snapped to

attention. "Sergeant. I agree with your assessment of the situation. Call in a Chimera hazmat team and bring Mister Lingoria to the secure biohazard containment and quarantine laboratory in Sector 5A."

Sergeant Li saluted. "Yes, ma'am. Right away."

She left the room and began the trek back to the surface. Her mind churned. Evan Lingoria had been a geneticist studying the intricacies of the vampire genome. House Cajon had given him the Rights in the 1960s because he'd fallen in love with one of their scientists clandestinely working at a research facility in Ashford. Incidentally, he'd been a genius when it came to genetics.

He had disappeared twenty years later. He'd already progressed to savant, which was impressive given the short timeline, but since it wasn't typical of Runners to be any level but initiate... Well, adults were adults. Evan wasn't *required* to live in Haven or with his wife. Anna Lingoria was left with a broken heart and a mystery.

A mystery that finding Evan's recently dead body among the lowest levels of the King's Archives did *nothing* to solve.

Valeria ground her teeth. This mystery was beginning to grate on her nerves.

CHAPTER TWENTY-TWO

The royal temple resembled a cross between a medieval cathedral with Gothic arches and dark stained glass windows and a sultan's palace. Sumptuous curtains and censers in the corners emitted faint aromas of unnameable spices and flowers.

I suppose the censers fit both, Elana mused. She was waiting for her retinue to arrive. The seven other vampires of varying levels, her sponsor and closest allies among them, would guide her through the First Progression. With only one exception, her entire retinue was above level five, sentinel. This had come up in her discussions with Cathy before the ceremony since there were traditional gifts to be given afterward that depended on the vampire's level.

"That seems high," Elana had remarked. "I'm not that special, am I?"

Cathy had laughed. "It's a mite out of the ordinary, yes, but then again, you're no ordinary vampire."

Elana nervously shifted her weight between her feet. Her robes swished around her knees and hung heavy on her shoulders. She felt like the world was weighing her down.

Arturo had outdone himself, according to Cathy. "With minor alterations, those robes would do you until well up the Nexus," she'd informed Elana the night before. "I suspect he planned it that way."

Elana had swallowed hard and continued staring at her reflection in the full-length mirror. "No pressure or anything, though," she tried to joke.

Cathy had put a hand on her forearm and gripped it through the dark red fabric. "I've met thousands of vampires in my life, dear. Trust me when I say you're a rare one."

That's not as comforting as you think it is, Elana thought in the present.

She rubbed the hem of her sleeve and let the pad of her thumb linger over the rich embroidery. She'd swear it *hummed* under her touch. She didn't understand how.

There was a lot about the rituals of the Nexus she didn't understand, even after all her reading. Vampires leaned *hard* into the mysteries here. Elana would have been more concerned about the whole thing being a Ponzi scheme if it weren't so clearly linked to keeping increased power in the hands of those able to wield it responsibly.

Her robes hung almost to the floor. They were long enough that they *should* have touched the floor, but much like Haven's floating traffic signs, the fabric hovered an inch off the ground and floated away from her feet so she couldn't trip.

It was impossible not to associate the dark red of the

fabric with blood. Elana had wondered if that was presumptuous, laying it on too thick, as it were.

Cathy had winked, and with a touch, the robes became a deep blue, then forest green, imperial purple, and back to dark red. Another time-saving measure from Arturo since it turned out that each level of the Nexus required a different color—and other shades of that color, depending on your specialty, something like academic robes.

Arturo had laid a finger aside his nose and smiled conspiratorially at Elana while Cathy had demonstrated this. "Not something they tell you ahead of time, *carina*, but it will be useful to you in the long run."

Dense embroidery in a multitude of colors covered the hem, arced up Elana's back to cover the hood, and snaked down the draping sleeves to encircle the wide cuffs. Hidden in the embroidery were symbols of Elana's family. Scales, a shield, and running children spread from the hem up the back. Construction tools and lightning bolts adorned the sleeves and cuffs. A late addition of badminton rackets and birdies hid within the designs on the hood.

"As you progress, we will add more to the robes," Arturo had explained. "They grow as you grow. They tell your story."

Elana wondered how much open fabric remained on Valeria's robes.

"Knock, knock," a pleasant male voice called. "Not interrupting, I hope?"

She turned to greet Lord Aldric, whose dark blue robes were over two-thirds covered in embroidery. The silver patterns appeared to shift and morph as she watched them, but that was nothing compared to Lady Vivian's. The head of House Ravenwood entered behind Aldric, and vine-like embroidery nearly choked her robes of iron gray. As far as Elana could tell, they *actually* slithered across the fabric.

"Only my nerves," Elana sheepishly replied. "I've done everything I could to get ready, but I still have a stomach full of butterflies."

Aldric nodded sagely. "Only the shallowest initiates don't. That's a good sign. It means you understand the gravity of what you're about to do."

"Progressing in the Sanguine Nexus is not to be undertaken lightly," Vivian remarked in her reedy soprano. She cast an approving gaze over Elana's robes. "It reflects well on you that you treat the rituals with care."

Aldric winked as they continued past her toward the inner chamber. "See you soon."

Belinda arrived next. Elana and Belinda had hit it off at the housewarming party. Since Elana had been short one person in her retinue for the ritual, she'd okayed it with Cathy and asked if Belinda was free. Music notes and dancing figures swirled in the golden embroidery along the edge of her deep yellow robes.

To Elana's surprise, Belinda was deep in conversation with Lucia Lambra Mor when she walked in. The slim Scottish matriarch wore robes of deep purple in a slightly different style than the others. Where the Havenite robes were rounded, the Scotswoman's robes had points on the sleeves and hood and had a longer train. Lucia's embroidery was an even darker purple than the robe, and the curling patterns made Elana's eyes cross like a Magic Eye puzzle.

Both women greeted Elana warmly on their way in, then followed Aldric and Vivian into the chamber beyond. Matt and Valeria arrived on their heels, with Matt in dark green and Valeria in white as usual. To Elana's surprise, instead of white on white, delicate black and gray embroidery covered Valeria's robes like smoke rising from white-hot embers. The lines were too thin and the patterns too dense for Elana to pick out any images in the nebulous mass of thread. Plus, she was reasonably sure they were moving as Vivian's did.

They paused before passing into the inner chamber. Matt gripped Elana's shoulder and held her gaze. "You've got this. You know that, right?"

Elana drew a deep breath, straightened, and nodded. "Yeah. I do. I've done my prep work. All that's left is to make it happen live."

Valeria slipped her hands into opposite sleeves, giving her the appearance of a monk. "You are ready."

While the encouragement was firm, something in her expression made Elana think part of the arbiter's mind was further away than usual, as though she wasn't fully here. She'd been that way ever since ducking out of the housewarming party. Elana desperately wanted to know what was happening but knew Valeria would tell her when and *if* she could. Until then, she had to be patient.

They continued into the temple proper, leaving Elana alone and waiting for Cathy. Her sponsor would escort Elana into the ritual room, signaling the beginning of the ceremony. Cathy was never late, unlike her dear partner, which meant Elana had less than five minutes before the next phase of her life would begin.

The exterior door slid open, allowing sunlight to stream into the dim atrium with the last arrival.

Cathy's robes were jet black but covered in sufficient rainbow embroidery that you wouldn't have been able to tell if not for the insides of the sleeves. Unlike the Havenite robes, hers had scalloped edges and functioned more as an intricate wrap dress with a headscarf than a hooded cloak. Instead of pictorial symbols, runes Elana didn't recognize hid within the complex geometric embroidery. Cathy's threads glittered and sparkled, unlike the subtle glimmer that shone in the high-ranking Havenites' robes.

For the first time, Elana glimpsed how foreign Cathy was. Her garb resembled something exotic in the ancient sense rather than the medieval vibe evoked by the Haven robes. She looked deeply out of place under the atrium's high arched ceilings, whose pinnacles were shrouded in shadow for those initiates who were more comfortable in darkness than light.

Elana still hadn't gotten a satisfactory answer for that. Why had she never been bothered by the sun? Her dad had always reminded her to use high-SPF sunscreen, but that was a good practice so you didn't get skin cancer. New initiates had to wear sunglasses if they left Haven, and if they were particularly photosensitive, some wore them *inside* Haven. Elana hadn't needed any of that, and no one would tell her why.

Cathy offered Elana her arm and a brilliant smile. "Ready, my dear?"

Elana slipped her arm through Cathy's and exhaled a long, slow breath. "Let's do this."

The temple was octagonal and consisted mostly of the

atrium, which formed a ring around the inner chamber. Since Elana was of the royal House, which was technically quartered in Premier, they entered through the Door of Light and Vision. The ebony double doors, polished to a lustrous shine with a full moon emblazoned in mother-of-pearl bridging the two doors, silently swung open on oiled black iron hinges at their approach.

No ray of dim light thrown through the stained glass in the atrium reached the inner sanctum. It appeared pitch black until Elana's eyes adjusted to the faint glows from the sixteen censers in the room. They occupied each corner of the octagon and a matching set encircled the center of the room. These censers shared the same aroma as those outside but glowed with a soft blue light.

The other six members of her retinue stood outside the inner octagon of censers. Their hoods were raised, hiding their faces in even deeper shadow, but Elana recognized them by the colors and placements. Clockwise from her position in the equivalent of Premier, there was Matt in green in Thani and Lord Aldric in blue in Etreta. Madame Lucia in purple was in Quarto, Valeria in white in Senkyem, Lady Vivian in gray in Shestoi, and Belinda in yellow in Octava.

Zevenda was unoccupied. That was where Elana would stand after the ceremony was complete, marking her continuation of her mother's line through her position as Arbiter of Sanctuary. Cathy would retain her position in Premier.

Elana paused for a heartbeat on the threshold of the inner circle, feeling her breath catch in anticipation, then stepped through. The moment the hem of her robes passed the edge of the circle, a deep red spotlight flicked on above her head. Its light engulfed the inner octagon perfectly, leaving her retinue in red-tinted darkness.

Elana swallowed. Her heart sped up. She stood in the perfect center of the octagon, and given that she'd walked in from Premier, she faced Senkyem. Valeria's white robe covered in embroidered curls of smoke faced her head-on. She could not see the Arbiter of Shadows' face in the darkness but knew those ice-blue eyes would be locked onto hers.

For an instant, she was back on the ring road in the rain, where those eyes pierced her soul and laid her bare for the first time. Then she was back in the warm darkness of the temple, and she gradually turned to face her sponsor. The glimmering and glittering of the embroidery on everyone's robes was entrancing in the dim light. Between that, her nerves, and the scent from the censers, Elana was beginning to feel light-headed.

While Elana had been turned away, Cathy had unwrapped part of her headscarf to obscure her face in a similar manner as the others' hoods. When Elana faced her, all she saw of her friend was the sparkling folds of fabric hiding everything but her eyes. A small part of Elana's brain threw up a pile of red flags at the terrifying sight of being surrounded by creepy hooded figures in a dark temple where they were about to perform a ritual on her.

It was way too late to back out now.

Elana tried to keep her breathing calm and waited for Cathy to start. It seemed like an eternity before she did.

"I present initiate Elana Bishop for progression to adept." Cathy's tone was smoother and calmer than

Elana had heard before, and something about her "sh" sounds seemed off—they were more like S's. Almost like she was speaking another language or in another accent.

"Name yourself, sponsor." This was from Valeria, who was acting as the ceremonial judge. *No pressure...*

Cathy responded to Valeria with a string of words that sort of sounded like *Cateriana* at the beginning but quickly segued into sibilant phonemes Elana had no hope of reproducing. That had to be Cathy's original name. It could have been an incantation.

Apparently satisfied, Valeria continued, "Retinue, name yourselves."

"*Mathieu Jean-Joseph Armand du Plessis de Richelieu, de la maison des Richelieux, membre du Conseil des cardinaux, sentinelle.*" Matt's voice was even sexier in French.

"Aldric de Rothschild of House Rothschilde, emissary."

"Lucia Lambra Mór." Lucia continued in a language Elana didn't recognize, full of H's and R's. It sounded vaguely Scandinavian by way of Scotland.

"Valeria Draven of House Scorpion, of the House of the SpiderKing, archon."

"Vivian Ravenwood of House Ravenwood, emissary."

A brief pause. Then, finally, "Belinda Leclerc of House Befonius, savant." If Belinda was fazed by being in a room with so many powerful vampires, she showed no sign.

Elana felt Valeria's gaze on the back of her head. She turned back to face her, and Valeria intoned, "Initiate, name yourself."

"Elana Danielle Bishop, of the House of the SpiderKing." Elana was deeply grateful her voice hadn't wavered.

"Do you, Elana Danielle Bishop of the House of the SpiderKing, seek to progress in the Sanguine Nexus?"

This line had been a tough one to learn. It had been like memorizing legalese. "Cognizant of the responsibilities inherent in progression through the Nexus, with full understanding of my duties and respect for those who precede me, I do."

Next came a series of questions from the retinue. Matt spoke first. "Being a vampire of the city-state of Haven, do you accept the rule of the SpiderKing?"

"I do."

Aldric queried, "Will you honor the best interests of your House in whatever vocations you pursue?"

"I will."

Lucia asked, "Will you seek always to understand more deeply your position, abilities, and privilege?"

"I will."

Valeria questioned, "Will you respect that some secrets are not yet yours to know, and exercise patience and restraint in your pursuits?"

"I will."

Vivian was next. "Will you build up the society in which you live, choosing progress over destruction?"

"I will."

Cathy spoke for Zevenda. "Will you choose to give rather than take whenever possible?"

"I will."

Belinda was last. "Will you seek balance and a life well-lived in all things, neither privileging work nor play?"

"I will."

A moment of silence passed before Cathy continued.

"You have heard her vows. I submit that Elana Bishop progress to the next level of the Sanguine Nexus."

"All those in favor, extend your dominant hand," Valeria proclaimed.

In unison, the seven people surrounding Elana reached toward her. The books hadn't been clear on what would happen next, so Elana was just along for the ride.

Her bare feet suddenly felt magnetized to the floor and the light shining down on her felt heavy and hot. The soles of her feet prickled, it was hard to breathe, and her vision blurred. She could faintly see swirls of blue light encircling Cathy's, Matt's, and Belinda's arms.

Then, those streams of light bridged the divide and touched her robes, and Elana's world exploded into a kaleidoscope of blue and red. It didn't hurt—it was more like pressure—but she couldn't breathe, and her arms and legs felt like they'd fallen asleep and were waking up with waves of pins and needles.

The prickling sensation intensified and spread up her limbs to her torso, which made her feel like her lungs had filled with fire and her stomach had turned to lead. Then the blue fire raced up her throat and into her skull, and she threw her head back in silent beseeching to the merciless red light that bathed her.

Time and space abandoned her. When her vision cleared of the bright blue and red afterimages, she had no concept of whether a minute, an hour, or a day had passed. It could have been longer. The fire was gone, and the inner temple had returned to its full darkness.

Cathy's voice swam out of the black, and her soft hands

pressed the stem of a goblet into Elana's. "Drink. It will help."

Elana knew what was in this cup, but nothing had ever sounded so good. She drank deeply from the goblet and trembled as the iron suffused her with warmth and energy.

When Cathy took the drained cup, Elana no longer felt like her knees would give out, and she could move to her place in the octagon.

"I ascend in the Nexus by the grace of my brothers and sisters," she breathlessly proclaimed. "I am Elana Bishop, of the House of the SpiderKing, adept."

CHAPTER TWENTY-THREE

Valeria slipped into the training room and silently closed the door. Elana and Gustav were locked in a fierce sparring match, and she did not want to distract them.

Elana slammed her fist into Gustav's stomach, then leaped back and to the side. Gustav retook the ground he'd lost in a heartbeat as he rushed Elana and tackled her by the shoulders. Elana fell back but curled her legs in and planted her feet in his chest, using the fall's momentum to fling him across the room upside down.

Gustav tucked and rolled into a backward somersault and came up on his feet. Elana was there to meet him with a flurry of blows, and student and teacher proceeded to parry, dodge, and punch their way across the training room floor.

Their movements would have been almost too fast to track to a less-trained eye. Each landed hits with strength that would have knocked a human out, and neither flinched. The spectacle resembled a choreographed fight sequence from any action movie you pleased, but this was unrehearsed and unplanned.

Elana bounced on the ball of her foot and spun into a flying kick. Gustav caught her ankle and hurled her at the floor. Elana caught herself with both hands and sprang up into a backflip. She landed on Gustav's shoulders and locked her legs around his neck.

He ran toward the wall, then a few steps up it, and launched them off the vertical surface toward the floor, aiming to slam Elana into the polished hardwood. Elana twisted in midair so Gustav hit first, then uncrossed her legs and scrambled away.

Gustav grabbed her ankle again and yanked her back. She flailed, and he caught her wrist and brought her to the floor with him. She rolled aside, but he followed and pinned her with a clever pivot.

Elana wouldn't give up that easily. She threw herself side to side to loosen his grip by a fraction, then drove her forehead into his nose at the same time as she got her knee up again and into his groin.

Gustav grunted and his grip slackened *just* enough that Elana was able to throw him aside. She rolled over and got one foot under her, but Gustav snagged the other one and unceremoniously brought her crashing back to the floor on her stomach. This time, he pinned her with her arms behind her back and a knee in her mid-back.

One breath…two breaths…

"Match." Elana panted.

Gustav hopped off her back and helped her to her feet. "Tell me what you did wrong."

Elana closed her eyes. Her chest heaved. After a second,

she replied, "You kept grabbing my ankle. My spatial awareness didn't extend far enough when I wasn't actively fighting you with my legs." She opened her eyes again. "Also, I'm still not fast enough."

Gustav chuckled and brushed some dust off her shoulder. "You are much faster than you were two days ago."

"Yeah, well, you were *clearly* holding out on me before."

He acquiesced with a grin, then nodded. "You are correct. You need to pay more attention to your lower extremities. Otherwise, you are integrating your new abilities admirably."

"You are indeed," Valeria remarked and approached the pair. "I can see the difference already. Your new status as adept is treating you well."

Elana was still mildly out of breath but bowed her head in acknowledgment. "Thank you, Arbiter. Did you need me for something? We didn't fight so long that I'm late, am I?"

Valeria shook her head. "I'm early. I wanted to see your progress after yesterday's ceremony. Shall we walk to our meeting?"

Elana eyed her sweat-soaked tank top and shorts. "Can I run myself through the shower first?"

"Yes. I will discuss the next phase of your training with Gustav."

"I'll be quick."

Elana jogged toward the locker room. When the door had closed behind her, Valeria looked at Gustav. "How long before she needs a new trainer?"

Gustav considered the question. "I can bring her to savant. *Possibly* to guardian, but not if her progress continues as exponentially as it has. Tamara would be better for her then."

Valeria nodded. "How far do you expect she will go?"

Gustav's eyebrows rose in surprise, then lowered again in thought. This time, it was a full minute before he answered her. "I would be surprised if she did not rise at *least* to emissary. She has great potential as long as it is adequately guided—although she is already making significant strides in guiding herself and in her focus. She has a goal. That much is clear."

Valeria hummed in acknowledgment. Her gaze remained riveted to the locker room door.

Elana entered the lobby of the Consorts' Training Grounds with her hands in her hair, busily tying it into a ponytail. Her gaze lit on the Arbiter of Shadows standing near the front door, and she changed direction. "Arbiter. Sorry to keep you waiting."

Valeria waved it off. "As I said, I arrived early. No need to apologize. Walk with me."

Elana fell into step with the white-clad woman, and they exited the building into the mid-morning sun. Valeria's outfit today was simple—white slacks with wide cuffs that swung around her heels and an equally loose white blouse. Elana caught glimpses of the subtle tattoos on her forearms, which seemed darker than usual today.

Valeria said nothing as she led Elana around to the back fields of the training grounds. They went past the trimmed lawns where guardian corps practiced field drills, beyond the line of trees that ringed the facility, and into fields nearly ready for harvest.

Elana glanced around them. She was reminded of her recent foray into the fields of Senkyem, where she'd stood in the wheat and awkwardly waited for some sign that Matt hadn't sent her on a wild goose chase. Was Valeria about to reveal one of her tricks?

The arbiter stopped after they'd walked for about fifteen minutes. As far as Elana could tell, they were in the middle of a field with nothing around them. She saw a building far to the east—probably the processing facility for this field—and the distant line of buildings that formed the Quarto cityscape. She had no idea why they'd paused *here*.

Then the ground moved underneath her. Moved *down*, to be specific.

She gasped and tensed, but Valeria was moving with her. They were descending into a shaft, slowly at first but faster with time, with a small platform around their feet still covered in vegetation. As soon as Elana's wits caught up with reality, she realized this *had* to be how Valeria had snuck up on her the other day.

They sank deep into the ground. The tunnel closed over them, but instead of being left in pitch black, dim strips of blue light appeared in the shaft walls and provided slight illumination. Not that there was anything to see. The shaft was unmarked, a sheer tunnel descending into unknown depths. The light strips had no markings either, meaning Elana could not gauge how quickly they were moving beyond the minor pressure in her ears.

The platform slowed to a stop and a door slid aside in front of them. Valeria stepped forward, followed by Elana. The light strips preceded them and illuminated a corridor with as many markings as the shaft—that was to say, none—but which had multiple branches.

Valeria followed the corridors on a path Elana could not fathom. She wondered if there were markings visible to the arbiter but not to her, perhaps keyed to Valeria's higher level in the Nexus.

Eventually, Valeria stopped and pressed a hand to the wall. Another door opened to allow them entrance into a chamber similar in style to the Mirabilis room in the consulate. It was Spartan, undecorated, and with walls so black Elana couldn't tell how big the room was.

Valeria motioned for Elana to sit at the large, featureless black table, then took the seat across from her.

Elana glanced side to side. "Am I allowed to ask where we are?"

"In the clandestine complexes of the Domain of Shadows," Valeria explained. "Any of my Domain's work that can't be public-facing for whatever reason occurs down here. There are multiple levels, none of which are accessible to anyone below the level of guardian, and you have to be on the privileged biometrics list, too."

Elana shivered. "So the entirety of Senkyem's subterranean space is a black site?"

"Essentially."

"God, that's creepy."

Valeria shrugged, but she had a tiny twinkle in her eye that read to Elana as pride. "Not being 'creepy' is functionally the opposite of my job description."

"Fair enough." Elana did her best to shake off the unsettled feeling and focus. "You must have something really important to tell me, then."

"I do." The arbiter waved over the table. A glowing blue square appeared, then lifted from the gleaming black surface to hover in the air and swiveled to face Elana. It showed a picture of a man in academic regalia whom Elana didn't recognize. He had an oval face, short brown hair and a beard, and large, round glasses.

"This is Evan Lingoria," Valeria told her. "He was a human geneticist who was given the Rights several decades ago when he became involved with a member of House X."

Elana frowned. "I know that name…" She scrunched her brow and thought for a moment, then inhaled sharply. "He went missing in the eighties. There was a *really* remote possibility that he was a victim of the East Coast Staker. Are you saying you found him?"

"My Shadowguard did."

"Wow. I mean, vampires must have crazy forensics teams. Identifying a decades-dead body probably isn't hard at all."

"He died less than a week ago."

Elana's jaw dropped. "You are… You're kidding. Where's he been all this time?"

Valeria's mouth tightened with displeasure. "I'm still working on that. *But*, after considerable investigative work over the past several days, I'm confident that whoever killed him is connected to the House Veridian conspiracy. I believe they're trying to send me—and by extension, you—a message."

"As in, 'quit fucking with us, or else?' That's usually what dead body drops mean, if the movies have taught me anything."

Valeria cracked a smile. "More or less."

"I assume we're not backing off."

Valeria's smile grew. "On the contrary. If they've progressed to the point that they're killing people they presumably disappeared for a reason, whether that's to work for them or as hostages, it means they're running scared and making stupid mistakes. The *smart* thing for them to do would have been to continue laying low, as they have been for the past few weeks."

"Right. Not like they're short on time, being vampires."

"Exactly. The fact that they haven't means they no longer believe they have the upper hand, and therefore have to intimidate you into backing off because they're no longer confident their plans are secure. They're scared of you."

Elana narrowed her eyes. "I don't follow. They dropped the body off somewhere *you* had to find it, didn't they? I'd have noticed if someone left a dead body on my front doorstep, unless you moved it before I woke up."

Valeria shook her head. "No, you're right. It was in the lowest levels of the King's Archives. The ones only accessible to very high-level vampires. It was a message for me, and by *extension*, you."

Elana frowned. "Now I'm *really* confused. You're the *Arbiter of Shadows*. I am a nobody adept whose only claim to fame is that my mother was really good at investigating shit and rose high in the Nexus super fast. Why are they scared of me? Why are they *more* scared of me than they are of *you*? That's just *stupid*."

Valeria shrugged. "Could be a number of reasons. First is that you're a newcomer who, yes, is technically a nobody, but you're a nobody who was immediately inducted into the royal House. Never underestimate the power of connections in Haven. They might not be so much scared of *you*, or even your mother, as they are of your perceived connection to the king."

Elana acknowledged that with an open palm. "Fair enough."

"Second, your mother *was* powerful and made as many enemies as she did friends. Add that to the propensity of vampires to presume that traits carry through House and family lines, which usually has a reasonable level of veracity when it comes to vampirism. They might not be so much scared of *you* as they are scared of what your mother found out and what you'll be able to do with it. Especially if you're anything like her, which you are."

"I'll take that as a compliment." Elana chewed on her lip. "Any other possibilities?"

"Many. They might hate you. They might think your mother didn't actually die, and you're her."

"Does that *happen*?"

"Do you want to know the answer to that?"

"Based on your tone, no. Go on."

"They might also be stupid enough to have forgotten how powerful I truly am, and they think they can get away with intimidating me. Since they're not doing much other than posturing, that explanation currently holds a lot of weight for me. If the lackeys they sent after you and Mister

Richelieu in the gardens were supposed to kill you, you wouldn't have escaped alive.

"My best guess, however, is that they're testing you."

Elana tilted her head. "Escalating and varying their tactics to see what I'll do? Or what you'll do?"

"Yes. They attacked you several times in different settings to test your abilities and priorities. They threatened your home to see if they could scare you away. Now they're leaving us both a message to warn us away from whatever they're doing. It's simple, and the simplest explanations are often the best."

Elana drummed her fingers on the table. "Normally I'd agree with you, but nothing about the House Veridian conspiracy seems simple, based on my mother's records. They have their fingers in every pie from Premier to Octava. I'm frankly astonished we haven't found any connections to the arbiters."

"I believe that's deliberate, based on their timeline. Judging by the pattern of implicated connections to House Veridian, I expect that if your mother hadn't shown up and thrown wrenches in their plans, they would have escalated their networking to emissary-level vampires. This would have happened by the turn of the millennium. After that, it would only have been a matter of time before they added an arbiter to their fold—or before one of their number became an arbiter."

Elana remembered the first video she'd ever watched of her mother, a C-PAN recording of her as a consort presenting to the consulate. "What about Arbiter Gow and Arbiter Zilmann? Neither of them liked my mother. She *replaced* Arbiter Gow, and Arbiter Gow took her position as Arbiter of Sanctuary back after she died."

Valeria pressed her lips together. "As unpleasant as Carlysle Zilmann can be, her connections are clean. Arbiter Gow's are as well. And believe you me, I went over them with the *finest-toothed* of combs."

Elana scowled. "Dammit. I thought we might have had something there." She sighed, leaned back in her chair, crossed her arms, and shifted her focus back to the picture of Evan Lingoria. "As usual, I'm hearing that we don't know what House Veridian wants other than for us to leave them alone to plot their dirty deeds. And we have no way of guessing what they're gonna do next."

To Elana's surprise, Valeria's expression of distaste shifted to one of anticipatory excitement. "That's true…but like I said, I *do* have a plan.

"If we have House Veridian on the back foot as I'm guessing, then they're nervous and more likely to make mistakes—and to jump at shadows," she continued. "We can take advantage of that, along with their tendency to arrogance. As you mentioned, no one *smart* decides it's a good plan to piss off the Arbiter of Shadows."

Elana snickered. "It's honestly, like, the second thing you learn about Haven."

Valeria cocked her head. "As a human? What's the first?"

"Vampires are better than you in every way and will just as soon kill you as drink your blood."

Valeria blinked. "Vampires don't make a habit of killing innocent civilians."

"I never said the common wisdom was *accurate*."

"Touché." Valeria tapped the tabletop several times. Evan Lingoria's portrait disappeared, and an image of an octagonal room carved of black and white marble and draped in dark red curtains replaced it. It resembled a small, semicircular amphitheater with a throne at the foot of the audience seating, facing the assembly with space in front of it.

Elana frowned. "That's the king's court. I don't get the connection."

"You're aware of the king's court's standard use," Valeria stated.

Elana nodded. The king's court was a rarely used chamber in the consulate, located a level beneath the central atrium. In theory, it was where the SpiderKing would hold court if he ever showed his face in public, which he did not. As such, it lay empty ninety-nine percent of the time, except for extremely uncommon judicial cases where the Arbiter of Shadows sat in judgment over the most heinous of crimes. In effect, she acted as the king's hand.

"It is also used for ceremonies involving the royal House, such as those that occur after a member of the royal House ascends in the Nexus."

Elana eyed the image of the courtroom with renewed intensity. "What kind of ceremonies might *those* be?"

"You are to be presented as your mother's lineal successor. This is an important tradition in all Houses, but especially as a member of the royal House. It will cement and legitimize your standing in the Houses, which will strengthen your alliances with Ravenwood, Stormhaven, Rothschilde, and Lucciola."

Elana chuckled. "Basically, I'm being named as my mother's heir, so I'm no longer a bastard vampire?"

Valeria smirked. "Something like that. I also hope it will lead to an assassination attempt."

Elana's eyebrows shot toward her hairline. "Uh, what? Run that by me again?"

The Arbiter of Shadows steepled her fingers and leaned in. "Your age is not common knowledge, nor is your lineage. It isn't *difficult* to unearth the truth about you if you know the right person to ask, but we haven't gone public with it.

"Announcing you in front of the consulate as your mother's successor, and therefore a legitimate and ranking member of the House of the SpiderKing, will *officially* make you as much of a threat to House Veridian as your mother was. It will also tacitly throw the weight of the entire royal House behind you.

"While your mother never made her pursuit of House Veridian public, my estimation is that they knew what she was doing by the time she became the Arbiter of Sanctuary. I don't know yet if they figured it out earlier. I expect that your mother receiving incontrovertible proof of support for her endeavors from the king when he named her Arbiter of Sanctuary was when House Veridian decided it had to remove her from the equation.

"Since House Veridian has escalated their tactics with you in exponential fashion, I expect they'll do the same with this," Valeria concluded. "We announce that you're following in your mother's footsteps genealogically. They'll jump to the conclusion that you're following in her footsteps in all other ways, and they'll mount their most sophisticated assassination attempt yet."

Elana pursed her lips. "You think they'll do it publicly?"

"I hope so. Even if they don't fuck up *that* spectacularly, any clear assassination attempt will be a ready-made opportunity for you to reveal your investigation into your mother's death. It will be a corollary to your obvious accusation that House Veridian just tried to kill you. The attempt on your life would allow you to formally challenge them."

"And then what? Pistols at dawn?"

"No. Then you go to court."

Elana made a face. "Aw. How boring."

Valeria smirked. "The appeals court involves swords."

Elana snorted. "That's more like it." She thought it over and frowned again. "Are we sure I'll be *able* to accuse House Veridian of trying to kill me? Do you think they're likely to misstep so badly that it'll be obvious it was them?"

Valeria shook her head. "It would be great if they did, but I'd consider it a remote possibility. Think of it more as bluffing and making them go all in, giving you a chance to play your full hand.

"We've been holding back, trying to gather information to prove it's them. They haven't been playing ball. Instead, we're taking the fight to them by goading them to act on you—at which point we'll call *their* bluff by revealing everything we know about House Veridian's clandestine activities and their connections to your mother's death."

Elana frowned. "But unless we get *really* lucky, there's no way the person who tries to kill me will be a member of House Veridian."

"No chance," Valeria agreed. "The plan isn't without risk. But it *will* look bad that House Veridian will be connected, however tenuously, with the murder of one member of the royal House and the attempted murder of another. If nothing else, it might make their allies uneasy, and uncomfortable friends make for excellent informants."

Elana thought this over as she stared at the black, white, and red picture of the king's court. The feeling of being a pawn in a game she didn't understand lurked at the edges of her mind. She'd felt that way for weeks and had only *stopped* feeling like that after her Chimera badminton tournament. She had no interest in letting the impostor syndrome back in, no matter how rational it seemed on the surface.

Her mother hadn't allowed her fear to get in the way of doing what needed to be done. She'd been courageous until the end. Elana owed her that much.

It occurred to Elana that she hadn't done nearly enough research into which Houses her mother had been *friendly* with. That was an unfortunate oversight on her part which she would have to rectify. Beyond not wanting to snub anyone unintentionally, it would be good practice. Life *was* all about who you knew.

Another thought struck her, and Elana frowned again as she snapped her gaze to Valeria. "I just realized we're making a really big assumption here."

"Oh?"

"You keep saying we want to goad House Veridian into making an assassination *attempt* on me. What if they manage it? They killed my mother, and she was way more powerful. I'm a baby adept. You said it yourself earlier. If they'd wanted me dead, I would be *super dead.*"

"That's correct."

Elana blinked, then raised her hands, palms up. "So? What do we do? What do *I* do? I'm not actually interested in dying for the cause just yet."

Valeria shrugged. "Simple. Don't die."

Elana rolled her eyes. "Oh, sure. You make it sound so easy."

CHAPTER TWENTY-FOUR

"A formal presentation is a bunch of stuff and bother," Cathy announced in the tone that generally meant she'd prefer to eat lunch in a pool of piranhas than do whatever she was talking about.

"I am *sure* you're right," Elana began. "But—"

"But you're a member of the royal House," Cathy finished with a sage nod. "It is what it is, darling. Don't apologize for that."

Elana cradled her cup of tea in both hands and waited for Cathy to continue. She had the contemplative look on her face that meant she was working something out in her head, and she didn't appreciate being interrupted.

Elana had shown up on Cathy's doorstep the day after Valeria's bombshell-drop of a *hopeful* assassination attempt. She'd cleared it with the arbiter first, but it was past time she told Cathy everything. So, over a pot and a half of tea and a spread of sweets chockful of pistachios and encrusted in sugar, Elana had filled Cathy in on the entire conspiracy.

She'd taken it well. Elana had expected no less. You didn't live for three or four thousand years without developing a keen sense of what was sensible. Elana still hadn't worked out exactly how old Cathy was, and honestly suspected she never would, because how could you verify it? Apparently, a decades- or centuries-old conspiracy to infiltrate and undermine an independent city-state, likely with the eventual goal of overthrowing it, was "sensible." Or not surprising, anyway.

Cathy hadn't been shocked by the revelation that House Veridian seemed to be behind it. "I never liked them," she'd mused. "Never had much reason to, but then, when you've been around the block a few times you learn to trust your gut."

When Elana had asked why Cathy hadn't done anything about it, the venerable vampire had shrugged. "Because I had no reason to look, and therefore I hadn't seen anything. Not enough to put any of it together, in any case. Your mother did an admirable job."

"She did. Which is why we've been so careful to safeguard the information since." Elana had winced. "I wanted to tell you sooner, I swear."

Cathy had waved off Elana's apology. "I understand entirely. You had no way to know whether I was friend or foe. Very sensible of you to act with caution."

The conversation had continued through Cathy's contacts and personal knowledge of House Veridian—not much, but she'd do some subtle asking around—then moved to the presentation.

Cathy tapped her chin with a finger. "They're usually

done quite soon after the First Progression. Has Valeria given you a date?"

"Not yet. There were other details she needed to settle first. How soon is 'quite soon?'"

"With prior planning, the day after, if not *immediately* after. But that's typically with heads of Houses who aren't as reclusive as our illustrious monarch. I'd expect her to schedule it within the next couple of days. Did she tell you what you would need?"

"Ceremonial robes, a well-catered reception, and official medallions of some sort to give to my closest allies. She said she'd get those and the robe for me. The reception is my responsibility. Can't I use the robes Arturo made me for this?"

Cathy shook her head. "Those are Nexus robes. These would be royal robes. Have you ever watched a coronation?"

"I've seen clips online. I was way more into vampire tabloids than royal-watching."

Cathy chuckled. "Terribly surprising. Well, even if all you've seen are clips, that should give you an idea of how ornate those will be. The king's court will be decked out in full regalia, and you and Valeria will be the same.

"The whole thing will be broadcast on Haven's primetime news program, of course—and the reception will be public," Cathy added. At the look of horror on Elana's face, she snorted. "I take it Valeria didn't include that part."

"She did not," Elana squeaked out. "I don't think I can *afford* that."

Cathy smiled and reached across the couch to pat Elana's hand. "Don't worry. I'll help. Keep in mind that it would be considered an extreme honor to cater a royal reception, and a *terrible* faux pas to turn you down."

"That doesn't mean they won't charge me out the nose," Elana lamented.

"Oh, certainly not." Cathy laughed gaily. "Like I said, I can help you there. I'd also recommend you reach out to your new friend Belinda—I suspect she would know the best places to hold a huge reception that aren't stuffy and boring."

Elana grabbed her phone out of her pocket and made a quick note to text Belinda later. "Good idea. On another note, do you know what these medallion things are? I haven't had a chance to get to the library and look yet."

Cathy nodded. "Formal recognition of allyship. You'd best be *very* certain of who you give them to. It's also traditional to present them with a letter that details the terms and benefits of your alliance."

Elana raised an eyebrow. "As collateral? Blackmail material?"

Cathy snorted. "Unscrupulous heads of royal Houses have certainly used them thus, yes. I'd recommend you craft them as invitations more than balls and chains.

"The letters and medallions don't mean you're required to maintain the alliances forever," Cathy clarified. "Think of them like a royal permit. As long as you both adhere to the promises set out in the letters of contract, and the alliance is mutually beneficial, the alliance will continue. If and when that changes, either party may seek termination. Obviously with some royal Houses that's more likely to work than others, but the legal precedent remains."

Elana nodded contemplatively, then frowned. "Who

would enforce that if the royal House broke the contract illegally?"

Cathy smirked, raised an eyebrow, and pointed at Elana. "You've hit the nail on the head, my dear. When something like that happens, the plaintiff's basic recourse is to get enough friends together and declare war. There's no United Nations of vampire city-states."

"Huh. I guess not." Elana considered this for a moment. "Is it weird that it strikes me as one way in which humans have figured life out a little better than vampires?"

Cathy shrugged. "I see your point. Councils of Houses and of city-states have existed over the millennia, certainly, which have functioned in similar capacity. The fact remains that vampires are far more capable of utterly destroying their enemies than humans are. *Yes,* even including humanity's recent developments in nuclear and biological weaponry. When you *can* annihilate the person you don't like without help, you're less likely to make friends. In sweeping generalizations, of course."

Elana shuddered. "Fair enough. Can we change the subject?"

"Slightly. What are your terms of contract for Ravenwood, Stormhaven, and Rothschilde?"

"I have no idea."

"Yes, you do. What do they most prize, how can you offer it to them, and what do you want in return?"

Elana sipped her tea. "Stormhaven is easy. They love information, the rarer the better. I can't offer them access to the royal archives—no way do I have clearance for that —but for now, the promise of the information my mother gathered is good credit. What I want back is just as simple.

Information *I* don't have. So, mutually beneficial information exchange, and I guess, privileged access."

"Barring royal interests first," Cathy pointed out. "Valeria will murder you herself if you trade information before she gets her hands on it."

Elana grimaced. "You're not wrong."

Cathy smiled and swirled her teacup. "I remember little Lucia when she took over from her aunt. She was a firecracker. Outmaneuvered her own father for the position of head of House. And a good thing she did, too. Robert would have made a *terrible* head, but no one had the guts to tell him so."

Elana leaned in. "I sense hot gossip. Spill the tea."

"Not on this couch," Cathy scolded, but she winked. "Robert Lambra Mor was a greedy bastard. He consolidated the Stormhaven finances into a veritable juggernaut in the early 1600s. Availed himself of a few connections to get in early on some colonizing expeditions. Made a fortune.

"But he hated his sister Mairi, because she saw through the pious act he gave their parents," Cathy continued. "Mairi knew he was a conniving twat who wouldn't hesitate to sell family secrets if it would get him more gold in the coffers. She dropped a few hints to young Lucia, who was already proving a much more capable information broker than her father even at the tender age of seventeen, and within a decade…

"Well, let's just say one of Robert's business deals went sufficiently awry that he was no longer an option for head of House when his sister decided to pass the torch," Cathy concluded.

Elana narrowed her eyes. "Did she *kill her father?*"

Cathy shrugged. "I'm sure I don't know."

"Right…"

"What about Rothschilde?"

Elana hummed thoughtfully. "I'm not sure, honestly. I don't have money to offer them, and I don't have anything they can invest in. The more time I spend with Lord Aldric, the more I think he's staying in this alliance because he likes me."

"How did you win him over in the first place?"

"The balance between humans and vampires," Elana explained. "House Rothschilde is one of the few Houses that has *truly* significant interests in both worlds—or rather, two branches of the same House with equal standing in both worlds. It's a complex arrangement, but I'm sure you know what I mean."

"I do. The Rothschilds and the Rothschildes maintain a delicate and conservative balance, and they are equally interested in maintaining the same in the rest of the world. So, how can you use that to your advantage and to theirs?"

Elana drummed her fingers on her thigh. "I suppose my whole mysterious existence speaks to the balance between vampires and humans. It's to my benefit to offer information to humans about vampires and vice versa, and I'm in a unique place to do that, thanks to my mom's work."

"Precisely. The thing you can offer to Lord Aldric to invest in is *you*. Also…"

"You have the gleam in your eye again that means you have secrets."

Cathy looked away. "It's not widely known, but Lord Aldric has no heir."

Elana's eyebrows rose. "You're right, that is *not* widely known. How did that happen? And why isn't it bigger news?"

"Because he has very good deals with very important people to keep quiet about it until he solves the problem," Cathy replied. "And because he's cashing in every ounce of reputation and respect he has to guilt everyone else into keeping their mouths shut."

Elana's eyebrows were just about to her hairline. "What the hell *happened?*"

Cathy's expression sobered, then saddened. "Aldric met his wife, Jacqueline, in the twenties. They married and had Miriam not long after that. Jacqueline was given the Rights a couple years later, and they planned to give Miriam the Rights when she turned twenty-one. They died of an unidentified illness three years early."

Elana gaped. "Both of them?"

"Miriam went two days before Jacqueline."

Elana clutched her teacup. "*God.* And the healers couldn't do anything to help?"

Cathy scowled. "The top healer at the time, Augustus Maxwell, tore most of his hair out trying to find the root cause. He found nothing. Sent him into early retirement. It's rare that an illness will harm a vampire and a human the same way, but this one… Jacqueline and Miriam wasted away. Aldric sat beside them as they died.

"It would have been the biggest tragedy of the century, but Aldric put gag orders on the media the day before Jacqueline and Miriam went into care, and they've never been lifted."

Elana processed this, sighed sadly, then frowned. "Wait.

What are you recommending I do here? I can't believe you're telling me to ignore his request for privacy. That's *not* who I am."

Cathy shook her head. "You'd never do that, and I wouldn't suggest it. I'm giving you context…and hinting at why Lord Aldric might want to invest in you."

Elana narrowed her eyes. "As an *heir?*"

Cathy shrugged. "It's possible. My connections across the pond say the European branches of House Rothschilde don't have much in the heir department either, and no great candidates have presented themselves in the human lines.

"Officially naming you as his heir would be a *stunning* move for the Rothschildes, granted—they rarely make alliances in the first place—but it's theoretically possible. He's been the next best thing to a hermit since his family died. Since you made friends with him, he's left the manor *multiple* times, even to social events."

Elana hummed and sipped her tea. It was getting cold. "I am *super* not ready to think about becoming the heir to a whole other House right now, so I'm just gonna swap over to House Ravenwood. I think my best bet there is again to focus on what I hooked her with. Truth. Justice. If I prove that I prioritize exposing the truth and acting with integrity, that's enough for Lady Vivian."

Cathy clicked her tongue.

Elana raised an eyebrow. "Share with the class."

Cathy chuckled. "Vivian Ravenwood is a clever old hag, which I say with all love and with the full knowledge that it takes one to know one. If that's all you give her, yes, she'll maintain her House's alliance with you, and it will bear fruit."

"I'm sensing a 'but.'"

"Bring her a plant." Elana blinked, and Cathy snickered. "I'm serious. Bring her a plant. It doesn't matter if she already has it. She already has exemplars of just about every species of flora on the planet. That's not the point.

"The point is that Ravenwood values *growth* in addition to truth," Cathy explained. "Not to mention that if you give her something, you'll show that you care about her as more than a pawn in the great game. That you want to be her friend, not just her ally—and trust me, if you have a chance to call Vivian Ravenwood your *friend*, you *take* it."

"Understood." Elana drained her cup and rolled her shoulders. "I'd better get moving, if Valeria could summon me to the court any day. Are there examples of these letters in the archives?"

"Absolutely. Ask to be let into the royal section."

CHAPTER TWENTY-FIVE

Elana finished coordinating the initial reception plans with Belinda not a moment too soon. She'd just sent the final go-ahead via text when a text from Valeria scrolled in.

Presentation two days from today. 3:00 PM. You'll be out by 3:30, so plan your reception accordingly.

Elana sighed in relief and texted back confirmation, then did the same with Belinda. It turned out that Belinda personally owned a bar with a huge patio in Shestoi, and was more than happy to host the reception there even on short notice. She also wasn't fussy about third-party catering.

She'd laughed when Elana had nervously brought it up. "Are you kidding? If I tried to give my back of house staff this menu, I'd have a mutiny on my hands. We do craft beer and peanuts, not afternoon tea. *That said*, girl, do I ever have some recommendations for you..."

Elana waited on tenterhooks until she received the

thumbs-up from Belinda. Then she slumped in her chair and rubbed her eyes.

She'd been up all night drafting the letters of alliance for Lord Aldric, Lady Vivian, and Madame Lucia, after running around to find the right manufacturing house in Etreta to make the medallions. She'd also had to design the medallions, which would also be used as the basis for her *official wax seal.*

Yeah, Elana was one of "those people" now, and she was constantly back and forth on whether she liked it.

On the one hand, having enough money that your money made money on its own was *very* nice. Her royal account with the Bank of Haven had a financial advisor attached to it, and Sir Lionel Gauthier, Esq., savant of House Beamot, was doing an admirable job investing her settlement money and personal assets as he'd done for all members of the royal House for untold decades. Elana could buy whatever she wanted, whenever she wanted, with very few restrictions, and the freedom that imparted still astonished her on a regular basis.

She was looking into starting a few charities on the human side of business, or buying up a ton of medical and student debt. Lionel had cautioned her against moving too fast. She'd given him a steely-eyed look and told him in no uncertain terms that she wanted him to use her money to help the largest number of people possible for the longest period of time possible. If he wouldn't do that for her, she'd find someone else.

A dry chuckle had ruffled his perfectly trimmed mustache, and he'd remarked that Elana reminded him of her mother.

Elana was getting a lot of that lately. So much so that she'd visited a hairstylist in Premier and requested a new look that would set her apart from her mother's memory. Something new, something that would stand out and mark Elana as her own woman.

She ran her hands through her shortened locks, which now fell to just below her chin. Still long enough to pull into a ponytail or braid for the gym, but a far cry from her mother's cascading brown waves. Elana suspected she'd grow it out again since she already missed the length, but for now, she needed to be different.

Word was getting around that Elana Bishop was setting trends, making waves, and breaking ground. She intended to ride that momentum all the way to the bank—or to the court, more accurately.

Valeria was keeping mum about anything to do with her investigation into Evan Lingoria's death. News of his body's discovery hadn't hit the public yet. Valeria intended to drop that shoe at the same time as Elana made her accusation against House Veridian for hopefully *not* successfully killing her, with the idea being to rattle House Veridian into fucking up more.

"Knock, knock," a pleasant male voice called, and Elana looked up to see Lord Aldric poking his head in the back gate.

"Come on in," she replied, and beckoned. Absent any office space of her own—a lacuna Elana was keen to remedy, but hadn't had time to implement—she was holding meetings in her backyard by the pool. Hardly the *most* professional location, but certainly in keeping with her burgeoning tradition of doing things differently.

Lord Aldric closed the gate behind him and strolled across the lawn to where Elana sat near the calm blue waters. He took a seat next to her and sighed gently. "It's very relaxing back here."

"Just the way I like it. Can I get you something to drink?" She stood.

"Coffee would be lovely, thank you."

"Sure. Back in a minute. Make yourself comfortable."

She disappeared into the house, allowing Aldric to relax in the yard. While she made coffee, she reflected on what Cathy had told her about Aldric's wife and daughter. It was a tragedy, to be sure, and she wondered if Aldric was still investing in research to try to find a cure —or simply an explanation. In his shoes, that's what she'd do.

Elana filed the idea away for later and returned to the yard with a tray of coffee, complete with cream, sugar, spoons, and a canister of chocolate-cinnamon wafer cookies. She deposited the tray on a table between their Adirondack chairs and sat.

She poured him a cup and nudged it toward him, along with a spoon. "Thank you for coming. I appreciate you taking the time."

"Happy to." Aldric stirred sugar into his coffee but didn't touch the cream. "It's a lovely day. Gave me a perfect excuse to take the Jaguar out instead of making it a conference call."

She grinned. "Ooh, a *Jaguar*. You'll have to take me for a ride sometime."

He chuckled. "You're welcome anytime. Now, rumor has it you're to be formally presented in two days."

Elana whistled under her breath and sat back in her chair. "And I thought human rumor mills traveled fast."

"The vampire grapevine never sleeps."

"No kidding. Yes, it's true. I asked you over for two reasons. One, to ask for your assistance with several tasks in the fight to take down House Veridian, and two, to offer you a formal letter of alliance."

Aldric savored a sip of coffee, then set his mug on the arm of the chair and nodded. "I expected as much. I'd be delighted to read it over. I expect I'll be equally delighted to accept, but I'd be doing you a disservice if I didn't read the letter first."

Elana nodded and produced the first letter from her handbag, which had been tucked beside her chair.

Lord Aldric took the proffered envelope and turned it over once before opening it. "Excellent choice of seal," he remarked as he slipped a pocketknife from the inside pocket of his light suit jacket and worked the tip under the wax holding the cream-colored envelope closed. "I appreciate the subtle spiderweb theme in the lightning. Very dynamic."

Elana smiled. "I appreciate the compliment."

Aldric slid the thick stationery out of the envelope, unfolded it, and muttered under his breath as he read. "Mutually beneficial alliance… Possibility of future investment… Prioritizing balance between vampire and human interests…" He paused near the end, then read, "And continued personal friendship with a surfeit of pastramis on rye. Sincerely, Elana Bishop."

Aldric looked up and met Elana's hopeful smile with a chuckle. "I've read many of these in my life, but none so personable as this. You have a knack for making friends, Elana."

"Thank you. I think it's important to have friends, not just allies. Allies are important too, don't get me wrong, but there's an extra value in a friend. I've really enjoyed getting to know you, and I respect your experience. I'd value you as a mentor and a friend, if you'll have me."

Aldric considered the offer. Elana tried not to show her growing nerves. Her words were truthful. It would be *stupid* to offer friendship that wasn't real. Insincerity was a surefire way to break an alliance.

"I'd be honored," Aldric finally told her. He refolded the letter and tucked it and the envelope into his jacket, then shook her hand firmly. When she gave him the brass medallion fashioned in the same spiderweb of lightning as her seal, he took it and slipped it in his breast pocket.

"I'll have it added to my robes tonight," he promised. "Now, about these tasks you were mentioning?"

"Right." Elana shifted forward in her seat and Aldric matched her increased focus. "I hope my presentation will kick the target House into high gear, and an attempt on my life might follow."

Aldric nodded seriously, entirely unfazed. Elana reflected that it was a *tiny* bit fucked up that vampires were so nonchalant about life and death situations.

"I need to push through a few legal safeguards in case they try to move on my assets," she continued. "There aren't many of them, but there's enough that I'd be seriously pissed if I woke up from a coma and found myself penniless."

Aldric chuckled. "Yes, that *would* be frustrating. Surely

you have a financial advisor who could help you with that? Isn't old Lionel working for you?"

"He is, and he already has things in motion too. What I want from *you* is to tie *them* up in red tape in the background any way you can. I know you've already been making connections with their companies behind the scenes—give them busywork and insist they finish *that* before anything else."

Aldric grinned, and a mischievous twinkle lit in his eyes. "Naturally, the first time they do it there will be something I've forgotten. Or to be more precise, something I definitely told them but they clearly missed and I'm being ever so polite by saying I forgot. But if they don't do it all over again I'll be very disappointed in them and will make sure they never do business with a Rothschilde again."

Elana smirked. "You are definitely picking up what I'm putting down."

Aldric rubbed his hands together. "Oh, you're *fun*, Miss Bishop. I look forward to the injection of life you'll undoubtedly put into this sleepy little city."

Madame Lucia arrived as Lord Aldric was leaving. As thanks for agreeing to remain in Haven the extra few days after Elana's Progression, Elana had arranged for the head of House Stormhaven to stay in one of Cathy's properties in Premier. The gorgeous penthouse apartment was in the second-tallest skyscraper in the city, only bested by the Citadel's Royal Towers.

The stay was treating her well, or maybe the North Carolina air was more to Lucia's liking than that of the Scottish Highlands. The information broker's skin had a rosier tint and she had tied her hair into a crown of braids rather than the long, demure hairstyle she typically sported.

"Elana. A beautiful afternoon for a chat." The tall, elegant woman draped herself into the Adirondack chair Aldric had vacated.

"It is," Elana agreed wholeheartedly. "Can I get you something to drink?"

Lucia requested tea, so Elana slipped into the house with the coffee tray to let Lucia have a few minutes to herself. When she returned to the deck, she was surprised to see the normally reserved head of House Stormhaven had kicked off her shoes, hiked up her skirt, and was sitting on the edge of the pool, dangling her feet in the water.

Elana sat cross-legged next to her and set the tray between them. "Makes me think I should have brought out lemonade," she joked.

Lucia laughed, a broad, gentle sound. "I find Haven much more relaxing with you around, Miss Bishop," she confessed. "I hope you don't mind my taking the liberty."

"Not at all. I'm glad you're enjoying yourself. Has your visit to Haven been pleasant?"

"Very much so. The accommodations you arranged are beautiful and private. They are thanks to your alliance with House Lucciola, yes?"

"My friendship with its head, actually, but functionally yes." Elana poured them both tea and motioned questioningly to the cream and sugar. Lucia gestured for a little of each, and Elana mixed their cups appropriately before handing the light blue china teacup to the other woman. "Cathy is a good friend of mine and a valued mentor. I'm very lucky to have her in my corner. As I'm lucky to, I hope, have you as well."

Lucia laughed again, still that loose and throaty chuckle. "That depends. What are you offering?"

Elana hopped up and went to fetch her handbag from her chair, then produced the second envelope from within it and offered it to Lucia. "A full formal alliance with all the rights, responsibilities, and benefits thereof. Go ahead and read it. I'll wait."

Lucia popped the wax seal off with a fingernail and turned it side to side in the light before removing and scanning the letter. When she came to the end, she eyed Elana. "I won't do you the discourtesy of questioning whether you have clearance to offer this on behalf of the royal House."

Elana inclined her head. "I appreciate that. I have an arrangement with my fellow House member, the Arbiter of Shadows. After ensuring the king's interests are protected, she will provide me, and therefore you, with access to multiple channels of information gathering to be consulted via keyword search or alert. In return, we'd expect the same preferential treatment.

"It's worth noting that no other House has received this level of access to Haven's surveillance network," Elana added. "Stormhaven would be the first House with this privilege. We consider this alliance to be deeply mutually advantageous in our active investigation of House

Veridian."

Lucia tapped the letter on her thigh and gazed at the gentle ripples in the chlorine-blue water. "Can you guarantee anonymity, or at least protection of source, should any information prove actionable in one jurisdiction but not the other?"

"To the best of our capability, yes."

The demure yet intense redhead nodded slowly, then firmly. She decisively folded the letter and set the seal on top of it and the envelope next to her. "I accept."

They shook hands, then Elana produced the brass medallion and passed it to Lucia. "I appreciate and honor your trust. On that note, I have a few bits of information about House Veridian's next moves, which I think you'll find *very* interesting."

Lucia's eyes lit up. "*Do* tell."

"Cone of secrecy?"

Lucia scoffed. "Goes without saying."

"Just checking." Elana winked. "Now... For one, they're getting anxious. They dropped a dead body in a location I can't share yet, but you'll know what I mean when I say *they shouldn't have been there.*"

Lucia hummed with interest. "Can you tell me who it was yet?"

"Evan Lingoria. Ring any bells?"

"*Oh*, yes." The hunger in Lucia's gaze sharpened. "I have a file in my desk about the East Coast Staker. In the interests of share and share alike, I believe they had victims globally, not just in the United States."

Elana's eyes widened. "You're kidding."

"I never kid when it comes to information."

Elana grabbed her notebook from her handbag. "Tell me everything you can. Now that we suspect House Veridian is connected to the East Coast Staker, we have a whole new avenue of investigation underway. Knowing that they were active elsewhere…"

Lucia grinned a nasty, predatory grin. "I *love* a good hunt. All right, you'll want to start in East Cambria in the 1950s…"

Elana's final visitor of the day was Lady Vivian. The venerable head of House Ravenwood arrived seemingly out of thin air twenty minutes after Madame Lucia left. Elana came out of the house after cleaning up the coffee and tea fixings to find the ancient vampire on the deck in the same chair she'd held court in at Elana's housewarming party.

"Lady Vivian, welcome," Elana greeted her with a courteous bow. "May I bring you anything to drink?"

"Something natural, please, and cold," Vivian replied. She was facing away from Elana, looking out through the thin trellis of the deck railing at the slowly gathering clouds.

"Right away."

Elana slipped back into the house and returned a minute later with two tall glasses of ice water infused with blackberries and mint. She set them on the table between the deck chairs and sat beside Lady Vivian. "Thank you for taking the time to come. I know it's quite a distance from Ravenwood Manor."

Vivian exhaled a tiny laugh through her nose and the corners of her eyes crinkled in amusement. "Not far at all, if you know the way."

Elana was reminded of Valeria's mysterious appearance in the fields of Senkyem. She'd thought that explained by the subterranean network of tunnels and shafts connected to the guardians' complex, but maybe there was more to it.

"I wish I understood the world and vampirism like you do," Elana admitted. "I can't tell you how honored I am to have you as an ally. I learn something every time you're around—*many* things, honestly, not just one per visit. You're fascinating."

Vivian's smile twisted the wrinkles of her face like the bark of a tree. "You probably talk that way to everyone you're allied with."

Elana chuckled. "Sort of, I guess. I'm privileged to have multiple powerful, wise, and experienced vampires among my allies. I *am* honored to know and learn from each of you. Not many new adepts can say they're so well-connected, and not just in name but in worth. I have a lot to learn, and excellent people to learn from."

Vivian nodded slightly. Her wizened hands, still wrapped in the thin wooden spirals that snaked around her fingers and palms and wound up her wrists, spread across the fabric of her dress. Its skirt was multiple layers of sea-foam green chiffon that shifted and rustled like leaves, but which had no adornment otherwise. The sleeves of the same chiffon were long and fell loose around her wrists, and the neckline of the stiff bodice came up below her chin.

Elana continued, "To that end, I'd like to offer you this."

She pulled the final cream envelope from her handbag and slid it across the table next to Vivian's glass.

Vivian took the envelope with two gnarled fingers. She did not look twice at the wax seal, which popped open upon being touched by one of the blue sparks that were sliding along the wooden whorls as she opened and unfolded the letter.

She was silent while she read. At last, she dangled the letter between her thumb and fingertip and glanced at Elana. "An acceptable alliance."

Elana reached down beside her chair and picked up the small pot she'd set out earlier that day. The terra cotta pot she set on the table held a sprig of mint and a long-stemmed mushroom with a creamy cap.

Vivian's eyebrow arched. "Interesting. Say more."

Elana pointed at the mushroom. "This is a *Mentasus reticuli*. It's a fungus that particularly likes growing in soil where mint is flourishing—and it chokes out the mint and leaves the soil ready to be planted with something new. Not much kills mint, but this little buddy does.

"The way I see it, House Veridian is a bit like mint. It grows anywhere and everywhere, spreads without anyone's help, and it's hard to get rid of. It's tasty, so we leave it alone and think it's fine, but the truth is that it's invasive and it takes up space for beneficial plants.

"I want to uproot House Veridian's quiet invasion, but I don't want to use a scorched-earth approach. I want to smother them, then use what they leave behind to build a better, truer Haven. I thought the *Mentasus* would be an excellent symbol. Also, a little birdie told me you like plants." Elana winked.

"Mushrooms aren't plants," Vivian corrected, but amusement glimmered in her eyes. "You have a clever head on your shoulders. Cleverer, I think, than even your mother."

Elana's eyebrows rose. This was the first time she could recall someone comparing her to her mother but placing Elana higher. "Thank you."

Vivian nodded and extended her hand for Elana to shake. When she had, a flicker of fire erupted from the wooden spirals on her arms and turned the letter into flash paper. Elana jumped, and Vivian laughed the creaky cackle of a dry tree swaying in the wind.

Elana recovered herself and offered the brass medallion to Vivian, who took it and turned it over in her fingers like a fidget toy. "Tell me your plan for Veridian."

Elana drew a deep breath and mustered all the details to the forefront of her memory. "Well, the first step is to draw them out, which we hope the presentation will accomplish..."

Lady Vivian left as she'd arrived, disappearing when Elana had her back turned. She took the potted mushroom and mint, so Elana figured the meeting had been successful.

She clambered up the deck railing and hauled herself onto her roof. She'd taken to coming up here as a fully quiet place to think for no reason other than she could, and something struck her as amusing about a vampire sitting on the roof of an unassuming bungalow instead of lording over their domain in a castle tower.

Elana strolled over the shingles and sat next to the decorative chimney with her back to the bricks, looking out at the wide cityscape of Haven.

From this vantage point, she could see the spread of the entire city. The many roofs of Zevenda stretched toward the Citadel at the center, its skyscrapers rising past the wall that encircled them. The monoliths of the King's Archives beyond in Quarto. The glints and glimmers from the architectural marvels of Octava far to her left. The green spaces of Shestoi and Senkyem to her right. Above her soared the spires and leaf-like projections of the canopy, turning Haven from an impressive city into true magnificence.

Beauty and weight settled in Elana's psyche in equal measure. The city's sprawl represented the fantastic wonders and opportunities her future promised, and the immense responsibilities and challenges that lay ahead. Elana flinched from neither, welcoming the awe and the portent. She was Elana Bishop, adept of the House of the SpiderKing, and she would meet and surpass her duties.

As long as she didn't die first, that was.

She slid off the roof and headed back inside. The last thing she wanted was to get sniped two days before her royal presentation. That would be embarrassing.

CHAPTER TWENTY-SIX

Presentation day arrived without any fanfare other than the immediate spike of adrenaline that hit Elana's bloodstream the moment she woke up.

She catapulted out of bed and zipped through her morning routine, making coffee, eggs, and toast like a woman possessed. Her phone was already buzzing with activity, and judging by the number of notifications piled up when she checked it, it hadn't stopped all night.

Elana answered as many messages as she could while cramming breakfast into her mouth. Belinda confirmed that everything was ready for the reception. Matt confirmed that the extra security details were booked for the same—plainclothes guardians who would join the guests and provide protection to Elana and the numerous high-ranking attendees.

Valeria told her not to skip her training session that morning. Elana scoffed at that one, then read the follow-up and blushed.

I said don't skip it.

Arguing with the Arbiter of Shadows was a bad idea, so…

Aldric sent an email with an update on all the clever ways he'd stuck wrenches in House Veridian's dealings so they'd be slow as molasses in trying to get anything done when she challenged them.

Vivian's daughter sent a message on her behalf with a recipe for a tea that Vivian recommended Elana drink half an hour before the ceremony. *Weird, but okay.*

Lucia sent a triple-encrypted file with more information on the East Coast Staker that had nothing to do with the day's events except the postscript, "Looking forward to seeing you today."

Elana chuckled. Lucia was all business, except when by the pool.

Cathy sent a short note letting her know she'd be by after lunch with Elana's robes. She'd gotten them from Valeria so Arturo could make the necessary alterations.

Vicky sent a text filled with party hat and grin emojis, then a follow-up saying she wished she could be there as Her Royal Spideriness' lady-in-waiting.

Elana chuckled. She also wished Vicky could be there. Her best friend's jet-setting lifestyle had never bothered Elana when she'd been busy day in, day out on job sites. Now, when she was neck-deep in high society instead, she wanted Vicky at her side making sage recommendations to keep her sane. Belinda was a great addition to her friend circle, but there was something about the people who'd gone through life with you.

Also, she suspected Vicky and Belinda would *adore* each other.

Elana drummed her fingers on her kitchen island, contemplated her toast crumbs, and wondered if Vicky would ever want to become a vampire.

She glanced at the little bubble reading **9+** on her messages app. She'd gone through all the messages from her friends and allies, but hadn't touched the million and one notifications and queries from the people she'd engaged for the afternoon's festivities. None of it was likely to be urgent, mostly heads-ups and requests for confirmation, but right now she felt a step from overwhelmed.

Elana tapped Matt's contact card and hit Call. The line rang for several seconds before it clicked and he picked up.

"Morning. Everything okay?"

She sighed and hung her head. "My feet are so damn cold and I am two seconds from calling all of this off, and I *just* woke up."

Matt hummed in understanding. "I hear you. It's gonna be okay. Deep breaths, all right? You've prepared *everything*. All you have to do now is walk in, kneel, say your piece, and walk back out. You'll be *fine*."

"As long as I don't get shot."

"A parahealer team will be waiting in the wings. I promise, you'll make it out of today alive. Don't let Valeria's doom and gloom get in your head."

"If you say so."

"I do say so. Now, tell me again about the menu for the reception. Rumor has it you ordered *octopus puffs*?"

Elana chortled. "Belinda's idea. They're a new thing from this avant-garde eatery in Shestoi…"

Elana focused solely on breathing and stared blindly at the back door into the king's court throne room. She had to wait for the eight chimes. Then she would enter.

This room was dark, almost pitch black. There was little need for light when you were a vampire, and when you were just waiting… She would have been nervous about someone sneaking in to kill her if Valeria hadn't posted Shadowguards *and* Chimeras at the entrance, and if the room wasn't tiny. There was barely enough room for *her* in here.

Her robes rustled as she nervously shifted. They weighed more than the ceremonial robes for the First Progression had—no surprise, since they were heavy velvet and fur. PETA would have a field day, but right now the smooth white fur at her collar was oddly comforting.

The black fabric garbed Elana in a complex pattern of wrapped and draped sections. Looking at herself in the mirror earlier, Elana had been struck by the resemblance to something caught in a spiderweb. She was trying to reframe it as her being the spider in the center of the web, which she suspected was the actual point of the design, but her continued worry about, you know, *being assassinated* colored the rest of her thoughts.

She would flip the long hood with its thin fur border over her head before she entered. The symbolism presented her as being in shadow, then revealed and illuminated. The black fabric would somehow turn white on cue. Elana had helped out behind the scenes at a couple of community theater shows and she'd never seen quick changes quite like that. The vampire insistence that what they did wasn't magic sometimes stretched the limits of the imagination.

The low pitch of a tolling bell interrupted her thoughts.

She closed her eyes and drew one last deep breath as she counted the eight chimes.

On what would have been the ninth, the door in front of her opened soundlessly and she stepped into the king's court with the eyes of all assembled glued to her.

The king's court was only accessible at the king's pleasure. An entrance platform would appear in the center of the king's sigil in the consulate's atrium, and attendees would descend one by one into the chamber. If the king didn't want you inside, the platform wouldn't move. It hadn't happened that day, thank God. That was a political disaster Elana didn't want to deal with yet.

The platform deposited people in the center of the court, which was a small amphitheater where the back half was filled with tall bleacher-style seating five rows high. A few dozen people comfortably fit in the room. The front half was empty except for the throne, a curving, arachnoid seat carved from a single block of black marble lightly shot through with silver and white. Anyone sitting in it would be dwarfed by its height, since it stood easily eighteen feet tall.

The ceiling soared another twenty-plus feet above, its vaulted heights invisible in the darkness. Similar to the royal temple, the room was largely unlit. Unlike the temple's censers, the king's court glowed with a faint red light that did not emanate from any particular location. The effect was incredibly creepy, and it was not mitigated by the thick red banners hanging on the walls behind the throne, emblazoned with the king's sigil in black. If anything, the banners made it creepier.

Elana entered beside the tiers of seats and slowly walked toward the throne. Scattered around the half-circle were seven of the eight arbiters, a selection of high-ranking consorts, and her closest allies. Everyone was focused on her except Valeria, who stood in front of the throne and stared straight ahead.

Valeria had been even cagier than usual about her role in the afternoon's proceedings. She was acting as the stand-in for the SpiderKing, who never showed himself in public. However, she hadn't made it clear whether she was acting in his name or if he was somehow telling her what to do during the ceremony.

Elana reached the center of the room. She turned to face Valeria and knelt on the polished floor. The loose fabric of her robes pooled around her and the silence pounded against her eardrums.

She glanced up at Valeria. Was it the weird light in the room, or were the arbiter's eyes glowing faintly?

"Elana Danielle Bishop, you are summoned before the king's court," the arbiter intoned. Her voice was naturally amplified by the room, her words bouncing off the marble walls without any seeming mitigation from the curtains.

"I answer the summons." Elana managed to keep the quaver out of her voice.

Something changed. The air became electric and Elana caught her breath as all the hair on the back of her neck and her arms stood on end. The light that suffused the room brightened a degree, and much like in the royal temple, Elana felt like her robes were lifting slightly. If she didn't have a hood on, she'd expect her hair to float off her shoulders.

The change was not limited to the atmosphere. When Valeria continued, her voice sounded as though it echoed directly in Elana's ears. "In the eyes of all gathered, today you shall be officially joined to the House of the SpiderKing as the issue and lineal successor of Tessa Marceline Hart, with all rights and responsibilities inherent therein. You will become an heir to the royal House of Haven. You will be responsible for its well-being and continued success. Your life and those of your Rights-given issue will be subject to the same.

"Do you consent to these terms?"

Elana's head swam. The red tinge over her vision was brighter than she thought it ought to be, and the floor under her knees vibrated. Again, like in the temple, *something was happening.* While part of her was awed by it, the other part was bothered that she wasn't allowed to know what that *was* yet.

Someday, she promised herself. *Someday, I will know.*

"I do," she responded.

"Then be it known to the consulate and consorts of Haven, to those allies who attend in your support today, and to all citizens of Haven that Elana Danielle Bishop is hereby presented as a full member of the House of the SpiderKing, royal House of Haven, to all those privileged to be given the Rights."

Valeria said something in a language Elana didn't recognize, and the warmth that had been growing within her surged to a fever pitch. When her vision cleared, her robes were white as snow and the red in the room was gone.

Elana stood on shaky legs and turned to face the assembly. Her allies and friends smiled and clapped, some more raucously than others. The arbiters all politely applauded—although Elana spotted several with mild distaste in their gazes and tension around their mouths.

They don't all have to like you. You just have to do your job.

She stepped forward and the platform rose underneath her. Elana would be the first person out of the court, marking her entrance into Haven society as a fully fledged member of the royal House. Valeria suspected this would be the prime moment for the assassination attempt—this, or Elana stepping out of the consulate's doors.

Either would be a monumentally stupid move on the part of House Veridian, considering Haven's ironclad law against weapons being used in the Neutral Zone of the Citadel. They were kind of banking on Veridian being idiots.

Elana was almost disappointed when she reached the consulate's atrium, then the exterior courtyard without anyone trying to kill her. Instead, she emerged to a crowd of clamoring reporters and cheering onlookers, and she was incredibly grateful for Matt's reassuring presence at her back a couple of moments later.

"No comment at this time, thank you," he kept repeating as he shepherded her through the pack toward the king's gate exit of the Citadel. From there, a royal car would whisk her off to the reception in Shestoi, where a group of merrymakers at least this numerous would be waiting. She'd have to talk to them, unfortunately, but hopefully by then she'd have her wits about her.

Matt guided her to the large limousine waiting outside the Citadel's wall, then followed her in. As the driver glided away, Matt indicated a garment bag hanging nearby. "Your reception outfit is there. Zizi outdid himself this time, I gotta say."

"Thanks." Elana mechanically exchanged the complex robes for the short, flowing dress Zizi had dreamed up. Its asymmetrical hem fell to her knees and moved with and past her as though it were dancing all on its own.

Elana never would have seen herself wearing this bright a red—it wasn't tomato red, it was candy apple—but the eye-popping color made a great contrast with her light skin and dark brown hair. The movement of the dress matched the movement of her new hairstyle. The simple, strappy, stiletto heels in the same color as the dress made her feel like she was a footloose, fancy-free *femme fatale* out on the town.

She slipped the ruby chandeliers into her earlobes, then clasped the matching pendant around her neck and argued with the bracelet until Matt took pity on her.

"You look amazing," he informed her. "You could have walked out of the pages of *Vogue*."

Elana absentmindedly fiddled with the bracelet. "Thanks," she repeated. "Do I look *royal*, though?"

Matt chuckled. "Yeah, because you *are*. It's in your eyes, when you stop looking like a deer in the headlights. Honestly, Elana, if I didn't know your parents were born human, I'd have pegged you for a Rights-born. This comes naturally to you, when you let it. So *let it*."

"Easier said than done," Elana muttered as the limo coasted to a halt.

Belinda's team had decked out the patio pub in red and black, the royal colors. Banners and streamers hung from every light post and all the table umbrellas had been swapped out for custom-made ones with black spiderwebs on red. The wait staff were in tuxedos with red ties and black gloves, and each table was covered in an original lace spiderweb tablecloth. No two were alike. They'd been a gift from Arturo, and as much as Elana didn't count herself among the goth girls, she'd fallen in love with them immediately.

Elana was proud of the themed menu. The aforementioned octopus puffs were an example of the theme of eights. Also included in that category were mini pizzas with toppings depicting the phases of the moon, as well as honest-to-God deep fried spiders. Elana knew she'd have to eat one for show, but she was *not* looking forward to it.

The next theme, less royal and more Elana, was electricity. This was being represented by an array of electric eel sushi, chicken wings that packed a truly thunderous amount of spice, and the signature cocktail, the Bishop. The latter was blue Curaçao and vodka in a glass rimmed with pop rocks. Vicky had thought that detail up, and it had made Elana laugh so hard she couldn't argue with it.

On the sweet side, guests could avail themselves of chocolate truffle spiders—which did *not* have real spiders in them—and cream puffs filled with tangy citrus crème…

and more pop rocks. There was also a massive croquembouche in the shape of the Citadel, because the dessert chef hadn't been able to keep from showing off. Elana didn't care. It was stunning.

She and Matt were the first ones there apart from the wait staff, security, and back of house crew. Although to be more precise, they were the first ones allowed entry. The queue for general admission after everyone on the guest list had arrived was already around the block.

Elana stared as they drove by. "I have *never* seen a lineup in Haven. Did I do something wrong? Am I gonna get written up in the tabloids for being a shitty host?"

Matt laughed. "Quite the opposite. No one's been talking about anything but your reception since the royal presentation was announced. This is the hottest event of the century, possibly even of the last three centuries.

"There are no lineups in Haven because there's rarely anything this new and interesting. Most high society parties are the same old, tired repetitions of banquets, ballrooms, and blowhards. Yeah, occasionally someone throws a rager, but those are almost always limited to your closest friends…or the ones you can trust not to kill you while you're so drunk you can't see straight."

"Doesn't it take a *shit-ton* of alcohol to do that to a vampire?"

"Oh yeah. Unless you're an initiate, in which case nobody goes to your parties because you're trying too hard."

"But I'm an adept. That's not much better."

"Ah, but you're a *royal* adept, and you're doing things differently without being a jackass about it. You're including everyone and respecting traditions while introducing new ideas."

They parked around the back of the pub, then entered through the back door and slipped through the kitchen and the closed front-of-house to get onto the patio without going past the line outside. It was showtime. If House Veridian planned to make a move, Elana suspected it would be here.

Belinda met them at the door. She wore what could only be described as a club outfit taken up to eleven—a tight leather jacket, a crop top, ripped jeans, and platform boots. She had accessorized with draping chains of diamonds, matching chandelier earrings hanging to her jacket collar, and enough rings to turn her hands into lethal weapons. The crop top featured her House sigil, an intricate floral design that resembled a peony with swirled petals.

"I'll give you ten minutes to get settled in your corner, then open the gate," she told Elana. "You ready for the craziest party of the year?"

Elana gave her a wide-eyed look of terror. "Yes?"

Belinda patted her on the shoulder and winked. "You'll be fine. Everyone's gonna tell you how wonderful you are because they wanna get in your good graces. Just be nice to everyone, smile and nod. Bask in the attention, don't promise anyone anything. Clear as mud?"

Elana nodded. "Yeah. I can do that."

"Perfect. Have a drink to loosen up, but no more than two. The more you remember from the people who drink too much, the better it'll go for you. Now get out there."

Belinda nudged Elana toward the door. Elana allowed

the inertia to propel her through and out onto the patio, where the line of hopeful guests erupted in cheers like the crowd outside the Citadel had.

Elana blinked in the sudden onslaught of flashing cameras. Matt's gentle hand on her lower back moved her forward and through the scattered tables and gathering areas to the raised platform at the other end, which was sheltered by subtly reinforced fences and covered by a bulletproof parasol. Any attackers would have to come at her from the front. The bouncer was a Chimera veteran who was almost wider than the patio gate and twice as scary as any gargoyle, so Elana didn't see that happening.

The guests of honor arrived first. The arbiters couldn't forgo attendance without looking terribly gauche no matter how much this wasn't their style of party, although Arbiters Amindóttir and Mélissand appeared mildly excited. Her allies were a different story. Cathy was game for anything as usual, Aldric had more color in his cheeks every time Elana saw him, Lucia seemed downright *ravenous*, and Vivian had a sly mischief about her face that intrigued Elana to no end.

The coterie greeted Elana formally, then Elana officially opened the party, and the *crème de la crème* of Haven's elite slipped away to socialize in typical fashion while the rest of the guests surged in.

Vivian stayed near Elana in one of the other secluded booths and rapidly gained another small court as she had at the housewarming party. Aldric started out with her, then ended up in a lively conversation about cryptocurrency alternatives with a handful of vampires who couldn't have been older than Elana. Lucia floated through the crowd making desultory conversation with everyone and undoubtedly gaining more insight from said small talk than any interrogation.

Cathy swooped in to welcome Arturo when he arrived twenty minutes late. They led the charge in getting everyone to try the deep fried spiders, much to Elana's chagrin, although it quickly turned into a drinking game with the wilder crowd.

This kicked off the party for real. The decibel level went from calm but steady conversation to loud laughter and cheering, and more than one chorus of "Hail to the SpiderKing!" went up in waves across the patio.

Elana raised her glass to each one and cheered along but did not move from her location on the dais. As Belinda had predicted, everyone on the official guest list and off it wanted to talk to her. The topics of discussion ranged from the ultra-mundane to the extremely specialized. The former included things like farming conditions in Senkyem and the best place to buy bespoke dimensional handbags in Premier. The latter encompassed the cutting edge of art curation in Octava and the most esoteric collections in Quarto.

In every case, Elana's guest wanted to express their best wishes on her presentation—Elana couldn't help but hear "coronation" half the time—and bring her attention to something they thought she ought to know about.

"They know I can't actually give the SpiderKing any advice, right?" she murmured to Matt behind her glass of pop rocks and Curaçao. "Like, they all *know* this is pointless?"

"They don't know that, actually." Matt was the sole

fixture at her table as her primary bodyguard. Valeria was "mingling," which would more accurately be described as constantly drifting around the perimeter while scanning for threats.

The other members of the security team were doing similarly or else engaging the guests in discussion to root out troublemakers. A couple had already been unceremoniously kicked out for not only not being on the list, but for being rude to other guests. Walk-ins were allowed, but only if there was room, and only if they played nice.

"No one knows how the SpiderKing picks who he talks to, or when," Matt continued. "You came out of nowhere and got inducted into the royal House almost immediately. For all they know, you *might* have the king's ear. Even if you didn't, your endorsement as Havenite royalty carries immense weight."

"No pressure."

"We'll get you set up with the royal legal counsel next week before you start making ill-advised comments."

A waiter circled up to their table with a tray of the themed hors d'oeuvres. There was no way they could get through the crowds of people wanting to talk to get any food for themselves, so they had a regular rotation of waiters checking in to make sure they were well-fed.

This time, Elana snagged a plate of assorted eel sushi and a trio of the citrus cream puffs. She thanked the waiter and he slipped away into the crowd to continue his rounds.

Elana polished off the sushi in due course while nodding through her latest guest's diatribe. This gentleman, appearing in his forties but speaking like a man from at least two centuries back and with a strong French accent, wanted Elana to understand the advantages of a certain method of kneading bread. He also wanted her to know why that made his Shestoi-based bakery the best in the city.

He was in the middle of explaining their exclusive rising process, and she was in the middle of the second cream puff, when her stomach flipped violently. A frigid chill ran through her followed by the hottest flash of heat stroke she'd ever felt, and the back of her mouth tasted like bile and salt. She was only saved from throwing up on the baker's pristine tan suit and navy waistcoat by Matt's timely intervention.

He whirled her out of the chair and came to his knees beside her as she heaved. The party went silent in seconds. While plenty of partygoers hadn't been actively keeping an eye on Elana, her security detail *had*, and they locked the place down in a matter of heartbeats.

Valeria was beside Matt a breath later. She uncorked a vial while the tattoos on her forearms luminesced and gleamed. "Get her head up," she barked.

Matt did his best to manhandle Elana into position, which was difficult while she was still dry heaving. The contents of her stomach were spattered across the wooden planks, but her body wouldn't quit.

Valeria tossed the contents of the vial down Elana's throat and slammed her mouth shut. She held it closed with both hands until Elana was forced to swallow the clear liquid. A few seconds later, the spasms stopped, and Matt grabbed Elana before she could topple over entirely.

The entire assembly instinctively shrank away from the

Arbiter of Shadows as she rose to her feet and surveyed them.

"No one leaves," she began, but she was interrupted by a reedy throat-clearing from the booth nearest the dais.

Lady Vivian stood next to her chair. She looked every bit the part of the ancient crone in the long, flowing robes, but her hold on the waiter who had served Elana minutes before was tighter than the roots of a centuries-old tree. Tighter even than the lianas of wood that snaked from her arm over his shoulder.

"He had the poison," Vivian calmly stated as the man vainly tried to wrench himself from her iron grip. "I can taste it in his air."

Valeria didn't question the old vampire's pronouncement. "Your House," she demanded of the waiter.

The man struggled in Vivian's grip a moment longer, then gave up and glared at the arbiter. "Veridian," he spat. "And since we have no quarter in Haven, there's nothing you can—"

Elana cut him off, breathless and hoarse but with a core of steel. "I accuse House Veridian of treason against the SpiderKing." She hauled in another breath, then added, "I accuse House Veridian of my attempted murder and of the murder of Tessa Hart. Two counts..." Another gasp of breath. "Two felony accusations means immediate extradition pending challenge. I will...see you...in *court*, you... *motherfucker*."

Elana wobbled, then slumped against Matt and passed out.

CHAPTER TWENTY-SEVEN

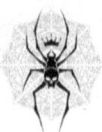

Elana floated in a murky haze. Voices murmured words she couldn't make out. She tried to speak a few times, but her body was sluggish and her tongue wouldn't move.

She felt heavy, as though she were weighed down by a thick blanket...or maybe gravity was stronger. Vampires could probably do stuff like that.

What had happened? Something had happened at the party. She sort of remembered it, like a dream she'd been having before she woke up, except she hadn't woken up. She'd been listening to someone talk about...something... She couldn't remember their face. What House had they been?

Bodes well for your tenure as Havenite royalty if you can't remember the people you talk to, she scolded herself. *That's gonna go over* great.

Elana shushed the tiny critical voice. There was a reason she couldn't remember, a legitimate one. She just couldn't *remember* it.

Matt had been beside her... Then she'd been on the

deck... Her body had gone haywire, she'd thrown up all the sushi she'd just eaten...

Oh yeah. House Veridian poisoned me.

With memory came relief. She remembered Vivian collaring the waiter who'd slipped her the poison. Belinda was no doubt having a field day with her staff, to say nothing of Valeria grilling the security crew. Then again, the point of the royal presentation had been to goad House Veridian into trying to kill her, so maybe they wouldn't get in *too* much trouble.

Mild, fuzzy alarm replaced the relief. She'd been poisoned, and she definitely wasn't awake yet. Was she dead? Was this vampire hell? Or worse, *heaven?* God, if the vampiric afterlife was floating in fog for the rest of eternity, she'd prefer death, thanks. This would get boring *fast.*

What if they'd dosed her with whatever had killed Jacqueline and Miriam de Rothschilde? What if she'd spent days wasting away to nothing in whatever ultra-secure hospital members of the royal House went to, with Matt sitting by her bed and hoping she'd wake up, and no one would ever figure out how she had died?

No, that couldn't be right. Vivian had said she could smell the poison. That would mean they could trace it. Also, Elana had painted a significant section of the pub's patio with the contents of her stomach, which would have had the poison in it. Matt was right there, and so were dozens of Chimeras and Shadowguards. They would have scooped some up for analysis, not that she envied them the job. *Ew.*

Maybe they couldn't find an antidote, or perhaps it had hurt her so badly that she would never wake up. Maybe she was doomed to be a vampire vegetable until someone put her out of her misery.

Hee. Vampire vegetable. The idea made her giggle.

"Welcome back," a familiar sexy voice said.

Matt? Was Matt in the mist too? Oh no, had House Veridian managed to dose him, too? Elana's heart sank. She'd been working so hard to keep everyone else out of the line of fire.

"I'm fine," Matt told her. "Nobody's tried to do anything to me."

Oh. That was good. Wait—had he heard her? Were vampires telepathic?"

Matt chuckled. "No. Well, I'm not. You're speaking out loud, Elana."

Elana blinked in confusion, and the haze cleared, revealing a sterile white ceiling and a number of medical machines lurking in her peripheral vision. Mild sunlight shone from her right, obscured slightly as Matt leaned in from that side and looked her in the eye.

"Good morning, sunshine."

She blinked again. "I'm not dead?"

"You're not dead. Congratulations."

"Thanks?"

Reality gradually settled in as the last bits of memory fell into place. Elana rolled her head side to side and took in the room. It resembled a standard hospital room except the machinery on the walls sported significantly fewer cords and looked like it had come from a sci-fi movie set. She wouldn't have been surprised to see a tricorder straight out of *Star Trek* sitting on a counter.

She attempted to sit up, but Matt put a hand on her

shoulder. "Nice and slow," he cautioned, then pressed his palm to the side of her bed. After a second, it hummed to life and the head of the bed rose at an angle, allowing her to sit without effort. "Better?" She nodded, and he released the interface.

"Thanks." Elana looked out the window behind him. Based on the cityscape beyond, she was in the Citadel, facing Senkyem. The view of the fields, orchards, and greenhouses under the gently undulating canopy relaxed her. *The wind must really be blowing for the canopy to move like that.* Usually, the sail-like leaves of the climate canopy stayed mostly immobile.

"You hungry?"

The question brought her back to Matt. He looked tired, which she didn't think she'd ever seen before. He had bags under his eyes and a crease in his forehead, and he wore the same clothes he'd had on at the party. The simple and elegant suit was in House Richelieu's colors and had a fleur-de-lis pocket square. The jacket wasn't wrinkled, but the pocket square was, and he'd unknotted his tie.

"Not really," she replied. "Have you not gone home?"

"Someone had to keep an eye on you."

Elana narrowed her eyes. "So call in a Chimera or a Shadowguard."

Matt avoided her gaze. "They're busy."

She crossed her arms. "They can't *all* be busy."

He sighed. "Yeah, okay, *fine*. I volunteered and I refused to let anyone spell me until you woke up."

"How long have I been out?"

"Three days," he admitted.

"*Matt—*"

"I was worried about you! That poison was…"

Elana frowned as he looked away again. The corners of his mouth pulled down, and his brow creased with concern. He looked pale and drawn.

"How bad was it?" she quietly asked.

"Bad. Really bad. It was in one of the cream puffs. It ripped through you in seconds."

Elana's heart skipped a beat. He wasn't exaggerating. She'd downed the first cream puff in one bite and the second one had been right on its heels. Seconds after that she'd been on the floor puking her guts out. If it had such dire effects after her body had summarily rejected it…

"That's a little scary," she confessed in a very small voice.

Matt made a sound that could have been a cough or a laugh and shook his head. "You're telling *me*. We got you to the healers in minutes and they still thought you were gonna die."

Elana fiddled with the edge of her blanket. "I'm sorry," she finally offered. "I know we wanted to pull them into the open, but I didn't want to die."

Matt laughed again and scrubbed his hands over his face. "Of course, you didn't. You don't need to apologize. It's *so* not your fault."

"I'm still sorry I worried you."

He gave her a rueful smile. "You might want to save that for Valeria. She's been a *tyrant* for the past three days."

Elana winced. "Uh-oh. Did the Veridian guy take a cyanide pill or something? Are we back at square one?"

Matt shook his head. "Nothing like that. He's in

suspended animation until the challenge trial so nothing like that *can* happen."

Elana's eyebrows shot up. "It shouldn't surprise me that vampires can do that, but *damn*."

"She pulled out all the stops. I think she likes you."

Elana scoffed. "I'm a means to an end."

Matt cocked his head. "Do you really think that?"

Elana blushed, considered her quickly chosen words a second time, then reluctantly shrugged. "It's probably more complicated than that, but I think that's one of the reasons she keeps me so close.

"My mom was her best friend. *Only* friend, depending on who you ask. I can only imagine how devastating it was for Valeria to lose her—then to find out that the people responsible weren't the ones she brought to justice? She's mad. *Furious.* I would be too.

"Me coming on the scene and shaking everything up is a perfect opportunity for Valeria to find out the truth about my mom and her death," Elana continued. "I don't blame her for that. I'd probably do the same thing. I might be a touch less *brusque* about it, but that's me. Valeria is who she is. She's the Arbiter of Shadows."

Matt nodded. "You're not *wrong*, but... You're more than that to her. If you ever tell her I said this, I will deny it to her face, but I think she feels responsible for you."

Elana blinked.

"I'm serious," Matt insisted. "Think about it. You're right, Tessa was Valeria's best friend. You're Tessa's *daughter.* Valeria always blamed herself for what happened to your mom. How could she not? She was already the Arbiter of Shadows then. It was her job to prevent anything from happening to the other arbiters—like, *literally* her job—and your mother was taken out in a *drive-by shooting*. That's not just awful, it's *insulting*.

"Then you show up out of nowhere. Yeah, part of her is mad that Tessa never told her about you, but if there's one thing Valeria understands, it's the need to keep secrets. She's almost certainly forgiven that one by now, ever since you've uncovered how deep this House Veridian conspiracy runs. Tessa was trying to protect you for as long as she could. Now that she can't protect you from Haven, Valeria feels like it's her job to protect you…to be the mom you didn't get to have."

Elana swallowed against the rising lump in her throat. She forced a laugh. "Valeria's not exactly known for her maternal side."

Matt chuckled. "Maybe it would be more accurate to say she's the weird aunt nobody knows how to talk to at family dinners. But she comes through for you with the kick-ass recommendation that gets you into the school you always wanted."

Elana laughed for real. "Yeah, okay, I can see that."

Matt sobered. "So, when I say she's been a tyrant for the last three days…it's not just because she's mad that House Veridian got through with such a dangerous poison. It's also because she feels responsible for not protecting you, and because she likes you and doesn't want you to die."

"And that's the closest Valeria Draven will ever get to an admission of warm and fuzzy feelings," Elana concluded.

"Oh, yes."

Elana ran her hands along the blanket. It was much softer and more comfortable than she would have expected for hospital linens. "I should thank the healers. From what you're saying, that poison should have killed me."

Matt's mouth set in a grim line. "You have no idea. I think I'm still underselling it, to be honest. That poison *should* have killed you. The healers did everything they could, but no one had ever seen it before. They worked through the night to make an antidote. Frankly, it was a miracle you survived until they could give it to you the morning after. Even then, it was still touch and go."

Elana frowned. "Why *didn't* it kill me, if it was that bad? I'm only an adept. It's not like I have much more than the basic regenerative powers."

"That is a *really* good question, and we don't have an answer for it yet," Matt admitted. "Valeria thinks it might have something to do with your vampiric lineage, but she hasn't shared any more of her ideas."

"My vampiric lineage? You mean my mom?"

"Your mom, and the vampire who turned her. We still don't know who that was, so it's damn difficult to trace."

"Can't we do a DNA profile? Doesn't Haven keep records of all vampiric genomes in any House quartered within its jurisdiction?"

"Valeria did that with the first sample you gave her, way back when you hit that Runner. That's how she found out you were Tessa's daughter."

"Okay, so can't we trace that back another generation?"

"Your mother's profile is the first one on file in Haven. Whoever turned her, their profile wasn't in the system. Which means they're either from a House not quartered in Haven, or…"

Elana grimaced. "Or their records have been excised, and we're back into conspiracy land."

"Exactly."

Elana let her head flop back onto the pillow. "Goddammit. Here I hoped this assassination attempt thing would give us more answers than questions."

"If only we were so lucky."

CHAPTER TWENTY-EIGHT

Elana cracked her neck as she walked into the training room, then waved at Gustav, who was tidying the shelves of sporting equipment.

He came over and clapped her on the shoulder. "Elana! Good to see you back. Congratulations on your presentation, and more importantly, congratulations on not dying."

She grinned and gave him a playful punch on the arm. "Thanks. I was almost disappointed the slimy bastard didn't just try to come for me. I didn't get to use any of the stuff I've learned."

Gustav chuckled and shook his head. "*Da.* We cannot punch poison. It is a shame. Ah, well. This means that the next time some unscrupulous soul attempts to do you harm, you still have the element of surprise. Will you be training today, or are you simply here to tell old Gustav you are not dead?"

Elana raised an eyebrow, then sank onto her heels and put up her fists. "Oh, I'm here to train. No taking it easy on me, either."

The trainer eyed her skeptically, then motioned toward the locker room door. "Go change, then. You might have to fight in streetwear someday, but not here."

Elana landed another punch on Gustav's arm and danced back. "What's the deal?" she teased. "I thought I was the one who got poisoned?"

Gustav rolled his shoulder and scowled. "You got lucky."

She laughed. "As long as you're not just being nice."

He scoffed. "When have you ever known me to be *nice*?"

"Well, you're nicer than Tamara…"

Gustav snorted and darted forward, then deked to the left. Elana matched him and swung a roundhouse kick at his head, which he ducked. She followed up with a right hook, which he caught on his forearm and deflected before delivering a jab to her solar plexus.

She grunted and took a step back. She braced herself for the tackle—any time Gustav gained ground, he usually pushed the advantage until she pushed back—but it didn't come.

Elana narrowed her eyes. *He is going easy on me. He's doing a good job of pretending not to, but he's pulling his punches.*

She feinted right, ran left, then hopped up on the ball of her foot and made as though to leap into a flying kick—but instead of doing so, she jumped over Gustav, twisted in midair, and came down on his shoulders with her legs around his neck.

Elana let her weight carry them both down. She absorbed the impact on her shoulder, which hurt, but not so much she couldn't handle it. She squeezed her thighs together and ignored Gustav pounding on them.

She could not ignore him shoving his thumbs into the backs of her knees. She yelped and let go, and he promptly scrambled away across the floor.

Elana was on her feet and after him in a flash. She pounced, aiming to tackle him to the floor and pin him again, but he rolled aside at the last moment and she slammed into the wood all by her lonesome.

She did the same, evading his returning tackle by inches. She hopped up and gave him half a second to get up too. When they were eye-to-eye again, she grinned.

"Told you not to go easy on me," she chided. "Or are you just getting old?"

Gustav growled, but he was smiling. When he squared off against her, she could tell the friendly Russian teddy bear was well and truly on the shelf once again.

Elana fell into the chair across from Matt and groaned. "Ow."

Matt snickered. "I take it you didn't let Gustav go easy on you."

"Duh." She stretched and grumbled again as her muscles complained. "The healers told me I was back to full capacity. It means I have to train that way. My muscles have to get used to it again, which won't take long—but only if I don't let myself slack off."

"You could have taken a *day*."

Elana shook her head. "House Veridian won't have. They've had a whole *week* to do their nefarious deeds without me on the case. I'm behind the eight ball again and need to catch up. No days off for me."

Matt put his elbows on his desk and leaned forward. "You do know that's a terrible way to treat yourself, right? Ever heard of work-life balance?"

They were in his personal office in one of the guardian complexes in Senkyem. One of the public ones, not the secret underground ones, although Elana hadn't seen any civilians in the halls here either. The room was simple with green walls and a large window to the right of Matt's desk. The desk was clearly a family heirloom and must have been a pain in the ass to get in here. Elana didn't envy the crew responsible for *that* moving job.

Elana gave him a look. "I will go back to balancing my life when I'm not facing down assassination attempts and a conspiracy that threatens the foundations of the city I love."

Matt's eyebrows rose. "You've changed a lot in the past couple of months."

"Oh?"

"You feel like you belong here. In Haven."

It wasn't a question, and the certainty of the statement hit Elana with significant force. "I do," she admitted, then repeated it with some surprise. "I do. Huh."

"Do you miss Ashford?"

She pondered this for a moment, then half-shrugged. "I miss not worrying about where the next assassination attempt was coming from, because no one was trying to kill me.

"In some ways, my life as a human was simpler, and I occasionally miss that. But here in Haven, I have a purpose beyond making enough money to pay my bills and my crew. I can make a difference here. I don't think I ever believed I could do that in the human world."

He smiled. "That makes sense. I'm glad to hear it. Finding a sense of purpose is integral to a satisfying life."

Matt hovered a hand over his desk. The familiar blue glow of the interface emerged. From this angle, all Elana saw was blue haze. A privacy filter, she figured. After he had tapped on the interface several times, he flicked whatever he was working on to her side of the desk. The hologram lifted off the dark, polished wood to stand on end.

"Your challenge trial begins tomorrow, as you know," he stated. "I'll be representing you."

Elana eyed him suspiciously. "I knew you were a lawyer, but are you really the legal counsel for the House of the SpiderKing?"

Matt chuckled. "No. But I'm most familiar with the ins and outs of this case, so I'm taking this one. Not to say Noreen couldn't handle it. She's the sharpest lawyer I've ever met. But we're short on time and she's been buried in an argument between the royal House and a subsidiary House of someone over in East Asia about shipping routes. Much easier this way."

"Fair enough." Elana peered at the hologram hanging in front of her. It showed a bullet point list of discussion topics. "Why are wigs on the list?"

Matt's chuckle turned into a deeply amused cackle.

"Because Haven's royal court follows the European royal courts in some ways. We all wear the black robes and wigs, for one."

Elana stared at him. "You're kidding. The ones that look like rolls of toilet paper?"

He snorted. "The very ones."

"Oh, my God. *Why?*"

"Honestly, at this point I think it's to keep us humble. You truly can't feel *too* self-important if you have to show up to work wearing a tent and a pile of toilet paper rolls on your head."

Elana raised her eyes to the ceiling and shook her head. "Has anyone tried to *change* it?"

"Yes, and they get vetoed by the king every time." Matt leaned in a bit more and gave her a conspiratorial look. "I think he thinks they're funny."

Elana groaned. "Okay. Fine. I will suffer the indignity of the silly wig. What else do I need to know?"

Matt gestured on his part of the interface, and the series of bullet points lit up in succession. "Vampire court is extremely orderly. I strongly suggest you only speak when I direct you to, or if the judge requests something of you specifically."

She nodded. "Seems pretty standard. The lawyers do most of the talking in human courts too."

"True, but in vampire court, breaking etiquette can get you killed or worse."

"Do I want to know what's worse than the death penalty?"

Matt grimaced. "Internment."

Elana tilted her head. "I have never heard of that before.

Explain?"

"You know how I told you when you woke up that the House Veridian assassin was in suspended animation?"

"Yeah…"

"Internment is in the same vein, but worse." He put his elbows on the desk again and swiped the glowing list to the side. "Essentially, your body is frozen for a length of time determined by the court. You exist within your mind for that time without any sensory input. You have no way of marking time, because your bodily functions are suspended. You're not asleep, you're not unconscious, you're just…taken out of time."

Elana stared at Matt while this sank in. At length, she stammered, "How… How long do they… How long is a typical internment sentence?"

Matt's grim expression didn't waver. "The worse the crime, the longer the punishment. Your body won't decay while you're interned since you're kept in a capsule that maintains the stasis. 'Small' infractions can result in one to five years."

"And *big* infractions?"

"The longest I've ever heard of was five centuries."

Elana's head spun. She steadied herself on the arm of her chair and gaped at Matt. "*Five centuries?*" she repeated, stunned.

"To my knowledge. Other jurisdictions might have handed down longer."

Elana shook her head in bewilderment. "How do you stay sane?"

Matt shrugged. "People who *have* say they eventually had to cling to one thing they knew for certain, or they would entirely lose themselves in the dreaming and eventual hallucinations. I don't know of anyone who survived beyond a twenty-five-year sentence."

Elana felt very small in her chair, small and insignificant in the face of the ruthlessness of vampire law. "What happens when they come out?"

"To the ones who don't hang onto their sanity? They go into care, if they're in jurisdictions that provide it for convicted felons. Some regain a modicum of their senses with time and exposure to their loved ones and familiar surroundings. Others don't, and they either wither away with the years or they're…quietly disposed of."

"Jesus Christ."

"The ones who don't receive care usually end up dying of exposure or getting into situations that get them back in trouble with the law. Or they're easy marks for unscrupulous vampires wanting a full blood transfusion. Not that there are many former interns on the planet at any given time. Sentences of that length are rare."

Elana swallowed. "I hear you loud and clear. I will not put a *toe* out of line in that courtroom. I will read whatever manual of rules of order is most commonly used and I will memorize every line."

Matt chuckled wryly. "You'd have to fuck up pretty bad to get yourself interned for disruption of the court—like, murdering the judge in plain sight, that sort of deal."

She glared. "Then why'd you even bring it up? You made it sound like if I so much as sneezed at the wrong time, they'd slap me in one of these stasis capsules!"

He sobered again. "Because it's very possible that the assassin will be sentenced to internment, and I wanted you to know what that meant ahead of time. It's also a distinct possibility that even if they're sentenced to death, Veridian will appeal and *request* internment."

"What? Why? I gotta agree with you, internment sounds a hell of a lot worse than death."

"For long sentences, yes. But if Veridian thinks they can argue for a *short* internment, then their guy gets out after a year or two and is free to wreak havoc again. They might think they can rehabilitate him if he goes nuts, or else they'll kill him themselves if he's not.

"There's also the perception of the level of punishment," Matt added. "A lot of vampires, especially younger ones, get hung up on the vampiric promise of immortality. To them, even the slimmest prospect of getting to live beyond your sentence is worth any risk. Not everyone sees the inherent horror as immediately as you did."

Elana shifted uncomfortably in her chair. "Understood."

Matt brought the list back to the center of the desk. "Now, I want to share my plan for presenting the evidence we've accumulated from your mother's journals."

Elana did her best to focus on Matt's game plan, but the butterflies in her stomach were multiplying exponentially. The moment of truth was at hand, where all the evidence against House Veridian would be laid out for everyone to see.

Even if they weren't judged guilty of her mother's murder, it would be damn hard for them to wiggle out of a guilty verdict on Elana's assassination attempt. That would discredit them in the eyes of every House in Haven. If nothing else, the surfeit of evidence would hopefully give the Havenite Houses reason to second-guess their involvement with House Veridian.

What stuck in Elana's throat was that they still didn't know what House Veridian *wanted*. What had they offered all of the Houses they'd secretly allied with, all these Houses who had accepted House Veridian operatives under their wings?

In the end, this was little more than a scare tactic. "We figured out what you were doing, so stop it or else." Or else what?

Elana didn't know. If Valeria knew, she hadn't told her. Elana suspected she would go to bed that night with a stomach still bristling with butterflies.

CHAPTER TWENTY-NINE

Elana did her best to ignore the urge to scratch the spot where the wig irritated her hairline. Overall, the wig was not the worst thing she'd ever worn on her head. That dubious honor went to the headdress she'd worn in her third-grade school play, where she'd played an onion. It was a Thanksgiving pageant and they'd run out of pilgrim costumes.

The robes, on the other hand, were the least pleasant of the ceremonial outfits she'd worn so far in her Haven adventures. They were heavy and didn't breathe. *Probably polyester,* she internally grumbled. *So much for Haven's advanced abilities and attitudes.*

The more she thought about it, the more it made sense. Between Matt's comments about the SpiderKing finding the wigs and robes "funny," and the sheer discomfort of them, she suspected the getup was supposed to make the process uncomfortable. It was an effective way to ensure that nobody wanted to spend more time than was absolutely necessary in the courtroom.

One could only hope that encouraged efficiency, not cutting corners. Although from everything Elana had heard, the SpiderKing was creepily good at knowing when his judiciary was acting in less than the public's best interests.

The courthouse was another building in the Citadel. It was adjacent to the consulate but without any adjoining walls or entrances to symbolize the separation of the legislative and judiciary branches. An odd insistence, Elana thought, since each arbiter took a turn as the head judge.

I guess it's not as obvious a potential overreach of power as it would be if all of them sat on a Supreme Court. This way, if one arbiter rules in a way another arbiter disagrees with, they have to take it up in the consulate rather than freezing up the court.

The courtroom was laid out like the kind you'd see on television, so much so that Elana wondered how many American legal dramas had taken their inspiration from the Haven Royal Courtroom's hallowed halls. Everything was solid wood polished to a honeyed shine, which was a distinct change from so many of Haven's official buildings of carved stone.

The presiding arbiter sat in a box raised about ten feet off the floor. The witness on the stand would sit to the judge's left in a box raised five feet off the floor. The court stenographer was in a matching box on the right—or that's who Elana assumed the slim woman with the handheld tablet interface was.

Haven did not use jury trials. The arbiter was the sole judge of the accused, and they rendered their decision based on the evidence presented by the prosecution and the counterarguments presented by the defense. In this case the prosecution was Elana, represented by Matt and Valeria acting in her capacity as senior representative of the royal House. No spectators were allowed, so no one else was in the courtroom.

Elana sat on the left side of the courtroom, across from the stenographer. Matt sat to her right and Valeria to her left at the huge oak prosecution's desk. Across the aisle, the assassin sat at the matching defense's desk, flanked by two vampires Elana didn't recognize.

The presiding arbiter was Arbiter Amindóttir, which gave Elana some hope. She'd seemed to like Elana well enough every time they'd run into each other, and she hadn't hated Elana's mother.

The door behind the judge's chair, below the king's sigil burned into the wood, opened silently. Elana rose to her feet, as did the others in the courtroom, as Arbiter Amindóttir took her seat.

"Be seated," she told them, and they obeyed. "Scribe?"

"Ready, Arbiter," the stenographer replied. Her voice was tart and reedy.

Amindóttir nodded. Not a lock of her flaxen blonde hair peeked out from under her austere white curled wig. Normally, Amindóttir had rosy cheeks and a faint smile, but today her pointed face was pinched.

"Let the record show that today, we hear the challenge of Elana Bishop of the House of the SpiderKing against Thomas Rysen of House Veridian," Amindóttir proclaimed. "Prosecuting counsel, your opening statement."

Matt stood. "Thank you, Your Honor." He stepped out in front of the large desk and motioned at Elana. "My client has suffered not only at the direct hands of the defendant, but also in an egregious miscarriage of justice by this court."

Arbiter Amindóttir's eyebrow twitched, but she said nothing.

Matt continued. "In the evidence I present to the court today, I will demonstrate how the assassination attempt on my client one week ago was the culmination of a decades-old vendetta by House Veridian against the House of my client. It included the murder of her mother, Tessa Hart, former Arbiter of Sanctuary.

"If the court will recall, this court accused and sentenced two members of House Ateles and two members of House Revidin for the murder of Tessa Hart," Matt reminded those present. "The court failed to consider evidence that House Veridian orchestrated an escalation of the standing disagreements between these two Houses and instigated the incident that led to the death of Tessa Hart."

Arbiter Amindóttir interrupted him. "That evidence was not logged in discovery, counsel. It is impossible to consider evidence of which we were unaware."

Matt acquiesced with a gesture. "An accurate statement, Your Honor, but the fact nevertheless remains that the judgment handed down by this court in the matter of Tessa Hart's unlawful death was inaccurate. I have with me today the Arbiter of Shadows, who will set the record straight with the evidence that *should* have been made available to the court at that time."

He raised a hand to forestall Amindóttir's incoming comment. "We will also explain why it was not entered into discovery in that case."

Amindóttir cocked her head. "This court questions why

counsel characterizes this court's judgment in the case of Tessa Hart to be a miscarriage of justice, if the evidence was unable to be submitted at that time."

Matt smiled. "If you'll indulge me, Your Honor, all in good time."

Amindóttir motioned for him to continue.

"Thank you, Your Honor. To conclude: I will prove today beyond a shadow of a doubt that House Veridian has been conspiring to kill my client for the last three and a half months. I will also prove that they likewise conspired to kill my client's mother for years prior to her death. Together, these proofs will provide sufficient cause to enter a charge of an unlawful blood feud on the part of House Veridian to the House of the SpiderKing."

Matt returned to his seat. "Nothing further, Your Honor."

Elana glanced to her right. The Veridian table appeared nominally calm, but the assassin looked paler, and the female lawyer had folded her hands tightly in her lap. The other lawyer, a short man with thin sideburns and long fingers, seemed unconcerned.

Amindóttir nodded, then turned her gaze to the Veridian contingent. "Defending counsel, your opening statement."

The man stood and moved in front of the desk. "Thank you, Your Honor." His voice was a resonant bass. If he hadn't been arguing on behalf of the man who'd tried to kill her, Elana would have found it soothing. Instead, it sounded portentous, and not in a good way.

He spread his hands in front of him in a placating, or perhaps imploring, gesture. "As high executor for House

Veridian, I can assure the SpiderKing's court that my House takes these accusations with the import they are due.

"While House Veridian has no quarter in Haven, we are of course familiar with the SpiderKing's laws and traditions since Haven is a global power with few equals. Our defense will show that at no time has House Veridian nursed a feud with any member of the House of the SpiderKing. *If* actions have been committed by members of House Veridian against members of Haven's ruling House, it has been without the blessing of our head of House. We have no quarrel with His Arachnoid Majesty."

Elana silently grumbled, *I bet you don't, you slimy bastard.*

Veridian's high executor took his seat again. "Nothing further, Your Honor."

Amindóttir nodded. "Very well. Prosecuting counsel, the floor is yours."

Matt stood, bowed, thanked Amindóttir again, then swiped a hand across his desk to launch the glowing blue interface and send it into the open space between the desks and the judge's box.

Then he dove in, starting with the attempts on Elana's life. He detailed, in chronological order, every time Elana's life had been threatened in the last three and a half months. Matt spent several minutes describing the circumstances of each incident and their connections to House Veridian.

The attack at the gala in Octava included stills from what Elana presumed to be drones or security cameras within the ballroom, showing the assailants first going for Vicky, then Elana as Matt got Vicky to safety.

Matt also submitted vials that *appeared* empty for

Amindóttir to examine. They were trace samples of the gas that had been filtered through the ventilation system to render the other guests insensate so the Veridian operatives could do their dirty work.

He added, "The gas should have made the guests turn on us, but House Veridian hadn't counted on a former Shadowguard being present. Not only am I immune to the mind-altering toxin, but I am capable of casting a shield of protection around a small number of individuals. As a result, I was able to circumvent the systems they had put in place with far less trouble than they had anticipated. After Miss Bishop had incapacitated the assailants, we were able to escape…"

After completing the detailed description of Veridian's tactics in Octava, Matt continued with a rundown of the attack in Senkyem and the vandalism on Elana's new house. Then, before finishing with the assassination attempt at the reception, he listed in rapid succession almost a dozen foiled attacks Elana had known nothing about.

"I anticipate that this extensive list of evidence will prove House Veridian's intentions toward my client without question," Matt stated. "But if the court needs further proof, they need look no further than the events of last week's reception, where the court was present at the time of the attempt."

Elana was too stunned by the revelation of *multiple other attempts on her life* to register much of Matt's detailing of the one she *had* known about. Clearly, Valeria and Matt had decided to shield her from a veritable influx of fuckery from House Veridian. Given how much she'd been dealing with already at the time, she was reasonably certain she appreciated the thought.

They seriously wanted me dead. They tried...thirteen times...to kill me.

Two thoughts struck her in quick succession.

One, they hadn't managed it yet, while they *had* managed to kill her mother.

Two, she had no idea how many times House Veridian *had* tried to kill Tessa before finally getting lucky.

That thought made ice drip down her spine. Elana swallowed hard to avoid betraying any discomfort in her expression. Matt was deep into the events of last week now, discussing the lethality of the poison that had been injected into the Cream Puff of Doom.

"Half the dose would have been enough to kill most vampires," Matt informed the court. "There can be no denying that House Veridian wanted my client dead."

A surge of uncomfortable warmth followed the icy dread as Elana recalled the horrific sensation of her body wanting to tear itself apart from the inside out. By the time she'd wrestled her thoughts back from feeling like she was about to die, Matt was sitting and Valeria was on her feet.

"Four years ago, I stood in front of this court to argue the case against House Ateles and House Revidin against the late Arbiter of Sanctuary, Tessa Hart," she began. "At the time, I could not deny based on my thorough investigation that these Houses were primarily responsible for her death. However, I never shook the conviction that the circumstances were too convenient.

"House Ateles and House Revidin had no personal quarrel with Arbiter Hart, as the court will remember, and gun violence is rare in Haven. For a sitting arbiter to be killed in a drive-by shooting in an inter-House war that had been largely dormant for decades was a strange occurrence indeed, yet I had no evidence to prove otherwise.

"That evidence has come to light over the past three and a half months, thanks to the investigation of Tessa Hart's daughter, Elana Bishop."

Valeria gestured with her right hand and the blue glow of the interface shifted to a portrait of Tessa Hart—a postmortem photo, which made Elana's stomach turn. She'd known Valeria would show the image and was grateful for the advance warning, because the picture was deeply unpleasant.

"Vampires kill each other regularly," Valeria continued. "Although perhaps not with the frequency that humans do. But we tend to opt for less *messy* methods. Had the arbiter's vehicle not been between the SUVs of House Ateles and House Revidin on that fateful day, it is most likely that those involved would have escaped with minor wounds.

"Those would have regenerated in due course. They would have been an annoyance, a message, but nothing more than that. Posturing between Houses with nothing better to do.

"Instead, an incredibly powerful woman was slaughtered without hope of resuscitation. Her gray matter was irretrievable, and thus she could not be healed."

Valeria stared at Amindóttir, but it was all too clear her mental focus was on the trio of Veridian members at the desk beside her. "In the years following Tessa Hart's death, I blamed myself for not being able to find the missing link

—the reason Tessa Hart had died so pointlessly and violently.

"Then her daughter came to my attention late one summer evening."

Valeria went on to explain the treasure trove of information Elana had discovered within Tessa's personal journals, and how she and Matt had pieced it all together to unearth the huge number of connections Tessa had been drawing between House Veridian and so many of the Houses within Haven.

Elana noticed one of the peculiarities of evidence discovery in vampire court. The interface was visible from this side, but it was mildly blurred. Images were clear enough, but text was illegible. Arbiter Amindóttir could read everything, but neither the prosecution nor the defense could.

You were expected to make your case on its own merits, Matt had explained the day before. If you couldn't prove your point, or if the other side presented something you didn't know about, tough luck.

As Valeria detailed the web of connections Tessa had discovered, Elana realized this was a huge boon for them. Valeria was *showing* more than she was telling, another benefit of having a trial with no jury. She didn't have to explain *shit*, because she could trust that Arbiter Amindóttir was smart enough to understand what was in front of her.

On the other hand, House Veridian would walk out of this courtroom *without* knowing exactly how much Elana and company knew about the extent of their conspiracy.

They would only know that it was a *lot*. That seemed like a *fantastic* side benefit to Elana.

It was also handy that chain of custody and the provenance of evidence were not of paramount importance in vampire courts. The onus was on the accused House to counter the charges. Also, arbiters weren't expected to reveal their trade secrets. That was bad business, understood by vampires worldwide.

Valeria sat after discussing Tessa's records and Elana's and Matt's investigations in precisely enough detail to illustrate to Arbiter Amindóttir how wide and deep Veridian's conspiracy went. She did *not* disclose enough detail to alert House Veridian to *which* of their operatives were made. Her face was impassive as ever, and she had delivered her diatribe as though she were discussing nothing of more import than the weather.

Matt stood and bowed to the judge's box. "The prosecution rests, Your Honor."

"Then this court will take a brief recess before hearing the defense's case," Amindóttir announced.

She rose from her seat and exited through the door at the back of her box. After the door closed, the Veridian cohort left the courtroom, then Matt gave it a beat before leading Elana and Valeria out after them. They said nothing until they had sequestered themselves in a small conference room down the hall in the opposite direction from House Veridian's corresponding room.

"How's it going?" Elana asked. She was far too antsy to sit still and was pacing the length of the room.

Matt shrugged. "Hard to say. Arbiter Amindóttir is almost as inscrutable as Valeria."

Elana caught Valeria's slight smirk and chuckled. "What do you think Veridian's case will be?"

Matt leaned back in his chair. "Based on the high executor's opening statement, they planned to pass the blame onto a patsy—someone who could be accused of acting outside of House Veridian's official purview. I'm not so sure they'll be able to do so effectively now."

Valeria laughed quietly, low and satisfied, and Elana raised an eyebrow. "Why's that?"

"They'd have to throw someone pretty high-ranking under the bus to make it believable, given the scope of the conspiracy we illustrated," Matt explained. "It would be remotely believable that some low-level Veridian lackey had it out for you, and even your mother, but to organize something on this scale… If they tried to pass off that it was anyone below a guardian—and in my opinion, even that would push credulity—they'd be stupid *not* to think we wouldn't believe them and therefore keep digging."

"And they don't want us to dig," Elana finished. "They want this done without repercussions."

"Exactly," Valeria confirmed. "They will want this to go away with a minimum of consequences, as would we all."

Elana nodded. "How long will the recess be?"

"Usually about fifteen minutes," Matt told her. "Long enough for Amindóttir to review what we gave her and make notes about anything she wants to follow up on before rendering judgment."

"Does that happen often?"

Matt shrugged. "In cases that aren't clear-cut, sure. Unless Veridian comes back with something that blows us out of the water, which I very much doubt will happen, I don't see her needing much in the way of confirmation."

He smiled in a warm way that made Elana stop pacing. "You've done *really* well, Elana. All the preparation and research you did to get to this point was worth it. Our case is the next best thing to airtight, and it's only *not* airtight because no case ever can be, in my humble and experienced opinion.

"So have a seat, take a breath, and relax. We are *well* on our way to having this Veridian business over and done with, and your mother's legacy given the respect and understanding it deserves."

Elana pasted on a smile, blew out a breath, and sank into a chair. She knew he was probably right, but she *also* knew you didn't count your winnings before the other guy at the table played his hand.

Back in the courtroom, after officially reopening the trial, Arbiter Amindóttir called House Veridian to the floor. The high executor stood, but he did not launch into an explanation of why his House was innocent of the crimes they were being accused of.

Instead, he announced, "House Veridian summons Marcus Favreau to the stand."

Elana glanced at Matt, but neither he nor Valeria made any indication whether this was as much of a surprise as Elana thought it was. The courtroom door opened behind them, and a tall, thin man who appeared to be in his late fifties strolled up the center aisle and up the steps to the witness stand.

Marcus Favreau's face was as thin as his frame. His dark brown hair was thick and short, and neither it nor his beard had any gray in it. The only clue to his biological age were the light crow's feet at the corners of his eyes, and a couple of creases in his forehead. His skin had a mild ruddy tint, and his overall demeanor hinted at a life with plenty of enjoyment.

He was nonchalant and unconcerned about being in the highest court of a foreign city-state. If Elana imagined herself in his place, she'd have been quaking in his Italian leather shoes, but he was as cool as a suited cucumber.

Amindóttir waved in front of her and a blue glow appeared out of sight behind the frame of her box. Based on where she was looking, Elana assumed she'd called up an interface that showed her Marcus' face so she didn't have to crane her neck down over the side of the box.

"Witness, state your name, House, and level for the court record," she instructed.

"Marcus Favreau, House Veridian, sentinel," he rattled off.

Elana kept her frown internal. This felt too easy. Something wasn't sitting right with her about this guy.

The scribe tapped their interface, and the blue glow below Arbiter Amindóttir's face brightened briefly.

"Sentinel Favreau, this court recognizes you as a guest witness on behalf of House Veridian in the matter at hand." Amindóttir looked at the high executor. "Defense counsel, you may continue."

The short man nodded. "Thank you, Your Honor.

Sentinel Favreau, if you would be so kind as to read your prepared statement."

Matt shifted in his seat, then stilled. Elana had caught it too. *Prepared* statement, he'd said. Were they so confident in their defense that they were still going with Matt's theorized plan of a scapegoat? Did House Veridian know something the House of the SpiderKing did not?

Marcus cleared his throat. "I, Marcus Amadeus Favreau, sentinel of House Veridian, hereby confess to ordering Thomas Rysen to kill Elana Bishop on the afternoon of October eighth, 2024. All previous attempts on her life were orchestrated by me and carried out by operatives acting on my behalf. I further confess to orchestrating the death of Tessa Hart four years ago in similar fashion.

"I was not acting at the behest of Cherry Vino, the head of House Veridian," he continued. "She did not condone my actions and was unaware of them. I am solely responsible for the charges brought before this court today and accept whatever punishment Your Honor deems appropriate."

When he finished, silence rang through the courtroom. It was all Elana could do not to let her jaw hit the desk. Matt had called it, but she was stunned they'd gone ahead with the ploy—no, *gobsmacked* was a better word.

Could a sentinel weave that web? Elana asked herself. She had reservations. Matt was a sentinel. He was undoubtedly well-connected and extremely good at his many jobs, but Elana thought they would need someone with power and experience like Valeria's to pull off a conspiracy the likes of which Tessa had uncovered.

Maybe House Veridian was stupid enough not to have

guessed how much they knew. Or maybe the conspiracy went so far that not even the high executor knew about it. Both options seemed more likely to Elana than them thinking this ploy would actually *work*.

"Let the record show that Sentinel Favreau has made his statement," Amindóttir announced. "Witness, you may step down."

Marcus did so and took a seat next to Thomas. The female lawyer had not returned with them, Elana realized. That struck her as odd, but she couldn't remember the finer points of vampire court etiquette to know for sure.

"Does counsel have any further evidence to add to their case?" the arbiter inquired.

The high executor bowed. "No, Your Honor. The defense rests."

He sat. Next, there would be another recess while Arbiter Amindóttir deliberated. When she called them back, she would either ask questions or deliver her ruling, then—

Amindóttir interrupted Elana's thoughts. "This court finds Marcus Favreau guilty on the charge of the attempted murder of Elana Bishop, adept of the House of the SpiderKing. It also finds him guilty on the charge of the murder of Tessa Hart, emissary of the House of the SpiderKing and Arbiter of Sanctuary. This court finds Thomas Rysen guilty on the charge of the attempted murder of Elana Bishop, adept of the House of the SpiderKing.

"This court further finds House Veridian guilty on the charge of conspiracy against the House of the SpiderKing.

"This court sentences Marcus Favreau and Thomas

Rysen to death for their crimes and their complicity in the crimes of their House."

Elana jolted in her chair. She couldn't help it. An immediate sentencing, and the *death penalty* at that? This was almost unheard of.

She glanced across the room at the murmuring and shuffling at the other table. Marcus' and Thomas' mouths were open in shock, and Thomas looked like he was about to protest. That was their right—a successful protest would take the case to the appeals court, where a second arbiter would oversee either a supervised duel or a second hearing of the case.

Before Thomas could get a word out, the high executor unsheathed a sword and whirled to his right. With a flash of green light, he beheaded Marcus and Thomas at the same time. Blood splattered on the gleaming wooden railing behind him and across the huge desk, then two heads hit the floor with a pair of almost-synchronized *thuds*.

Elana jumped. She stared at Marcus' unblinking eyes. He still looked surprised. She couldn't blame him.

The high executor wiped his sword on his robes, then slid it back into its scabbard and bowed to Arbiter Amindóttir. "House Veridian bows to the king's justice."

Elana's heart pounded. She tore her gaze from the corpses, which had slumped in their chairs, and looked at Matt and Valeria. This was a good thing, right? It had to be. Maybe Marcus had *thought* he was getting away with it, but House Veridian *hadn't* actually condoned the conspiracy and *did* want to root it out at its source.

Based on the tiny narrowing of Matt's eyes, that was not the case.

Elana forced herself to return her attention to Arbiter Amindóttir. Technically, she wasn't supposed to look anywhere else at any time, although how you were supposed to *not* look when two people got beheaded with one sword stroke was beyond her.

Arbiter Amindóttir regarded the high executor of House Veridian levelly. "This court recognizes the fulfillment of its sentence in the matter of Marcus Favreau and Thomas Rysen. Today's business is concluded."

She stood and left through the back door. The high executor strode out the main entrance, leaving the bodies of his compatriots behind without a second glance.

Matt, Elana, and Valeria followed a moment after, although Elana lagged when her gaze caught on Thomas' disembodied head. A week ago, he'd tried to kill her.

Valeria cleared her throat behind her, and Elana hurried to follow Matt out of the courtroom. She couldn't shake the feeling that this wasn't over yet.

CHAPTER THIRTY

"I don't understand," Elana protested once they were all back in Valeria's office. The moment the door had closed, Matt's and Valeria's faces had turned to thunderclouds. "I mean, I *sort of* understand why we're pissed off. They 'got away with' the scapegoat plan, which means they snuck something by us. Right?"

Matt sighed heavily. "Essentially. That Arbiter Amindóttir sentenced them both to death is no surprise. They killed one scion of the royal House and tried to kill another. Death was kind of the minimum.

"But we expected Veridian to protest and appeal for internment rather than execution, and for the sentencing to be carried out by Haven."

He growled under his breath, and Valeria exhaled sharply in response.

Elana frowned. "Why would anyone request internment instead of execution? It's horrible, and nobody comes out okay."

Matt grimaced. "It's like we talked about yesterday. A

lot of people believe that as long as you're *alive*, you still have a chance."

Valeria scoffed. "They would have pushed for internment for the 'chance' to try springing their poor idiot from the guardians' holding cells. Utterly futile, but people still try."

Elana crossed her arms. "Except they didn't do any of that, so all of this is immaterial. Instead, they killed *both* their lackeys without blinking and walked out like they didn't care. *Why?*"

"My best guess is that they want us to believe they're above board," Matt replied, then raised his hands placatingly at Elana's incredulous look. "It's the only thing that makes sense."

"You *almost* have it, Mister Richelieu, but not quite," Valeria corrected. "That is the *public* ploy, yes. To anyone who does not know the full story, what happened today shows that House Veridian abides by Haven's laws without question. When faced with accusations of crimes against a foreign city-state, they complied entirely with extradition, induced confessions from those involved, and excised the problem promptly and without complaint. *Now*, in the public eye, we have no grounds for further action.

"*But*, if you'll recall, Arbiter Amindóttir *was extremely* specific in her judgments," Valeria added. "Do you recall them, Miss Bishop?"

Elana thought back. "She said that the court was satisfied with the outcome of the sentences against Marcus and Thomas."

"What did she say about House Veridian?"

Elana's frown deepened as she racked her brain, then

the answer hit her like a poisoned cream puff. *Too soon? Nah...* "She said the court found Thomas and Marcus guilty, but she *also* said the court found *House Veridian* guilty—and she didn't say anything about *that* verdict being satisfied before she dismissed court!"

"*Exactly.*" Valeria's disgruntled scowl transformed into a predatory grin. "She *also* said nothing about an actual *sentence* for House Veridian. She left that wide open. It's hardly our fault that the high executor was so pleased with his little plan that the big picture went right over his head."

Matt chuckled. "Somebody at House Veridian will be *very* angry when they review that record."

Elana frowned. "Does that mean we can do anything we want to them? That seems too good to be true."

Valeria shook her head. "It means we keep digging. I showed Arbiter Amindóttir everything she needed to see to know that House Veridian was planning *way* beyond killing you and your mother. I expect she delivered the swift sentence in the hopes that the high executor would be spurred to move just as swiftly and miss what she hadn't said."

The Arbiter of Shadows' eyes gleamed with dark promise. "It is the arbiters' duty to protect Haven at all costs. We will not allow this rot to go unchecked. The high executor's hasty act will show anyone with two brain cells that Marcus and Thomas were scapegoats, made an example of so everyone else keeps their mouths shut. Luckily, I am *very* good at making people share secrets without them realizing it."

Elana shivered. Whoever was on Valeria's hit list... Well, she certainly didn't want to be them.

"I thought I might find you here."

Elana started and looked over to see Valeria standing on a second floating platform next to hers. You couldn't hear footsteps coming without footsteps to hear, unfortunately. "Hi. Am I late for something?"

"No, no." The arbiter turned to admire the portrait of Tessa, which Elana had been staring at moments before. "I was on my way to a meeting and wanted to see you first if I could."

"Oh? Something I can help you with?"

Valeria shook her head. "Not today. You've already helped more than you can imagine, honestly, and I trust you know I don't give praise lightly."

No shit. "Thank you. I'm glad to help." She glanced at the portrait. "I have to. For me—I couldn't leave this unsolved and not put right—but also for her."

Valeria hummed and nodded. "I understand. For what it's worth, Elana, you've done very well the last four months. Your mother would be proud."

Elana blushed, and her throat tightened. "Thank you," she repeated, then swallowed against the growing lump in her throat. "Do you really think so?"

Valeria looked Elana straight in the eyes, ice-blue to warm brown. "I don't just think so. I *know* so. Your mother never told me about you, but I know what made her happy, and fighting for justice and truth topped the list. She would be *extremely* proud of you."

Elana couldn't speak. She nodded instead and blinked to hide the tears.

Valeria gazed at her late friend's portrait a heartbeat longer, then inhaled sharply and nodded. "Well. I need to get to that meeting. I'll see you at the training grounds tomorrow."

The Arbiter of Shadows descended to the gallery floor, leaving Elana in the company of the late Arbiter of Sanctuary's portrait.

A few moments after Valeria had left, Elana took a shaky breath. A single tear slipped down her cheek as she stared at her mother's face.

"That's all I want," she whispered. "To make you proud."

Valeria waited until precisely ten seconds to noon, then strode across the Citadel courtyard with purpose. At the moment the clock struck twelve, she crossed the exact center of the open circle, and between one footstep and the next she descended several hundred feet.

Her foot landed on smooth marble instead of cobblestone. When her second foot joined it, she stopped moving and stood silently in the near-black tinged through with red, like the color inside your eyelids if you closed them on a sunny day.

She saw nothing in this place and did not expect to. She did not know if there was anything to be seen, and she was either kept from seeing it or simply unable to do so. Perhaps she would have been unable to comprehend what lay around her if she had been able to see. She did not know. It was not her job to know.

It *was* her job to listen.

Valeria stood in that central place and listened. After some time—she could not have told you how long. Sometimes when she left here seconds had passed, sometimes hours—a voice deeper than the ocean with a rough, vocoder-like edge emanated from all around her. It made her sternum buzz and her insides quake. Although she had been doing this job for centuries, there yet remained a sliver of her brain that told her to prostrate herself before this being, for what else could it be but a god?

She remained upright and listened to her king's words.

"I am pleased. Your work with young Elana is commendable. She progresses well."

"Thank you, Your Majesty."

"More enemies lurk within my city. The sentinel and the savant were pawns."

"Undoubtedly, Your Majesty."

"Follow them. Uncover their trail of lies and burn it out at its source."

"It will be done, Your Majesty."

"Make sure young Elana is prepared to protect herself. Do not allow her to be lost."

"Yes, Your Majesty."

"Go now, my Arbiter of Shadows, and balance the light, that all may find balance and peace within my walls."

"I serve at His Majesty's pleasure."

A breath, a blink, and Valeria stood once again in the center of Citadel Plaza, the red room having melted away as though it never existed.

Valeria swallowed against the lingering taste of iron in the back of her throat as she continued toward the consulate and the next meeting on her endless list.

AUTHOR NOTES - MICHAEL ANDERLE

OCTOBER 7, 2024

First, thank you for not only diving into this story but also taking the time to read these author notes at the back. I appreciate you hanging around to let me chat with you, just a little!

The Quest for WriteHalla

So, the other day, I told someone they'd accomplished enough in their career to earn a seat in 'WriteHalla'—that's right, escorted by Odin himself to a grand hall where wine and keyboards abound, and the party lasts until the end of time.

But then I got to thinking—what would WriteHalla actually look like? Let's be honest, keyboards as table settings don't quite do it for me, and wine isn't exactly my drink of choice (unless you count that very, very occasional Drambuie when the mood strikes).

How about this instead: chili and Big Red? Yes, you heard me right. Or maybe pizza and an ice-cold Coke?

Perhaps a hearty roast with a tall glass of iced tea? Now we're talking!

Imagine a massive, sprawling castle with endless wooden bookshelves housing over a million books. A haven where we authors can lose ourselves—rooms filled with stories waiting to be discovered or written. There'd be areas of complete silence for when you need to noodle over a plot twist, and zones buzzing with energy for when you crave a bit of company.

Trust me, authors are a diverse bunch. I've been to some of the parties and get-togethers, and let me tell you, the romance writers know how to make even the most seasoned among us blush.

(I had to step out quick more than once. I blush really easily!)

Back to WriteHalla.

We'd have all the technology we could dream of, with ways to read anything and everything we want. And here's a fun twist—the weather changes depending on which direction you go. North, south, east, or west, you pick the climate that suits your fancy. Fancy a snowy backdrop while you delve into an epic fantasy? Head north. Craving some sun and warmth? South it is!

WriteHalla... I'm definitely down for it.

It's a delightful thought, isn't it? A place where we can indulge in our favorite foods, surrounded by endless stories, with the perfect weather to match our mood. Maybe it's a bit of escapism, but isn't that what we do best? We create worlds we'd love to inhabit, even if just in our minds.

Here's to dreaming big, to chili and Big Red, and to the

hope that one day we might just find our own version of WriteHalla.

Until then, I'll keep writing and sharing these adventures with you. I hope they bring a bit of joy and perhaps a smile or two.

Ad Aeternitatem,
  Michael Anderle

BOOKS BY MICHAEL ANDERLE

Sign up for the LMBPN email list to be notified of new releases and special deals!

https://lmbpn.com/email/

For a complete list of books by Michael Anderle, please visit:

www.lmbpn.com/ma-books/

CONNECT WITH THE AUTHOR

Connect with Michael Anderle

Website: http://lmbpn.com

Email List: https://michael.beehiiv.com/

https://www.facebook.com/LMBPNPublishing

https://twitter.com/MichaelAnderle

https://www.instagram.com/lmbpn_publishing/

https://www.bookbub.com/authors/michael-anderle

www.ingramcontent.com/pod-product-compliance
Lightning Source LLC
LaVergne TN
LVHW091700070526
838199LV00050B/2222